# Praise for Dylan Newton
## *How Sweet It Is*

"Newton's debut romance is laugh-out-loud funny, with enough antics, fast pacing, and chemistry to keep readers as engrossed as any of her hero's bestselling horror novels would. A hilarious rom-com romp that delivers on both sweet and heat."　　　　　　　　*—Kirkus*, starred review

"Brimming with witty banter, sweet characters, and sizzling charm."　　　　　　　　*—Woman's World*

"The funny moments had me laughing out loud. The end of this book was super romantic and very fitting! *How Sweet It Is* exceeded my expectations."　　　　　　　—Nerd Daily

# ALL FIRED UP

ALSO BY DYLAN NEWTON

*How Sweet It Is*

# ALL FIRED UP

Dylan
Newton

FOREVER

New York   Boston

Forever
Hachette Book Group
1290 Avenue of the Americas, New York, NY 10104
read-forever.com
twitter.com/readforeverpub

First Edition: May 2022

Forever is an imprint of Grand Central Publishing. The Forever name and logo are trademarks of Hachette Book Group, Inc.

The publisher is not responsible for websites (or their content) that are not owned by the publisher.

Library of Congress Cataloging-in-Publication Data
Names: Newton, Dylan, author.
Title: All fired up / Dylan Newton.
Description: First edition. | New York : Forever, 2022. | Summary: "As a
  successful book publicist, Imani Lewis prides herself on being prepared.
  But nothing can prepare her for seeing Zander Matthews again after she
  ghosted him a year ago. Their chemistry was so hot that her only
  option of not getting involved is to avoid Zander at all costs. But in a
  town with only four stoplights, avoidance isn't an option. As manager
  and artist-in-residence of a ceramic's studio, Zander Matthews seemingly
  has it all: he creates all day and throws clay with strangers at night.
  But his carefree lifestyle hides a serious side. After his tour as a
  Marine, his life goal is simple: enjoy the present, as tomorrow is not
  promised. But lately he's thinking a future with Imani might be exactly
  what he's been missing. His proposal: spend time together just as
  friends. After all, she needs his help anyway in fixing up her
  grandmother's house. After weeks of totally platonic fun together, she
  finally caves to his request for a first date in a hot air balloon. But
  since her small-town stay is temporary and Zander can't be tied to
  anything beyond the most tenuous plans, will she be able to handle it
  when things get all fired up?"—Provided by publisher.
Identifiers: LCCN 2021059188 | ISBN 9781538754429 (trade paperback) | ISBN
  9781538754436 (ebook)
Subjects: LCGFT: Novels.
Classification: LCC PS3614.E74 A79 2022 | DDC 813/.6—dc23/eng/20211203
LC record available at https://lccn.loc.gov/2021059188

ISBNs: 978-1-5387-5442-9 (trade paperback), 978-1-5387-5443-6 (ebook)

Printed in the United States of America

LSC-C

Printing 1, 2022

*In memory of my grandmother,*
*Leah Folts Dillon.*
*I hope I did you proud.*
*Save me a seat at the May-I table.*

# CHAPTER 1

It's only vomit. It'll come out," Imani Lewis said with far more confidence than she felt. She dabbed regurgitated kiwi from her vintage Hermès white silk shirt with the last of her emergency wet wipes, waving away the distraught mother's apology. "What with the bumpy landing and watching dance recitals on my phone, Jasmine got motion sick—used to happen to me all the time as a child."

Jasmine's mom—whose name Imani hadn't caught in the chaos of entertaining her daughter during the flight from JFK to Buffalo—grimaced as they deplaned.

"You're so prepared," she said, as Imani deposited the vile pile of used wet wipes into a plastic bag she pulled from the left zippered pocket of her purse. "And you've been so tolerant with my little bundle of energy."

The culprit, a three-year-old who had escaped her own *Exorcist*-like projectile vomiting without a drop staining her daisy-printed shirt, smiled. She skipped ahead of them on the ramp leading to the airport terminal. Her Princess Tiana backpack acted like a bumper, pinballing her off other passengers.

"Watch me! I can twirl like those ballerinas, Ms. Imani."

The elfin toddler's yellow-and-white beaded braids flew out like rays of sunshine as she whipped around in a joyful string of full-body-flinging pirouettes. Whatever she lacked in grace she made up for in vigorous enthusiasm, and Imani's heart squeezed as it did every time she watched young dancers. Her Tuesday/Thursday volunteer gig at the Bronx Barre Belles was the highlight of her week and probably the only thing she'd miss during this unpaid leave of absence.

Well, that and the paycheck from her publicist job.

Her cell phone buzzed like an angry nest of wasps in her purse. She'd turned it back on as they were taxiing, but before the device had synched up, she'd gotten a chestful of vomit. She pulled out her phone and peeked at the display, stumbling in her only pair of Louboutin heels.

She'd racked up twenty texts during her forty-five-minute flight.

A glance revealed fifteen were from her number one romance author about some snafu with the book-signing itinerary, four were from her contact at the Florida bookstore asking where their scheduled author was, and one was from the man filling in for her during her leave...wondering where she kept the stapler.

Then she saw she'd received a voicemail from her boss at Cerulean Books.

Crap. Trisha never called unless things were seriously off the rails.

Imani sucked in a breath through her teeth. Dread coiled like a serpent in her guts, constricting her in a way that had become hideously familiar these past few months. Her mind skittered into action, crafting a checklist:

☐ Call star romance author. Take ownership of any problem, including acts of God.

☐ Resolve itinerary issue.

☐ Call bookstore manager. Grovel until everything is back on track.

☐ Call assistant publicist to see why he isn't assisting. Tell him where to find stapler. (Note to self: Breathe. Resist urge to tell him where to shove said stapler.)

☐ Craft email re-explaining itinerary, highlighting how EASY it is to follow because it's color coded, for heaven's sake!

☐ Delete the snark. Then send email.

☐ Call Trisha to reassure her the issue is resolved. Fend off questions about the promotion to publicity manager she's offered you. Remind her Wellsville has poor reception. Find polite way to make boss understand that, for a few weeks, communication will be spotty at best. (Note to self: Maybe compare Wellsville to the Bermuda Triangle in terms of cell reception?)

☐ Hang up before boss hears your voice go up at the end like it always does when you stretch the truth.

☐ Call Katie and relax for the summer. (Yay!)

Her inner list maker was interrupted as the toddler grabbed the edge of Imani's overstuffed purse. Her eyes sparkled and she grinned in expectation.

"Did you see my good twirling?"

"Jasmine, she doesn't have time now," the mom said, catching hold of her daughter's hand. "She's going to visit her grandmother, like we are."

Imani blinked at the mention of her grandmother. Her Gigi.

Releasing her death grip on her phone, Imani dropped it back into her purse. She fixed her face, smiling at the tiny, frenetic ballerina and shoving back the exhaustion from last night's sleepless, pillow-flipping extravaganza.

"You are so talented, Jasmine!" Imani bent down to clasp the girl's hands, still so small you could see tiny dimples instead of knuckles. She formed the girl's arms into a round hoop in front of her daisy-shirted chest. "Now, pretend like you're hugging a giant, fluffy panda bear who is so big your fingers can barely touch! Then we have to imagine a string holding you up nice and tall, and then we raise up on our tiptoes and twirl with nice round arms, like this!"

She spun Jasmine in a pirouette, clapping as the child held the form for three in a row.

"You've got a natural here, Mom," Imani said to the mother, who gave her a thankful smile as she gathered up her still-spinning daughter and headed toward baggage claim.

Peeling off to the bathroom, Imani hauled her phone out again. She rapidly scanned the texts and surmised the problem: Leann Bellamy's limo hadn't arrived at the Sarasota location to take her to the Tampa signing, forcing the popular romance author to take a cab. That wasn't typically an emergency; however, the cabbie decided to take the Skyway bridge en route from Sarasota to Tampa, unaware that Leann Bellamy had gephyrophobia—a raging fear of bridges.

Her star romance writer was currently sitting on the side of some road that led to the Skyway, hopefully still inside the cab. But maybe not.

Knowing this conversation was going to take a hot minute, she mentally rearranged her to-do list, opting for the most enjoyable task first: calling her best friend.

Shutting herself in the handicapped stall so she could use the sink in privacy, she hit Kate Sweet's face in her Favorites menu, then began working on her shirt's stain.

"Well, finally! I was beginning to wonder if Gigi decided not to get her knee surgery, or if she'd somehow talked you out of coming. That woman has mad persuasion skills." Kate's rapid-fire patter was like a sliver of sunshine in this crap-tastic morning. "But then Drake told me he'd had a call from your boss letting him know you were on your way to go over his book signing and movie cameo trip next week. I knew you'd never dare to ditch both Gigi and my husband!"

"You know I'd never keep anyone waiting, regardless of their infamous reputation. So sorry, Katie. The flight got delayed with the rain." Imani dabbed at the splotch of green yuck with a wad of toilet paper and water, grimacing as it did little to fade the stain on her vintage white blouse. Neither did a fierce scrubbing with her emergency Tide pen. Instead, it made the whole section below the pattern of keys printed along the neckline practically transparent over her left nipple. Blowing out a breath, she abandoned the effort, the urgency of her next bunch of calls squeezing her chest. "I'm heading to baggage claim in a sec. I got barfed on during the flight, and then I deplaned in time for a major work crisis, so I'm doing some cleanup. Literally and figuratively."

"Oh no!" Kate's voice wavered between a laugh and a cry of dismay. "Well, take your time, and let me know if I can help. We're unstoppable when we team up, and although it's been a while since I broke out the Roy G Biv gel pens, you know I've got your list-making back. I'm so glad you're here, Imani—I can't wait to catch up and tell you the plans for the gender-reveal-slash-baby-shower tomorrow."

Imani smiled at her friend's enthusiasm. She'd never imagined her busy, event-planning best friend to be the one married and expecting so soon, but Drake Matthews's charms had evidently proven too hard for Kate to resist.

"I'm honored you chose me as the baby's godmother. I saved the reveal envelope with the sonogram results, still closed like you sent it to me. I'll open it at the party, and we'll both be surprised on the same day. It's right in my purse."

"Where else would it be but in the Mary Poppins bag?" Kate joked. "And that's sweet. I'm so happy you're going to be here for Baby Matthews as Auntie Imani."

A warmth spread in Imani's chest at the name.

"Aw, really? The baby can call me Auntie?"

"Well, we've lived together on and off for years, so we're sisters in every way but genetics," Kate said with the easy, breezy way that only someone who already had siblings could manage. Then Kate gasped. "Oh, I forgot to tell you! The venue I reserved had a plumbing issue, so we're having the shower at Zander's studio. He's got this ceramic thing we can smash after you fill it with the appropriately colored starch for the reveal. I was freaking out when my original place canceled, but this is so much better! You remember Zander, right?"

At the mention of Drake's youngest brother, Imani felt her face tingle with pricks of heat, and the cleansing breaths halted in her chest.

Zander Matthews.

Yep, she remembered him, all right. He was her first and only one-night stand. Well, technically, it was two nights, two mornings, and one long, glorious afternoon, nine months and twenty-five days ago. But who was counting?

Kate must've assumed her memory had sinkhole-sized gaps, as she quickly supplied details. "He's the taller, beefier Matthews brother who has the smoldering Jason Momoa vibe that's broken hearts all over this county. Oh, remember? He's the guy you did that fun dance with at my wedding—what was it called again?"

"Bachata." Imani felt the tension in her guts move up into her chest, constricting the breath there. No. Not so soon! She'd thought she'd at least have a week to tell Kate about her hookup with Zander and, more importantly, explain why she'd kept this secret from her best friend whom she'd confided everything to since elementary school. And Zander—she thought she'd have more time to figure out how to explain why she'd never answered his texts and calls, how the intensity of that weekend had sounded every alarm bell in her heart...

But she was facing him tomorrow. At his studio. In his element.

Inhaling, Imani figured she might as well just plunge

in. "Yes, I remember him. Listen, I've been wanting to tell you something but haven't known how to—"

"You can tell me about it in the car," Kate interrupted, "because I've got to pee again. I swear, these next six weeks can't go by fast enough. I need to meet this child who is making a punching bag out of my bladder! I'll see you when you get done with baggage claim."

"Wait, I need to—" Imani realized Kate had already disconnected. "Damn."

She winced, anticipating the confession to come, gazing into the airport bathroom mirror. Before locking up her tiny Bronx apartment this morning, she'd tied her long brown hair back in a low ponytail and taken care with her makeup, going heavy on the concealer. But the dark smudges under her bloodshot brown eyes were like a billboard screaming *Insomniac!* Her normally olive complexion—a credit to her half-Hungarian heritage—looked pale and washed out, and coupled with the sheer, almost nipple-revealing wet spot on her boob...well, suffice it to say she wouldn't be 'gramming this look.

She snagged her favorite red lipstick from her purse and applied it generously. She'd read once that people perceived you as "put together" as long as you had on lipstick.

She was about to challenge that perception.

Her best friend was a stickler for details, so she'd notice Imani's fatigue and maybe go easy on her for keeping such a secret from her for this long. Anyway, it wasn't like Imani would be spending a lot of time with her two-night flame. They'd see each other for maybe a couple hours? Although Wellsville was a small town, it was big enough to avoid the youngest Matthews brother, if she tried.

Besides, Zander was all about the casual lifestyle. Her discreet inquiries to Kate after her weekend fling revealed that while he'd dated dozens of women in the past, he was still friends with them post-breakup. She figured he'd moved on from their weekend long ago, which was for the best.

Imani shrugged off the worry. This trip wasn't about her. It was about her best friend's baby shower first, followed by Gigi's double knee replacement. Then she could relax! Something she hadn't done in...she couldn't remember how long.

She smiled, imagining her leisurely summer. It was worth taking the unpaid leave from work, worth the hit to her pocketbook, and worth putting a bookmark in her career, as long as she got to chill out for a while. She'd bask in the cooler, Western New York summer temps, enjoy the food that was tied to happy memories, sit on Gigi's front porch, and figure things out.

Like her life.

Imani replaced the lipstick and stain-removal pen in her tote, zipping it with finality. Soon she would no longer be worried about puke stains, authors stuck on the roadside, massive career decisions, or wondering if her red lipstick was distracting enough to hide the widening cracks in her armor. She'd be with her best friend in a town from her past, spending all summer with her grandmother—the woman who was the closest genetic relative to the mother she'd lost more than a decade ago.

It was going to be amazing.

As she rode the escalator down to baggage claim, Imani multitasked, calling the bookstore to let them know Leann

Bellamy was stuck in traffic. Then she dialed Leann's number as she searched for Kate in the crush of people surrounding the revolving luggage carousel, maneuvering to the front so she could spot her bright-turquoise suitcases. The number for the romance author's cell rang busy, and Imani juggled with her phone to hang up, just as she spotted her luggage trundling toward her.

Suddenly, a tall white man whose broad shoulders strained at his fitted T-shirt stepped in front of her, snatching her big bag, along with the smaller matching one, off the belt.

"Excuse me! Those are mine," Imani said to the back of the six-foot-five guy.

Something in the way he moved gave away his identity before he turned to flash her with his sparkling, devil-may-care grin.

Her jaw dropped.

It was Zander.

Zander freaking Matthews.

He of the hot bachata moves, and the hotter under-the-covers moves, stood in front of her at the Buffalo airport. Kate had been right—if you darkened his dirty blond, surfer-like curls, the guy could be a stand-in for Jason Momoa in *Aquaman*, as they had the same broad shoulders, bulging biceps, and legs like tree trunks.

"It's you," she breathed.

"It's me." His low voice and sexy smile hit her square in the libido. "The car is parked outside, and Kate's waiting for you there. You set?"

Her mind noted with dismay that he was just as scrumptious as he'd been that weekend. It hadn't been her imagination embellishing his solid frame, the thick, corded muscles that said he did more physical labor than throwing clay in his studio.

"I—I've got everything," she squeaked, dazed. For two hours, she'd be stuck in a car with the guy she'd slept with and then practically ghosted, plus her best friend who knew nothing about it? Could this be any more awkward?

Imani followed as Zander hefted her luggage and carried both of her bags on his back, refusing to roll them for some reason known only to him. He stopped shy of the exit's revolving doors, gesturing to the restrooms.

"We've got time if you need to towel off." Zander aimed a pointed look at her chest, his expression amused. "So...did you win?"

Imani blinked. "Did I win?"

"The wet T-shirt contest. I'm guessing you were a shoo-in for your flight. The other passengers didn't stand a chance against that lacy bra."

Imani scowled, refusing to laugh. "A gentleman would have politely averted his gaze."

Zander shrugged, leading the way through the revolving door.

Was that all he had to say to her? Not "Hi" or "Nice to see you again" but some crack about her wet blouse? Imani's eyes narrowed as she spoke to his back.

"A gentleman would have said how nice I looked, even if I'd been puked on by a kid who'd just eaten a sliced kiwi. A gentleman would not—"

"Let me guess." Zander's smile became razor sharp. "A gentleman wouldn't call out the woman whose only reply to his texts and voicemails following their amazing weekend together was 'Yeah, that was fun.' He wouldn't ask why she'd blocked him from her life without a *single* conversation. No gentleman would put the woman who'd practically broken his heart in that awkward position. Would he?"

"Broken your h—" Before Imani could finish, a car beeped behind them. She spun, and her anger was replaced by a spasm of embarrassment as she recognized the driver.

It was Drake Matthews. Bestselling horror writer and her number one client.

Next to him, hanging out of the window, waving like a goon, was Kate, his wife and Imani's best friend.

Imani forced a smile. "H-hi, Kate. And Drake. It's good to see you. I didn't think you'd have the time to pick me up, with your book's deadline. And you *all* came. I feel so...special."

"I always have time for my publicist." Drake peered out Kate's open window, pushing his dark glasses up his nose to give her a warm smile as he gestured to the Prius. "Sorry about the tight squeeze, but Kate's car is in the shop and my truck doesn't have a back seat. My brother offered his car as long as I agreed to drive and take him with us to get some wings. Hop in! My wife is dying to talk sex with you and Zander."

Imani sucked in a breath.

Zander chuckled. "That's my favorite kind of talk. Although I have to say, you're a little late. Dad had that talk with me twenty-some years ago. But I appreciate the thought."

Kate rolled her eyes.

"Drake, why do you purposely set Zander up like that?

No, I want to talk to you about the sex of the *baby*. I think I've changed my mind. I want you two to tell me tonight. But not now—over dinner." Kate's green eyes lit up. Her auburn hair had grown longer and more luxurious, and she glowed with pregnant happiness. "I'm dying for some Buffalo wings, and trust me, this restaurant's homemade blue cheese is Lactaid-worthy."

Imani crossed to the car, her face aflame. Apparently, Zander hadn't told Kate and Drake about their hookup. Yet. Maybe this was karma warning her to come clean to her best friend?

Kate's face went from shining to dim, reading something in Imani's body language.

"What's wrong? And why are you soaking wet?"

Imani's forehead felt as though it had its own sprinkler system. Brushing away sweat with her free hand, she opened her mouth, unsure of what she was going to say but determined that if her best friend and her famous client were going to hear of her sleeping with Zander, they were going to hear it from her.

Suddenly, Zander spoke in her ear. "You're lucky I'm a gentleman."

Imani felt Zander's arm around her shoulder, but before she could say more, he was talking to Kate and opening the back passenger door.

"Aww, she's just mad because I pulled her out of the wet T-shirt contest before she could show skin to win." Zander shoved her bigger bag in, then swept his hand as if sending her into a throne room instead of the squished back seat of his car.

"I don't think my suitcases will fit." She ducked inside,

holding her tote on her lap like the little old ladies did on the subway.

"My car's like your purse. It holds more than people give it credit for." Zander tossed her smaller turquoise bag into the trunk and piled in next to her, somehow closing the door. "Told you we'd fit! Let's get the momma-to-be some wings!"

Without warning, Zander reached across Imani, tugging the seat belt out from under the suitcase and hooking it over her. He clicked it home, his thick fingers grazing her hips, perilously close to her ass. Zander's body filled the back seat, and she found herself bending toward him, like a sunflower to the sun. His smell—Irish Spring soap and a hint of something warm and spicy—enveloped her. Despite everything, she breathed in deep, sucking him into her lungs.

Damn. How did he always smell so freaking good?

His blue eyes met hers as he fastened his own seat belt. He grinned, as if sensing his effect on her.

"Buckle up," he said in a low voice. "It's going to be a bumpy ride."

# CHAPTER 2

Zander settled into the back seat with Imani, who seemed to be pretending he was a cactus, leaning away to avoid brushing shoulders.

Her cherry lips curved in a forced smile.

"Thank you so much for taking time out of your workday to pick me up. Had I known I was going to warrant such a...large welcoming party," she said, glancing sidelong at Zander, her eyes as shimmering and splendid as a new can of chestnut-tinted stain, "I would have ordered an Uber so I didn't inconvenience anyone."

Zander grinned. His plan was working already. "As soon as Kate told me you were flying into town, we decided we should welcome you properly. Can't have you thinking we don't *care*. Because we *do*."

Imani speared him with a glare and then turned to Kate, who was trying to pivot her pregnant body in the passenger seat to look at Imani while she spoke.

"Zan's right." Kate offered her friend a huge smile. "Besides, none of us have seen you, outside of video chats, since the wedding. I can't believe it's already been almost a year."

"Boggles the mind," Zander said, determined to needle Imani as payback for leaving him hanging after what he'd thought was the start of a new relationship. But more importantly, getting under her skin was part of his larger plan—the one he'd concocted once he'd heard Imani was spending the summer in Wellsville. He needed to find out whether they were more than one weekend's fantastic chemistry. And the only way to do that was to spend as much time together as possible. If they weren't compatible, he'd be able to evict her from his brain, where she'd lived rent-free since his brother's wedding reception.

Imani ignored his comment, focusing on her best friend. "Kate, you have to tell me about your last ultrasound! Weren't you tempted to glance at the monitor? You have such restraint, waiting the whole eight months until your shower..."

The two women chattered on, and Zander's eyes met his brother's in the rearview mirror. While his brother telepathy—something the three Matthews boys called their "bro-lepathy"—wasn't as strong with Drake as it was with Ryker, it was clear enough for him to know what his oldest brother was asking.

*What in the hell is happening?* In Zander's head, Drake's voice sounded exactly like his stern, responsible big-bro voice.

It was a valid question.

You'd have to have the empathy of a doorknob not to sense the awkward vibe in the back seat. Or, in his sister-in-law's case, you'd have to be so preoccupied with the task of making a small human, planning the impending gender reveal, and being thrilled your bestie was in town that you were too distracted to notice those stuck in polite purgatory two feet away.

These thoughts seesawed through Zander's mind as he met Drake's gaze in the rearview mirror. He shrugged his shoulders, bro-lepathy for: *I have no idea what's happening. Beats me.*

Some of this was true. But most of it was a lie, and he was pretty sure Drake knew it. His writer's attention to detail missed damn little, and he read body language as easily as one of his research books. His brother knew he was up to something. He just didn't know what yet.

Drake shook his head, bro-lepathy for a mini-lecture that likely sounded something like: *Whatever. I hope you know what you're doing. And you'd better not piss off my publicist, or you'll have hell to pay from both me and my wife.*

Maybe Drake hadn't put *all* those words into his gesture, but he didn't have to. Zander knew what was at stake—she sat right next to him, her arms crossed over her wet shirt as she listened to Kate update her on every single thing that had happened since they last spoke. Which seemed to be yesterday.

Zander nodded along, pretending to follow Kate's plans. But inside, he wasn't listening.

He was plotting.

While Drake didn't know of Zander's past with Imani—nobody did, as far as he could tell—his brother had likely guessed he had a thing for his publicist. First, when he'd met her at Drake's horror-novel launch party two Halloweens ago, they'd ribbed him for his obvious interest. Then, last August, at Kate and Drake's reception in the swanky Niagara Falls hotel, everyone had remarked how "cute" he and Imani looked together...and then had to abruptly shift to another adjective after watching their impromptu bachata.

Dancing the bachata was a skill he'd acquired completely by accident. He'd thought he was signing up for a cooking class that exclusively focused on bruschetta, one of his favorite appetizers. He'd put his name in for it at the arts center, hoping that by improving his culinary skills and serving appetizers to his clients before workshops, he'd be adding an even classier vibe to All Fired Up, his ceramics studio chain. It was because he mistook a bachata dancing class for a bruschetta cooking class—and then went through with it for the whole six weeks—that he'd been able to hit the dance floor when the wedding DJ played the Shawn Mendes song "Señorita."

Zander remembered that night. He'd been subtly flirting with Imani the whole reception, but Kate's maid of honor hadn't been picking up what he'd been throwing down. In the obligatory wedding party dance, she'd been so stiff in his arms during "Unforgettable," he'd wondered if one of his relatives had already warned Imani against him. It wouldn't be the first time Mom's church buddies had cockblocked him with an eligible bachelorette, and he distinctly remembered shrugging off Imani's disinterest, determined to have a good time at his brother's wedding regardless.

Once the DJ started playing pop songs, the previously full dance floor emptied like someone had lobbed a grenade into their midst. Zander saw his new sister-in-law's face fall as the older guests started checking their watches, trying to figure out if now was the time to make an exit from the hotel's ballroom. While he didn't know Kate well, he was certain of one fact: she was an event planner to the core. Her goal was for others to have a good time, and the DJ's unfortunate choice for the mostly older crowd was like a big ice cube down the back.

So he'd done his best to save the moment. He sauntered onto the dance floor, took off his coat and tie, unbuttoned the first two buttons of his shirt, and began dancing the bachata by himself. His older relatives clapped and chuckled—they'd given up on lecturing him on his zany life choices long ago. And after being lubed up by the three rounds of toasts, Zander had given up on caring what anyone thought.

He made "c'mon" gestures to various friends and cousins in the crowd, but they waved him away, laughing. Suddenly, to his surprise, the woman he'd been crushing on since he met her at Drake's book launch twirled herself into his arms.

Imani's fire-engine-red dress flared as she spun into him, stopping as her shoulder grazed his chest. She'd smelled of a zesty, sunshine-bright perfume, and she'd raised an eyebrow in challenge, speaking in a low voice.

"I'm not sure you can handle this song by yourself."

Zander had grinned at Imani's flushed face. So the straitlaced publicist wanted to let her hair down, did she? Hell, yeah. He was all in for that. He matched the playful expression in her deep brown eyes as he put his hand out for hers.

"I heard you were a dance teacher on the side. Maybe you'd better help me out? If you can keep up, that is."

Her cherry-tinted lips had curved into a smile of wicked delight. "You're on."

What came next was nothing short of miraculous.

He'd been so startled he'd kept his mouth shut, focusing on the dance, mentally reciting eight counts. It was like guiding a flame around the floor, simultaneously mesmerizing and dangerous. He twirled her into him, his body finding a rhythm with hers so quickly, it was almost as if they'd practiced. After the first few bars, it seemed he could read her intentions in her eyes, which glittered like onyx in the half-lit reception hall.

By the end of the dance, they both knew where they'd be heading at the end of the night, and what came after in his hotel room...

The Prius hit a pothole, and Zander was jerked back to the present. Memories swirled through his head, mixing like two paints from opposite sides of the color wheel.

Suddenly, Kate gripped the seat, using it as leverage to tug herself into the middle console and spear Zander with a green-eyed glare. He'd thought he was keeping his nefarious plan on the down-low and that nobody guessed he wasn't here to innocently welcome Imani back to town. But he'd underestimated his sister-in-law's ability to sense when things were off. "You were a chatterbox the entire trip up to get Imani, but you haven't made a peep these past ten minutes," Kate said accusatorily as her husband pulled into the parking lot of the wing place, keeping his eyes studiously on the white lines, as if parking the Prius required his complete attention, so he couldn't possibly come to his youngest brother's rescue. "What's wrong? Are you having second thoughts about hosting the gender reveal at your studio tomorrow night?"

Zander stammered a reply. "N-no, it's—"

Kate talked over him, her face screwed up in earnest consternation. "Zander, don't be offended we named Ryker as the baby's godparent, along with Imani. You know we adore you! You'll be the cool Uncle Z who shows the baby how to make pottery, harvest honey, and do axe-throwing tricks so they can win a contest like you."

For the first time since the luggage carousel, Imani looked him in the eyes, and he was trapped like a fly in amber. "Wait. You won an axe-throwing contest?"

Zander couldn't tell if Imani was impressed or horrified. "Only in my age group." He shrugged, downplaying the axe-throwing, just in case. He wrenched his gaze from those gorgeous chocolate eyes of hers, focusing again on his sister-in-law. "Look, Kate, I'm not offended—"

"I think you are!" Kate's voice went up an octave, and her face and neck turned red in magnificent blotches. "I don't want there to be hard feelings. We felt Ryker needed the title more than you did, you know? Although he's doing so well with his business, we worry his life is so...empty. Our choice didn't have anything to do with you or your abilities as a godparent, whatsoever."

Zander stuttered over some words until Drake came to his rescue.

"Kate, honey, I don't think Zander has hard feelings about that. He's glad not to be on the hook for parenting in any form." Drake put the car in park and flashed a smile to dial down any rancor his statement may have caused. "Those were your exact words, weren't they?"

Zander winced. Those had been his exact words. Why did his penchant for trying to lighten the mood always come back to bite him in the ass?

In truth, he had been a little jealous they'd named Ryker over him for godparent, but he understood. Given the choice between him—the guy who made his living partying with strangers as they created ceramic art—and his military hero middle brother, it was an easy decision. Uncle Ryker would take the godparent title as seriously as he had his Marine rank. He'd do whatever the online guide said were his responsibilities as godfather. Probably even take the kid to church.

In contrast, Uncle Zander would be in charge of supervising the farm animals at the kid's birthday party or playing with his niece or nephew on the Slip 'N Slide. As if he were only competent enough for the fun shit. Sure, Zander had changed his outlook on life after his own tour of duty—he'd been brutally introduced to how short and precious life was—but that didn't mean everyone should automatically discount him as a responsible adult.

Hearing his own words thrown back at him stung.

He mustered his most casual air, desperate to find something pithy to say that wouldn't reveal his inner turmoil, when, to his surprise, Imani spoke.

"Zander would have made a great godparent." Although her voice was barely above a whisper, her words shocked everyone in the car into silence, including Zander. She didn't look at him, but instead rubbed at her throat with one hand as she finished her statement. "He's not upset about that. He's upset with me. I might as well tell you and get it over with. Zander and I—"

Zander put a hand on her knee. "Imani, don't—"

But Imani squelched his objection with a cascade of words. "—slept together after your wedding in Niagara

Falls. It was a one-night thing. Well, two nights. So if he's offended by anything, it's that I've all but ghosted him ever since."

Kate sucked in a breath.

Drake groaned, slapping his forehead.

What followed was twenty seconds of awkward silence.

Finally, Zander mustered a fake hearty laugh.

"Okay. Now that we've exhausted the topic of my feelings...who's hungry for some wings?"

Before anyone replied, Imani's cell rang in a series of piano tones that even Zander recognized from Tchaikovsky's *Swan Lake*.

"It's Leann Bellamy. I've got to take this," she said, before wrestling past her suitcase and jettisoning herself from the car.

Zander took his time getting out, allowing Drake to help Kate from the car first before exiting the Prius and loitering so everyone could precede him into the restaurant. His mom didn't raise a fool. If he walked with his brother and sister-in-law, they'd read him the riot act for keeping such a big secret. Time enough for that later. Plus, being the caboose meant he could shamelessly eavesdrop on Imani.

Her voice was as calm as chamomile tea as she put the author on speakerphone so she could text as they talked. Her thumbs flew over the screen in a frenetic display of technological prowess.

"Leann, I just got off the plane and saw your messages. I am so very sorry about the car snafu. I've contacted the bookstore and said you were stuck in traffic, and I'm texting Brian now to ensure your detailed itinerary

is obeyed to the letter for the rest of this book signing tour. I will take care of everything, I promise. Are
you okay?"

"No, I am *not* okaaaay." The woman's voice on speakerphone was so agitated that her syrupy Southern accent
stretched her vowels further, making "I" sound like "ah" as
she rattled off her tale. "Ah'm freakin' the fudge out! The
limo didn't come, so ah'm takin' some rando cab to Tampa,
when the man started going toward the 'new' Sunshine
Skyway Bridge! Imani, do you know why they call it the
'new' Sunshine Skyway Bridge?"

The woman paused in her babble-shout long enough for
Imani to speak.

"No, Leann, I don't."

"Because the original Skyway fell into the fudgin'
ocean!" Leann shouted on the heels of the response. "You're
gonna have to cancel this signin' and get me somewhere
landlocked."

Zander felt as if he'd been invited to watch the Wizard
of Oz behind the curtain as Imani proceeded to tame her
author's fear, convince the cabbie to make an illegal U-turn
onto the other side of the highway leading away from
the bridge, and conduct a frantic texted conversation with
someone named Brian—whose name she muttered in anger
when on mute with her author—all the while smiling at
Kate and mouthing, "It's okay," whenever her best friend
looked her way.

It was amazing to watch.

But exhausting.

Imani finished up with her author, then took the phone
off speaker to have a quiet, apology-laced conversation with

someone named Trisha as the group stood in line waiting for a table.

"Does your publicist put out fires of this magnitude on a daily basis?" Zander asked, sidling up to Drake as he pretended to browse the wing T-shirts. Really, he was hiding in the tiny in-restaurant store. Kate had disappeared to use the bathroom, and without Zander as a buffer, Drake was likely to be overrun by fans eager for an autograph from the Knight of Nightmares. Zander positioned himself so he faced the crowd, folding his arms over his chest in his best bodyguard impersonation. "I thought you were her only pain-in-the-ass author."

Drake pushed his black glasses up, his expression heavy with disapproval. "Imani has been gobbling up promotions at Cerulean Books like jellybeans these past few years, getting bigger authors and bigger responsibilities. It was only a matter of time before they promoted her to manager. I've been damn lucky to work with her, and although I'll miss her, I can't hold her back from her dreams."

Zander's eyebrows rose. He cast a glance at Imani, still talking on her cell. Her pale, thin-lipped expression conveyed none of the happiness he'd associate with a woman working toward her dreams.

Before he could say as much, Kate returned, and a hostess guided them to a table in the back corner—the most private place they could put his famous horror-writer brother so they weren't accosted all dinner long.

Imani had finished her call but was busy texting as they sat down and menus were handed out. She looked up long enough to order a glass of water with lemon, and Zander wondered if maybe it had been a blessing she hadn't returned his call and his texts last year.

Despite the fact he hadn't been able to stop thinking of her, maybe it was best that she'd thrown up relationship barriers and kept everything surface level with the "Yeah, that was fun" text she'd sent. Clearly, she was intent on reaching the summit of her industry's career ladder, whatever that was. And clearly, he'd abandoned that stupid climb years ago, promising himself he'd only expend energy on those things that filled his bliss bucket. He and Imani were like arrows shooting in opposite directions.

So what was the point of trying for anything more long-term?

As soon as the server took their orders, Kate pivoted to Imani. She cocked her head to the side, as if contemplating the origin of the universe, and released a bomb. "Why didn't you tell me you slept with him?"

Zander snorted and gave a finger wave. "Hi. Um, the 'him' you're referencing is sitting right here."

Both Kate and Imani ignored him.

"I don't know. I guess I felt it would put you in a weird position?" Imani shrugged, her hand fluttering down to press against her chest before focusing instead on Drake. Her voice was breathy as she spoke. "I'm sorry, Drake. It was unprofessional to...complicate things. I made a reckless decision, and I should have told you both sooner."

"N-no, you didn't...erm, I mean, I don't need to know about—"

Kate interrupted. "It's okay. I mean, I totally get that Zander's a giant thirst trap."

"The giant thirst trap has ears and is still listening," Zander said, and was again ignored.

"I just—we've been best friends since second grade. I tell you everything." Kate's green eyes filled with tears. She grabbed Imani's hand, holding it between her own. "I've been a crap friend, haven't I? First, I was obsessed about my wedding, then I went off on my honeymoon, and before you know it, I was pregnant...no wonder you didn't tell me. It's been all about me-me-me for a year. You probably couldn't get a word in edgewise!"

Then, as if the words were a plug in a dam, tears burst from Kate's eyes, cascading down her face in an impressive stream. She snatched a napkin from the dispenser and leaned against Drake, sobbing.

Drake wrapped Kate in his arms, tucking her head under his chin as he murmured soothing words in her ear. His amber eyes promised murder and a closed-fist type of conversation with Zander later.

Imani recoiled as if she'd been slapped. Her hand shook as she patted her best friend's back. "That's not true! You're—you're amazing, Kate." Imani's voice was papery thin. "Please don't cry. I...can we talk about this later? I'm not...I'm not feeling so well. I can't breathe. I think I need some air."

Imani stood, then stumbled, her hand fanning her pale face, her chest rising and falling as if she'd just finished a 5K and clocked a personal best. Her pupils were tiny pinpricks in her brown eyes, and droplets of sweat beaded on her forehead and the bridge of her nose.

Zander had seen more than one new Marine recruit—fresh bullet catchers—'coptering in with these same symptoms to know what was coming next.

A panic attack.

Acting without thought, Zander shoved his chair back. He pulled Imani to him, and they were halfway to the door to the ladies' room—him mostly carrying her upright, as if she were a store mannequin—when she looked at him with panic in her eyes.

"Outside. I—I can't breathe. I feel dizzy. I need...air!"

He pivoted from the bathroom, spotting the emergency exit down the service hall. He shoved the bar on the door, ignoring the high-pitched alarm as he barreled out, almost carrying Imani outside. His Marine training kicked in as he used his sneakered heel to slam the emergency door closed behind him, cutting off the alarm as his eyes scanned the restaurant's back alley. No danger. The paved space was empty but for a plastic crate and a stack of wood pallets.

"Holy shit, I'm so hot. This shirt..." Imani unbuttoned her sleeves, shoving the white, almost sheer blouse up her arms, fanning her hands at her face and neck. Then she attacked the first three buttons, opening the collar about four inches south of decent.

Zander rubbed a hand on the back of his neck, then shook his head.

"It's the fabric. Silk. That's what you wear under ski clothes because it holds your body heat." Making a decision, he pulled off his T-shirt. In one smooth motion, he popped it over her head, yanking it down before she could put her arms inside the proper holes. "Take off your shirt under there and wear mine until you cool down."

Imani's gaze roved over his bare chest and then rapidly away.

Her flushed cheeks grew darker pink.

*Hmm.*

Maybe she wasn't as uninterested as she'd seemed? Maybe dating could still be a thing?

"I have other...shirts in my suitcase," she protested, gasping like a fish plucked from a lake.

Zander looked at her with exasperation. "I'm trying to be a gentleman here and get you cooled down so you don't pass out. Quit being difficult."

Her gaze returned to him, and after two more gasping breaths, she unbuttoned the rest of her shirt, and under the cover of his tee, she slipped it off and threaded her arms into his cotton sleeves. "I guess...this is better. To get my shirts...I'd have to get the keys...from Drake and Kate. Dying...is better than facing them."

He held out his hand, and to his surprise, she handed him her stained shirt, stumbling slightly in her heels.

He spotted an overturned blue milk crate some employee had likely used on a recent smoke break, if the cigarette butts littering the ground were any indication. He moved it under the building's awning and helped Imani to sit on it.

"Well, you're not dying, but having a panic attack is one way to end an awkward conversation." He crouched down, giving her his best grin. Bringing her hands up, he formed them around her mouth, his fingers barely brushing against the smooth skin of her jawline. "Cup your hands like this and breathe into them. Three counts in, hold, then five counts out. You're hyperventilating."

"Is...is that what's happening?" she asked, her gasping voice muffled behind her hands. "Everything is...crackling in my sinuses, like I just ate...peppermint. Are you sure I'm not having a heart attack?"

"Do you have any cardiac history?" he asked, and when she shook her head, he continued. "Any pain radiating to your arms, jaw, or neck?"

"N-no."

"I'm no doctor, although my family jokes I've taken enough college credits to be one, yet still don't have a degree." His self-deprecation earned him a tiny gasping snicker of a laugh. Progress. He smiled in reassurance. "But I don't think you're having a heart attack. Just a garden-variety panic attack. Breathe in for three and out for five counts. Do it with me."

He counted as they inhaled together, but her exhale was too fast.

"I don't have time...for panic attacks," Imani said, abandoning the calming breaths and throwing up her hands. "I made a fool of myself in front of a dining room...full of strangers. Now I'll have to call my boss...and confess why I'm resigning from the Drake Matthews team. I hurt...my best friend's feelings, and to top it off...I ruined this Hermès shirt my Gigi bought me that I wore to surprise her!"

Her voice grew in volume and desperation with every confession. He ignored her words and focused on the tone.

Upset. Alone. Overwhelmed.

Lord knew he'd been all those. More than most people knew, family included.

What she needed was a little coddling. Some tenderness. Just for now. Then, when this crisis was over, his quest would once again resume to see whether they were compatible beyond one weekend. If not, he'd forever banish her from his thoughts.

"We need to get your breathing under control—you're sucking in way more oxygen than your lungs can handle, and you need some of that carbon dioxide. It's all about balance. Breathe into my hands for a count of three." He cupped his hands over her face as he counted. Imani made a noise of protest but didn't speak. To his surprise, she was holding still, letting him minister to her. "And now out for a count of five."

Her brown eyes gazed into his, wide and trusting, while her hand came up to steady his hands cupped over her mouth as he counted out the series four more times.

"It's working," she whispered on the exhale. "It felt like an elephant was sitting on my chest...but it's starting to ease."

"You have a stressful job. It happens. When I was in Afghanistan, we saw it all the time. You just need a break from your stress." He shrugged, ducking his head to look into her eyes to show her, with the power of his gaze, that it was okay. *She* was okay. "And you didn't embarrass yourself. As for the Drake situation, he doesn't care that you slept with me."

Imani gave him a dubious look, her muffled voice doubtful.

"I don't know about that—"

"I do. He's my brother. Oh, don't get me wrong. The dude is going to ream me up one side and down the other about how I took advantage of you that weekend—"

"It wasn't like that."

"Yeah, I know. I was there. Remember?" He grinned

to soften the words. "If I recall, *you* took advantage of *me*. Seven times, to be exact."

She swatted at him, her hand connecting playfully with his bare shoulder, then stalling there. Her thumb moved in a tiny circle. It was as if his nerve endings caught fire, and he clenched his jaw against the tidal wave of physical and emotional sensations at her touch.

"Zander, I—"

"Shh. Breathe in for three counts." He cut off her apology for that weekend, not ready to rip off that scab yet. She dropped her hand, and he was able to focus once more. "As for your shirt, when we get to Wellsville, you take it over to Ray's Dry Cleaners in the plaza by the McDonald's. Tell him I sent you. He's a miracle worker with stains. If anyone can get puke out of your shirt, it'll be—"

The door flew open, and the alarm shrieked again. Kate stuck her head out, followed by her belly. Her green eyes scanned the scene, saw Zander's hands cupped around Imani's face. He scrambled to stand, feeling somehow guilty, as if he and Imani had been caught doing something naughty.

"Imani, are you okay?" Kate asked.

"She was feeling a little overheated," Zander said, hoping to help deflect attention from Imani.

It worked. His sister-in-law glared at him.

"Why are you half-naked?"

Zander put on what his brothers jokingly referred to as his "smoldering smile" and reached for his wallet. He gave Kate everything he had—forty bucks.

"Can you do me a favor?" he asked, leaving Imani's side, holding out the bills with as much suave charm as he could muster. "I need you to find me an XL shirt. I gave Imani mine because hers was too hot and had vomit on it."

He held Imani's shirt up as evidence of his good deeds. Kate's green eyes narrowed. Then she snatched the money from his hand.

"Fine. But Imani is coming with me."

"B-but why am I taking your shirt?" Imani asked. "Shouldn't Kate get me a shirt, and I can give you yours back?"

To Zander's surprise, it was Kate who nixed the idea.

"It's quicker if I just grab Zander a shirt, then we can all sit down and eat. I'm freaking starving!" she growled, ushering her best friend into the restaurant. Then, before closing the emergency door, she gave Zander one last glare. "I'll be right back."

True to her word, Kate was back in five minutes.

Zander tried to act chill, as if it were totally normal to be shirtless in the alley of a wing house. He cranked the wattage of his smile.

"Thanks, Kate."

"I don't know what you're up to, Zander Matthews, but Imani is not in town for you, and she is not your plaything. And if you hurt her, I'll gut you." Kate tossed a plastic bag at him then smiled sweetly. "Here's your extra-large shirt. See you inside."

He caught the bag one-handed, and as the emergency door clanked shut, he pulled out the shirt.

It was a women's XL.

It was bright pink.

And it had rhinestones on the front.

He shrugged, tossing it over his shoulder as he plopped

Imani's dirty blouse into the now-empty plastic bag. Kate thought she was giving him a little payback for her best friend, did she? Well, he could pull off a tight, pink rhinestone shirt. No sweat.

Plus, giving Imani his tee was brilliant. She'd want to return it...which meant she couldn't hide from him in Wellsville. He'd have at least one more chance to determine if they had a future together, or if he could sweep her forever from his mind.

He tugged the shirt over his head with effort. Shoving his melon through the opening was a bit like he imagined the birth canal might be—a tight squeeze that mashed his nose against his face and made him claustrophobic until he was finally expelled on the other side. With considerable effort, he dragged it over his chest, bits of those sparkly crystals scratching his skin until he yanked the fabric down to his belly button. It lay against him like a spandex half-shirt, with a good four inches of his stomach exposed.

His happy trail was on full display under the pink fabric.

It was almost worse than being shirtless.

He rolled his neck to the right, then to the left, popping the vertebrae as if readying for a grueling workout. Then he pushed in the bar on the restaurant's reflective glass door...and paused, squinting at his reflection.

"What the..." He dropped his chin to his chest to read the upside-down sparkly words next to a perverted picture of a chicken wing. Drake was going to wet himself when he spotted this shirt, and God help him if he sent a picture to Ryker. His middle brother would never, *ever* let him live down the fact he'd appeared in public like this. He groaned. "Well played, Kate. Well played."

Taking one of those calming breaths for himself, he opened the door, resigning himself to his fate. He crossed the restaurant, ignoring the titters as diners read his shirt and pointed. When he got to the table, neither his brother nor Kate bothered to hide their grins.

He gave them a sour look.

Imani turned. Her face was beautifully composed, her red lipstick reapplied, the terrified look in her eyes gone. His blue shirt hung loosely on her frame, and she'd spiraled one side of it into one of those tiny knots girls tied in oversized shirts to make them more formfitting. Then, she smiled at him.

Genuinely smiled at him.

Suddenly, he didn't care if he was wearing a pink minishirt with an obscene saying and a chicken wing that looked like a dick on the front. It was worth it for that one smile.

Damn.

He'd better recalibrate his plan, or this woman was going to break his heart.

Again.

# CHAPTER 3

$I$mani was set to grovel. She'd already created a to-do list in her head for the ways she was going to apologize to her best friend and her biggest author for her lie of omission. But surprisingly, they had moved on as easily as Zander had promised.

"It's okay," Kate said, patting Imani's hand in reassurance after returning from the gift shop and then back outside to Zander. "I understand how my brother-in-law lured you into bed at the reception, and how awkward that must've been for you afterward. But you don't have to worry. Zander may be a thirst trap and a goofball, but he's a good guy. I swear, he's still friends with every ex-girlfriend and their families, as well. He probably couldn't resist playing us for its comedic effect, and I just gave him a taste of his own medicine to settle the score."

Imani thought her face would burst into flames as Drake agreed.

"My youngest brother has a definite joie de vivre, and while that's his superpower, it's also his kryptonite." He shook his head, pushing his glasses up on his nose. "He's always had trouble discerning when fun time is over and real life begins."

Imani frowned, thinking their assessment seemed a little harsh. But they knew the man better than she did. All she had to judge him on was an amazing weekend, during which her brain was mostly turned off.

Even so, as she followed Kate and Drake's table chatter, she searched for the words to thank Zander when he returned. She appreciated his quick thinking during her panic attack. It had been kind of him to give her a dry, non-puke-stained shirt—one that smelled deliciously like Irish Spring soap—and she'd lined up the perfect phrase of acknowledgment, when he approached the table.

The words died on her lips.

Zander wore a pink half-shirt that bulged at the seams. But what stood out were the words on the shirt, written in rhinestone letters: *I Like Mine BONE-IN.*

Under the proclamation jutted a bedazzled drumstick that looked like...

She burst out laughing.

"Oh my God. Is that a deep-fried penis on your shirt?"

Her whole body shook with laughter.

Her mood shifted from heavy, shame-filled resignation to hilarity-filled lightness so fast, she wondered if he'd worn the ridiculous shirt Kate had bought him as payback just to make her laugh.

It was a sweet thought, and she held it to her like a warm blanket.

"What?" Zander asked, adopting a superhero pose, with his thick legs set wide apart and his hands on his hips. He puffed out his chest, which made the pink shirt rise to a few inches below his nipples.

Imani's eyes were drawn to his rippling abs. She yanked her gaze away before it followed the path of hair from his belly button to where it dipped, tantalizingly, into his jeans.

Zander must've sensed her intent, because by the time she'd dragged her gaze up to his, he was grinning, one eyebrow rising in a silent question. Mercifully, he shifted his attention, speaking to his sister-in-law instead. "Kate, I'm sending you shirt shopping for me more often. Check out the looks I'm getting right now."

He gestured to the party of women at the bar, whooping it up in bridal sashes proclaiming *Bachelorette* over their chests. A busty blonde took his gesture as invitation to catcall.

"Hey! You with the glittery shirt!" she shouted, cupping her hand over her mouth. "Give us a show!"

He waved good-naturedly at the bachelorette party, ignoring their wolf whistles as he took his seat.

"What?" Kate asked, in what a stranger might interpret as a tone of total innocence. "You asked for an XL, and that was the only one they had in stock."

Drake chuckled. "I'm not sure who's being punished more by this shirt—Zander or the rest of us who have to watch him strut around in it."

"You only wish you could fill out a woman's shirt this well," Zander said, picking up his menu. He'd evidently thought the catcalling would stop once he showed he wasn't interested.

He obviously didn't comprehend the power of ladies liquored up in a pre-wedding pack.

"C'mon, give us a flex. Flex!"

Imani looked over.

Zander's face was buried in the menu. Which was upside down.

"I don't think they're going to be satisfied until you give them what they're asking for." Imani tapped the menu with a fingernail until he lowered it. She smiled at him, feeling her stomach unclench as she laughed at his expression. "You're the one who got them all riled up."

His blue gaze latched on to hers, and she felt herself drowning in the pool of his regard as his mouth widened into the same smile that had lured her into his bed last year.

"I was trying to be a gentleman," he said, then speared her with a grin. "But let it never be said I leave a woman riled up with no...resolution."

With that, he shoved his chair from the table and stood. Turning to the bachelorette party, he did a good Arnold Schwarzenegger–as–Mr. Olympia double biceps flex. The pose burst the seam under both of his sleeves with stereo ripping sounds, and Imani heard several stitches at the sides of the shirt pop as he flexed his pectorals—the same ones that had been under her hands as she'd leaned over him, naked, their bodies moving in rhythm...

Imani twisted away, picking up the wing menu to shield her vision from Zander's chest and Kate's raised-eyebrow glance that said, *Ooh, I saw that. We are so going to talk later.*

Despite its awkward beginning, dinner was surprisingly fun. Zander did much of the conversational lifting, regaling the table with stories from his and Drake's childhood, complete with him doing impersonations of Drake the year he chose to be William Shakespeare for Halloween.

"He drew on a terrible mustache and beard with Mom's eyebrow pencil, and wore one of Nana's lace blouses under Dad's black suit coat, popping out the collar in an attempt to be Elizabethan. He looked like a kook. Nobody knew who he was, and instead of saying 'Trick or treat' like a normal kid, he launched into an obscure Hamlet soliloquy." Zander waited for Imani and Kate's snorting laughter to end before adding, "Best Halloween ever. People dumped loads of candy into our bags just to get the sweating kid yelling about flesh melting and resolving itself into dew off their front porch."

Imani was thankful for Zander's goofy antics. His playfulness was like a breeze, whisking away her worries and giving her mind a break from creating mental to-do lists, as if he were a human version of her meditation apps. Apparently, he'd had the same effect on her best friend, as Kate didn't bring up the baby shower at all.

By the time dinner was over, along with her last Lactaid pill so she could have the wings with blue cheese, Imani's belly was full and her heart felt lighter than it had in months.

"Listen, Katie," she said, pulling her friend aside on the way out. "I'm sorry I kept the fling with Zander a secret."

Kate waved away Imani's apology. "It's me who should be apologizing for putting you on the spot. I hate to be the preggo who blames hormones, but, honestly, I cry at mayonnaise commercials. I didn't mean to make you feel like a shit friend, and I'm sorry for not being there for you."

"You've *always* been there for me. You let me bunk in

your bedroom every night for a whole year in high school, listening to me as I grieved for my mom. You've always had my back. I guess I just wanted to keep it to myself. Zander was...me stepping outside my comfort zone. A spur-of-the-moment thing."

Kate nodded. "I get it. You know I'm a crap liar, and you didn't want me knowing and inadvertently telling Drake, because then it would get weird and awkward."

"Weird and awkward?" Imani scoffed. "Never!"

They both giggled and got into the car.

Zander piled into the back seat with her moments later, his torn pink sleeves flapping at his shoulders like tiny capes over his biceps.

"Best wing crowd I've ever seen. It's a good thing I had some business cards with me. Those ladies know how to party." Zander's blue gaze scanned Imani from head to toe, and she felt hot as that familiar smile slid over his lips. "Need some help with your seat belt?"

"Nope." Imani tugged the nylon strap, leaning into Zander's side to get the thing latched, his clean smell tickling her nose. She swore he purposely took up more room in the back seat so she'd have to invade his personal bubble to buckle in. "I've got it."

Drake started the Prius, and Kate—ever the event planner—began ticking off the list of things they still needed to do before tomorrow's party, speaking mainly to her husband. He nodded, humming in assent every once in a while.

Imani was intrigued by their relationship. At Cerulean Books, Drake was known as the writer who hated the spotlight, yet here he was, adding to the list for the big shower-slash-gender-reveal without so much as a squeak of protest.

As they chattered, Imani's eyelids grew heavy. It was dark inside the Prius, and they had the windows cracked for air circulation, which created a hypnotic, whooshing white noise.

Imani let her head fall back. It was hard to get comfortable, as the stupid seat belt cut across her neck, and with every bump it felt like she was being garroted with a piano wire. Fed up, she pressed the release, easing the restraint off. She'd take her chances—what with the luggage on one side and Zander on the other, she wasn't likely to get better safety measures. She let her eyes drift closed, listening to the whoosh of the air, the wipers on low as they went through occasional rain, and the murmur of voices from the front seat, along with Zander's occasional rumble as he commented here and there. It was almost as if he were picking up the conversational slack from the back seat to allow her to rest.

Her lips curved. The guy was clever, she had to give him that. She'd let him take over while she closed her eyes for just a second . . .

"Imani? We're almost there." The voice at her ear was low, calm, and easy to ignore as she returned to the delicious cocoon of slumber, burrowing her head to better hear the steady heartbeat under her ear. *Lub-dub. Lub-dub.* The soothing sound made her sigh, her cold hand wriggling its way to someplace warm.

"O-okay, that's one way to get me to let you sleep longer." A deep baritone rumble of soft laughter vibrated under her head, as someone cupped her shoulder, jostling her awake. "But I draw the line at going to third base in the back of my car. Wake up, Sleeping Beauty."

Blinking her eyes in confusion, Imani saw she was in the Prius's back seat. They were driving through an area with bright streetlights that illuminated the inside in camera-like bursts of light. It took a couple of streetlights before she became aware of two embarrassing facts: She'd fallen against Zander Matthews. And the warm place she'd stuffed her hand... was between Zander's thighs.

Directly against his crotch.

Imani's body spasmed as she launched off Zander, crashing into her suitcase with enough force to knock it against the window with a sharp *bang!*

"Everyone okay back there?" Drake asked from the driver's seat.

"Fell asleep and had a nightmare," Imani said, her voice gravelly with sleep.

"That's harsh," Zander whispered, clutching his chest as if wounded.

Thankfully, moments later, Drake pulled into the driveway of Gigi's nutmeg-colored 1920s bungalow, and Imani's relief was palpable.

She shoved around the suitcase on her side and flung herself out of the Prius the second Drake put it in park, her soul doing consecutive pirouettes as she stretched her legs into long strides up the driveway.

"Gigi!" she called, using the nickname for her grandmother, Georgina Foltz. "Gigi" had been easier for Imani to pronounce as a toddler, and it had stuck.

"Well, there's my girl!"

Beaming, Gigi levered herself up from the porch glider.

She wore a zebra-striped housedress that zipped up the front, and her feet were stuffed into a pair of fuzzy blue slippers. Her sparse, blond-brown hair was up in curlers, pinned in neat rows over her scalp and covered by a wispy purple head scarf. It was the same thing she'd done with her hair at night for as long as Imani could remember, and the sight of those orderly curlers made her weepy with nostalgia.

Her grandmother held her arms open. "Get over here and give me some love. Watch your step—the porch light is out, and I don't want you breaking your neck, Shypoke."

Imani grinned at the childhood nickname. She bounded up the porch steps, soaking in the sight of the woman who had taken on a mother's role in her life, starting in high school.

"Gigi!" She enveloped her grandmother in a fierce hug, breathing in the familiar, nose-tickling scent of her grandmother's curl-setting spray and rose-scented body powder. Imani was startled to feel the bones of her grandmother's spine sticking out like little knobs through the back of her zebra housedress.

Imani's mind went on high alert. Had her grandmother lost weight? She felt so spindly and frail. Gigi must've needed help but was too proud to ask. The realization struck her like a blow. She'd thought she'd been on top of things by calling a couple of times a week, but clearly, her grandmother's health had gone downhill.

What else had she missed, not having visited for almost a year?

Imani swallowed the ball of guilt, vowing to be a better granddaughter.

"Gigi, I brought you a little something." Imani reached into her tote for the parcel she'd wrapped in tissue paper. "A lady was selling these on the corner of Fifth Avenue, and while I'm sure it's a knockoff, I thought you could show it off to your card-playing buddies."

Her grandmother unwrapped the Coach wallet and squinted down at it.

"I can't see a damned thing with that light off." Gigi scowled up at the offending fixture above them. "Can't get anyone to fix it, either, because my ladder's broken and I haven't been able to bribe anyone to come over and do it for me."

"I'll take care of it, don't worry," Imani assured her, guilt knotting again in her stomach. Her grandmother hadn't told her about any repairs she needed done, yet glancing around the porch and the small patch of lawn visible in the car's lights, there seemed to be an abundance of things that needed doing. She felt neglectful. She felt ashamed, wishing she'd visited more. "Here. I'll shine my cell light on it. See? It's leopard-print. Isn't that fun?"

"You're sweet to your old Gigi." Her grandmother grasped her hand, squeezing it. "I'm so glad you're here. Now, who is this in the sparkly muscle shirt? You didn't tell me you were bringing your boyfriend. Don't just stand there, introduce us!"

Imani spun and noticed Zander had followed her up the porch, his steps cat-quiet in spite of his size.

He set her turquoise suitcases down on the dimly lit porch. Then he stuck his hand out to her grandmother, as formal as if he were dressed in a suit and tie instead of a pink shirt with a penis-like drumstick so bedazzled that the rhinestones caught the streetlights and reflected them like a million tiny disco balls.

"I'm Zander Matthews, Patty Matthews's youngest son. My mom used to bowl with you in the Ladies' League. She said to say hi and to tell you she's got a molasses cookie with your name on it whenever you can get over to the bakery."

"I recognize you now," Gigi crowed, snatching Zander's hand and yanking him toward her, temporarily abandoning Imani. "I haven't seen Patty in a month of Sundays. After your father died, I'm the one who told her to open a bakery after tasting those cookies every Friday night, don't you know? And look! PattyCakes is still hopping all these years later."

"She is my hero," Zander said, his expression polite despite the fact that Gigi's hand had drifted up to his biceps. Her fingertips—nails painted electric blue—were squeezing his muscles, as if he were a melon she was testing for soft spots.

"Feel him, will you, Imani? He's like a lumberjack," Gigi said, peering at his biceps, then zeroing in on his exposed abs under the women's half-shirt. She patted his abdomen. "Well, would you look at that! He's a big boy, but there's not an inch of fat on him! Are you on one of those protein diets?"

Imani intercepted Gigi's groping hand before it could drift south to examine the goods there. When she did, her hand brushed against the faint trail of hair pointing like a neon sign toward his crotch. Her cheeks burned as she captured her grandmother's hand safely in her own.

"Okay, Gigi. I think we're done fondling Zander for

the night. Let's get you in the house. Um, Zander," Imani said, focusing on the suitcases sitting by his sneakers so she didn't have to look him in the eyes. She knew he'd have that amused grin on his face—the one that always made her want to cuff him. Or kiss him. So she avoided his gaze as she spoke. "Thanks for the help. If you could stick those inside, please? I'll take them upstairs later."

She assisted Gigi and her walker through the door and flipped on the light to the foyer.

It was all she could do not to cry out in dismay.

The place was a disaster!

Gigi's walker could barely maneuver around the bins piled in the entryway. The original pocket doors to the pink parlor were pushed open, and she could see inside the place standing in for Gigi's bedroom until her knees healed.

It was like a Container Store bomb had gone off in there. Bins, bags, totes, and boxes were stacked strategically in the parlor, spilling out into the foyer. The bins were clean, but they were piled almost to the ceiling of the ten-foot-tall Craftsman-style room, making the passage unsafe.

Noticing Imani's look, her grandmother stood belligerently next to a pile of boxes.

"Most of these should be in the attic. I had Noah Nowakowski bring them down for me so I could decorate for the holidays, and then I had other visitors grab some from the spare bedroom for my winter clothes, then my summer clothes." Gigi pushed out her lower lip at Imani's incredulous expression. "They're *my* things, and I have a right to be able to get to them. Once I feel better, I can put them upstairs where they belong."

Glancing at the stairs, Imani noticed that nothing and nobody had been up the beautiful, original wooden staircase in a long time, if the bags, boxes, and debris crowding every step were any indication.

In fact, the only thing getting through the rubble was Lancelot, Gigi's African gray parrot, who swooped down from the upstairs banister. He perched on Gigi's walker like a raven from one of Poe's stories.

"BIIITCH!" Lancelot screeched, ruffling his gray feathers as if the mere sight of houseguests offended the old bird. "Damned FOOLS!"

Zander snorted behind her, and Imani blew out a breath. "Nice to see you too, Lancelot."

She'd sort of been hoping her deceased grandfather's wretched pet had decided to join him on the other side, but the bird looked spry and able for his twenty-seven years.

She focused on her grandmother. "It's fine. I'm here, and I'll put everything back to rights while you're recovering from your surgery at the rehab center. Once you return home, I promise it'll be spick-and-span."

"Rehab center?" Her grandmother spat the words. "Why would I pay to sleep in a lumpy bed, eat garbage food, and have people poking me day and night, when I can stay in my own home and recover with you for free?"

Imani's jaw dropped. Before she could question this change in plans, Kate knocked and popped her head into the foyer.

"Hi, Mrs. Foltz. I wanted to invite you to the baby shower tomorrow. I didn't send you a separate invite, because I figured you'd be coming with Imani." Her best friend grinned at everyone, oblivious to any tension. "And no gifts. It's just a chance to get together, eat, and have some fun at Zander's studio."

Zander gave his trademark lazy smile. "Fun is my middle name. I've already stocked up on libations for Saturday." Then his face momentarily looked unsure. "But for Sunday, are you sure you only want orange juice and herbal tea? I bet some of the helpers would appreciate some champagne chilled for mimosas. You'd want something stronger than tea, wouldn't you, Imani?"

Kate smacked Zander's arm. "She doesn't know about Sunday. I haven't had a chance to ask her yet."

Zander flashed his pearly smile at Gigi. "You'd think eating an entire dinner together, she might've found a spare thirty seconds? These two make chatting an Olympic sport."

"Always been like that, ever since they met in dance class," Gigi agreed. She sidled over, taking the support arm Zander offered with a rapacious look, her hand settling on his biceps once again. "Those girls' mouths flap like the tail feathers on a goose's hind end."

Imani ignored them, looking at her best friend.

"Ask me what?"

Kate's green eyes widened in that beseeching look Imani knew so well.

"I'm sorry I didn't ask sooner. I was going to attend alone because I didn't want to take you away after you'd just arrived. And it's only because Drake's out of town for his—"

"Signings. I know. I set them up for the *Memory's Lane* paperback release months ago, followed by a flight to Los Angeles to film his cameo in *Halloween Hacker*. He wanted to do it now so he wouldn't miss the baby's birth." Imani mentally reviewed the checklist of publicity events for Drake's first romance going from hardcover to paperback, followed by the filming timetable for his tenth horror book's movie adaptation. It was perfect. "What do you need me to attend? Is something wrong with the baby?"

"No! Nothing like that." Kate's hand rubbed her belly, as if to ward off anything bad happening. "With Drake leaving Sunday morning, I need someone to fill in for a couple of...Lamaze classes."

Imani swallowed. Kate was her best friend. There was only one good answer.

"Of course," she said. "I'll hyperventilate with you anytime."

And just like that, between Zander, Gigi, and Kate, Imani's plan for a peaceful, rejuvenating summer cartwheeled out the door.

After they left and she'd had a chance to catch up with Gigi, Imani's constant yawns finally prompted her grandmother to send her upstairs to bed.

"The doors to the rooms have been closed, so while I can't vouch for the dust up there, at least Lancelot hasn't left any grenades to step in." Gigi directed Imani to the hall cupboard under the staircase. "Grab a set of fresh sheets and a blanket, and strip off whatever's on the bed now."

"I'm sorry I'm pooping out on you so early, Gigi."

Her grandmother waved the words away. "Nonsense. I need my beauty sleep too, don't you know? Tomorrow's card night, and I'm hosting." Gigi's dark-brown eyes lit up. "Do you think you might be able to—"

"Give your regrets to Kate for missing her shower? Sure." Imani set down the armful of bedding to draw the covers up to her grandmother's chin. "She'll understand, with your knees—"

"Well, yes. But that's not what I need help with." Gigi pushed away the tuck-in to prop herself up on one elbow. "Can you help me clean the kitchen so we can play cards in there? I can't get the floors as good as I'd like with these damn knees...and if you could get down my good bottle of Jack and my highball glasses, I'd appreciate it."

Imani laughed, giving her grandmother a kiss on her forehead. "Done and done."

Thanking her mother's side of the genetic pool for her long legs, she ascended the staircase. She leaped over bags and straddled boxes of her grandmother's stuff, going as carefully as a rock climber picking out holds on a cliff. She reached the second floor without dropping the armload of clean linens and used her knee to open the spare bedroom door. Walking sideways, she shoved a couple of bins aside to get to the bed, where she set down her load, heading back for her suitcases.

By the time she'd made it up the stairway gauntlet the second time, rain plunked against the metal roof, coming down like a car wash. Thankfully, the problems with Gigi's house did not extend to leaks. No rain came through, and Imani found no wet spots on the floor—at least what she could see of the floor with the boxes, old furniture, and clothing bags piled everywhere.

She flicked on the light switch, took a deep breath of the stale room, and sneezed.

"Gesundheit!" Gigi yelled from downstairs. "Is it terribly

dusty up there? Maybe you should sleep down here? I think I have a cot in the garage somewhere."

"It's not bad at all," Imani said. "I'm heading to bed as soon as I get these sheets on."

"Suit yourself. Sleep tight, and I'll make you a nice breakfast in the morning!"

"Night, Gigi," Imani said, shaking her head. There was no talking her grandmother out of waiting on her while she could, so she didn't bother trying.

With considerable effort, Imani cracked open the only window she could reach without moving bins and a dresser, allowing cool air to flood the room. Unfortunately, along with the breeze came the dried-up carcasses of at least twenty flies, which must've been lying on the inside of the windowsill. The reason for the dead flies was immediately evident as she spotted a palm-sized tear in the screen that made it whip back and forth in the wind of the approaching storm.

"Got to add a screen-repair kit to my list." She used her sock foot to sweep the dead flies into the corner. She held her hand to the opening and couldn't feel any water coming in, so she thought she could risk keeping it open all night without destroying the sill.

Squeezing through the bags of her grandfather's old clothes, dilapidated boxes of Christmas decorations, and a bunch of dusty old drapes, she stripped the twin bed of its comforter and sheets, tossing them on some stacked bins. She thought briefly about fighting her way to the bathroom to wash up, then decided she'd survive dirty hands, face, and teeth tonight.

Fatigue hit her like a wave as she made up the bed with

the fresh linens. She pulled some lightweight pajamas from her suitcase and changed for bed.

As she slipped between the sheets, her phone chimed with a text notification.

Zander.

She debated not looking at it, but her traitorous eyes had already scanned the preview, and she felt compelled to read the rest.

> Zander: Okay, one thing is bothering me. Your grandmother called you a Shypoke. What the hell IS that?

Imani smiled in the dark bedroom, her phone's display light making the boxes and bins around her look more like a fun fort rather than a hoarder's wet dream. She texted back.

> Imani: The only reason I'm telling you this is because I owe you for earlier. Shypoke is the colloquial name of a local green heron, and Gigi's nickname for me.

> Zander: How did you end up being named after a water bird?

> Imani: Because I have disproportionately long legs. A gift from the Hungarian side of my family tree.

Imani debated whether to tell him the whole reason, then shrugged. He'd asked, and she did feel as though

she was the one in the "owe him big time" category. She
texted the rest.

> Imani: Plus I went a long time undiagnosed
> as lactose intolerant. For the record, I have
> an unrequited love for milkshakes. The green
> heron's common name is 'shitepoke' because
> the bird is known for its...loose bowels when
> startled.

She added the poop emoji followed by the See No Evil
monkey and then hit send, biting her lip as she waited for
his reply. Besides Kate and her dad, nobody else knew the
meaning behind Gigi's nickname, and she felt exposed by
telling him, like she was posing nude at his studio instead
of texting fully clothed. Posing nude...

She jumped as her phone chimed with his reply.

> Zander: Better than what kids called me growing up.
> Besides, your legs are perfectly proportioned.

> Imani: No fair! What nickname could you have
> possibly had growing up?

> Zander: That's a story for another time. But I
> guarantee Shypoke is sweet in comparison. Hope
> you're feeling better and can get some rest.

Before she could answer, he followed it up with another
text, changing subjects abruptly.

Zander: As awkward as it was, I'm glad Drake and
Kate know about our past. Makes it easier for both
of us to move on.

Imani's eyebrows went up.

*Move on?* He'd felt the vibes in the alley behind the wing
place as surely as she had!

She snorted, feeling like he was playing with her. She
texted back, wanting to see how far she could push his
charade before he revealed his ulterior motive.

Imani: I agree. Now we can go back to being just
friends and be there to help Drake and Kate with
the baby prep.

She finished with an emoji of a baby girl and a baby
boy face, then waited as the three dots did the wave on her
screen, indicating he was replying.

Zander: Being friends is a great goal. Speaking
of goals, I overheard your grandmother say the
porch light needs to be changed. I've got a ladder
you can borrow. Happy to bring it over in the
morning.

*Aha!* Imani grinned. He *had* felt the chemistry. But as
much as she might welcome the physicality of being with
Zander again, nothing good would come of another fling.
Best to keep it casual. Uncomplicated, like he did with
the rest of his exes. Her thumbs tapped the keyboard on
her phone.

Imani: Don't know when I'll be around. Have a long list of errands to fix up/clean out Gigi's house. I don't think Grandpa's old car runs, so we'll be grabbing Jimmy's Car Service to head to the home improvement store over in Hornell.

Zander: I figured you'd be busy. I'll leave the ladder in the back next to the garage.

His reply came back so fast, Imani blinked in surprise. He wasn't upset about not seeing her?

Another message popped up.

Zander: Keep it as long as you'd like. When you're done, text me. Either Drake, Ryker, or I will come pick it up.

He'd send one of his brothers to pick it up? She frowned. That was unexpected. Sure, it fit with her decision to keep it uncomplicated, but a tiny part of her couldn't help but feel hurt that he wasn't at least *trying* to get with her. At the airport, he'd said she broke his heart, only to flirt incessantly in the car...yet now he was all for missing an opportunity to see her? She tried to goad him, pretending she was ending the conversation.

Imani: Perfect. Thanks again! Good night.

But all he sent back was a thumbs-up.

Wait. That was it?

She glared at the phone, expecting those three dots to dance.

But they never did.

She punched down the pillow and yanked the covers to her chin.

"Fine." She glared at the popcorn ceiling. "We'll just be friends."

She muted her phone and set it facedown to charge, fuming. This past year, she'd been keeping tabs on Zander, directing conversations with Kate to casually discover his whereabouts. For months, she'd been high-key questioning her decision to ghost him after their fling. Had his talk of a broken heart been a ruse—or worse, a joke?

It pissed her off. Worse, it was keeping her awake. After forty pillow-flipping minutes struggling to sleep, she gave up.

"Might as well be productive." She flung herself out of bed and downstairs to the kitchen, keeping quiet until she was at the back of the house to avoid waking Lancelot. She knew Gigi slept like the dead.

She got out the cleaning supplies from under the sink and started scrubbing the kitchen floor. As she worked at the old linoleum, she listed the reasons to stay away from Zander Matthews this summer.

She hoped that at least one of those would stick.

# CHAPTER 4

It took every ounce of Zander's Marine-strengthened fortitude to send only a thumbs-up to Imani's lukewarm texts. He'd hoped for a larger opening in her replies, some indication she'd felt the same zing in the restaurant when they'd teamed up to distract Kate and Drake from the bombshell announcement about their one-weekend fling. But two hours later, the only idea he'd had to further his plan with Imani was...a ladder.

So, after changing out of the pink sparkly dick shirt—which landed squarely in the dumpster behind his studio—he headed over to Ryker's garage. He knew his gearhead brother would still be awake, and Ryker had a way of putting things into proper perspective.

"Damn," Zander said, after pushing open the door to Ryker's garage and spotting his brother shirtless, doing lat pull-downs on the Smith machine he kept next to his bay of car lifts. "You've got to lay off those bro-tein shakes, dude. If your lats get any bigger, they're going to bust out of your back like angel wings."

"It's work out or lash out," his brother grunted, completing his set and grabbing his towel. He chugged some of whatever post-workout mix was in his metal Tervis, then leveled a look at Zander. "At least, that's what the shrink at the VA is always preaching to me. Besides, any wings that sprout out of my back are likely to be scaled and dragon-like."

"True. I've seen you unhinge your jaw to eat your lunch on more than one occasion." Zander approached the closest car lift, admiring the sleek, matte-black beast of a car held aloft as if on a pedestal. He gave a low whistle. "Isn't this the same bile-green '68 Impala that was covered in rust last week? I like what you've done with her. The blacked-out wheels are sick. Is she your only date tonight, then? I thought your doctor had given you some social homework. Told you to get out a little more and join the rest of us in the world beyond this garage."

Ryker stood. His prosthesis popped further into the socket as he put weight on his left leg, which ended in the black carbon spring-like blade he used for running.

"Don't you have a mud pie to make in your 'studio'?" he asked, putting air quotes around the word "studio" as he moved to jump up on the Smith machine's metal bar, his hands shoulder-width apart for wide-grip pull-ups. "Or a plate-painting party or some shit like that? Because I don't need life advice from the guy whose personal manifesto is about as deep as a three-word Nike ad. All I need is to be left the hell alone. I don't know why that's so hard to understand."

Zander rolled his eyes. "I need to put a damn mood ring on you, dude. You're a lot these days."

"Copy that. Don't let the door hit you in the ass on your way out."

Zander opened his mouth to give him hell, when his gaze snagged on his brother's tattoo. The black and gray of the eagle, globe, and anchor on Ryker's shoulder bulged with each flexion, the other permanent reminder of his brother's time in the Marines.

As if he needed something more permanent than missing some of his left leg.

Initially when Ryker had returned from his second Marine deployment in Afghanistan to recover from a below-knee amputation and other wounds from an exploded IED, he'd seemed fine, facing his surgery plan with stoic realism. Almost unfazed by the partial limb loss, the painful stitches, the staples, and the wound VAC he wore to heal his shredded body, Ryker was more focused on when he'd go back to Afghanistan. He pestered the doctors at Walter Reed and his platoon sergeant, pushing for a return to active duty. He knew other guys who had returned after a BKA, and he was eager to get back into his combat role.

But the days turned into weeks, then into months as his wound refused to heal. Eventually, the Marine medical board decided against his return to combat, offering him lateral moves instead.

Ryker turned them down. If he couldn't serve his country the same way he had before his injury, he would take the honorable discharge and return to civilian life.

It was this, more than the wounds themselves, that had turned him from a happy, dedicated serviceman to a person who preferred to be around cars over people. Drake, Zander, and their mother took turns watching out for their middle brother—never allowing him to slink too far into his world of gears and grease, yanking him out, by force when necessary, to join in the world and be social.

Tonight was Zander's watch.

Zander rolled his head side to side, his vertebrae popping, releasing the tension that came whenever he thought about those dark days as Ryker's recovery coach at Walter Reed. He did the same relaxing breath he'd shown Imani earlier, then spoke.

"Sorry, bro. You're right. We're not trying to be up your ass. We're just worried about you."

Ryker dropped down from the pull-up bar, his Nike landing with a splat while his prosthetic hit the concrete with a barely a whisper of sound. He closed the few steps between them, grabbing his shirt from the top of the massive rolling toolbox.

"You're afraid I'm going to stick a hose from the exhaust pipe to the window, climb inside the car, and fall asleep, like Aunt Beth did." Ryker's blue eyes blazed as he yanked the T-shirt over his head. "But I'm fine."

"That coming from the guy who's living like a hermit. Kate told me you weren't sure if you were coming to the party tomorrow night, and Drake's pissed."

"I've got work." Ryker made as if to walk past him, but Zander grabbed his shirt.

"You're the godfather of this child." He got up into his brother's face, meeting force with force so Ryker couldn't retreat. "Surely you want to see if the newest Matthews kid has dangling bits or not?"

"But what if it does?" Ryker whispered, making no move to pull away. He wore a tortured, pained expression, his blue eyes wild as he touched the crescent-moon-shaped nick he had on his ear from the same piece of shrapnel that had smashed through his left leg. "What if it's a boy and he feels compelled to follow in our footsteps? Take on the family legacy?"

"You mean be a Marine?" At his brother's terse nod, Zander shrugged, releasing his brother's shirtfront. "So he joins the fleet. We all chose our paths. Nobody ever forced us to go to the recruiter, and I'm sure if it happens, Drake and Kate will make damn sure the kid is doing it for the right reasons—not for some tradition. By the way, dude, you do know if it's a Matthews girl, she can be in infantry, too."

Ryker groaned, slapping his palms to his eyes.

"I didn't think about that possibility. I remember the pressure, and I don't want the kid feeling some stupid obligation after learning that all Matthews men were Marines, almost since the Corps began. I want him—"

"Or her."

"—or her to make the choice without fearing any disappointment from anyone living, or for some dead legacy." Ryker took his hands from his face, shaking his head. "I know it's not my child. But with all this damn radiation treatment to curb the cells in my body from growing bone everywhere except where it's needed, I'm not likely to have any of my own. I feel this sense of responsibility to not screw up my nephew. Or niece."

Zander gazed at his brother for a minute.

"You know I'd do anything for you, right?" he asked. When Ryker nodded, he clapped him on the back. He gripped his brother's shoulder, putting all his love and support into his expression before saying, "And I mean this in the nicest possible way: you're being a neurotic douchebag. Do you know that?"

Ryker scoffed, shoving Zander's hand off.

"I was being serious, Zan."

"So was I. You need to let Drake and Kate know you're coming to the shower and quit that talk about screwing up your niece or nephew. That's my job." Zander puffed out his chest. "Kate promised they'd call me Cool Uncle Z and said I could teach the kid axe-throwing, beekeeping, and how to sculpt a kick-ass mug before the age of three. I've already got the title I wanted—you can be the 'godfather' who attends the kid's boring science fairs. You can be in charge of the pinewood derby car, then be there to pick up the pieces when your car loses and you have to admit to your niece or nephew that you only know how to make cars pretty. All show and no go."

The last was enough to warrant a punch in the arm.

Ryker glowered at him.

"Fine. I'll text Kate." Ryker tossed the dirty towel into a wheeled bin of the same in the corner and snagged a new one from a neatly folded pile on top of his metal workbench. "Now, are you going to ask me what you came to ask me? Or are we going to dance around it all night?"

Damn. He'd hoped to ask with a little more subtlety, but he should have known: his brother did subtlety like a hungry T. Rex.

"The thing is. I need a wingman," Zander blurted.

"I heard about the shirt Kate bought you as payback for seducing her best friend at their wedding. Sounds like you've got 'wingman' pretty much covered."

Zander groaned. "Drake called you already?"

Ryker grinned, and his "resting bastard face" was transformed into the face of the brother he was a decade ago, before the injury. "Sent a picture, too. Honestly, it's a weird way to come out of the closet, man. I'd opt for something a little classier than 'I like mine bone-in' when you tell Mom."

"Har-har," Zander said, not flinching when Ryker gave him a not-so-joking double tap with his fist on his arm. "No, I need a wingman for my plan to work with Imani."

"What's your plan?"

"Date her or forever hate her," Zander said, giving him what he'd come to think of as his Imani Manifesto in Rhyme. Then he explained his theory as he checked his phone to see if Imani had texted. Still nothing. He shoved the device back into his pocket.

Ryker heard him out, then shook his head. "Hate is a little harsh, isn't it? Considering you've apparently been pining over her since last August, are you sure you've thought about your options?"

Zander fingered the leather cord around his wrist, brushing the black piece of ceramic tied on it. The oval depicted the Chinese calligraphy characters for the concept that had become his way of life: mindfulness. Living in the moment.

"I haven't exactly been *pining*. And *hate* isn't really the right word. I just...something clicked for me that weekend with her in Niagara Falls. And I can't..." Zander blew out a breath, unable to vocalize to his brother that he'd felt connected in a way he never had with any other woman. He felt seen. While Ryker was an outstanding problem solver, he wasn't sure his brother's EQ could withstand that much bro-fession. So he kept it simple. "Look, she's living in my head, dude. I need to know if what I felt was a fluke or not."

Ryker snagged his Tervis and drained it, the ice clinking against his teeth. "So, you've decided if you give Imani some sort of dick-ultimatum, she'll fall hopelessly in love? That's your game plan? 'Cause it sucks."

"She quit on *me*. Never gave what we had a chance, assuming I was some sort of shallow…" Zander trailed off, his hands moving in the air.

"Thirst trap?" Ryker laughed at his brother's glare, using the lever to lower the Impala until it was about a foot off the ground. "Drake told me, with Kate pleading in the background that I should talk sense into you. Imani's not here for *you* this summer. She's here for Kate's shower, then to help her grandmother."

"I know. I just want to take her out. Dinner or something. She used to be a dancer, so maybe to the ballet? But I'd settle for another dance or a night talking over drinks."

Ryker used his spring-like prosthetic to snag the green-and-black padded creeper. He lay on it and wheeled himself under the front of the car, with only his right Nike sneaker and carbon blade sticking out.

"Hand me the three-eighths wrench."

Zander found it in the rolling toolkit and plopped the tool into Ryker's outstretched hand.

After a few moments working on some unseen bolt, Ryker spoke again. "So you think this date will clear it up? Tell you if your weekend in bed with her was some sort of reflexive reaction to watching your older brother tying the knot, or if it meant more?"

"Yeah, but without the snarky spin you're putting on it." Zander heaved a breath. "Look, I want to know if Imani Lewis is renting space in my head because she's 'the one' everyone says will someday appear, or if she's only intriguing because she ghosted me. Let's be real, most of the women I've dated start out all sparks but then flame out, and the whole 'relationship' shatters like a piece of wet clay in a bisque kiln."

"I understand your goal, Zan, but I'm not sure if you're reading the room." Ryker rocketed out from under the car to chuck the wrench back into the toolkit so hard it clattered. "You know how much it takes out of a person to be someone's legs after a surgery. I don't think you've thought about how available Imani is for a relationship. With anyone."

Zander's jaw dropped. He *hadn't* thought of that.

"Don't I owe it to both of us to try? If it's crap timing, then it'll go down in flames, but if there is something there—isn't it worth the risk?"

"You really like this girl?" Ryker asked, his left leg making a *thunk* of metal against cement as he got up. He leaned against the car. "Because Drake's going to kill you if you screw with his publicist. Plus Kate's her best friend, and if our sister-in-law murders you, it'll be done in such a complete, spreadsheet-perfect way, they'll never find your body. Be sure this isn't another one of your harebrained plan-of-the-week ideas."

Zander wanted to reach out and punch his brother so badly his fingernails dug into the palms of his hands. Yet at the same time, he recognized it was a legitimate question.

Was figuring this out worth the possible collateral damage?

He relaxed, plucking an answer from the emotional maelstrom. "I'm not sure how I feel. We've only had a weekend together. Last August. But she makes me want to explore the dirty c-word."

"Mmm. There are so many dirty c-words to choose from, but from the context of your past failed relationships, I'm assuming you mean 'commitment.' Or is it 'chastity'? It's not 'Catholicism,' is it? Because Mom's gonna be pissed if you leave the Methodist church."

"You're such an ass." Usually, Zander was the one his brothers wanted to strangle for not being serious. Having the tables turned on him was uncool. "I'm looking for your advice, Ry. I don't want to screw this up, and if I ask Drake, he'll give me some weirdo, wordy answer that involves three historical references, and I'll have to do a freaking research paper before I can figure out what he means."

"So you're asking me? The guy who—in case you haven't noticed—has no girlfriend? Hasn't had one, in fact, since before I became bionic?" Ryker shook his head. "Scraping the bottom of the barrel, but okay. I'll give you my opinion, but you're not going to like it."

Zander leaned forward. He wished he had a notebook and pencil. Based on the intense expression on his brother's face, he was going to be serious, and he'd only say this once.

"My advice: let her make the moves. Demonstrate that you're interested. Hell, tell her point-blank that you like her, but then also tell her she's got to be the one who takes it to the next level." Ryker paused. "You've dated a bunch of women, but Imani—she's got the whole control thing going on, and she knows her own mind. I think if you don't make a move on her, you're going to see better results than if you do that incessant flirting thing."

"Incessant flirting?" Zander clutched his chest. "Why you gotta be so judgy? I'm friendly, dude. Something you should try sometime if you want a date. Your RBF— resting bastard face—is intense. Just sayin'."

"I meant you've got to let her control the pace. Don't make a move to kiss her—let *her* kiss *you*. Repress your caveman instincts. Don't be such a typical baby-of-the-family hedonist."

"I am not a hedonist," Zander said, pretending to be offended. "I only want what I want, when I want it."

"Just hang back." Ryker gave him a challenging look. "You're man enough to let her drive, aren't you?"

"Hell yeah." Zander ran a hand through his hair. "But what if she never calls me? What if, after we see each other at the baby shower tomorrow, she avoids me until she returns to New York City?"

"Ask yourself: What does she need most right now?" Ryker shrugged, as if it were the simplest question in the world. "And then make it happen for her."

Zander looked at his brother, confused. "I already offered to drop off a ladder. What else can I do?"

"Like I said, my garage is no set for *Bachelor in Paradise*," Ryker said. "Go deeper, Zan. What does she *need*? If you can help her post some wins on her scoreboard, she might take you seriously."

Zander's heart danced with the possibility of Imani agreeing to date him. Although he'd played it off in his head that he'd be able to "hate her" if she didn't give him the time of day, having spent most of the evening with her, his memory of that weekend last year seemed more truth than fantasy.

They *did* have a connection.

And he was going to do his best to show her he was worth a second look.

"Hey, can I borrow your ladder in the morning? And I need you to follow me in your work truck over to Mrs. Foltz's house on Grover Street tonight. I've got an idea."

# CHAPTER 5

Imani jolted awake as her phone chimed a text notification.

She squinted, bleary-eyed, out of Gigi's upstairs bedroom window. Sunlight filled the room as if it were high noon. Flipping over her cell, she groaned. It was only seven a.m., which meant after fuming about Zander Matthews and his damn sexy smile, then stress-cleaning Gigi's kitchen, followed by a shower, she'd logged four hours of sleep.

The text preview showed Kate's grinning profile picture, and Imani clicked it open.

> Kate: Heyyyyy. You up? I got some deets for you.
> Can you talk?

Imani yawned, stretching as she pulled the phone to her, unplugging it from the charger.

> Imani: I'm up, but the parrot is a light sleeper, so
> I'll have to whisper. Deets about what?

The phone trilled in her hand a second later and she answered.

"So," Kate started, as if they were already mid-conversation, "Drake heard from Ryker that Zan's been holding a torch for you since the wedding. I know my reaction sucked at first, but now that I've had a chance to absorb the fact you two slept together, I think you'd be a cute match."

"It's not a thing, Katie," Imani whispered, clearing the sleep from her throat. She closed her eyes against the bright sun and tuned out the sounds of birds chirping outside her window, tugging the covers over her head. "I've got time for only two life goals this summer: make sure Gigi gets through surgery and rehab, then figure out what I'm doing about the publicity manager promotion. If I take it, I'll be shedding some of my smaller authors, but I'll also be dealing with more sales pressure in addition to figuring out how to manage a staff of publicists. I'll barely have time to read books in that role, and that was the whole reason I got into the publishing industry in the first place."

"Are you sure it's not your impostor syndrome talking? You'd be an amazing manager. You're so good at your job and always mentoring others. Drake loves you as his publicist, and we both know he's a tough sell on anyone pushing him into the spotlight." Kate laughed as Imani snorted in agreement. "You even have Leann Bellamy—the Diva of Romance—twirling to your tune, like one of your rec-club ballet kids."

"Aw, don't remind me. I miss my kiddos! Tuesdays and Thursdays were the highlight of my week. And I know. I used to think I wanted to be a manager, too. But lately…" Imani trailed off, wishing she knew what, exactly, was the reason her guts churned every time she thought about the fabulous promotion.

"Ohhh," Kate's voice dipped, and Imani heard the unmistakable sound of pages being turned in a book. She didn't have to be there to know Kate was looking at the second most important tool in her life, next to her spreadsheets: her planner. "I'm so sorry, Imani. I forgot Sunday is the anniversary of your mom's death. You don't have to come to the Lamaze class tomorrow—I'll ask Drake's mom. Patty would love to be there, I'm sure!"

Guilt gnawed at Imani as she realized that with the hectic move-out of her apartment for the summer and the trip to Wellsville to care for Gigi, she'd forgotten that tomorrow was June 27. Sixteen years ago, at dance camp, she'd gotten that call from her dad, his raw sobbing almost more painful than the news he delivered. For so long, this date had brought a sense of dread and a wave of sadness so deep, it would make her physically ill. But this year, she'd almost forgotten. Or had she? Maybe somewhere in the recesses of her subconscious she'd remembered the terrible significance of Sunday's date, and that's what was throwing off her mojo lately?

Imani refocused on her friend's words. "Are you kidding? I haven't seen my bestie in months, and although our Margarita Mondays are on pregnancy hiatus, I think Birth-Ready Brunches are a great substitute."

Kate sighed. "Okay. You win. I appreciate this, Imani." It seemed she was going to accept Imani's reluctance to talk about either Zander or her mother. For now. Kate's voice brightened. "In other news, I can't wait to show you what I planned for Drake's second annual wreath-laying event at Arlington National Cemetery."

"Which, by the way, is my favorite annual event for him,

and that's saying something. Your husband has officially claimed millions of hearts with this new genre," Imani joked. Then she sobered. "I miss being excited about work. Lately, it feels like the better I get at my job..."

"The less you love it?" her best friend asked. "You know, you could always come work with me. Shifting Sweet Events to incorporate brand management for Drake in addition to my regular wedding clients was a fantastic idea, but with the baby coming, I'm starting to wonder if I've bitten off more than I can chew."

"Please." Imani brushed away the concern. "You've got the plans on your detailed spreadsheets. Plus Carl's a great assistant, and he'll take care of things until you're back, so you can enjoy the rest of your time before the baby. My summer, on the other hand, is booked with taking care of Gigi and putting her house to rights again."

"Ha, you can't fool me. Your organizer-lovin' heart is going pitter-pat right now. I'll bet you cleaned before you went to bed last night, didn't you?" Kate laughed as Imani remained silent. "I knew it! I sense a Container Store shopping spree in your future."

They chatted a few seconds more, and then Kate had to go pee. After hanging up, Imani entertained the idea of going back to sleep. It was Saturday. Who wanted to get up before eight on a weekend? But every time she closed her eyes, her mind went to Zander.

Probably because she could smell him.

She'd gotten floor cleaner on her pajamas, so she'd pulled on Zander's T-shirt after her shower and spent the night wrapped in the comforting scent of Irish Spring soap and the warm, unique spiciness that was him underneath. She thought she'd excised him from her life, but her brain, her very nose, zeroed in on the guy the moment he entered her orbit yesterday.

She knew she should've taken that shirt off last night, but it had been so comfortable. Now it smelled like she was lying in bed with him...

To distract herself, she toggled into her work email. Despite the fact she'd turned on her out-of-office notification on Thursday and cleaned her inbox out after yesterday's debacle with Leann Bellamy, she opened it to find twenty-eight unread emails, fourteen of which were marked urgent.

Imani groaned, flipping off the covers. She was officially up.

Fifteen minutes later, dressed in an old pair of shorts and a T-shirt that was *not* the property of her former one-night stand, she was ready. Her morning's to-do list included tea, breakfast, and then tackling her inbox before getting ready for Kate's shower.

After making it down the staircase gauntlet to the first level, she tiptoed past the front parlor, afraid of waking Lancelot. The bird could stay with a sheet over his cage all day if it would sweeten him up.

As if psychic, the bird gave a low wolf whistle from the dark room.

"Shh," Imani scolded as she maneuvered the tight walkway through the dining room into Gigi's tiny kitchen, which glowed in the morning light, thanks to the bleach wipes and the hour she'd spent scrubbing at the old mint-green linoleum floor. Situated at the back of the house, the room was lit by two windows: one over the sink and one next to the back door. While she hadn't gotten to clean the outside of the glass yet, the inside sparkled, and the smell of cleaning supplies gave her the feeling of a fresh start.

She filled Gigi's metal kettle with water and put it on the gas stove to heat, reveling in this morning ritual that was so different from her grab-and-go lifestyle in New York City. There was so much birdsong in the sound of wind blowing through the oak tree in her grandmother's backyard that Imani checked her phone to make sure her relaxation app hadn't accidentally started playing. She wasn't used to hearing nature in the morning and had forgotten how tranquil it was here, compared to home.

Imani made her tea and sat at Gigi's old wooden kitchen table, now polished to a lemony shine, its top traced with burns from long ago when it had stood in for an ironing board here and there. She cupped her mug and savored the warmth of the June sun as it draped over her shoulders, thawing something within her. She'd needed this break. That much of what Zander said was right.

Zander.

His name made her insides whirl like a series of piqué turns. She sipped her tea, relishing the hot sting of the liquid as she vowed to put him from her mind. She was busy enough without that distraction.

"Aw, thank you, Shypoke," Gigi said, startling Imani into spilling her tea. As she cursed and mopped at her shirt with a napkin, her grandmother laughed. "Looks like a cleaning fairy came—everything is sparkling in here. I'll bet you stayed up all night doing it too. Have some coffee. That'll wake you up."

"It's not waking up I have a problem with." Imani

bustled to the coffeepot, having already prepped it with her grandmother's favorite—Folgers—the night before. "It's the falling asleep and staying asleep that eludes me."

"Sure you don't want to skip Kate's shower and stay here for the May-I party with the girls?" Gigi asked. The contract rummy game had been a longtime staple in her family. "I'm making Foltz's Fiery Fizzers to drink. You'd like it. It tastes like a root beer float with a couple shots of Fireball whiskey to give it some oomph."

Imani chuckled. "Be careful how much oomph you're doling out, Gigi. Especially if they're driving. But maybe I'll take you up on one when I get back tonight. I'll try anything."

"Have you seen a doctor for your insomnia?" Gigi asked, as the smell of fresh coffee filled the tiny space. "They'll charge you up the ying-yang for every cotton swab they use, but sometimes they're right."

Imani nodded. "When I went for my yearly checkup, I told Dr. Kent I wasn't sleeping, and she ordered a full blood panel. Ruled out anemia, my thyroid is fine, and every marker was within normal ranges. She thought..." Imani paused, snagging a clean mug from the dishwasher, then opting—like she always had since childhood—to tell her grandmother everything. "She thought there might be psychological reasons, like stress. She asked if I might be depressed, as that often manifests itself in sleeplessness and fatigue."

Gigi was quiet while Imani poured coffee, setting it in front of her with the crystal jar of sugar cubes.

"Tomorrow will be sixteen years since Amira's passing. While I still feel her loss, the pain isn't as intense now.

More of an ache." Gigi dropped a sugar cube into her coffee, stirring thoughtfully. "I'm wondering if Kate's pregnancy is making it all fresh for you, with her about to be a mother."

Imani blinked. "I hadn't thought of that. Maybe. Seems like more than that, though. I barely function without gallons of tea, and then I can't sleep at night because of the caffeine. It's a vicious cycle."

Gigi patted at her curler-laden head, sipping her coffee. "I think I know what your problem is, Shypoke."

Imani smiled at the nickname, thinking about how she'd told Zander its origin last night. She sipped her tea. "What?"

"You need to get laid," Gigi said. "The boy who brought you home last night seems like as good a place to start as any."

Imani snorted in her tea, coughing and laughing. "What grandmother talks like that to her granddaughter?"

"One who happens to know a few things about a few things." Gigi stood, holding the table for support before limping over to the breadbox and toaster. She paused for a moment, then turned, her gray eyebrows raised in surprise. "Well, well, well. Speak of the devil. Your boyfriend is already here."

"Huh?" Imani leaped up, peering out of the window. Sure enough, Zander's car was in the bungalow's driveway. But there was no sign of the man, with his surfer good looks and casual-sex vibe, and she was surprised by the slight dip of her heart.

"What the hell is that?" Her grandmother pointed at something secured with silver duct tape to the garage door handle.

Imani was out the kitchen door and onto the back porch in an instant, eschewing shoes as she loped over the dewy grass to the Prius. Empty. She gingerly stepped over the gravel driveway to the garage, using her fingernails to peel away the edge of the duct tape and reveal a ziplock bag with a white piece of paper inside.

She opened the baggie and unfolded the paper until an electronic key plopped in her hand. Glancing at the paper, she read the short note:

> Heard Jimmy's Car Service is on vacation, so a cab might be hard to get. I'm working at the Wellsville studio, so I won't need my car. Thought you might want to borrow it for your errands. You can return it tonight at the baby reveal, and either Kate or I will give you a lift home. I'll bring the ladder over later. —Z.

She handed the note to Gigi.

"Well, that was thoughtful." Gigi pinned Imani with a look. "What exactly is going on with you two, Shypoke?"

"Nothing." She bit her lip as she tried to puzzle out his intentions. "At least, that's what I thought. I'm going to head downtown for some supplies. Do you want to come?"

"Nah. I'm going to sit in this clean kitchen and drink my coffee. Then before Noreen comes to pick me up for our hair appointment, I plan to mess it up by making you some gulyás," Gigi announced, grinning as Imani sucked in a breath of pleasure at the mention of Hungarian goulash. "What? You didn't think I'd forget your favorite meal, did you? Your grandpa taught me that recipe, but I only know how to make it to serve ten people, like he used to do in the old country. You're here working your backside off, and if you take the leftovers to your friends, we can justify a pot of it."

Imani raced upstairs to brush her teeth and slap on some mascara, her thoughts returning to Zander. He'd been the last guy she'd slept with, or even spent more than a few hours with, this entire year. Lately, it had been more exhaustion than fear of relationships that had kept her out of the dating pool. The whole rigmarole of courtship—finding the perfect outfit, waiting for a reservation in the best restaurant, hell, even shaving her legs—seemed way too much effort for a guy she probably wouldn't vibe with, statistically speaking.

It was so much easier to finish work, do the obligatory hour at the gym, grab takeout, and spend the evening vegging out in front of the TV, watching the moon scuttle behind the rooftops as it rose amid the city's few visible stars.

By herself.

Gone were the days when she'd stumbled to bed after too many drinks with friends. Now she'd stumble to bed after binge-watching too many rom-coms. Maybe her grandmother was right? Maybe she needed something more than just relaxing this summer?

She examined herself in the mirror. Her hair was up in a utilitarian ponytail, and she wore a pair of denim cutoffs and a yellow Bronx Barre Belles recital T-shirt. The bags under her eyes looked like bruises, but she didn't feel like wrestling through her suitcase for the rest of her makeup kit, so she smoothed on a cheerful, red-pink lipstick she found in Gigi's medicine cabinet, aptly named Summer Fling.

Maybe her grandmother's words, the vibes at the restaurant, and even the freaking lipstick was the universe's way of telling her something? Zander was a chill, laid-back kind of guy, and if she had to bet, he'd be cool with a summer fling.

But then she thought about the text last night. His insistence they be friends. Was he purposely trying to mess with her mind?

Twenty minutes later, Imani settled herself into Zander's car. She had to move the seat forward about a foot to reach the pedals and spent a good while adjusting the mirrors so she could see something other than blue sky, but once she'd put the tiny car into gear, it was remarkably smooth and easy to drive. Fun, sporty, and close to the road, like a bumper car.

Plus it smelled like Irish Spring soap.

She cursed her Pavlovian response to the scent—it was ridiculous. She drove through Wellsville's tree-lined streets toward the McDonald's plaza. Heads turned as she passed people out for a morning walk, and she felt as conspicuous as a thief as they tracked her movement in the Prius.

Imani's paranoia was confirmed at her first stop: Ray's Dry Cleaners.

"Thought I'd see you today," said a bald Black man behind the counter of the neat-as-a-pin dry cleaning shop. He wore gray-and-peach Hawaiian shorts with a stylish, perfectly tailored white polo shirt. He grinned at her confusion. "I'm Ray Taylor. Zander called and said you had a close encounter with partially digested kiwi while wearing a vintage shirt?"

She nodded and introduced herself, sticking out her hand to shake before plopping the plastic bag on his counter. "As my grandmother says, it's all over but the crying. But Zander told me you were a miracle worker with stains, so I figured I'd give it a shot."

Ray peeked into the bag, nodded, and pulled a slip from under the counter. He handed it to her. "I'll do my best. But for the record, I'm not the miracle worker in this town. That'd be Zan, even though he's too humble to say so."

"Humble?" Imani scoffed. "You sure we're talking about the same Zander Matthews? Granted, I haven't known him long, but I would hazard to say anyone who's met Zander wouldn't choose 'humble' as the first adjective to describe him."

"At first blush, I might agree. He's easygoing, and let's face it, girl," he said, winking at her, "the man is easy on the eyes."

Imani felt her face heat. What was she going to say? She was driving his car, smelling like his soap, for the simple fact that he had been both easygoing and easy on the eyes last year. She gave a nod of agreement.

Ray continued, "Few years ago, I had a...vandalism problem." His friendly smile dimmed until it vanished entirely. "No. Let me call it what it was: a hate problem. Bunch of homophobic, racist assholes spray-painted my shop's windows, doors, and outside wall with every slur imaginable. Most of them were spelled wrong, but still— the sentiment was there. Each time, I'd clean it up and open for business, but by the fourth instance, they'd gotten smarter and carved their hate into the glass so I couldn't scrub it away."

"How horrible." Imani's lips thinned in outrage. "What did you do?"

"I flipped my sign to *Closed* and headed home. I hadn't decided if I was packing up and leaving town, but some desperate plan was forming in my mind. I had reached my limit. Then Zander spotted me." Ray shook his head, his face devoid of its previous animation, lost in the memory. "He flagged my car, and we pulled into his mom's bakery. He treated me to one of those Pumpkin Maniac cupcakes and dragged the whole saga from me. I'm not gonna lie— there may have been some dramatic declarations on my part, but when my rant was over, he told me not to worry. He said this town wasn't built from hate, and the perpetrators were a misguided minority. Said to take the day off, and by tomorrow it would be handled. He made me promise not to, you know—get *extreme* in my reaction."

Imani's heart ached for him. She'd had some pretty extreme moments back in high school after her mother's death.

"What happened the next day?"

"Your guy knows everyone here," he said, prompting her to immediately shake her head to refute the "your guy" part, but he'd already moved on. "Everyone owes him a favor, including me now. Because when I drove to work the next day, the glass was sparkling. No scratches. No nasty names. Apparently, he knew a man who fixed windshields, called in a favor, got every scratch filled in on my plate glass, and buffed my metal doorjamb. But here's the best part. He asked the McDonald's manager to turn in his security camera records to the police for the days I'd been vandalized. By nine o'clock, not only was my business spotless, the dickheads responsible were in jail for destruction of property and vandalism."

"So satisfying when people get what they deserve," Imani said, nodding her approval. "I truly believe you reap what you sow. Did they do time?"

Ray's smile returned.

"They were fined and made to do community service—scrubbing buildings, park benches, public bathroom stalls of all graffiti and hate language. Ever since then, I've been waiting for a chance to repay Zander. He won't take a dime, so I'm tickled you're here. If there is a solvent in this world that will get this off your beautiful Hermès blouse, I will find it. No charge."

Imani protested, but when it became clear it was a losing battle, she thanked him and took her pickup ticket, climbing back into Zander's Prius, half-amused and half-amazed. She took out her phone. She was overdue in giving Zander a thank-you text and was ashamed she'd waited. Her fingers flew as she typed.

Imani: Thank you so much for lending me your car.

Then, before he could respond, she double-texted, unable to resist teasing him.

Imani: Soooo...I hear you're good at getting out scratches in metal?

His reply was super fast.

Zander: Uh-oh. What happened? Are you okay?

She snickered. But she noted his first concern was for her safety. Still, after messing with her last night, she thought turnabout was fair play.

Imani: And I heard you might know a glass guy? For some minor scratches?

Zander: Jesus, Imani, ARE YOU OKAY?

Two seconds later, the phone rang, and she picked it up.

"I'm fine," she said, assuming without looking it was Zander.

It was. He sounded frantic.

"Where are you? Are you hurt?"

"I'm fine." She put the call on speaker as she pulled out of the McDonald's plaza. "I was in Ray's, and he was telling me some stories about your heroism. He seems to think you've got a big 'S' tattooed on your chest."

"You're not wrapped around a tree somewhere?"

"No. I'm sorry." She felt like a jerk for scaring him. She'd thought he'd find it funny, like he seemed to find most other things in life. "I was just yanking your chain."

"Hmm. If I weren't a gentleman, I might say something crude about yanking my, erm, *chain*." His low chuckle made her nipples stand at attention. "But since I am a gentleman, I'll only say I'm glad you're okay and in a joking mood. I'm all about keeping it lighthearted. You feeling better?"

She put on her blinker to turn onto Fassett Lane, heading to the only store in town likely to have what she needed to fix the bedroom window's screen.

"I am, and thanks again for letting me borrow your wheels. I have to say, you were impressively unconcerned about your car when I pretended to have wrecked your pretty Prius."

"Ryker has a great philosophy. He says don't ever fall in love with a vehicle, because it won't love you back. Plus, it's a bed hog." He chuckled when she gave a surprised laugh. "Oh, hey, that reminds me. You said your grandpa's car wasn't working. How bad of shape is it in? Do you want me to have Ryker take a peek at it? He could see if it's an easy fix, or if it might be better to take it to the wrecker for its weight in steel."

"That's...too much," she said, settling on the words. "Look, I appreciate you rolling out the red carpet and lending me your car, but—"

"Say no more," he broke in, his voice not sounding offended in the least. "I understand. I don't mean to make you feel...indebted in any way. I just remember being in your shoes, and I know how emotionally draining being a caregiver can be."

Her eyebrows rose. Zander had been someone's caregiver?

Before she wrapped her mind around this alternate version of Zander, he spoke again.

"Gotta bolt. Holler if you need anything. And Imani?"

"Y-yeah?" She felt so whiplashed she could barely follow the conversational turn.

"Don't wrap yourself around a tree, okay?"

Imani drove down Fassett Lane to the local lumber

and home improvement store, still mulling over the call, Zander's actions, and what she'd learned about him from Ray. It was like a wall-sized jigsaw puzzle: no pieces fit where you thought they would. Pulling into the parking lot, she put the puzzle on hold as a leggy young blonde jogged over, a smile plastered on her tanned face.

Imani got out, and the girl waved.

"Are you Ms. Lewis?" At her confused nod, the girl continued. "Good, 'cause we have an order waiting for you. I'll get some guys to load it up."

"An order?" Her brain sluggishly moved through the options—her grandmother hadn't seen her to-do list, and she hadn't told Kate about her errands this morning. "I think there's been some mistake."

But the woman was speaking into a walkie-talkie. "Bruce, can you bring out the stuff Zander ordered and put it in the back of his Prius? Thanks." She beamed at Imani. "All set! He said you needed to do some other shopping as well, so go on in. If you want to pop the trunk, we'll take care of it."

Feeling as though she were three cups of tea behind everyone else, Imani nodded dumbly. Maybe Zander had phoned in stuff for his shop, betting she'd be heading for household supplies today? It was Wellsville—there was only one home improvement store—so the bet wasn't a long shot.

Imani searched the key fob for the trunk logo and pressed, opening it as a man—Bruce—came around with two gigantic potted floral arrangements.

"Perfect fit," the woman chirped as Bruce nestled the vibrant blue, yellow, and red flowers into the back of the

Prius, having to lean the back seats forward to do so. "Tell Mrs. Foltz we hope she gets those knees feeling better so she can get back into her garden. She gave me a cutting from her vintage rosebushes last year, and it's already blooming. That woman can make anything grow, but lucky for you, these plants are past the delicate stage and you can pop them right in her planters."

Imani thanked her, inwardly shaking her head. There went that theory. Zander bought these for her—or rather, for her grandmother—on purpose.

What the hell was she supposed to do with that information?

Her mental checklist made a giant addition:

☐ Figure out if Zander wants friendship, a fling...or more.

An hour later, armed with groceries, a new lightbulb, and a screen-repair kit, she pulled into the driveway. Despite the warm June day, Gigi was dressed in a red-and-white argyle sweater with matching red pants, red sneakers, and a red purse as she sat on her porch glider, waiting for her friend to arrive.

She gasped as Imani popped the trunk.

"What floral shop did you rob?" she asked, delighted. "And why didn't you take me with you? I had time before my hair appointment, and I'm a good lookout."

"They were a gift. For you." Imani refused to think Zander had bought them for her. He was...just being kind to Gigi. "You have a secret admirer."

"Hmph," Gigi sniffed. "Tell me something I don't know."

Imani took the groceries and supplies inside, then hauled the potted arrangements one by one to the front. Walking around the house, she saw that while the yard was freshly mown—a testament to the wonderful lawn service—the rest of the exterior looked unkempt. Weeds overcrowded Gigi's normally immaculate flower gardens, and the rhododendron looked like the creature from *Twenty Thousand Leagues Under the Sea*, with long, gnarled branches grasping like arthritic fingers to strangle the poor bungalow.

Imani removed the limp, root-bound begonia from the decorative stone planters by the porch steps and inserted the new flowers. She wrestled with them until they stood straight in the old urns, putting her at eye level with the porch, which was showing its age. Gray paint peeled from the wood like a month-old manicure, and some bird had made its nest in the trim above the front door. The second step sagged in the middle; the underside had rotted and it needed to be replaced.

The entire house was suffering from neglect.

And it was all her fault.

Gigi grunted, startling Imani. "I know the place has gotten run-down. Harder and harder to find kids who want to work 'round here. Noah Nowakowski is at college, so I do what I can when my damned knees let me."

Imani stood, brushing off her hands. "Well, you've got me, and I work for cheap." She tacked a smile to her face as she bounded up the porch, noticing the spongy second step, and kissed her grandmother's wrinkled cheek, breathing in the powdery scent of her face lotion. "Just keep whipping up your gulyás, and I'll make this place look as swanky as the Matthews mansion."

"The Matthews mansion? Hmph!" Gigi wrinkled her nose. "If you put those god-awful spiderweb gates in my front lawn, you're going to catch the dickens! Drake Matthews let those creepy books go to his head. Now, your boyfriend, Zoolander—"

"He's not my boyfriend," Imani corrected, shaking her head and hiding a smile. She couldn't tell if her grand-mother was purposely screwing with her about his name, but to laugh would only encourage her teasing. "And his name is Zander."

An old blue sedan pulled up to the sidewalk, and Noreen Nowakowski got out. Gigi gave her oldest friend a finger wave and stood, using Imani's arms as leverage and wincing when she got upright.

"Well, whatever you call him, your Zoolander is a nice boy—a little wild, but he can be tamed. Like a stallion, you've gotta keep riding him—"

"Who are we riding?" Mrs. Nowakowski stepped up the porch steps dressed in a pink T-shirt with a massive, embroidered red rose smack in the middle of her chest, a bumblebee hovering to one side with a tiny smile on its bee face. Her gray hair blew in the breeze as she peered at them through a pair of spectacles held by a chain around her neck. "Spill the tea, ladies. Who is the stallion? And who's riding him? And don't tell me it's a horse—I may not be one of you millennials, but I know about casual sex."

Imani blanched. "N-no, Mrs. Nowakowski, we weren't talking about—"

Gigi waved away Imani's protests. "She's got the hots for

that wild Matthews boy. Patty's youngest. You know, the artsy one who looks like he might be a pro football player on the side?"

"Oh, you mean Zander?" Mrs. Nowakowski nodded knowingly. "He's a sweet boy—he's the one who talked to the dean of admissions over at Alfred University and got my grandson Noah into their ceramics program. He might flit from job to job and girl to girl, but Zander is always there to lend his friends a hand. Those Matthews boys have good genes, but Zander—well, he puts the pop to my weasel, if you get my meaning."

Imani grimaced. "Oookay, I think it's time for you two to scoot, or you'll be late for your hair appointments."

As soon she got Gigi loaded into Mrs. Nowakowski's car, Imani went inside, determined to clear out the front parlor Gigi was using as a bedroom. It was a large, light-pink room with a pretty plaster decoration of roses along the edge of the ceiling. But the room's showpiece was the corner fireplace with its hand-carved maple overmantel. A mirror was built in above it, and it had columns on each side that embraced the original rose-and-green decorative tile surround. The fireplace was Gigi's favorite thing about her bungalow, which was why she hadn't resisted moving her bedroom a few years ago when the staircase had become a challenge. The sweet, pink room made the transition from front parlor to downstairs bedroom gracefully.

Gracefully, that was, except the room's eyesore: the large, square metal birdcage.

"Bitch," Lancelot said in his oddly feminine voice, like a man trying to talk in falsetto.

"Bite me." Imani ignored the parrot as he went through

the rest of his repertoire, tossing curse words like confetti at her back as she headed to the kitchen.

After ladling out a giant portion of Hungarian goulash, she sat at the scarred wooden table, making a list as she scarfed the comfort food. In addition to the all-over scouring Imani had planned, she wrote her other tasks:

☐ Clear a path/rearrange Gigi's room to fit walker

☐ Label bins and boxes with contents

☐ Haul them to attic

☐ Fix guest bedroom screen

☐ Scrape/paint porch

☐ Weed/spruce up flower beds

☐ Check into Grandpa's car—possible to fix?

☐ Repair front step and replace light

Imani tapped the top of the pencil against her lip, debating on making two lines out of repairing the porch step and replacing the light. They were two different items, and she was likely to get the light changed before fixing the porch step. She flipped the pencil over to the eraser side, then she made herself stop. Creating, revising, and color-coding to-do lists was her superpower . . . and her kryptonite. They helped organize her, but it was easy to get lost in the weeds making, reevaluating, and revising them.

"Done is better than perfect," she reminded herself, thinking—not for the first time—that she should get that tattooed on the backs of her hands so she'd constantly be reminded.

She washed her bowl and downed the rest of her iced tea.

She stashed the to-do list in her shorts pocket, and after collecting cleaning supplies, garbage bags, a water bucket, and paper towels from under the kitchen sink, she got to work.

She started with the windows by Lancelot's cage, but as she reached the large metal enclosure, she saw its door was open.

And the bird was gone.

"Oh no!" Imani groaned.

Using the pointy end of the dusting brush, Imani poked at the faded blue pair of jockey shorts Gigi put in there, because Lancelot didn't sleep well if he wasn't tucked in like Grandpa used to do; the resulting parrot freak-outs kept Gigi up, so she put a new pair in when the old ones got too ratty or crappy.

Nothing squawked or came flying out at her from inside the men's underwear.

Lancelot had vanished. And he'd gone missing on her watch.

If the bird got hurt or killed, her grandmother would be devastated. The African gray parrot was Grandpa's pet, and it was the last thing Gigi had alive to remind her of him.

Imani swore, casting her gaze around. When he wasn't in his cage, Lancelot liked to hang with Gigi in what she called his gym. Imani craned her head to look at the makeshift parrot workout area, with its wooden blocks and twisted branch with a bird-sized rope ladder dangling off it.

No Lancelot.

That meant he was either hiding or...she gasped as another thought hit her. Maybe the beast went upstairs and found the gaping hole in the guest room's screen?

"Please be hiding, you little creep." Imani raced upstairs,

shutting the window with its torn screen. She peered at the ceiling fixture and the top of the dresser. Lancelot preferred high perches. He delighted in sitting in wait above you and then releasing a huge stinky mess on your shoulder or in your hair.

She checked the bathroom.

Nothing.

Then she swore she heard the whistle sound of a fake fire alarm—Lancelot's favorite noise—coming from downstairs. She levered herself over the junk, heading back into Gigi's parlor.

"Lancelot?" she singsonged. "Want a treat?"

This time there was a clicking noise, but it sounded like it was in the kitchen. Knowing he was safe, and that ignoring him was the likeliest way to draw him out, she filled the laundry basket with dirty clothes from the hamper in Gigi's closet and started a load of laundry.

Next, she sorted the pile of things that appeared to be broken or just trash, like an oscillating fan with a frayed cord and stacks of gossip magazines. She stuffed the garbage into bags, placing them next to the back door to haul out later.

Then she tackled the things that needed a new home, like the shoeboxes of loose photos, many of them of Imani as a child.

She found one of her and her mom.

"Oooh," she breathed, picking the yellow-edged picture up as if it were an antique. She had few physical pictures of her mother, and to this day, she always uploaded every picture to the cloud, backing it up on several photo-printing sites and in her email account for good measure.

She'd never come across this one, and she examined it greedily, drinking in the details.

She was in an early ballet recital costume—a white swan from *Swan Lake*—and her mom was crouched down next to her, hugging her and grinning with pride. Flipping it over, she didn't spot a date, but in Gigi's scrawling cursive, it said, *Amira and Imani after dance recital 5th grade.* She knew by the braces on her teeth that it was the end of fifth grade, four years before her mom died. She studied her mother's face. They looked more alike now that Imani had grown her dark-brown hair out, especially when she wore it loose like her mother had, and they both had the same juicy-lipped smile.

Imani took her phone out, snapped a picture, and attached it to a text to her father. While she'd sent him a brief message before her flight left New York City, she hadn't had a chance to call since she'd arrived, so she crafted a longer note than their typical one-liners.

> Imani: Gigi decided she's not going to a rehab center because I'm more fun and will give her ice cream every night.

She inserted a rolling eyes emoji.

> Imani: I'm cleaning out her room to allow her easier access. Check out what I found.

To her surprise, her father—who worked as a surgery tech and wasn't usually available to text during the workday—replied immediately.

Dad: I figured as much. Gigi will use every excuse for more time with you. Nice picture! What a beauty I married—thank God you inherited her genes and not mine.

Imani smiled. While she and her dad had grown apart when she'd gone to college and then further apart when he'd remarried a woman with two kids of her own, texting with him made her feel like she was little again, running to him for a hug.

Her fingers hesitated, then rushed along the keypad.

Imani: I still miss her so much.

Only a beat went by until her dad's reply.

Dad: I know. She was a hell of a lady. In spite of her personal demons, she'd be tickled to see you taking care of Gigi like this. Call if you need anything. Love you, sweetheart.

Aaand the hug was over.

She texted back a heart emoji and pocketed the phone. Taking one last glance at the picture, she stacked it with the others she found and hauled it to the guest room, refusing to take a detour down memory lane. She'd go through and put them in an album later so Gigi could look at her old photographs. Plus she'd scan each one and upload it to her photo server.

Nothing would steal *these* memories.

Imani dusted, cleaned the glass, made the bed with fresh

sheets, and swept the floor. Finally, she gazed around with satisfaction. The pink room glowed without the clutter, and it would be so much easier for Gigi when she came home from surgery. Her grandmother would be so happy.

Imani sighed in pride and then frowned as she noticed Gigi's side table. On the top was a massive assortment of nail polish. Imani piled the bottles inside an empty lacquered box she'd found, fitting the collection in every which way.

"Jeez, Gigi," Imani said aloud. "Did you rob a nail salon?"

"STOP!" a screeching voice came from behind her. "YOU'RE HURTING ME, OOOUCH!"

Imani shrieked. She spun, tossing the lacquered box of nail polish toward the man's voice as if it were a shot-put.

Except it wasn't a man.

Lancelot flew off the fireplace mantel in a flash of gray feathers as the lacquered box exploded against the front, sending bottles of nail polish flying. Like colorful missiles, they smashed into every hard surface, leaving glass shrapnel and riotous paint colors splashed everywhere. The sharp, pungent smell of acetone filled the room.

Imani clutched her face, moaning as she gazed around her. "Nooo! You bad bird!"

"You're hurting me," the bird repeated in a conversational tone, mimicking what Gigi and her grandfather would say when admonishing the bird. Early on when they'd purchased him, the parrot had a bad habit of nipping people with his sharp beak when he got hangry or nervous, or whenever the mood struck him. While Lancelot rarely bit anyone now, the words used to scold him had become part of his lexicon.

Imani shook her finger at the parrot, who was using his

beak and dexterous feet to climb to the top of his cage. Once he got up there, he turned to face the window so his red-tipped tail feathers were pointed directly at her. Then the bird squatted and shat a stream of white, peppered with bits of something green and lumpy. She hadn't had a chance to put papers down outside the cage, so the poop splatted onto the gleaming hardwood floors, and the scent of overripe fruit assaulted her nose.

"BITCH!" Lancelot shrieked, whirling back around on his two legs, as graceful as a prima donna as he sidestepped along the driftwood atop his cage. His head cocked, looking at Imani from one eye, then dipping his head to glare at her with the other bead-black eyeball. "BA-AAD bird."

Imani's attention veered from the shouting bird back to Gigi's favorite thing in the bungalow.

"Shit," she whispered, taking in the destruction and mess. In addition to the glass and nail polish everywhere, she'd broken three of the historic, handmade ceramic tiles on the fireplace surround. Maybe she could find some superglue or caulk or some freaking sticky chewing gum— anything to put the pieces back together before Gigi came home and lost her mind? But first, she had to clean up the nail polish so it didn't destroy the floor and the other fireplace tiles. "Shit, shit, shit!"

She raced from the room, intent on getting more paper towels. But before she got two steps, her toe caught on the discarded lacquered box, and she went sprawling, chest and belly first, directly into the debris. Something poked her belly, and polish immediately soaked into her shirt and shorts, cold and wet against her skin.

"Ow, damn it!" she yelled, gingerly brushing aside

broken glass to leverage herself up on one arm. Before she got to an upright position, she saw something reflected in the mirrorlike gloss on the unmarred surface of the fireplace tile surround: Lancelot had swooped down onto the floor and was trundling toward her.

And toward the broken glass.

"No!" she shouted and spun. Glass poked her in the butt as she heaved herself into a crouched position, like a bear guarding his den. "Get back!"

Lancelot's feathers puffed, and his bird head did an exaggerated, swaying *no-you-didn't* motion before he screeched, "STOP! You're HURTING ME!"

Suddenly, someone pounded at the front door.

"Imani? Mrs. Foltz? Are you okay?"

Zander.

She looked down at herself, covered in nail polish and smelling flammable. Worse, her grandpa's old bird was taking cautious steps over to the nearest bit of broken glass, his beak already open and his upper and lower mandibles coming together in little grinding and clicking motions. Lancelot's dexterous gray tongue peeked out of his beak, and Imani sensed he was determined to discover what that bit of pretty pink in the glittery glass tasted like. While she wasn't a bird expert, she knew if Lancelot got cut, he could bleed out in matter of minutes. Birds didn't have much blood, and a small loss could end him.

Under ordinary circumstances, Zander was the last person she'd want to see right now.

Clearly, these were not ordinary circumstances.

"Come in!" she shouted.

And she resigned herself to her fate.

# CHAPTER 6

The first thing that entered Zander's mind after he climbed Mrs. Foltz's front steps was that someone was murdering Imani, her grandmother, or both.

"No! Get back!"

"Stop, you're hurting me!"

The screaming from inside was full of terror, anger, and...something he couldn't quite put a finger on.

He dropped Ryker's ladder on the porch, using a fist to pound against the door. Adrenaline charged through his body, and his mind cycled through rescue scenarios: First, get Imani and her grandmother out. Then deal with whoever or whatever had put the fear in their voices.

"Imani? Mrs. Foltz? Are you okay?"

He'd half opened the door before hearing Imani's shout to enter. He burst into the foyer, his fists clenched. He blinked in the relative darkness, willing his eyes to adjust. When his vision cleared, he blinked again, trying to process what he saw.

Nobody had Imani in a chokehold.

Nobody was threatening to carve up her grandmother with a knife.

Instead, the sight greeting Zander was Imani on all fours, covered in dripping wet paint. She was frozen in a tense face-off with a parrot that was squawking and whistling, swaying his weight from one clawed foot to the other.

"Huh. I came over to drop off the ladder, and I'm not sure what's happening here." Zander cocked his head to figure out what the sparkly bits were on the floor. "But leaving my cell phone in Ryker's truck was a tactical error. Can you hold this pose one more minute while I get it? This is bound to go viral in some sort of Angry Bird meme."

"Zander!" Imani sputtered. "Don't just stand there and crack jokes. Help me! Get this twit back into his cage before he steps on a broken bottle and bleeds to death."

The wood floor creaked under his sneakers as he crept into the pink room. He crouched down a few feet from both the parrot and Imani, who alternately glared at each other and side-eyed him with what seemed like equal amounts of wariness. He thought for a moment and came up with the name of the swearing parrot that he'd seen yesterday when bringing in Imani's luggage.

"Hey, Lancelot. You ready for a treat?" Although Zander captured the gray bird's attention with the word "treat," Lancelot swayed faster. His throat worked up and down as he emitted a loud, smoke-detector-like squeal, followed by a series of raptor-like clicking noises that seemed territorial in tenor.

Time to deescalate.

Maybe he should whistle back?

Zander put his fingers in his mouth and blew a piercing whistle he usually reserved for when he was in the stands watching a Buffalo Bills game. The bird stopped moving, cocking his head. Progress. Zander whistled a few bars of "Take Me Out to the Ball Game" and then used his most enthusiastic falsetto to say, "C'mere, boy!"

The parrot fluffed his feathers, shuddering as if he had a bad case of the willies. He took one step in Zander's direction, followed by another, and then froze as Zander put out a finger he hoped looked like an attractive perch for the feathered beast to fly toward.

The bird hastily backed away. No dice.

Zander rose, shaking his head.

"Nah, he's scared of me. Must be intimidated by my size. Most males are," Zander said, shooting for a joke. By the annoyance on Imani's face, he could tell he'd missed by a mile. "Don't worry. I'm going to get between him and the glass, and he'll fly toward the cage or out of the room. Then we can get it cleaned up."

He stepped between the bird and Imani, who was still on all fours—a fact he did his best to put out of his mind—and when the bird cocked his head at him, Zander tried the last animal noise in his repertoire. Pursing his lips together, he made a loud smooching noise followed by several shorter kissing sounds, the universal call to cats everywhere. Then, he made an "up" gesture with his hand.

"Let's go, Lancelot."

To his surprise, the bird flapped its wings, flew up, and landed directly on Zander's left shoulder.

Zander froze as Imani gasped.

"Watch out! When he's scared, he bites. Hard!"

For a bird as long as a shoebox, he was light. Zander recalled from a long-ago biology class that birds' bones were hollow, which allowed them to fly. The parrot's feet gripped his trapezius muscle for balance, the curved talons at the end piercing the thin cotton of his shirt and grazing his skin like a set of long, pointed fingernails. It didn't hurt. But the wicked curve of those claws and the hooked black beak were disturbingly close to his eyes.

Lancelot re-fluffed his feathers with a whispery rustling sound.

Zander turned his head, his neck creaking with the effort of moving in infinitesimally small increments, to gaze into the creature's beautiful, cloud-gray eyes.

The bird bobbed his head once as if to say, *I got you. We're cool.*

Imani's whisper came from his right—a direction he didn't dare look in, as it would have presented his jugular to the bird—but he could hear her hissed directions.

"Put him in his cage—the door's open."

"Good boy," Lancelot said, his tone conversational. "Good boy get a treat?"

"Where are his treats?" Zander moved toward the cage, amazed at every step that the bird wasn't flying off. Instead, Lancelot perched there, alternately gazing at Zander's face and then cocking his head to examine the sparkling bits of glass on the floor.

In a low voice, Imani directed him to an old, red cracker tin on the shelf underneath the vast metal birdcage. It sat next to a bundle of newspapers, some wooden blocks...and a puzzling array of neatly stacked men's underwear.

He wasn't even going to ask.

Zander bent, performing a deep stretch to the right, reaching to snag the cracker tin while keeping his left shoulder aloft. The bird scrambled to the point of his shoulder, the claws gripping harder at the unexpected movement.

Grunting with the effort of balancing in this position, Zander retrieved the tin, careful not to touch the jockey shorts. Straightening, he opened the container and was thankful to see it was filled with a twist-tied baggie of pistachios in their shells.

"Okay, Lancelot." He tossed a few of the nuts onto the newspaper-lined bottom of the bird's massive cage. "Soup's on, buddy."

Remarkably, the bird flapped once, launching from Zander's shoulder to the outside of the metal cage. Using his strong black beak and nimble feet, he climbed into the cage and fluttered to land on the comic page. With one last look at Zander, he used his foot to hold down a nut, shelling it with his beak with a single-minded ferocity that made Zander glad to have the bird away from his eyes.

Zander swung the door shut, locking the outside bolt mechanism before turning to Imani, who sagged on all fours, head drooping.

"Not that the view isn't enticing," Zander said, moving to Imani's side, his sneakers crunching on the glass shards littering the floor, "but I don't think this is the best position for you. At least not now."

"This is the second time you've rescued me." Imani, her hair in a ponytail, peered up at him with a resigned laugh. Her face was spattered with tiny specks of neon green, and her buttercup-yellow shirt was streaked with so many splattered hues, she looked as though she'd just finished a Color Run race.

"Yep. I'm the hero you didn't know you needed." Zander

extended his hand to Imani, and when she put her wet palm in his, he tugged her to her feet.

And then she screamed.

"My foot!" Imani held up her right leg, stork-like, and it was only then he noticed she was standing sock-footed in the aftermath of a glass cyclone.

Zander cursed. Acting quickly, he swept her up into his arms. While the mental side of him was laser-focused on getting her somewhere he could set her down and tend to her foot without boxes, bins, or glass in the way, the physical side of him took note of how, despite her long legs and stature, she was willowy and light. While he was as dense as a boulder, his gait like a marauding troll, Imani was more like the parrot he'd held—as if nature had meant for her to fly in this world.

"Okay, set me down," Imani said, after he carried her into the white kitchen.

While her arms were not exactly thrown around his neck—in fact, one of them was crooked and cocked against his shoulder, like a bike's kickstand—Zander noted her other hand rested against his chest.

"One of the chairs . . . okay, the counter is fine."

Her voice trailed off as he set her on the kitchen counter and knelt down by her foot. He cupped her right ankle in his hands, peering at her bloody sock.

"I don't see any glass poking through. I'm going to slide this sock off just to see what we have going on here."

Imani grimaced as he gently eased the fabric over the wound. "Sounds like another Zander Matthews line. First my right sock, next my pants, right? I mean, 'just to see what we have going on here'?"

Zander catalogued and dismissed the wound on the bottom of her foot as superficial. It was already clotting and only needed to be cleaned off and bandaged. But as his gaze lifted from her ankle to her eyes, his plan for a snappy retort vanished as he spotted a blot of dark red on her yellow T-shirt that wasn't nail polish.

"Nope. Next is your shirt. How in the hell did you get scratched on your stomach?" He gestured to the blood on her side, standing so quickly his knees popped in the quiet kitchen. "Where are your grandma's clean towels? Or, better yet, does she have a first aid kit?"

Imani frowned, gazing down at her shirt.

"It must've happened when I fell," she said, lifting the hem of the shirt to reveal an inch-long cut below her ribs. She hiked the buttercup fabric up to her bra to better see the wound.

Her lacy white bra. Not that he was looking...but then he did look.

"Oh shit, Imani. You've got glass still in there. Hang on." He shook his head as he pivoted around the kitchen, his eyes taking in the countertops with clean dishes in the dish rack, the simmering pot on the stove, the black cat clock on the wall whose tail twitched back and forth, marking off precious seconds while she was probably losing blood. "Where's a damn set of tweezers or some sort of first aid kit in this godforsaken pla—"

"No need to cuss. I got it."

He spun back around in time to see her holding up a triangular-shaped piece of glass between her thumb and index finger, turning the bit as if examining the red blood staining the surface. Then she set it carefully next to the soap dispenser by the sink, hefted her shirt again, and probed the bleeding skin with her fingertips.

"I think that was it."

Zander's mouth hung so far open, he figured it could double as a fly trap. "You couldn't wait for me to find something...I don't know...sterile? You just pulled it out with your fingers, like some Navy SEAL? Did Steve Irwin's death teach you nothing? You're never supposed to yank shit out of your own body. You let the professionals do that!"

"You're being a little dramatic. It's just a tiny piece of glass. Not a barb from a massive stingray." Imani scooched herself over on the kitchen counter to the sink, where she ran the tap and snagged the roll of paper towels his panic-stricken gaze had missed earlier. She expertly wiped up the blood. "I think I got it all, but the skin is ragged here. Can you...can you check if I got everything out?"

Somehow, Zander managed to close his mouth before she spotted him gaping at her again like some Neanderthal.

"Yep." He stepped up to the sink next to her. "Hand me those paper towels."

She did, then leaned to the other side, holding up her shirt to expose her cut side. Zander ran the water, dipped the paper towel in, and gently swiped at the cut, flicking his gaze to her face to see if she was wincing.

"I'm fine." She gave him that sexy smile where she only tipped up the edges of her full lips, as if she were holding in a secret. "Stupid bird. Did you see the mess out there? I'm going to be spending all day getting that polish out of the fireplace and floor. Damn. It's like two steps forward and five steps back with my life. You ever feel like that?"

His face was a couple inches above her skin—that beautiful caramel color that she'd told him last year was thanks to her half-Hungarian heritage—as he swabbed at the cut, using the paper towel to lift the edges of the ragged skin's edge on either side of the small slice in her side. He was distracted by the task and answered absentmindedly.

"Not usually, no. My life trajectory isn't linear. It's more...fluid. But this year, things have felt...off."

She was quiet for a moment.

"Is it because...like you said the other day? That I broke your heart?" Her words were soft, tinted by either sorrow or guilt, he couldn't tell which. "Or was that hyperbole?"

"You sound like Drake with your fancy writer-type words." He avoided her gaze as he held pressure to her side. "Yes, I was exaggerating. My heart wasn't exactly broken. Just bruised."

"I'm sorry I hurt your feelings. Truly. After that weekend, it got hectic at work. I kept meaning to reply to you, but before I knew it, three weeks had gone by. I felt stupid replying after all that time, so I texted that weird one-liner." She frowned. "It wasn't my best look. It's just...I figured you'd already moved on. You give off this good-time-guy, dancing-through-life vibe, you know?"

He felt her ribs expand as she inhaled...and then stilled as if she were holding her breath, waiting for him to answer. He glanced up and her face was so close he could see the individual hairs of her exquisitely formed brows. Her gaze drifted down to his mouth, and before he could decide if he should kiss her, she was there, pressing her lips to his.

It was as if the kiss breached a levee in his mind,

there was such an immediate torrent of emotion flooding through him. The hand not holding pressure on her ribs came up to cup the back of her head. He eased her up into a sitting position, his fingers threading through her hair as he deepened the kiss. Her lips were soft, and when she sighed against his mouth, every blood cell in his body made a simultaneous decision to migrate south, where they held an impromptu rave.

In his pants.

He shifted, pivoting his hips so his erection wasn't pressed against her knee. But she countered his move with one of her own, hooking her long, long leg around his hips and recentering herself. Right. There.

"You smell so good," she breathed. "Why do you always smell so good?"

"Mmm," he replied. "You smell like...acetone."

She snorted a giggle against his lips, then pulled her mouth away and laughed, looking down at the front of herself.

"Oh, crap. I'm a mess."

"In all the best ways." He smiled, and when he leaned in for another kiss, she winced. He halted an inch from her face, searching her brown eyes. "Am I hurting you?"

"No," she said. "But I'm afraid I might hurt you. Again. We should stop. Stay friends, like you said."

Suddenly, there was the sound of a car. Glancing out the window behind Imani's head, Zander spotted a headful of orderly blond-brown curls popping up out of the passenger side of a blue sedan as another woman came around the back of the car, wheeling a walker.

"I'm not sure I agree with anything except the stopping

part, at least for now." He nodded toward the window. "Your grandmother's home."

"Oh, screw me sideways!" She swore under her breath, and in one crazy athletic movement, she swung her leg entirely over his head so she wasn't straddling him and jumped down from the kitchen counter.

"Well, I'm game if you are," he joked.

Panic flitted across her face as the women approached the back porch at a snail's pace.

"The fireplace!" She gripped his arms with both hands, as if her touch made the non sequitur more logical.

"It's kind of dirty in there. Maybe your bed instead?"

"Can't you stop joking for one second? I've got to fix the mess on her fireplace before she gets in. Quick, help me!"

Like a flash, she'd cleaned up the kitchen and was off, sprinting toward the front of the house with the roll of paper towels tucked under her arm. She thrust the broom into his hands and began wiping down the front of the fireplace, her hands moving in a wax-on, wax-off series that would make *The Karate Kid* look like a punk.

Zander swept the glass into a pile. Imani wielded the dustpan and hand brush to pick up the little bits and dump them into a flimsy plastic grocery bag. The women were clomping up the back stairs, moving slowly and chattering the whole time, as Imani scoured the floor and the fireplace surround with a spray cleaner.

It was an impressive and effective display. In less than seven minutes, she'd single-handedly cleaned the whole mess of shattered nail polish bottles.

She stuffed the dirty paper towels into the bag, hissing as she shoved the bag full of cleaning garbage at him.

"Take this to your car. Do you have any caulk adhesive on you?"

"Fresh out." He shook his head, baffled. "Why?"

"I'm trying to figure out how to stick those tiles on temporarily. How about chewing gum—would that work? Then she won't know I broke anything. I mean, the tiles are broken, but if I put them back together, like a puzzle, maybe I can disguise it until I get them fixed?"

The back door jiggled, and they both heard the sound of keys in the lock.

"I don't think gum is going to work, but I have some grout—"

"No time! Quick, take off your shirt!"

Zander felt as if he'd been around too much paint thinner.

"Um, okay. Are we back to the 'screw me sideways' part again? Because you may want to rethink your timing."

Imani whipped the shirt off her body in a single swoop of yellow and a whiff of acetone. She tossed her blood-and-paint–covered shirt into the plastic bag, while making a "gimme" sign with the other hand.

"Hurry, they're coming."

Dropping the bag at his feet, he stripped off his tee, unable to help his gaze roving over her as she wrestled with it, putting it on backward, then fighting on the inside of it to twist it around so the All Fired Up logo was facing front.

"There." She hustled him to the front door, whispering, "Now go outside, and in a couple of minutes, you can knock at the door and pretend you just arrived to drop off the ladder, okay? Oh, and take these."

She shoved the three broken tiles at him. Then the door slammed in his face.

He stood there, shirtless, shifting his weight from one foot to another, his body like a ship after a rogue wave, attempting to right itself. He dropped the plastic bag on the porch behind him and stuffed the rectangular, broken tiles in one of the many pockets in his cargo shorts.

After a moment, he heard the older women in the house.

"Someone's at your door." That came from Mrs. Nowakowski, he was pretty sure.

"Who is it?" Mrs. Foltz asked, and he vaguely heard Imani's voice rambling about a ladder, but before she'd gotten too far in her excuse, the front door opened.

Mrs. Foltz stared out at him, then grinned.

"Hey, Shypoke, you didn't tell me your friend did strippergrams! Hell, I heard Patty's youngest had a bunch of jobs through the years, but I'll bet this is a lucrative side hustle. Noreen, come here and record this with your phone, will you? We can upload it to TikTok later."

Zander brought the adjustable ladder up between them, trying unsuccessfully to hide behind the metal contraption.

"I . . . I'm here to drop off a ladder."

"Hurry, Noreen. He's starting his act!" Mrs. Foltz shoved the door open with her walker and crowded him into one corner of the front porch. She grinned, showing off pearly-white dentures. "Go ahead, Zoolander. You were saying you had to carry in a ladder . . . and then I'm supposed to say something like, 'How did you know I needed a strapping young man today?' Is that right?"

"Gigi! I let Mrs. Nowakowski out the back door." Imani appeared behind her in the doorway, breathless. "What are you yelling about?"

"Get me my purse, Imani. Give us five seconds, young

man, and let me get some dollar bills. Between me and my granddaughter, we're gonna make it rain."

Zander burst out laughing.

He had to lean the ladder up against the house as he went weak with the silliness of it all. The disappointment on the older woman's face when Imani explained Zander wasn't, in fact, a strippergram, but was coming over to drop off supplies, was priceless.

"Oh." The older woman scowled. "Well, how was I to know? With all those muscles and the chest hair and with his shorts hanging so low…are you sure you don't want to do a little show, Zoolander? For an old lady who's not gotten out in forever?"

"Gigi!" Imani said, blushing. She shook her head, giving Zander a dark look as he laughed louder. "His name is Zander, and he doesn't want to strip anything else off."

Gigi widened her eyes at her granddaughter. "How do you know, unless you ask?"

"Zander, come on in. I need that ladder, um, in the laundry room. Off the kitchen. I'm trying to find Gigi's hidden stash of paint for the porch, and she thinks she put it there or in the garage."

Zander composed himself, grabbing the ladder again. "No problem."

"Hey." Mrs. Foltz blocked the front door with her walker. "We got news that our typical fourth for May-I— Ginny White—has the trots. She can't come tonight, and we need someone who can play cards and wants to party with a bunch of wild old women. You game? I can teach you—it's contract rummy. Easy-peasy."

Zander shook his head, regretful. "Your party sounds

way more happening, but I have to be at Kate and Drake's baby shower and gender reveal. They're having it at my studio, so I'll be cleaning up afterward, too."

Mrs. Foltz pushed her lower lip out in his direction, then shrugged, turning. She guided her walker back inside with Imani's help. "Well, get in here before you let the flies in. What about your mom? Would Patty want to come, after the reveal? You know, back in my day, we didn't find out the gender until the child was born, and the world still turned."

"I'll have to check." Zander hid a smile and followed Imani and her grandmother toward the back of the house. He got up on the stepladder in the cottage's tiny laundry room, trying not to feel self-conscious that he was still shirtless as he peered into the deepest recesses of the ceiling-height cupboard. There was an old bottle of whiskey, which he handed to a triumphant Mrs. Foltz, but there wasn't any paint.

"I might have gray paint in my studio," he offered, knowing he didn't, but he had an unused bucket of white outdoor paint he could take to the hardware store and have it tinted to match. "I can bring it over—"

"Absolutely not." Mrs. Foltz wiped the dust from the bottle of whiskey, placing it carefully in a lower kitchen cabinet. "I have some. It's just a matter of finding it."

Imani massaged her temples. "Maybe the garage?"

He followed Imani as she led her grandmother laboriously down the three back porch steps to the garage, and he stepped in front of the ladies, hauling the door open when it stuck.

Inside was a dark-green Chevy Monza with a decade's

worth of dust on its hood. Beyond that, the place was stuffed with tools and various items, but what caught his attention was the side wall. It was completely covered in a variety of bowl-like metal contraptions. It took him a full thirty seconds to recognize the collection.

They were old bedpans, nailed up in a massive, mandala-esque array.

Mrs. Foltz saw him take in the collection, and she gave a rueful smile. "Yep. Those are bedpans. My late husband, Arlo, said this space was 'Men's Island' to do with what he wanted."

Imani pinched the bridge of her nose, as if warding off a headache. "He could've chosen car parts. Or deer antlers. Why bedpans?"

"Same reason he taught Lancelot bad words. He thought it was funny as hell." Gigi shook her perfectly curled head in disgust.

Zander grinned. "You've got to love a collection that gives the owner joy."

Twenty minutes later, Zander had helped Imani empty the top of the garage crawl space looking for her grandmother's paint supplies. They found about three hundred empty Cool Whip containers, a pair of old stereo speakers, and several Ball jars with something fermented inside, but no paint. They loaded the items into Ryker's truck, and Zander promised he'd take them to the recycling center.

"She won't let me go and buy a new bucket," Imani said, blowing a lock of hair off her forehead as she leaned against the top of the ladder. "She doesn't want anything to go to waste, and she's convinced she has extra around here somewhere."

There was a smudge of dirt on her cheek, and Zander wanted to take his thumb and rub it off. But she'd said they needed to stop—and she was in charge. That was the plan.

"We'll grab the old paint in my studio and put it in your garage clandestinely. Then you can 'find' it in the morning." Zander grinned as her face lit up. "We'll stash it tonight after the shower. What time does your grandmother go to bed?"

She gazed at him, as if debating something, then shrugged. "Ten-thirty on the nights she plays May-I. But Zander?" She came down off the ladder, giving him a hard look. "It's not a date. And we're not kissing again."

"If you say so." He folded the ladder and hefted it to his shoulder. "You're the boss."

# CHAPTER 7

Cleaned up and wearing a lilac sundress and a strappy pair of espadrilles, Imani walked with Kate and Drake in the light sprinkle of rain, her head under their large, black umbrella to protect the beach waves she'd spent so long on in Gigi's upstairs bathroom. She'd driven to Kate and Drake's house first to help Kate get ready, then followed them to the studio. Now she felt like a third wheel, the conspicuous single girl tagging along with a couple into All Fired Up.

"My mom has been relentless for months about this reveal," Kate said. "She was upset I gave you the envelope and not her, Dad, or Kiersten, but my parents have no filters, and Kier can't come because she's got exams next week. You have the sonogram results, right? If Mom doesn't find out today, she might stroke."

Under normal conditions, Kate would never ask if Imani had forgotten something as important as the sonogram results—her best friend knew when something went into the Mary Poppins bag, it was as good as a vault. But these weren't normal circumstances. Imani had read enough "What to Expect When Your BFF Is Expecting" articles online to know her job: don't drink margaritas in front of her, keep the snacks within reach, and overlook any hormone-induced panic.

Imani unzipped the left-hand side of her black purse, pulling out the sonographer's envelope containing the baby's gender.

"I got you, don't worry. And the two little plastic containers you just gave me, with pink and blue cornstarch, are safe in the other compartment." Imani patted the larger right side of her purse. "All we'll need to do is insert the proper color into whatever ceramic thingy Zander has created for us to smash for the reveal."

An auburn lock drifted down from Kate's chignon, and she tucked it behind her ear, blowing out a laugh.

"I'm getting neurotic, aren't I? If it weren't raining, we could've done the reveal outside. Zander's not super jazzed to have this cornstarch flying around his studio, so you'll have to help him figure out the least messy way to pull off this change."

"Don't worry. We'll make this epic for you and Drake, and get the perfect pictures for your baby book. You relax and soak in the celebration." Imani felt a twinge recalling her grandmother's earlier wisdom about her insomnia and stress. Kate was going to be a mother. She was embarking on the least plannable thing in the world—having and raising a child—yet knowing her best friend, Kate was going to rock it.

Meanwhile, Imani's own life was spinning in circles. Even with a straight career trajectory before her, she was uncertain about everything, from her promotion to whether kissing Zander had been a good idea.

Kate patted her belly in her forest-green maternity dress,

her face glowing with excitement. "He or she is so lucky to have such a thoughtful auntie. I'm excited to see what Baby Matthews will be. Quick, what's your prediction?"

"A boy. Those Matthews brothers have waaaay too much testosterone to allow any X chromosomes out." Imani stifled a yawn. She was bone-tired after last night's cleaning extravaganza, then the disastrous save-the-bird episode in Gigi's parlor. The last thing she wanted to do was coordinate starch colors with a guy who she'd swapped spit with—on purpose or by accident, she still hadn't decided which—earlier today.

As if reading her mind, Kate squeezed her hand as they stepped under the building's awning and Drake put down the umbrella. Thunder rumbled in the distance, and there was a tang of earthy wetness in the evening wind.

"I know it's awkward with you and Zander, but he's a good guy. He won't hold it against you or tell anyone you slept together," Kate said.

"Yeah. I did that all on my own, didn't I?"

"Zander's got a knack for life. For enjoying the moment. He doesn't hold grudges, pass on gossip, or worry about the future. When something isn't serving him, he bails and starts anew." Kate beamed as if this were good news.

Drake waved them both inside. He'd cuffed the sleeves of his black button-down dress shirt below the elbow, which was as casual as the horror-turned-romance writer got. "Zan's got a happy-go-lucky relationship with the present that I lack," he said.

Imani's eyebrow rose at her client's envious tone, but she figured Drake was biased. Zander was his baby brother, after all.

They walked into the studio, and Imani halted.

The place was stunning.

The lower floor was industrial chic. Sweet-smelling pine shelves loaded with ceramics lined the white walls. There were beautiful glazed mugs, pitchers, vases, and earthenware crocks of every size and color. Some were stamped with designs, some had "Wellsville" engraved on them, but most of them had the same blue-green glaze and a certain similar flair.

"Zander made all of those," Drake said, beaming with familial pride. "He's really talented. He even makes the bisque-fired ones over there for people to paint at his parties. He's had his fair share of jobs, but this studio is my favorite of his enterprises to date."

Imani gawked at the shelves full of white bisque pottery. There was everything from piggy banks to plates, with the occasional painted and finished piece interspersed, as if to provide inspiration. Next to the bisque collection were shelves holding plastic pump bottles of paints in every color of the rainbow. They were not in Roy G Biv order, she noticed, but they were placed neatly on the shelves.

The middle of the room was a long, bar-like cement countertop lined with stools. Coffee urns, carafes, and buckets of ice with water bottles were spaced along the bar, which acted as a divider for the place. The area to the right of the countertop looked like the painting workshop and party area. It was filled with sturdy wooden tables, covered in white butcher paper and mason jars bristling with clean brushes.

But it was the left side of the workspace that drew Imani. There were pottery wheels—about six of them, spaced a few feet from each other—and unbidden, the scene from that old romantic movie with Patrick Swayze and Demi Moore came to mind.

"You're picturing *Ghost*, aren't you?" Kate whispered in her ear after Drake walked inside, searching for his brother. A naughty, knowing smile dawned on Kate's face as Imani blanched. "I know. I had the same thought the first time I saw this place. Of course, I was picturing Drake behind me, not Zander. But still. Momma knows." Kate rubbed her belly in smug satisfaction as she headed to the center bar, snagging two glass Evian bottles, and handing one to Imani.

"No, I was thinking of how chic it is in here," Imani said, squinting one eye at Kate, although they both knew she was lying. She opened the water, taking a long drink to stall her reply. "From your description of the place, I'd pictured more of a bar with a folding table for the occasional art project in between rounds of shots. This is . . . unexpected."

"Zander's not the total renegade you think he is. Not even the total renegade *he* thinks he is. I'd go so far as to say he's not even aware he's bought into his own mythology a bit."

Imani gave her a look. "Don't do the matchmaker thing."

Kate snorted. "Matchmaking now is like putting the toothpaste back into the tube."

"Look, I was going through a drought. With the exception of our failed night of speed dating, my last relationship was Armand. Remember him?"

Kate scrunched her nose. "The one who thought it was a good idea to send dick pics? To me? While he was dating you? He was a real treat."

"Yeah, after spending almost a year with Armand only to find out he was a cheater, you can't blame me for being wary about relationships. But at your wedding, with Zander...I mean, the guy's freaking hot. All I was looking for was a diversion. A night of..."

"Mind-blowing sex?" Kate supplied with a wicked grin.

"He made me feel...alive. But I'm not interested in getting involved. Apparently, he isn't either, because he sent me a text last night that said us being friends was 'a good goal,'" she said, using air quotes.

"I think he's playing a longer game. And you should join in. I mean, why not? You still find him attractive, don't you?"

Imani wanted to say, *Hell, yes! You can't imagine the accidental kiss we had today!* Instead, she opted for a shrug. She'd tell Kate after the shower. Maybe. Because what did the kiss mean, anyway?

Her gaze landed on a large mural in the back of the studio. To her surprise, it featured a quote from business leadership guru Dale Carnegie, written in bold black letters next to a beautiful painting of a seashore sunrise.

TODAY IS LIFE—THE ONLY LIFE YOU ARE SURE OF. MAKE THE MOST OF TODAY.

She pointed the quote out to Kate.

"That is so Zander. Mr. Live-in-the-Moment." Imani scoffed, feeling once again as if she were on firm ground. "I mean, don't get me wrong. He's a good dancer, and he's a great lay. But his whole dancing-through-life thing is not for me."

"No?" Kate asked, sipping her bottled water. Then to Imani's surprise, her spreadsheet-loving friend shrugged. "I wish I were more like Zander."

Imani's eyebrows lifted so high her forehead muscles strained. "Really? But he's always so chill, like none of it matters. Everyone's told me how many different jobs he's had, and even Drake wondered how long this art phase would last. He's too commitment-phobic for me."

Now it was Kate's turn to look surprised. "Ha, that's rich coming from the woman who won't even watch a Netflix series with me because you don't want the weekly pressure of following a show."

"That's different. I'm protective of my free time. Movies are easier to schedule."

"Oh yeah? What about the fact that you debate accepting page Like requests on social media, because that may obligate you in some way? Or your habit of always clicking Maybe on online invites?" Kate laughed, giving Imani's shoulders a squeeze-hug. "C'mon, Imani. I mean, I love you, but you're projecting your own issues onto him. Patty brags on her boys and their philanthropy, but even she says Zander takes it to another level. He'd give someone the shirt off his back if they needed it."

Imani laughed, but it was forced. He'd given her the shirt off his back. Twice, in fact. Was her best friend right? Was Imani the one with commitment issues?

"Well, you've nailed it with the shirt part. I still can't believe he wore that pink top you got him, but you said it yourself that he can't resist doing things for comedic effect."

"Sometimes. But he's…different with you. The Matthews boys go big with their grand gestures. Believe me, I know—first, it was making me Cobb salads, next it was a helicopter flight over Niagara Falls. With Zander, it might be a shirt now, but next he might be signing a mortgage with you."

"As if," Imani scoffed. "Didn't you say Drake holds the mortgage for the studio and that the seed money Zander borrowed still hasn't been repaid?"

The skin between Kate's brows puckered. "Yes, but it was a tiny amount to lend, and the studio space ends up being an easy tax write-off."

Sensing she was gaining ground, Imani rushed on. "Even so, he can't even keep consistent hours for the studio here, or the ones in Cuba and Friendship. His website says 'By appointment only.' I mean, how can you run a business like that?"

Kate jabbed her in the ribs, speaking low. "Imani!"

"Ow! I'm not trying to be mean, but this dancing-through-life thing is like some kind of Peter Pan syndrome. Someone who can't adult isn't fit for a long-term relationship with me."

Imani had been so busy trying to make her point, she hadn't picked up on Kate's subtle clue. It wasn't until she'd finished speaking that the spicy, fresh scent of Irish Spring soap wafted to her nose.

Damn.

Zander was standing right behind her.

She turned, pasting an "I wasn't just talking about you" smile on her face. "Heyyy. We were saying what a great job you've done with this place."

Zander returned her smile, nodding. "For someone with Peter Pan syndrome, you mean?"

Imani's cheeks blazed with heat, but she was saved as Drake approached, letting them know Kate's mom and dad had arrived. Kate waved guiltily to Imani as she walked off with her husband, leaving her alone with Zander.

"I, um, didn't mean for that to come out the way it sounded." Imani's gaze locked onto her espadrilles—and the Band-Aid still wrapped around the bottom of her foot. She juggled her water bottle to the other hand to pull a set of keys and a neatly folded T-shirt from her purse. "I wanted to thank you again for your car. And for helping with Lancelot. And for the ladder, and taking the broken tiles, and then helping me clean out Gigi's garage, and your offer of paint. And...lending me your T-shirts. Wow—I'm going to owe you some Hungarian goulash or homemade cookies or something. Until then, I filled the Prius with gas, and I, um, washed the shirt you gave me at the wing place last night."

He scooped up her hand in his, and she stopped babbling. Dragging her gaze up, she was surprised to see he was grinning. He held her hand a moment before pocketing the keys and taking the shirt, snapping it open and out of the crisp rectangle she'd folded it into, draping it over one shoulder like a dishtowel.

"You don't owe me anything. I've never had Hungarian goulash, though, so if you do make it, count me in for a heaping bowl. Thanks for washing yesterday's shirt. Which means I'll have to see you again for *today's* shirt I so gallantly let you borrow. How's your side, by the way? And did your grandmother spot your deception?"

"My deception? I didn't lie..." She trailed off, grimacing. "Yeah, I totally lied. I said the fireplace tiles fell off when I was cleaning. But I'm going to find replacements online. It'll be fine."

He raised his eyebrows.

"Sounds like you have it figured out. Well, good news. I wore a black T-shirt tonight, knowing your tendency for getting half-naked in my presence. I figured this color would match whatever outfit you wore. Great forward thinking on my part, right?" He tilted his head, grinning maniacally at her until she cracked a smile, unable to hold a straight face any longer. "Now when you have another wardrobe emergency and simply *must* strip down, you won't have to worry about clashing. Plus, it'll camouflage me when I drop off your clandestine paint. Although, for the record, I think you should tell your grandmother you got paint and end this tangled web of lies."

It was pointless to carry on a serious conversation with him, so Imani sipped her ice-cold water, trying to make her lips quit twitching into a smile.

"It's gorgeous in here," she said, switching topics. "Perfect for today's party. I'm assuming Kate and her spreadsheets visited at least once this week?"

Zander nodded, folding his arms on his massive chest to survey the room with her. Most of the guests had arrived, filling the space with chatter, laughter, and the sound of cutlery against plates as people swarmed the beautiful charcuterie boards set up along the middle bar.

"All done to Kate's specs. She was very...precise on how she wanted things. My only job was to follow directions. A skill I possess. Believe it or not." He turned to face her, arms still crossed. A smile curved his lips but did not reach his blue eyes. "Which is why I never reached out to you after the lukewarm 'that was fun' text you sent two weeks after I called. I took the hint and followed your unspoken directions. To set the record straight—it wasn't for lack of interest. On my part, at least."

Imani wasn't sure her face could feel any hotter.

Thankfully, Ryker chose that time to approach. Zander's brother wore a garnet-red T-shirt over a light-washed pair of fitted Buckle jeans perfectly tailored to hit an inch above the bottom of his Chuck Taylor sneakers—which he'd chosen to wear on both his prosthetic and his foot. For once, he wasn't wearing a baseball hat, and she noticed his dirty blond hair was the same color as Zander's—albeit much shorter.

"Look what the cat dragged in," Zander said, clapping his brother on the back in welcome. They stood about the same height, and with their matching blue eyes and blond hair, they were like two Viking bookends—one with a perpetual come-hither smile on his face, and the other with a stern, talk-to-me-at-your-own-peril expression. She watched as the two exchanged a glance—one that conveyed entire conversations with a single eyeblink—and she was instantly envious. She'd always dreamed of having a sibling, and during the times when she'd lived with Kate, she'd sometimes pretend they were sisters who'd been separated at birth.

"I'm here, aren't I?" Ryker stared daggers at Zander, but then he turned to Imani, and his expression thawed. "Hey, Zan tells me you have a 1975 Chevy Monza in your grandmother's garage that's on the fritz. I love a good challenge, and I've never had a chance to see a little car like that under the hood. Mind if I swing over sometime and take a peek? Those Chevys will run forever. I bet what it needs is a good tune-up, and the old gal will be back on the road for you and Mrs. Foltz in no time."

"That's—that's such a nice offer. But," she said, swallowing her pride as she admitted, "I, um, don't have the funds right now to fix up the Green Grabber, and honestly Wellsville is so small, I can pretty much walk wherever I need to go, or call Jimmy's cab. He loves Gigi and doesn't mind fitting her in to run to the grocery store."

"The Green Grabber?" Ryker asked with a hint of a smile. "Hold up. I have to know the story behind that name."

Imani shrugged. "Grandpa Foltz had it forever. It's forest green and old as dirt, but he was the only owner, and proud as punch of that fact. Gigi said you'd get into the thing and have to grab your butt when you went over the potholes, hoping it would hold together. So it got nicknamed the Green Grabber."

"Better than our nickname for Zander's car. Mom dubbed it the Clown Car. Because of the driver. Obviously." Ryker winked, waving away Zander's objection. "As for cost, if I don't have the parts in my junk pile to fix it for free, I'll let you know. But trust me, I've got more spare parts and scrap metal than most. In more ways than one."

Although it made Imani squirm to accept charity, she remembered the bigger picture. Once Gigi was healed, there wasn't any reason she couldn't drive. She hadn't driven in years, because her knees made it too painful to push the gas and brake pedals, let alone walk anywhere once she got to a destination. Her grandmother having the independence to drive again after her surgery—well, that was worth Imani sucking up her pride and accepting some help.

"Thanks. I'd appreciate your opinion on whether the car has any miles left in her."

"Good, then it's settled," Zander said, looking pleased.

"I'll grab the keys from you tonight and we'll push it out of the garage so Ry can tow it to his place for a look-see. Now…" He crooked his finger at her. "I believe we have an unfinished pottery piece to fill?"

"Ooh!" Ryker waggled his eyebrows. "Filling a piece—is that code for a quickie? I like it. Subtle, yet vulgar and cringey at the same time. Although, I doubt you could describe anything about Imani Lewis as 'unfinished.' You're the classiest woman Zander's ever met."

Zander punched him in the arm but looked at Imani. "Have you got the sonogram results?"

She pulled the envelope out of her tote, waggling it at him. "Of course."

He nodded, then refocused on his brother. "Can you make sure Mom gets to Mrs. Foltz's house after the shower? She's been invited for cards."

He gestured to their mom, who stood next to Kate and Drake. She was dressed in a smart, short-sleeved pink pantsuit and appeared almost as excited as her son and daughter-in-law, who both stood gawking at the finished shower cake made to look like—what else?—a tower of baby books. Imani was quite proud of this detail—one she'd concocted with Kate a couple months ago—and was pleased to see her favorite book as a child, *Angelina Ballerina*, among the piped titles on the frosted spines of the stacked cake books.

"Sure, no problem, but I thought you might need help cleaning up afterward." Ryker turned to Imani. "Oh. I get it. Are you staying after to help, then?"

Feeling put on the spot and getting the strong vibe Ryker was purposely setting her up, she speared Zander with a look. "Apparently I am. I do owe him for...pretty much everything lately."

Ryker headed across the studio, leaving her to follow Zander up the spiral staircase that led to the loft where he lived. The steps were winding metal, and she had to switch the envelope to the same hand as her drink so she had one hand free to clutch the railing as she climbed. No way was she going to tumble down these stairs in a sundress and wedges and embarrass herself.

She was looking down, ensuring each step, so she didn't pick her head up to see the living space until she was at the top.

"Oh my," she said, caught off guard. "It's so beautiful and...tidy up here."

She'd thought his home would be messy and bohemian, with piles of clutter, a hammock in a corner, and a big tie-dye tapestry tacked on the wall. What she found was altogether different. The vibe was more library–meets–World Market, with neat shelves of the same industrial sort as downstairs, but these were stacked with books intermingled with odd objects. She spotted several throwing axes, an antique globe, a deer's antler, and a massive bamboo plant that had taken over one entire shelf.

In lieu of a dresser, Zander had a massive steamer trunk, complete with leather handles and old brass latches. Atop that was a vintage suitcase, open to reveal T-shirts folded in compact envelope squares, Marie Kondo–style.

On the room's main wall was a world map, with colored pins stuck in various places. Other walls contained a handful of family photos in a framed montage, and a massive beehive—unoccupied, she hoped—was tacked to the space above the room's only door, which presumably led to a bathroom. His bed was a king-size monstrosity made up with a fluffy gray comforter whose matching sheets were turned down, as if ready for a magazine shoot. The ginormous, down-filled pillows made her yearn to snuggle under the covers, slip on her sleeping mask, and drift away for a good ten hours. No, she wouldn't be greedy—eight would do. And if an hour or so of that time in bed happened to be shared with a certain Viking with a bearded shadow on his face, all the better...

She jumped as Zander cleared his throat behind her.

"I can't help but notice you're staring at my bed in a way I can only describe as longing. I'll admit, it's not the best timing in the world, and I warn you, sound travels spookily well in this place, but maybe if we're quiet..." He trailed off, then laughed at her expression. "Kidding. Except you did look like that when you saw my bed. Am I lying?"

"It's not what you think." Imani juggled her glass water bottle, awkwardly crossing one arm in front of her sundress. She hated the way her nipples always seemed to snap to attention when his voice got low and gravelly.

"Bullshit," he breathed, taking a step toward her. "I didn't hallucinate that kiss earlier. I may not have a degree, but I'm not stupid. You can argue all day long about hating my...what was it...my Peter Pan lifestyle? Yet I think, subconsciously, you know we could work. But you're too afraid to try, and I'm not sure why."

Imani wasn't sure whether she was angry or turned on. Maybe both?

"I'm sorry if it hurt your feelings, but I've got goals. Plans." She made a conscious effort not to lean into him, to keep her arms between them as she spoke. "I feel like your whole flirt game is an elaborate punishment for me doing the adult thing after our hookup. Most guys would be thankful I just wanted a strings-free weekend."

"I think you owe the concept of 'us' another chance. One *real* date, where I take you out to dinner, followed by something fun to do as a couple to see if we work. You know. Outside of sex. We already know we're good there."

"Shh!" She elbowed him in the gut, looking past him and over the loft's railing to the studio below to see if they were being overheard. People were milling about, and nobody glanced up.

"Ow! Violence is not the answer, Imani." He clutched his belly, pretending she'd hurt him. As if she could put even a tiny dent in those rock-hard abs. "Use your words."

She fought against the smile he always seemed to coax from her. "Someone's going to hear you."

"Which is why we can't test out my bed. But we can check out what I made for Baby Matthews."

Before she could call him on his constant flirting, he pointed to a game table with two chairs sitting in the farthest corner.

A beautiful ceramic fox sat on top, painted glossy white. The detail on its eyes and the carvings for the fur on its face and tail made it look like he'd taken a real fox, dipped it in plaster, then painted it a beautiful arctic white.

Imani crossed to the table and set down her water bottle. Then, noticing it was an antique-looking wood table, she doubled up the gender reveal envelope, sliding it underneath as a makeshift coaster so she could pick up the fox with both hands.

"Wow. This is amazing! You made this?"

"Yep." Pride rang in his voice as he elaborated. "I carved the mold myself. Took several castings until I got the facial expression right. The first few looked like something out of one of Drake's horror novels. Cool Uncle Z isn't about to give his niece or nephew bad dreams."

Her fingertips traced the snout. Then she examined the details on the fox's back and the tail curving around its paws, all puffy and catlike. She flipped it over to see that he had, indeed, signed it "Uncle Zander" with the year in his precise, draftsmanlike printing.

"This is exquisite. It seems a shame to have to break it."

Zander snorted. "We're not breaking this. I spent weeks getting the piece perfect, without a single flaw or bubble. This is my gift to them, so we'll find another way to do the gender reveal. Like dump the colored starch into the garbage or something."

Imani set the fox carefully back onto the table, shaking her head. "Uh-uh. No way are we deviating from Kate's plan. She wanted something dramatic and exciting—she's waited eight months for this, and if you know my best friend at all, you'd know that going so long without knowing a major detail, like the sex of her firstborn, has been torture." Imani recalled the shelves of unglazed ceramics downstairs. "What if we smash one of the piggy banks instead? You must have a couple dozen of those, and it'll be easy to get the cornstarch in its belly."

"We are not smashing anything inside my studio—I don't care how pissed Kate gets. Do you have any idea how many pieces will go flying when it shatters on my concrete floors? It's one thing to toss it out my back window into the yard, where it would safely break in half, and make for an easy cleanup. But in here, with cornstarch inside?" He gestured to the studio, where the voices of the guests below increased, as more people arrived. "Nope. We'll do something else and ask for forgiveness, not permission."

Imani spun, jabbing her index finger at Zander's chest. He caught it in one big fist, squeezing gently as she hissed at him. "If you don't help me come up with something epic to replace Kate's dramatic gender reveal plan, you are in big trouble, mister."

"Mister?" Zander rounded his eyes. "There's no need to name-call. We'll get this figured out. I have an idea. Are you allergic to body paint?"

Five minutes later, Zander had Imani seated on his toilet, lid down, while he hovered over her with a thin paintbrush and balanced a used package of Halloween makeup on the vanity next to her.

The face makeup was left over from a Cowardly Lion costume—a fact she picked up on immediately.

"I'm not sure how painting me as a jungle animal is helpful," Imani said, scowling at him. The beach waves she'd worked so hard on this morning were going to be ruined as she'd grudgingly capitulated to Zander's request to pull her hair back in a ponytail.

Zander went to work on her face with the kit's black, crayon-looking applicator. He began at the bridge of her nose, moving up to her hairline in a squiggle.

"It's our new and improved gender reveal. I'm writing 'It's A' on your forehead and eyelids, and the sex of the baby will be on the rest of your face. I'm envisioning writing it in this Banksy-inspired, graffiti-like font, and then I'll fill it in with the bright red, yellow, and white to make it bright and fun. For the gender, I'll mix colors to make pink if it's a girl, and use the blue if it's a boy," he said, stopping in his drawing to explain but not pulling away from her face.

She inhaled deeply. How did he always smell so good?

"What's the reveal part, then? You're going to have me walk in backward and then spin me around in a dramatic twirl?"

He grinned. "Or a bachata-like dip? That would be awesome. But I was thinking of something simpler—we can clip one of the masks I use when I'm working with stains and paint thinner over your nose and mouth, covering the gender, and you can whisk if off when the time comes. Way better than smashing pottery on my studio floor. Now close your eyes and relax your face. You keep frowning."

Imani huffed a breath. "It's because you're taking so long! Can't you scribble it on and be done with it? They're going to be wondering where we are. And what we're doing."

"You can't rush a masterpiece. Now close your eyes." He gave her a stern look until she shut them once more. He used a finger to rub at the spot between her brows. "Smooooooth this out...there! Besides, you're making a scrapbook thing, so you'll want great reveal pictures to put in the book, right?"

"Fine," she grumbled, fixing her frown line after he squished it down. "But hurry. My best friend is down there, putting up with her mom and stressing about this reveal."

"Will do. Don't move your eyes—the bottoms of 'It's A' extend to your lids, so you'll have to keep your eyes closed during the initial reveal."

She sighed and obeyed. His hands were warm and seemed to be everywhere on her. One was lightly cupping her jaw to steady it, tilting her this way and that as he drew, and his drawing hand rested against her cheek as he used the black crayon to outline, then color it in. It was like the makeovers she used to have with her mom long ago, when she'd close her eyes and let her mother apply eyeliner and shade her lids, then use her trademark red lipstick to draw a heart out of the bow of her lips, like a Parisian clown.

It felt nice to have someone touching her—warm, soothing hands in her hair, against her face—and after a few minutes, her shoulders relaxed and her palms lay in her lap. Her breaths were long and even, and she no longer jumped when the paintbrush touched her eyelids.

"Have you fallen asleep?" he asked, coloring something on the left side of her forehead. "Your eyelashes are motionless against your cheek, like the soft, feathery end of one of my nice brushes. You look as serene as a painting."

Her inner high school girl was blushing furiously at the elaborate compliment. "It's nice to have this little slice of serenity," she managed, sighing. "I feel like all I've done is sprint at work, then flew to Gigi's, where I raced to clean her house until about an hour ago, when I took the fastest shower of my life to rush here..."

"Mm-hm." He swept aside a wayward strand of hair to color something next to her ear, and she suppressed a sigh. His touch felt so wonderful. "I sense a theme, with all those action verbs. Makes me feel like I'm running on the treadmill, just listening. And I hate that freaking machine."

Her lips twitched upward, but she didn't open her eyes. Rain pelted down on the roof, and the whooshing, rushing sound of it lent a cozy, intimate feeling to his little studio space. She wished like hell there weren't a couple dozen people downstairs. Not that she was envisioning sex— not exactly, although the thought sent a delicious shiver through her body. But being here, chilling with Zander, letting him touch her face with his callused but gentle hands, his fingers combing slowly through her hair while he massaged her shoulders...that would be some kind of wonderful.

Kate was right. Zander was a good guy. He didn't deserve to be jerked around.

"Zander, earlier today—it was my fault. I kissed you first. I didn't mean for it to happen. You're just always so..."

"Kissable?" he provided.

She cracked open one eye, then closed it when the paint-brush approached her pupil.

"You're hard to resist, even when I know I should. You're like a good cheese. Except without the gas and bloat."

He pulled the paintbrush away, and she opened her eyes to see he was chuckling. "I've been called many things, but this is the first I've been compared to...cheese."

"I'm lactose intolerant, so you're like milkshakes, ice cream, and dairy for me. If I indulge, there are major GI consequences."

"At least I rate right up there with Gouda and milk-shakes. Now I just need to figure out the relationship equivalent of Lactaid to get you to date me." He laid the paintbrush across the Halloween palette, dropping the conversational thread like a hot potato. "It's time for the gender. Tell me if I'm writing 'girl' or 'boy' across your cheeks and lips."

Imani felt her face flush at the dating comment and hid the reaction by hopping up from the toilet to gaze into his vanity mirror. Although the words were backward for her, the font and lettering of 'It's A' looked like the puffy, spray-painted letters on city buildings where an artistic tagger took some liberties. Her heart lifted—Kate was going to love this more than smashing ceramics. She was sure of it!

"I don't know the gender. I promised Kate I'd wait to open it at the reveal, so I wouldn't accidentally slip and use a pronoun. The envelope is on the table by my drink."

Zander left the bathroom, and soon she heard a ripping noise.

Then he poked his head into the bathroom, handing her a piece of paper.

"Imani, we've got a problem."

She looked, and the ring of wet condensation from her water bottle happened to be right after the words:

*Congratulations! You are having a—*

Smear.

Panicked, she held the paper up, staring through it at the bright lights of Zander's bathroom. Exactly where the gender was printed was a mess of black, melted ink. The warbly outline of letters that could be a "B" or "G" was as indecipherable as the last bunch of letters that could be an uppercase "Y" or a lowercase "L."

She couldn't be sure if she was reading "boy" or "girl."

"What do we do?" She rattled the paper at him. "It's all a puddle of ink! How am I going to tell Kate I screwed up my one job?"

Zander scanned it once more, his eyebrows creased. Then

he grinned, pointing to the paper's letterhead and phone number.

"We'll explain what happened to the sonographer, and they can look it up and tell us the sex over the phone."

Imani rushed to her tote and had her phone out, dialing the number, in a matter of a few heartbeats. Then she got the office recording and remembered one crucial fact: medical offices were closed on Saturday nights.

Zander seemed to deduce the same, because his face fell.

"Do you know the name of her ob-gyn? Maybe we can call that number? We wouldn't get a recording, because, you know, babies come at all hours, and she could—"

But Imani shook her head. "HIPAA. They're not telling *us* anything, and probably neither would the sonographer's office." Then she brightened. "But we could paint the obstetrician's number on my face, in place of the gender. I'll still go down in a mask with it covered, and I'll...I'll admit I smeared the gender, but that makes it more exciting. It's like opening a gift to find out there's another box inside, and another inside that."

"Drawing out the suspense. Turn it into a happy mistake. I like it." Zander nodded, his eyebrows lofted in that pleased arch he got when he was vibing with something she'd said.

Imani knew it was some throwback to when she was a child, but she loved it when he gave that "I'm impressed by you" look. It was a gold-star-on-your-paper type of reaction that gave her an irresistible hunger for more, like the feeling she used to get working with authors and getting a national media hit or helping to launch them to a spot on the bestseller list. She'd always loved reading books, but these days her joy in her job stemmed more from snagging those gold stars than from the job itself.

The thought erased her earlier contentment, reminding her of what was awaiting her at the end of this summer.

She brushed the feeling aside, looked up the number for Kate's ob-gyn, and wrote it on the paper for Zander. Then she retook her place on his bathroom's closed toilet lid, eager to have his hands soothing her into a Zen-like state once more.

"There," he said, after what could have been hours but might have been five glorious minutes of that gentle touch-touch-touch on her face. "We're ready. Don't move. I'll get the face mask I use when I'm working with paint thinner. It'll be huge on you, and I'm not confident it'll stay hooked on those bitty pixie ears of yours, but we'll make it work. I'm going to get my phone so I can take pictures for you. Keep your eyes closed so you don't smudge the paint."

"Mm-hm," she said, unable to form syllables. Vaguely, she wondered what it was with this guy that always rocked her equilibrium, taking her off her stress mountain and whisking her away, making her think anything was possible. Irish Spring–laced pheromones, maybe?

The guy was like a mellow two-shot buzz, smoothing away her worries.

Intoxicating, euphoric... and addicting.

It was too bad they'd never be a thing. She could get used to this. But she knew more than most that nothing perfect could last forever. Eventually, it all went up in flames.

The floaty, half-drunk feeling propelled her downstairs with Zander, giving her the courage to stand in a giant, paint-splattered N95 mask with her eyes closed as he announced how the reveal was going to work. Lucky for Imani, the guests were relaxed, having demolished the charcuterie board and some of the gorgeous cake, so they thought the whole thing was fantastic. But it was Kate's face that Imani searched for as she peered through her lashes. Her best friend's brow was furrowed, and her hand rubbed the forest-green fabric stretched over her belly in an unconscious soothing gesture.

"Kate is going to count down from five, and when she gets to one, Drake will drop this side of the mask off Imani's face," Zander instructed, positioning his brother on her left, leaving Kate in front so she'd be the first to read it, straight-on. "And...we'll see what we'll see."

Imani watched through her lashes as Drake positioned himself, his hand on the left elastic loop. But Kate stood, stock-still, her teeth catching at the inside of her cheek in a gesture Imani knew was her version of the *Thinker* pose.

"Count us down," Zander said to Kate as if nothing was amiss.

Imani noted she should be nervous, considering she was about to disappoint her best friend. Strangely, though, she wasn't. What was done was done. And as Zander said, they'd turned it into a happy mistake.

"Five," Kate said, her voice loud. The rest of the crowd joined in as she continued. "Four. Three. Two...wait!"

Drake's hand on the elastic twitched, but he held, waiting.

Kate's hands moved from her belly to her chin, coming together like the prayer-hands emoji, fingers pressing into her lips, elbows out.

"Don't take it off," she whispered. Then she looked at

Drake, her green eyes pleading. "You were right. There are so few true surprises in life. I don't . . . I don't want to know."

Drake exhaled in what sounded like relief. Then he dropped his hand from her mask and moved to his wife's side.

"This is going to be the luckiest baby in the world, having you for a mother." He placed a kiss on Kate's forehead. "Now let's open those gifts."

As they moved away, Dr. Kasey Sweet, Kate's mom, snagged Imani by the elbow.

"Imani, honey. So nice to see you." She wrapped Imani in a fast hug, then squinted at her face mask. "They may believe in surprises, but I believe in being prepared."

Kasey's hand inched toward the N95 mask, and Imani was unable to say no to the woman who'd taken her in and given her a home until her father could get his feet back under him after her mom died. A strangled sound came out of her throat, but she was frozen in place as Kasey began to unhook the elastic from her ear—

"Sorry, Doc," Zander said. "The boss said no, and I'm not about to argue with my pregnant sister-in-law. I have a pretty well-honed sense of self-preservation."

Placing a hand at Imani's back, he spirited her away, nodding toward the curved staircase to his loft.

"Washcloths and towels are stacked on the shelves outside my bathroom. You go ahead and wash off the evidence. I'll hold down the fort."

Turned out, taking face paint off was harder than applying it. She rubbed at her face with the washcloth, but the black eyeliner-like crayon outlines were still vaguely visible after scrubbing her face almost raw.

A knock came at the door as she was finishing up.

"Imani? I'm leaving, and I wanted to thank you for such a perfect night. It's so like you to know me well enough to give me a second chance to decide before the reveal," Kate said, giving Imani an immediate knot of guilt in her stomach. Zander's words about the webs of deception came back to her.

"Katie, wait." Imani opened the door, and Kate clapped her palms over her eyes. Imani pried them off. "I don't have words on my face. I got water on the sonogram results. We couldn't read them, so Zander put your ob-gyn's number on my face instead. We were going to have you call her for the results in front of the group. I'm so sorry."

"Oh, thank goodness!" Kate said, throwing her arms around Imani's neck, hugging her tight. "I know you can keep a secret, but I didn't want Zander to slip and say 'he' or 'she' when referring to the baby. I was so stressed, figuring out how I could avoid him for the next few weeks!"

"You and me both," Imani muttered. At Kate's look, she shook her head, grinning. "But the guy's like fungus. He grows on you."

She walked Kate downstairs, chatting with her as Zander and Drake loaded the last of their gifts into the truck.

"You sure you don't need a ride?" Kate asked, her question holding multiple layers.

"I'm fine," Imani said, this time believing it. "Looking forward to hyperventilating with you at Lamaze class tomorrow."

After they left, Zander tossed her a roll of paper towels and set her to work with a wink. "Time to clean. Unless you decide you'd like to try out my bed instead?"

"Cleaning it is," she said. "I told Kate everything, by the way, and she was cool with it—thrilled, actually, that neither of us knew the gender."

"We make a great team. I keep telling you that." He cranked up some classic rock hits on his studio sound system, and they chatted and laughed as they worked. All too soon, the place was spotless and set up for the next day's Lamaze class. Zander took the broom from her hands, setting it with the mop and vacuum in the supply closet by the first-floor bathroom. "You ready to head home to Gigi? I'll bet the card game is in full swing now—it's raining too hard for anyone to want to leave."

He was right about the weather. The cold rain was coming down in sheets, the wind propelling it toward the building's tiny overhang. While it sounded soothing inside, it was much fiercer standing outside behind Zander as he locked the doors, and she shivered at the growing intensity. Thunder rumbled as the storm moved toward the village and settled into the valley.

"Once I get this up, we're going to have to run for the car." Zander locked the door, then faced her, holding what appeared to be the world's wimpiest umbrella in his hands. When he opened the rainbow-striped thing, she could see a broken rib caused it to sag on one side. "Are you sure you don't want to stay here and I'll come get you? Then you won't have to get wet."

"No. I'm sweet, but I'm not made of sugar," Imani said, using Gigi's favorite saying. "I won't melt."

"Let's go." He leaned into her, putting the umbrella almost completely over her head, and began to walk.

Cold rain hit the skin on her bare arms and the back of

her neck, and she squinted as the wind gusted, blowing a chilly sheet of it onto her face, making it tough to see his Prius parked in the nearby lot in the deluge. She gasped, laughing as she picked up the pace, his long legs keeping up effortlessly with hers as they sprinted, their feet splashing into puddles, soaking her feet and the backs of her bare legs under her dress. The whole thing was breathless and silly and...

Suddenly, out of the corner of her eye, Imani caught a flash.

There was a trio of candles, still lit, in Zander's studio window.

"Wait!" she shouted, halting so fast she skidded in her wedges on the wet pavement. "We've got to go back. You've left the candles burning."

"No, it's okay," he shouted to be heard over the rain and thunder. "I'll get them when I get home."

Imani spun, and the flames were shooting up from the wicks now. They were getting out of control!

"Hurry!" she yelled, retreating to the store's overhang as a crack of thunder boomed loud overhead. The noise made her yelp and cringe, but she kept running, heedless of the water filling her eyes, cold against her head, her face, her body. She blinked back the rain, but her worst fear was coming true. The flames weren't just at the top of the candles—they flickered high above the wick. Too high.

"Zander, we've got to get inside!" She'd reached the protected overhang of his storefront and began yanking on his door, twisting the knob and tugging, then pounding on the wooden door, then the glass. She heard his footsteps splashing in the street's gutter, and then he was up on the sidewalk with her, holding the stupid, broken, rainbow umbrella up as if he were a circus tightrope walker.

"Whoa, hold up. Stop pounding, Imani, you're going to hurt yourself. It's not a big deal, they're—"

"You didn't blow them out before you left. They've gotten out of control. We've got to get in there!" She turned to him, her heart hammering so hard against her ribs she could hear the *boom-boom-boom* in her ears. Or was that the thunder rolling through? She couldn't be sure. "Don't you know you never, *ever* leave a candle burning unattended? Look! It's already spreading—but we can still stop it. Open the door, Zander!"

"Okay, okay. Give me a sec—" Zander fumbled with the keys, but he was slow. So slow...she wasn't going to get in there in time.

Rain drenched her face, gusting against the glass but not disguising the fact that the flames on the candles grew. Fire rose from the wicks, devouring the wax, burning it down to nothing with every gulp of oxygen as it searched, starving, for more fuel. More fuel. More fuel. It was all going to burn. It was all—

Then the door was open, and Imani shoved past Zander, her breath heaving, her lungs sucking in choking gasps of air. She smelled smoke as she looked frantically for water, or a big rug, or cornstarch—anything to douse the flames!

Her eyes lit on the shelving unit and its colorful plastic jars of paint.

"The paint—is it water-based?" she asked, snatching down the blue plastic container. It was heavier than she thought, and she almost dropped it as she lugged it to the windows, gasping as she twisted and twisted on the top, her palms rain-slicked and sliding over the ribbed lid, unable to budge it open. "We can use this if I can—I can't get the top off. Quick, help me get—"

"Imani." Zander's voice was quiet. Eerily so. And instead of dashing over to help, he stood right next to the candles.

"Watch out!" Imani used her free hand to wipe the rain from her eyes. "You're going to get burned—"

"No, I won't." His hand reached into the bright flames, and he grabbed a candle, holding it in his hand. Upsidedown. And it was still burning. Yet, oddly, the flames weren't spreading . . .

He flicked something on the bottom, and the dancing flame went out.

There was no smoke. Not even a tiny ribbon of it trailing from the extinguished wick.

He grabbed the next, and then the third one, repeating the procedure, and she heard the tiny click above the din of her own heartbeat.

Then he brought all three to her, holding them stacked in his arms like white logs. Zander eased into her personal space, lowering the candles in slow motion, as if afraid he'd startle her. His voice was gentle.

"They're battery-operated."

She stopped twisting at the blue paint canister, panting. Her heart still hammered in her chest as she looked around, surveying the rest of the candles in the place. While the candles around the art studio flickered, none of them smoked.

Nothing was on fire. Nobody was burning.

It was . . . only in her head.

She dropped the blue paint canister and it thudded onto the floor between her feet. She looked at the dead candles in Zander's arm and dragged her hands down her face.

"I've got—" She stopped speaking, sobs rising in her so fast she knew she had only moments before the tidal wave hit. "I've got to go."

Imani sprinted to the door, then heaved herself out into the night.

As she stumbled down the sidewalk, rain pelted her face, mixing with her tears until she wasn't sure who was weeping more: the heavens or her.

# CHAPTER 8

Imani, please get in the car," Zander pleaded for what felt like the thousandth time.

After her odd candle scare, she'd rushed into the rain, heading toward the bridge that spanned the dark, churning waters of the Genesee River below.

At first, he'd run after her. Then, after a huge crack of lightning burst overhead, he'd cursed, sprinted back to the parking lot, and jumped into the Prius. Peeling out of the lot, he caught up to her as she scurried over the four lanes of traffic on 417, not waiting for the pedestrian light.

She'd reached the street that wound around the back of the David A. Howe Public Library by the time he could pull the car up next to her. He slowed the car to her pace, rolled his window down, then threw the passenger door open.

"Imani, whatever's going on, we can fix it. Please, just get in the car."

While he couldn't hear sobbing over the rain pelting down, her shaking shoulders and the way her head drooped conveyed such tragic sorrow, his own eyes welled up in empathy.

"Imani!" In desperation, he played to her only weakness—

family responsibility. His voice turned firm as he tossed his only grenade. "You're not going to be much help to your grandmother if you get struck by lightning or catch pneumonia."

She stopped.

Her face was a study in misery, her eyes pools of despair.

"Don't be a martyr," he said, hiding the fact his heart broke seeing her pain. "Get in the car and I'll drive you home."

She trudged to the car, her hair matted to her head and her dress stuck to her legs. She plopped into the passenger seat, closed the door, and clutched her purse to her chest as he rolled up the windows and blasted the heat.

Her teeth clattered as they drove, and he might have thought there was rain running down her face, if it weren't for the soft sound of her sobs. He gripped his steering wheel, focusing on the road as he turned onto Main Street and headed south, racking his brain for something—anything—to say that would comfort her.

"You're okay," he said in his most soothing voice. "I've got you. I'm going to take you home to your Gigi, and then I want you to get in a hot shower. I'm not sure what I did, but whatever it was, I'm so sorry."

Imani waved his apology away. "It doesn't have anything to do with you."

Two minutes later, he came to a halt on Grover Street in front of the bungalow. He sprinted around the car to the passenger side to help Imani out. He guided her up the sidewalk, shielding her from the rain as much as he could with his body, having left his broken umbrella on the street by his studio.

The front door was unlocked, and Imani went inside. She headed for the staircase, taking the steps two at a time.

"Shypoke? That you?" came Mrs. Foltz's voice from the kitchen, where Zander could hear the women gathered. "C'mon in here and I'll make you a drink that'll curl your hair."

Reluctantly, he headed toward the back of the house, noting the tile gaps in the parlor fireplace as he went by. Lancelot eyed him from his cage.

The kitchen was alive with light and energy. His mom was there, of course. He also recognized Mrs. Nowakowski, and Aggie from down the street. The women were all smiles and easy conversation, the cards pretty much abandoned for drinks and snacks as they sat on chairs or leaned against the kitchen counter. An old AM/FM radio was playing the Ariana Grande song "No Tears Left to Cry" in the background. The conversation ceased when he entered the kitchen, rain dripping off him onto the mint-green linoleum floor as he answered the women's unspoken question.

"Um, Imani's upset. Crying. I'm...not sure why."

The mood in the room abruptly shifted, as the women exclaimed at once.

He winced, directing his words to Imani's grandmother. "She's okay, but we got stuck in the rain," Zander said, by way of explanation. "She headed upstairs. I think for a hot shower. Afterward, she might need some cocoa or tea, or..."

"Bottle of Jack?" Mrs. Foltz nodded in understanding.

"Tell me you didn't do anything to make her cry, Zander Hollis Matthews," his mom hissed, tugging him aside as Mrs. Nowakowski and Aggie got their belongings. "I've known Imani since she started working with Drake. She's kind, and she isn't looking for heartache, son."

Before he replied, Imani's grandmother wheeled her walker toward them.

"Mrs. Foltz," he began, running a hand through his sopping wet hair. "We were cleaning after the baby shower. Talking and catching up. When we left, I had some candles—battery-powered ones—that I left on in my display windows and—"

"Say no more." The older woman patted his arm. "Amira—my daughter and Imani's mother—died in a fire sixteen years ago tomorrow. She fell asleep with a candle burning and a window open. By the time the firefighters arrived . . . the whole house was engulfed in flames."

Zander felt his skin go prickly hot, then icy cold. "I—I had no idea."

"She doesn't talk about it much." The woman's sad, pensive expression was in direct contrast to her leopard-print shirt and bright lipstick. "Imani wasn't home. She was away at dance camp, so she blames herself. Amira was struggling with bipolar disorder. She'd have manic episodes, followed by a surge of depression. Ethan did the best he could, but he worked during the day, and as a surgery tech, he also had some night and weekend shifts. Much of Amira's care fell to Imani. We should have recognized Amira was spiraling and done something. A few weeks earlier, Imani had come home from school and found her mom asleep. In the shower."

Zander's mom clucked her tongue, reaching out to rub Mrs. Foltz's back. "I'm so sorry."

Zander winced. "I didn't know, or I would have tossed my candles. I didn't mean to . . . trigger her."

Mrs. Foltz shook her head, patting his forearm. "It's the stress that's triggering, not the candles. That's why I asked her down here this summer. I don't need a damn babysitter. But Imani does." She peered up into his face. Her dark-chocolate eyes, so similar to her granddaughter's, searched his for a moment, and then she nodded. "What she needs, young man, is a distraction. Some kindness and fun. Plus, you have one other very, *very* big thing she needs right now."

Patty sucked in a breath, giving Imani's grandmother a scandalized look. "Georgina! That's my son you're talking about, and I'm standing right here."

"I'm talking about his strength. His ability to lift things. We need someone to get these boxes back up to the attic." Mrs. Foltz put on an offended air, but her eyes sparkled with mischief. "Although I'm sure—"

"Zander, honey, it looks like you've got this under control," his mom said, giving him a look as he held back a laugh. "I'll see you later. Don't forget, you promised to help Cathy fix up the old Super Duper building so she can get it on the market. While I love your Aunt Cathy, the woman has been into PattyCakes a dozen times 'reminding' me, so do your poor mother a favor and help her out."

"Thanks for stopping by," Mrs. Foltz said. "You should be a regular for May-I—you're a natural at it. Plus you bring the best snacks."

Patty gave Zander a "good luck with her" look and left as the other ladies joined her, giving their goodbyes.

"Now it's time to put you to work." Imani's grandmother took charge, directing Zander to the boxes and bins piled high in the doorway to her room and stacked on the stairs and in the foyer. "We need those hauled to the attic. Go up the stairs, turn right, and you'll see a pull cord. Yank that and quickly step to the side, or the collapsible stairs will take your fool head off."

"Goddamn FOOL!" Lancelot yelled from the darkened room off the foyer—the one that earlier in the day had been covered in various shades of nail polish and dangerous shards of glass. "Good boy get a TREAT?"

"Gimme a minute," Mrs. Foltz hollered over her shoulder, as if reasoning with a person and not a twelve-inch gray bird.

Lancelot made a few clicks, followed by a few bars of convincing birdsong.

"Once you get up in the attic, there's a lightbulb in the center. Some of the rafters have nails sticking down, so watch your head. And for the love of God, keep the holidays together, or my granddaughter will have a stroke."

Zander nodded, glad to be of use. "No problem."

He heaved the first box up the stairs. In front of him was an open door with a bunch of other boxes and bins. By the turquoise suitcases stacked by the bed, he guessed this was Imani's room. On the opposite side of the hall was another closed door, and the last room was at the end of the hall. This one had light shining from the crack underneath, and the sound of a running shower inside— the bathroom.

He yanked the overhead pull cord, and the trapdoor stairs unfolded like some sort of multi-jointed alien. Clambering up and wedging himself into the attic, he began stacking bins in the tiny space. He started on the right side of the room, carefully facing out the *Christmas* label, which was handwritten in alternating green and red letters. Imani's handiwork.

Imani.

As he hefted box after box to the attic, the physical labor made his muscles complain, but what he ached for most was Imani—for what she must have gone through as a child. The loss, the responsibility. No wonder she was a list-making fiend. It probably gave her a sense of control, pushing back the chaos always lapping at her toes. It was exactly the same reason he lived for the now.

They'd both been the ones to survive, unscathed.

And that shit left scars.

The shower was off, but a hair dryer flipped on behind the closed door at the end of the hallway as he started emptying the upstairs room of its boxed items. The stack in the attic was neat and orderly; every box was lined up, labels facing out, organized by holiday: *Easter* on the far left, followed by *Fourth of July/Summer*, then *Halloween/Fall*, and finally the multiple *Christmas* boxes to the right.

He'd just lifted the last massive box and was lumbering out of the bedroom with it when he heard a little sound, like a gasp.

"Zander?" It was Imani. Her voice was tentative.

He stopped. Although the giant box he held didn't allow him to see her face, he was focused entirely on her as she next spoke.

"Are—are you okay?"

"Me? Yeah. I'm good. Why?"

"You've marched by carrying bins twice and didn't see

me." Imani's oval face peered around the side of the box. Her hair was still damp, hanging down in loose, wavy tendrils, and her face was devoid of any makeup.

She was breathtaking.

He lost the grip on the box he'd been holding, and it thumped down between them.

She leaped back, her dancer's agility making the movement graceful and evocative, although all she'd done was avoid a broken toe. From him.

"Sorry," he mumbled. "Once I get into Field Day mode, I'm in a zone."

She walked around the box and into the bedroom, setting down a bundle of things on the vanity before turning to him with a half smile.

"I'd hardly call hauling boxes to the attic a field day."

"Marine term." He rubbed a hand on the back of his neck as a quick glance revealed Imani was in a loose-fitting green shirt that ended mid-thigh, showcasing legs that went on for miles. It took a full second before he recognized why it looked so familiar—it was his shirt. The one he'd loaned her in the parlor after hers had gotten splattered with nail polish.

In that millisecond-long glance, he noticed two disconcerting things: she wasn't wearing a bra, and the soft fabric draped against her breasts and erect nipples in a way that made his mouth water. He lifted his chin like he was standing at attention. His eyes focused on her hairline so they wouldn't betray him and glance down at all of her goodness on display.

"A Marine thing?" she asked, and out of the periphery of his vision, he saw her put her hands on her hips, the gesture making her breasts sway under the shirt. *His* shirt, under which she was braless.

"It's a twisted joke. They make you deep-clean like crazy for hours once a week in boot camp, and they called it having a Field Day. Although I've been out years now, once I get into the cleaning mode, I'm still hardwired not to stop until it's done."

"Hmm. Good to know." She edged over to him.

He stared at the fixture over her head.

He would not look at her chest.

He would not look at her nipples.

Those nipples...

"Look," Imani said, startling Zander into glancing at her face. But not her nipples. The ones under his shirt. He wouldn't stare at those, but they were branded on his frontal lobe as she continued speaking. "I'm sorry I freaked out on you earlier. It wasn't your fault or anything. I just...had a weird moment. From my past—when my mom died in a fire. I'm sure it must've looked crazy..."

Her eyes were wells of shame, and he wanted to wrap her in his arms. Hold her and show her it was okay. That *she* was okay.

But he had to use his words.

"You don't have to explain." He captured her sad gaze. "I lost my dad when I was ten years old. Heart attack. Ryker was twelve, Drake was fourteen, so we all mourned him a little differently. Drake became a father figure to me, Ry rebelled, fighting in school and failing classes because he skipped out most days to hang with the local mechanics and tinker with cars."

"And you?" she asked, gliding a little nearer. "How did his death affect you?"

"I ate." He grimaced. "Everything. At all hours. Mom had to literally lock up the food at night with chains around the handles of the cupboards, because I'd sneak down and eat until I puked, then eat more. My nicknames in middle school were way worse than yours—they called me Carbzilla and Thigh-tanic. I took the idea of comfort food to a whole new level—it was the only thing that made me feel better. I got big—not in a good way—and it wasn't until I joined football that I discovered the transformative joy of the gym and turned some of the fat into muscle that got me a spot on the JV team. Soon, football became my life."

"What position did you play?" She flipped her damp hair over her shoulders. The motion sent a wave of her scent his way: something floral combined with some sweet, buttery lotion.

"Lineman. Specifically, left guard. My number one job was protecting our quarterback—which, when they moved me up to varsity, turned out to be my older brother."

"My favorite author played football?"

Zander snorted. "I love Drake, but he's more of a track-and-field kind of dude. No, Ryker was our star quarterback, and I got to play during his senior year, when I was a sophomore. Best football of my life, playing with Ry. He was a great leader, and his arm was a rocket that sent us to the state championship that year. After Ry graduated and joined the Marines, both of my brothers were gone. Although Mom and I are close, football wasn't the same. I struggled with food again—still do."

He patted his belly, giving her an "it's okay that I'm thick" smile, but to his surprise she was shaking her head.

"Don't do that."

"Do what?"

"Put yourself down." She scowled so fiercely that his self-deprecating smile evaporated. "You're perfect."

"I'm not," he said, then decided to throw it all out there. Open the vault to his shame. "I'm trying to say I get how you feel. After Ryker got hurt in Afghanistan, I got lost in that same well of misery I had when Dad died. I hated myself. See, my brother—the star quarterback who'd already won one Silver Star in service and wanted to rise to the level of master sergeant in the Marines—got injured in combat. And here I was, a dumb lineman who'd joined the Marines for shits and giggles and left the fleet without a scratch. I was whole, and Ryker—he wasn't. It didn't seem fair. It should've been me."

A beat of silence stretched out between them, full and round with emotion. Memories coursed through his head: the picture of Ryker with his arm thrown around him, both of them with smeared eye black as the sweat—or tears— from their championship victory poured down their faces. Ryker in his dress blues, coming home to drive Zander to the Marine recruiting office to sign his contract. Ryker arriving at Walter Reed, his face pale, his body criss-crossed by tubes and wires leading to machines keeping him in a medically induced coma as they worked on his injuries...

"Survivor's guilt is a bitch," Imani whispered, bringing him back into the bungalow bedroom where she stood, looking so soft yet so resilient—a combination he found irresistible. "That's one thing we both know pretty well, isn't it?"

He nodded, averting his gaze again to her hairline, loving the fact that her part wasn't perfectly straight. "Too well. That bitch doesn't know when to take the hint and get out of my head."

Imani flinched. "Sort of like me. What we did—how quickly it fell together for us in Niagara Falls, it wasn't me. It was...some other Imani. A version who does what she wants and doesn't think about consequences." Her voice was only a whisper as she gazed at him. "It wasn't fair to put you in that position, and I've sensed this lingering...resentment from you. I don't want you to be angry with me for my momentary lapse of reason."

He shook his head. "I'm not angry at you. I'm worried you won't grant me the honor of an actual first date— to decide whether we're as good together as I believe, or whether we're only a momentary lapse of reason, as you say. But I'm not angry."

"Then why won't you look at me?"

His gaze flicked to her annoyed expression, and he wanted to take his thumb and smooth out the crease between her knitted eyebrows, as if she were as malleable as the clay he worked with every day. Instead, he kept his hands by his side.

"I'm trying to be a gentleman." His gaze focused once more at her adorably crooked part. "I'm ignoring the fact that you're high-beaming me. And it's hot as hell."

"High-beaming you?" She looked down.

Zander dislodged his gaze from her forehead long enough to see her cross her arms over her erect nipples. To his surprise, she started to laugh. It started as a snorty chuckle, like she was holding back amusement but it was burbling out. Then the giggles escalated to full-out belly laughs so infectious he couldn't help but join in.

Before he knew it, his arm encircled her waist, and then her other hand was on his chest, and they were clutching each other, laughing like loons. She pressed against him, her breath unsteady from the unexpected hilarity.

"You—you're a good guy, Zander Matthews."

"Whoever told you that," he replied, "was a liar."

Her gaze traveled to his lips, and suddenly she was kissing him. Her mouth was all soft, minty lushness—a pool he could sink into for hours. Her breasts pressed against his chest, and he wanted so bad to cup that flesh. But he had a plan—she had to initiate *everything*.

"You taste delicious," he growled.

She pulled away to kiss his cheek, then his neck, her mouth sending delicious zings of sensation directly to his groin. She returned to his lips again, her tongue finding his—an action that made him reach out to steady himself against the wall as he let her explore him with her mouth.

He hissed a breath through his teeth as her hands found their way under his shirt and went skating over his abs, making him shudder with the effort required not to put his hands on her in return.

"Touch me," she breathed against his ear.

And it was go time.

His hands were up her shirt so fast, he was sure he set a Guinness record. His left palm pressed against the silky smoothness of her back, holding her steady as his right hand cupped the soft flesh of her breast, gently at first, then roughening his touch as she pressed hard into his touch, moaning. His thumb had just found her nipple, dancing over the pebble-hard top when a voice sounded from the doorway.

"You taste delicious," said a man in a husky, nasal tone.

Imani leaped away from him with a small cry, shoving the green nightshirt down as Zander spun to the doorway. He stepped in front of her, ready to block the guy's view of—or access to—Imani.

But the doorway was empty.

Then a whistling noise came from the dresser next to the door, followed by a series of raptor-like clicks. Lancelot sat on top of the dresser's mirror, cocking his head to one side then the other as he peered at them.

"You taste delicious," the bird repeated in a reasonable facsimile of Zander's voice. "Good boy get TREAT?"

The last word was more of a screech, and Zander barked a laugh, shaking his head at the beast. The thing had balls.

"Is that Lancelot I hear up there?" Mrs. Foltz yelled from downstairs. "I lost the fool when I refilled his water bowl."

Imani let out a shaky half laugh, adjusting her shirt and hair, looking guilty as hell though her grandmother hadn't seen a thing.

"Yes, he's here, Gigi. I'll shoo him down after I help Zander with this last box. Be there in a sec." She lowered her voice, speaking to him. "Talk about timing, huh? I— I don't know what got into me. Same thing that always seems to get into me when you're around."

He refrained from the obvious joke, opting instead for

the high road. He shrugged, grinning. "You don't hear me complaining." He hefted the last box, glad for something—anything—to conceal his obvious arousal. "I'll get this into the attic and let you two get some rest tonight."

By the time he'd adjusted the boxes to allow for anything additional that needed storage, switched off the light, and folded up the attic stairs, he'd managed to tamp down his desire so he didn't embarrass himself once he rejoined Imani and her grandmother downstairs. The former wore a bathrobe over the green T-shirt, and the latter wore a zebra-print housedress zipped up to the neck. Perched on the woman's walker was Lancelot, his head contorted as he preened the bright red streak of feathers at the base of his tail.

Sensing he was being watched, Lancelot sat up straight, his eyes bright with interest as he fixed his gaze on Zander.

"Good boy, get a treat?"

"He's a cool pet," Zander said to Mrs. Foltz as he showed his empty hands to the bird. "Hard to believe they live so long."

"You're telling me." The older woman pursed her lips in loving disapproval at the creature. "He's just like Arlo. Swears like a sailor, expects to be waited on hand and foot, and makes a damn mess everywhere he goes. But you love him anyway."

"Thanks again for the help with the boxes," Imani said, prompting an immediate agreement from her grandmother. "You did that so fast—I'd planned on spending all day tomorrow hauling those up there, but I can check that one off my to-do list. Now I'm freed up to do another project."

The bird gave a high-pitched, fire-alarm-decibel whistle, which Zander ignored. Instead, he squinted an eye at Imani.

"Well, you're freed up until ten o'clock, anyway."

She looked puzzled. "But tomorrow's Sunday. What's going on?"

"Oh, nothing big," he said, waving in dismissal. "Only your best friend's Lamaze class where she's counting on you to sit in as coach. You know, in case she has this baby while Drake's away."

"TREAT!" Lancelot screeched, and was immediately shushed as he paced back and forth on the front bar of Mrs. Foltz's walker.

"Oh no!" Imani clapped a hand to her forehead. "I completely forgot. I'm so glad—"

Suddenly, the bird flew in the air to Zander's shoulder.

"You taste delicious," Lancelot said in a husky male voice. Then the bird immediately changed tones, his voice softening to a breathy, female cadence. "Touch meeee," the bird whispered. "Touch me, touch me! TREAT!"

Imani gasped, her face reddening.

Her grandmother's eyebrows rose. She turned to level a quizzical glance at her granddaughter. "My, seems as though Lancelot's learning some new words. Wonder how?"

# CHAPTER 9

With the day's emotional drama, Imani figured she'd conk out after Zander left and she'd told Gigi all about the night...except for the kiss upstairs. She left that out, although she had a feeling her grandmother knew.

"I'll give you a cocktail that'll send you right off to sleep," Gigi said, waving Imani's insomnia worries away with one gnarled hand. "It's the best recipe for slumber. Next to sex, anyway. But I guess that's off the plate tonight?"

Two hours later, the house was quiet. Lancelot was tucked in the jockey shorts, fast asleep in his cage, and Gigi's snores echoed from downstairs. Yet, despite Gigi's drink with a healthy shot of Fireball, Imani lay in the upstairs twin bed.

Wide-freaking-awake.

Her embarrassing performance at the studio played on repeat in her mind, as did Kate's comments about Zander and her best friend's opinion that it was Imani, not Zander, with commitment issues. Her face would alternately flame with shame that she'd had some sort of PTSD moment with the candles, and then her body would ignite when she re-lived Zander's kiss. Kisses. They'd done that twice today—

and even the memory of his skilled mouth and hands made her libido tick to life.

It was as if she couldn't keep her lips off the man. Clearly, she'd touched a match, reigniting the raging inferno that had consumed them for an entire weekend after Kate and Drake's wedding. She had no intentions of starting anything with the guy—it wasn't listed on any spreadsheet, bullet journal, goal board, or bucket list to string along a man with no way to bring that relationship into the realm of reality.

But she couldn't seem to stop.

The kissing happened without any forethought, and damn, it had felt wonderful. It was like in dance, when she'd practiced a routine so well her body knew the motions without any mental prompts. Muscle memory. Time spent in Zander's arms was as effortless as if they'd been together forever.

Which, considering they had no long-term possibility, was terrible.

"Don't be a shit," she whispered to herself, flipping the pillow to the cool side for the ninety millionth time since lying down. "Don't start what you can't finish."

She screwed her eyes closed, focusing on her breathing, trying to recapture that Zen state she'd had earlier, that calm that had enveloped her when Zander was painting her face—that glorious touch, touch, touch...

She groaned, her body choosing to remember other Zander touches instead, and that made her want to call him over to finish what he'd started. The thought of him was like a shot of caffeine, making sleep a distant memory.

She peeked at her phone. Midnight. Mentally, she counted

the hours of sleep she had left—seven hours if she stopped thinking about Zander and fell asleep immediately.

As if.

After another pillow flip, she gave up. Hitting the light switch, she dragged over the only boxes left in the room—the shoeboxes of photos she'd spotted in her grandmother's parlor this morning.

"This is pointless. If I can't sleep, I might as well organize," she mumbled to herself.

From downstairs came the sound of a low train whistle, and Imani cursed, remembering to be quiet unless she wanted to wake Lancelot.

Starting with the shoebox of pictures on top, she began to sort. She made three piles. The first were pictures from her mother's childhood and older pictures of Gigi and Arlo, easy to sort as they were mostly black and white or Polaroids. The second pile was pictures of Imani's childhood. It was the largest. The third pile was the easiest to organize, as they were mostly still in the same Kodak envelope sleeves Imani had sent to Gigi over the years.

These photos were from after Amira's death.

As the self-assigned memory keeper, Imani printed a stack of photos for Gigi whenever they were together, in addition to uploading them to her cloud server and external drive. The envelopes had everything, from her dance recital pictures to the ones she'd taken a few years ago when she'd brought Gigi to New York City. Most were labeled with the date and subject, like *Broadway Show* and *Statue of Liberty Tour*. The rest were categorized by season. Imani flipped through a few, chuckling at how many times Gigi clandestinely flipped off the camera—giving the bird and not getting caught was one of her running jokes with the world.

By the time Imani had sorted the piles, it was 2:30 in the morning. Her head buzzed as if she'd had a Red Bull and not a shot of Fireball, so she reached for the largest pile. The prickly, painful one with the invisible daggers attached to it.

And she dove into the pool of memory.

She sifted through pictures of her as a baby being held by her mom, as Gigi stood behind them both—showing all three generations together. Then candid shots of Imani's first day of kindergarten, and the time her mom and dad came down to camp with Gigi and Arlo in their old RV at Letchworth State Park.

She peered at each picture of her mother, as if it held clues to her eventual unraveling. Amira's dark hair and deep brown eyes, so similar to her own, stared back. Like a lake, her mother's gaze appeared calm and clear on the surface. But Imani knew once you dove down, you saw the strong current at the silty depths where her mind was muddled and disconcerted.

"I'm all wrapped up in a world I can't explain," her mother had said once, cryptically, when Imani asked why she was so unhappy. If you pressed her too much, she'd "go dark"—a term her father had coined for how her mother acted during her depressive cycles when it was all eggshell-walking for fear of sending her plummeting further down the rabbit hole.

Imani had morphed into a comforting caregiver at those times.

"You bring her light," her dad would say, encouraging her to tiptoe into her mother's room and sit on the edge of her bed, chattering softly to her and showing off every single good grade she'd earned, every compliment she'd received, and every sunshiny detail of her day. Imani often stopped at the library on the way home from school to pick up one of her mom's favorite romance author's newest titles to read to her.

Often, she was able to bring her mom around, or at least get her to the dinner table. Toward the summer after her freshman year, before the fire, there had been so many weeks with her mother going to work, reading, creating scrapbooks, making homemade meals, and acting, in general, as if she'd never flaked out before. It lulled them all into thinking her mother was better. That the new regimen of medication was working.

Then, two days before Imani had left for dance camp in the Catskills, Dr. Jekyll transformed into Mr. Hyde. Amira became sad and vacant, looking through Imani as if she'd become invisible.

Imani picked up the photo she'd seen downstairs, taken after her *Swan Lake* dance recital in fifth grade. She examined their matching hair, eyes, and smile. While she'd had braces, you could tell by their similar expressions they were mother and daughter. But beyond those physical traits, were they alike? Was Imani's insomnia a precursor to depressive episodes ahead?

Exhaustion hit her like a dump truck, and Imani blinked owlishly as she looked at the clock on her phone.

6:20 a.m. She'd spent all night organizing photos into piles.

Imani shuddered, flipping her phone over to gaze at the sky through the bedroom window, already turning from black to light gray.

"I'm not my mother," she whispered, placing the piles of photos on her dresser. Flipping off the overhead light, Imani burrowed under the covers. While she'd put away the dance recital picture, as she closed her eyes, the image appeared like a screen saver behind her lids, seeming to symbolize something larger.

She squeezed her eyes shut so hard that tiny white sparkles danced in her vision, momentarily replacing the mom-daughter screen saver. She wasn't her mother. She'd been to the doctor, and everything was normal. Resting was just as important as sleep.

She repeated those three facts to herself, like counting sheep, until her eyelids relaxed.

Imani woke what seemed like five minutes later to the sound of her grandmother's quavery voice calling from below.

"Anybody up, up there?" Gigi had used this phrase to wake her every morning Imani slept over for as long as she could remember.

"I'm up." Imani's voice was as rough as a gravel pit, and when she opened her eyes, the sunlight streaming through the window stabbed her vision like the sharp edge of a garden trowel. Her head throbbed in time to her heart as she cleared her throat, pressing her temples with her palms as she called down to Gigi. "I'll be right there."

She staggered out of bed and down the dim hallway to the bathroom. Keeping the lights off, she brushed her teeth carefully, as if her head were made of delicate porcelain, liable to shatter at any moment. Cracking open one eye, she checked her phone as she brushed.

9:32 a.m. And a missed text from Kate.

Clicking on it, she read quickly.

Kate: I'll be there at 9:45 to pick you up for Lamaze class. I'll bring my whole birth plan to review with you, just in case. I'm so lucky to have you as my BFF! ☺

Imani groaned, spitting toothpaste foam into the sink and rinsing her mouth with as little head movement as possible. She glanced down at her bed clothes—Zander's green shirt—then wished she hadn't, as the vertigo made her want to spend the morning leaning her forehead against the cool porcelain bowl of Gigi's upstairs toilet.

Moving as if her head were a live grenade, she managed to dress in a pair of black capris and a red top. She shoved her feet into sandals just as Kate beeped outside.

Walking downstairs, she leaned against the railing like a drunken debutante, her neck stiff and her head unmoving. She met Gigi at the bottom.

Gigi scanned her stem to stern, then pursed her lips and shook her head. Pink curlers rustled underneath the wispy purple fabric of her headscarf. "You look hungover. Like you need a little hair of the dog that bit you, Shypoke."

Imani grimaced. "I wish. The birthing class will only be an hour, and I have some ibuprofen in my bag. There will be food there. I'll be ... fine."

"Hmph," Gigi huffed, unconvinced. "That's a pretty impressive set of luggage under those fibbing brown eyes of yours, but I know better than to try to talk you out of it."

Slipping sunglasses on, Imani used her ballet skills to transport herself, without moving her head, down the porch steps. She eased into the passenger seat of Drake's matte-black 1950s-style truck.

"Hi." Kate grinned at her from the driver's seat. She wore a pair of denim shorts with a cute gray T-shirt that said, *Can I get the Wi-Fi password in here?* over her beach-ball-sized belly.

"Funny." Imani gestured to the shirt. "Drake get you that?"

"No, Ryker gave it to me at the baby shower. He's the king of rude gifts, so apparently this one is tame in comparison. How are you? I heard things went awry after the shower last night."

"Awry. That's pretty accurate. The CliffsNotes version is I saw candles burning in Zander's window after we'd left...and freaked out. Turns out, they were battery-powered."

"Ooh." Kate bit her lip, wincing. "Triggered memories of your mom, I'm sure. How did...what happened with Zander? And how are you?"

"He was chill about the whole thing. Really kind. And I'm okay. Headache and no sleep, which seems to be my new normal." Imani forced a smile at her best friend's concerned expression. "Nothing that a lot of deep-breathing exercises and some food this morning won't cure. So, what's this birth plan you were telling me about, and why am I only hearing about it now?"

Imani had pushed both questions out at once, hoping to

derail her best friend from asking more about last night's events. To her surprise, Kate acquiesced, and Imani sank gratefully into the truck's seat, thankful to not have to speak more than a few hummed assents until they arrived.

Zander had delivered, so to speak, for the Lamaze class, and the spread laid out on the ceramic studio's center bar was impressive. Sliced bagels, mini-muffins, and delectable mini-quiches Imani suspected were from his mother's bakery were loaded on platters, along with cream cheese spreads and fresh fruit. Regretfully, Imani skipped the quiches. She had no Lactaid pills left and with the amount of floor work involved today, it was best not to tempt the gas gods. Arming herself with an orange juice and a plate with half a bagel, a muffin, and some fruit, she settled onto the chair next to Kate in the side of the studio Zander normally had set up for painting classes. Right now, the tables were shoved behind a portable screen and projector.

Imani nibbled on the muffin—it was blueberry and quite good. If she'd been in a normal headspace, she'd have done some damage on the breakfast in front of her. As it was, with her head pounding in time with her heart, she didn't dare eat for fear she might get nauseous. She used the orange juice to wash down the three caplets of ibuprofen from her purse and prayed they'd work soon.

Around them were various couples, mostly husband-and-wife teams, except one couple of two women, like she and Kate, although she gathered the other same-gender couple was married from the sweet, loving gestures they exchanged. All were first-time moms, so the room hummed like a beehive of nervous excitement.

Imani searched for Zander and spotted him puttering, refilling carafes, making fresh pots of coffee. She needed to tell him the kissing yesterday had been a mistake on her part. She hadn't meant to lead him on when she had absolutely no intention of starting a relationship, and since he'd been hurt by their fling last year, she didn't want a repeat of that either.

She closed her eyes briefly, trying to muster the strength for this explanation.

Then Kate grasped her hand, chatting excitedly about the plan she'd printed out for the baby's birth, and Imani changed her mind. Today was about her best friend. Her own drama could wait.

Later. She'd eventually talk to Zander, just not now.

"Okay, everyone! If I can have your attention, we're about to start. Let's begin with introductions. My name is Shama Patel, and I'm a retired labor and delivery nurse who's seen more babies born than I can count," said the petite, white-haired woman standing in front of a projector screen. She wore a pair of blue scrubs with storks carrying babies on them. "Why don't we go around, and you can introduce yourselves and let me know a little bit about your birth plan and how committed you are to having a natural, drug-free childbirth?"

Imani pinched the bridge of her nose with one hand, willing the pain to recede as each couple gave their intro and a brief summary of their birth plan. By couple three, they were all starting to sound the same: they wanted to do this naturally, with no drugs, and were planning various birth scenarios from traditional hospital births to home doulas and underwater births.

"Don't worry," Kate whispered, noticing Imani's shocked face. "I'm not having my baby in the tub."

When Kate's turn came, she gave a brief rundown of her birth plan. "I have my best friend on earth with me." Kate grinned, throwing an arm around Imani, who attempted to look thrilled. "She's always been my rock. God forbid something happens and my husband can't be there, I know I can count on Imani."

Next, Shama had them position themselves on the floor, with the pregnant moms lying on their yoga mats. The support coaches were positioned behind them; most, like Imani, were cradling the mom's head in their lap, but some had the mom lying against them as if the coach were a chair.

"We will be watching a birth movie, but first we're going to practice the core of the Lamaze method—the *breathing*." Shama demonstrated this breathing, stringing syllables in a pattern of *hoo*s, *ha*s, and *hee*s, followed by a cleansing breath between contractions.

As they practiced, Imani noticed her vision was funny. While her headache wasn't as vicious as before, the edges of her vision seemed to be graying out, as if her brain were using a vignette photo filter. Four rounds of Lamaze breathing later, the filter's lens had narrowed alarmingly, leaving only a pencil dot's worth of vision in Imani's eyes.

"Kate," she whispered into her best friend's ear as they practiced one last time. "I...I think I have to, um, go to the hospital."

"What?" Kate tilted her head up, halting her *hee*s and *hoo*s momentarily. "Did you say you needed to go to the hospital? What's wrong?"

"I need to go to the bathroom," Imani mumbled, unwilling to freak out in front of everyone. "My eyes are...I think I have something in them."

Kate squinted into Imani's face, her gaze searching her friend's.

"I don't see anything, but they are red. Hurry back—they're starting the movie next, and I need you to convince me I won't poop in the delivery room like they always do in these clips. If I do, promise me you won't tell me later they had to call a code brown, okay?"

Imani gave a wan smile. "Deal. Be right back."

Standing and walking was almost a trust exercise, as so much of her vision was eclipsed by the strange filtering. However, Imani managed to find the bar-like table and used it to feel her way to the other side of the studio next to the pottery wheels.

"Zander?" she stage-whispered, afraid to let go of the concrete bar but knowing she'd never make it to the bathroom unaided.

"I'm standing right next to you." Zander's voice came from her right, and she jumped, reaching out blindly, as her vision had narrowed to a pinprick. She felt his arm and stepped inside his reach, as if readying herself for their next bachata. She welcomed his warmth as she tilted her head to whisper.

"I think I'm going blind."

He didn't answer right away. She poked him in the ribs, and he grunted in response.

"Ow, I heard you. I'm just trying to understand." Zander's low, throaty rumble sounded like a lion's purr. "One of my Sunday school teachers told us boys that masturbating would make us blind. Is this...code for that?"

She clicked her tongue in disgust. "Damn it, can't you ever be serious? I literally can't see anything. It's like everything got..." She trailed off, squeezing her thumb and forefinger into a teensy opening. "...super narrow in scope. I think I should go to the hospital. What if my headache is some crazy brain bleed, and my blindness is the last sign I'll get before I die?"

He grabbed her hand, and his arm wrapped around her shoulders as he guided her toward the back.

"Sorry. Joking is my knee-jerk reaction when I don't know what to say. What I should have said is this: Don't be scared. You're okay. It's likely just a visual migraine." His scent, spicy notes riding on the soothing wave of his Irish Spring soap, wafted to her as he turned them both to the left, and she resisted the urge to bury her nose into his neck for comfort as he continued speaking. "Ryker got them a lot when he first came home. Sometimes they can be accompanied by pain, and sometimes they're weird optical things, like sparkling, colored lights or a dimming of vision."

"What should I do? Do I need to see a doctor?"

"Best thing for it is sleep. That's what always worked for Ryker. Why don't you lie down for a twenty-minute cat-nap?" he said, guiding her to the staircase. Without waiting for an answer, he helped her onto the first stair, cutting off her objections. "I'll sit with Kate for the movie. You've already done the heavy lifting with the breathing stuff—this is the easy part. I'll close my eyes if it gets too graphic."

"But what'll you tell Kate?" She allowed him to lead her upstairs. She wanted to lie down so bad, but she didn't want her best friend to think she was abandoning her.

"That you had to lie down because you've got a migraine," he said, and she didn't have to see his face to know by his tone that he was rolling his eyes. "Life is less complicated if you tell the unvarnished truth and don't try and make every moment a perfect version of itself."

"Wow." She frowned at the top of the stairs. "Tell me how you really feel."

"Lie down and quit arguing."

He guided her to his bed, and as she sat, he swung her feet up and onto the covers, flipping off her shoes and tossing a throw blanket over her as she reluctantly snuggled against his downy-soft pillows.

She sighed, closing her eyes as soon as her head lay back, like one of those sleepy-eyed dolls. His pillow smelled like him, and her insides unclenched as they always did in Zander's presence.

"I'll just take a catnap. Wake me up in twenty?"

He mumbled something in response and then clicked something next to her. Moments later, the smell of lavender filled her nostrils. She cracked open her eye, curious as she focused her tiny pinprick of vision in on the noise. Was that...?

She snorted, closing her eyes again.

"Of course you have an essential oil diffuser," she mumbled, her mouth curving in a smile. "You're way too bougie, Zander Matthews."

"Sleep," he said.

His hand cupped her cheek briefly, and then he was gone.

# CHAPTER 10

Zander shut and locked the front door to his studio, flipping the sign to *Closed* after the last of the Lamaze class attendees left, along with his sister-in-law.

"I checked on Imani. She's still out," Kate had said, before leaving herself. "I've called her grandmother and let her know she's sleeping off a migraine. Gigi told me Imani hasn't slept well in months, and it's catching up with her. I...I didn't know she was suffering from insomnia so bad. It reminds me of when she was in high school right after her mom died. Do you think she's okay?"

Zander's eyebrows rose. How in the hell was he supposed to know? He'd been with her not even three full days this calendar year, and he was the expert? But he sensed Kate needed more generic reassurances.

"Don't worry, sis," he said, as he carried her yoga mat out to Drake's truck. "I have a bunch of work to do in the studio, so she can sleep as long as she wants. I'll have her text you when she wakes. I don't offer Sunday classes, so I can run Imani home whenever she's ready."

After Kate reluctantly left, Zander got to work cleaning up. He covered the food but didn't toss anything, in case

Imani was hungry when she woke—she'd barely touched her plate from this morning. Then he dug around in his tea stash to find the bags of chai, recalling her breakfast-beverage order from room service during their weekend at Niagara Falls. He set those out where Imani would see them when she woke and came downstairs, making sure his hot water carafe was still full and piping hot.

Once everything was put away, he didn't feel like messing it up by getting out his clay and beginning the set of mugs he'd promised a client. He gazed out the studio windows at the sun-dappled area of his narrow backyard. It was such a beautiful summer day—perfect to be outside. Figuring he'd be quieter if he were outdoors, he crept upstairs to grab his throwing axes.

He was proud of his ninja ways, as Imani didn't stir when he carefully picked up the four metal axes from his bookshelf. He glanced at her still form, an arm thrown over her eyes, her luxurious mahogany hair splayed out on his pillowcase like a mermaid's. Not wanting to be a creeper who stared at a sleeping girl, he retreated downstairs and out the back door, closing it quietly.

Zander set up his target in the tree-shaded plot behind the studio, away from the beehives. After a brief stretch, he started tossing axes. He'd created the spray-painted wooden target from an old bunch of pallets he'd disassembled and nailed together, attaching it to a hay bale situated on the opposite side of the lot, toward the river. After a few minutes of throwing, he started to loosen up, and his muscles got warm as he found a rhythm.

He'd retrieved his axes for another go when he heard a noise different from the sound of the Genesee River tripping over stones in its rush north toward Rochester. Casting a glance over his shoulder, he spotted Imani's head poking out of the studio door, gazing around at his backyard, curiously.

"How's your vision?" he asked, making his way to her. She looked refreshed, and her eyes weren't squinting as they had earlier, although she blinked like an owl as she came outside.

"Normal again. But it's the afternoon. What happened to a twenty-minute catnap?"

"Kate and your grandmother said to let you sleep." He had the excuse already prepared. "You're supposed to text Kate when you're awake. Your grandmother said she was going to run some errands with Mrs. Nowakowski and for you not to hurry home." At her expression, he hurried to say, "But I can take you whenever you're ready."

She nodded, then surprised him by saying, "I'm in no hurry."

Huh. That was a first.

But he wasn't one to squander an opportunity.

"Want to toss some axes?" He displayed all four in his hands and was rewarded by a spark of interest in her brown eyes.

"Thought you'd never ask." She joined him, reaching for an axe.

He gazed at her sandals and pointed to a pair of his work boots sitting by the door.

"Slide your feet into those. I don't want you dropping an axe and chopping off those cute toes while I teach you everything I know."

"That shouldn't take long," she joked, winking to sand

the edge off her words. The sultry gesture put a stupid smile on his face, threatening to derail his plans. Again.

He taught her the basics, demonstrating the proper throw, and set her up in front of the target.

"Let the hatchets fly."

"That's what Kate said at Drake's Halloween book launch two years ago, when I first met you." She threw the first axe, and it landed two feet from the target, sticking into the grass.

"Take a giant step forward. Try again." Then, because he was curious, he had to add, "I remember the day we met, but I'm surprised you did. I didn't think you knew who I was until Drake's wedding."

She tossed the second axe, and it bounced off the target, the flat side of the axe hitting the wood with a clang as it encountered the head of a nail.

"No, I remember. You were wearing a white dress shirt with the cuffs folded up, and you had a little bit of a beard. You introduced yourself as the 'best Matthews brother' and then got flustered when I questioned your title." Her smile got soft. "I'm starting to think maybe you were right. You've been kinder to me than I've deserved."

He debated, then decided she was well enough. "Well, you know I have a goal—"

"Date me. I know. But I think...we should cool it down between us. I feel like I've been unfair to you. Leading you on in some way."

"All the kissing on me, you mean?" He cocked an eyebrow. "For the record, you kissed me. Both times yesterday. I was merely the recipient."

She threw the third axe, but her aim was off, and it

sank into the hay bale behind the target with a crunch
of straw.

"Merely the recipient? I think we're both guilty of it
getting physical. We can barely be in a room together,
it seems, before our lips are locked. All I'm saying is we
should cool it down. Quit the physical part. Try being
friends—you said it was a good goal, right?"

She aimed the last axe and it hit, dead center, with a *thunk*.

"I did." He scowled as he retrieved the axes. He threw
all four, but none landed close to the bull's-eye. It figured.
"Okay, friends. For now. But that doesn't mean I'm giving
up on our first date."

She clomped in his work boots to retrieve the axes, and
they got into a rhythm of throwing and picking them up,
chatting about other things. She asked about his flowers—
the sunflowers, zinnias, and purple asters he had in the
back—and he told her about his beehives, and how he'd
planted the bees' favorite flowers. She never scoffed when he
told her how he'd read a philosophy book about the neuro-
biological process of the apian mind, and how trippy it was
to know that when he harvested a pound of honey, he was
taking the lifetime's work of almost eight hundred bees.
The conversation was easy, light, and not as awkward as he'd
thought, considering she'd shut him down on the dating.

He remembered what Ryker had said: He needed to go
at her speed. Let her drive.

Damn. It was hard.

Soon, the sun got too hot in the backyard, and they retired
to the shade of his patio. He slipped inside and grabbed
a pitcher of iced tea from the fridge, and two glasses,
snagging the box of PattyCakes goodies just in case.

"Here—make sure you hydrate." He handed her a glass, then set the box of bagels and muffins on the tiny wrought-iron table between them. "Dehydration is the most common cause of headaches. Also red wine. And chocolate."

"And stress. And lack of sleep." She nodded, sipping the iced tea. "All that kind of rolls together, doesn't it? Being June twenty-seventh doesn't help my cause much, either."

Zander nodded carefully. "Your grandmother told me it was the anniversary of your mother's death when I dropped you off. I'm so sorry. That must've been so hard on you."

"Not as hard as being in the service in Afghanistan. War has always been…sort of an abstract for me. That's a luxury your family doesn't have," Imani said, her voice pensive. "I can't imagine what you and your brothers…"

Zander shook his head. "Not me. Not as much as Ryker. I was in four years—did one tour as a combat engineer, but saw no real action except for some pop-off fire every once in a while when we were blowing up walls or clearing a path for guys like my brother." Zander tasted the desert dust in his mouth, recalling his sweat-stained, days-without-a-shower stink, and hearing the incessant sound of choppers in the distance as they dropped off new meat or carted another Marine to the nearest triage hospital.

"Is that how Ryker lost his leg?" she asked, and at Zander's nod, she continued. "Were you there? Did you see it, um, happen?"

"No. Thank God. Watching Ry recover was hard enough. I can't imagine my therapist's bills if I'd seen my brother getting blown up." He glanced over at her, and instead of the weird look most people got when he mentioned

PTSD, he saw only understanding. "You didn't see your mom..."

She shuddered. "No. Neither did my dad. All that was left of our house was ashes. Oh, and the toilet. Somehow it survived."

"Weird how things stick in your head. I remember when my dad died, what stuck in my head was he hadn't finished his lunch. He died in the middle of his ham-and-cheese sandwich."

Imani nodded. "Of anyone, you can relate to losing a parent when you're young. The grief stays with you."

"Funny thing about grief." Zander opened the PattyCakes box, angling it toward her until she took a mini blueberry muffin. "In my experience, it's always accompanied by re-silience. While I waited for my brother to be released from his multiple surgeries and physical therapy requirements at Walter Reed, that's what I saw. No matter how a man or woman was battered by grief—whether it was the loss of limb, or opportunity, or life—instead of being crushed by emotion, you saw people buckle under the weight. But then, somehow, they managed to rise again. It made me humble, witnessing their strength. I sense that same strength in you, Imani."

She chewed quietly, staring down at her feet in his massive work boots. Although they were alone, when she spoke, her voice was barely above a whisper. "I...my doctor thinks survivors' guilt is the reason for my stress and insomnia. Probably so is my preoccupation with preparation. The Mary Poppins bag, the constant lists and organizational urges. I worry, sometimes, that I'm turning into my mother. They say bipolar isn't necessarily genetic, but..."

"We all worry we're turning into our parents. That's a normal feeling," he said, wanting to reach out to hold her, but refraining with effort. "I'm no expert. But here's what I think: You're lost. You've got a ton on your plate, with your grandmother needing surgery, fixing up her house, and trying to ensure your job isn't going away while you tend to those things. Your mind is a busy place. Hey, you know what? I've got something for that—the perfect solution to stress."

Imani's eyebrows rose, and she gave him a sassy smile that made him want to kiss her. Then again, what expression could she wear that didn't evoke that knee-jerk reaction from him?

"Let me guess—it's in your pants and rhymes with 'flick'?"

"God, you and your Gigi have dirty minds. She said almost the same thing the other day. That's not what I meant." He pretended to consider. "Although it's not off the table, either."

He reached into the cargo shorts pocket where he'd stashed it earlier, hoping for this conversational opening, and pulled out one of her broken tiles.

"Come to my studio this week, and I'll teach you the stress-busting art of throwing clay. You can make tiles to replace the broken ones on your grandmother's fireplace." He handed her the tile. "We'll make twenty of them, and hopefully after we fire, paint, and glaze them, a few will make it through the process. When we grout them in, it'll be like the accident never happened."

Her delicate fingers traced the jagged edge of the broken tile, her face wary.

"I'm not sure that's a good idea. We don't seem to...do well with unsupervised time. Thank you, but I think I might try something else to burn off this stress. Gardening or maybe organizing Kate's massive cloth diaper collection by size and color. Something's gotta work."

On a whim, he unknotted the leather cord around his wrist and motioned for her arm. "Here. Try this."

"What is it?" she asked, as he tied the bracelet around her slender wrist.

"It's the Chinese calligraphy characters for mindfulness." He scooped up the engraved black ceramic charm with one finger, angling it to catch the sun. "It's a combination of the characters for 'now' and 'heart.' I made it years ago when I got out of the Marines. It helped me remember to enjoy the present. No matter if you're gardening or sorting baby diapers, do it with a full heart. Because nothing is guaranteed other than right now."

She gave an unsteady smile.

"You're so...that's so...it's perfect. But I hate to take it from you."

He shrugged. "I don't need it anymore."

"You sure?" She cocked her head in that playful way he loved. "Wait. Never mind. You live in the moment more than anybody I've ever met."

Her phone trilled with a text notification, and she read it.

"Kate's coming to pick me up and we're having dinner together—something we haven't done in ages. I miss time with her...and I owe her an apology for sleeping through the birth film and for not being present lately. I had fun, and I'm going to take your advice. Be more mindful." She stood, stretching, and blinked for a second. Her smile grew.

"I don't have a headache anymore. It's the first time in three days I haven't felt at least a little niggling of pain in my head. What did you put into this tea?"

"Only lemon," he said, walking her around to the front of the studio where Kate pulled up, beeping, in Drake's truck. "No sugar. You're sweet enough."

"Aaand he's still trying to get into my pants." She laughed, waving him off as he looked offended. "We're doing the just-friends thing, remember? It's better that way."

He greeted Kate, then opened the truck's passenger door for Imani.

"Thanks again for...everything," Imani said, her hand reaching out for his, then pulling back. "I appreciate you. And our talk."

"See you soon," he said, closing the door. Then he stuffed his hands in his pockets, forcing himself to smile and act chill and confident.

As the woman he was falling for was whisked away. Again.

# CHAPTER 11

A week later, Imani put the tiny American flags in the planters out in front of the giant brick-red Victorian so the place would be as festive as the rest of the block for the Fourth of July. She sat back on her heels, wiping her brow with her forearm.

"Damn. You have outdone yourself!" Kate sat in a rocking chair on the massive wraparound porch of her home, a lemonade in one hand and her feet up on a stool. Her bestie looked like she could pose on the cover of a maternity magazine, her pale skin glowing in a navy-blue maxi dress, despite the fact she was about four weeks until her due date. Imani, on the other hand, knew she herself resembled a filthy garden gnome in her paint-stained cutoffs and an old black Bronx Barre Belles T-shirt. "Our front gardens are now officially the best-looking ones in the neighborhood. And what's that sound I hear?"

Imani grinned as Kate mimed putting her hand to her ear. It had been a running joke between them since high school, doing humor that only type A's found funny.

"The melodious sound of another of my to-do items being checked off." Imani mimed a giant check mark in the air as she climbed the steps. Removing her gardening gloves, she tossed them on the porch where Sasha, Drake and Kate's caramel-and-white shih tzu, pounced and promptly dragged them off to a corner to gnaw on contentedly.

She slid her phone from her back pocket, giving it to Kate to scroll through the before-and-after landscaping pictures she'd taken. While Kate oohed and aahed appreciatively, she looked over her friend's shoulder to admire her work.

The timothy grass, weeds, and random ferns that had been clogging the hostas, coneflowers, and lilies now lay in the dented aluminum garbage can she'd dragged beside her this morning as she'd worked. Now the perennials could breathe.

She was high-key jealous.

She'd been trying to breathe, trying to weed out the mental clutter this week since arriving in Wellsville, without much success. But at least she was productive in her tasks.

Taking the sweating glass of lemonade next to Kate's, Imani leaned back in the adjacent rocker, brushing some dirt off her forearms, and felt the rush of pleasure she got after completing another task. She couldn't help listing this week's accomplishments aloud to the only person in this universe she knew who would appreciate the recitation.

"Today we weeded the garden, got the baby's room situated, and cut the tags off the clothes and crib sheets so you can wash them. I worked my ass off this week scrubbing Gigi's house from top to bottom, put in her summer annuals, repainted her front porch, fixed the sagging second step, replaced a lightbulb, and mended a torn window screen." A pleased smile came to her lips as she pictured gold stars next to the items completed. "That was all done between work emergencies and the just-this-once-and-then-we-won't-bother-you-again conference calls."

"Wow. That's...quite a list." Kate continued to scroll through the pictures on Imani's phone. But her voice was more factual than impressed. A beat of silence stretched between them before her friend added, "You know, there's a fine line between never-ending helpfulness and martyrdom."

Imani's eyebrows shot up. "You think I'm a martyr?"

"I think you need to slow down. Gain some perspective. Throw up some damn boundaries. Get a different personal cell phone, like I did, and then you can turn this one off when you're not on duty." Kate waggled the phone, her green eyes kind as she reached her other hand to Imani. "With your panic attack and the migraines and insomnia, your body is begging you to make some changes. While it's okay not to be okay, you can't ignore your mental health. Never-ending kindness is great—God knows I've appreciated having you here helping me—but remember this: martyrs only achieve recognition once they're dead."

Imani's jaw dropped open. She'd been expecting kudos and praise. Not a lecture. Some of this must've crossed her face, because Kate squeezed her hand. "You're my best friend—my person—and I love you. Don't let your happily ever after happen only in your eulogy."

Unexpected tears filled Imani's eyes, clogging her throat. She let go of Kate's hand, gulped lemonade to ease the lump of emotion until she was able to talk.

"I love you, too, Katie. You're—you're right. I've put off making a telehealth appointment, even though my primary care doc gave me a referral ages ago. I don't know what it is with me lately. Maybe it's my confusion with this work promotion, or maybe cleaning out Gigi's stuff brought up too many memories of Mom? And now with you having a baby, the fact that you're going to be a mother yourself, it's got me so—"

Good grief, had she really just blamed some of her mental health issues on the fact her bestie was going to be a mom?

But Kate nodded.

"This pregnancy is so surreal. I've never had a situation where I couldn't control a single thing. I mean, this is happening, whether I'm ready or not. I've read every freaking book out there on babies and motherhood, and they contradict each other on everything from pacifiers to co-sleeping."

Imani and Kate were distracted by some commotion at the front gates by the sidewalk. A tour bus had just opened its doors, letting out some random fans who chattered excitedly, pointing at the house, hoping for a picture of Kate's horror-writer husband.

"And then there's them," Imani said.

"Exactly. Where is the guide for how to raise a child with the guy the whole literary world dubbed the Knight of Nightmares? How will Drake's fame, or even my work away from home, affect the baby?" Kate took her feet off the stool and slid her rocker to face away from the crowd. "I feel like this is the most important thing I'll ever do in my life, yet there are so many ways to fail. And a whole audience of people out there, ready to pounce with their judgment. How do I not screw this up?"

Imani reached over to squeeze Kate's knee. "Love. No matter what mistakes you or Drake may make, it's love that'll keep it together. You are destined for a happily ever after with that guy—I knew it right from the day you returned from that awful research trip with him to the mausoleum. I mean, you only lie down in a crypt with bats if he's the real deal. Everyone knows that."

Kate laughed. "Drake definitely had a unique way of charming me. Not unlike another Matthews brother we both know. The youngest one. A tall Viking-looking guy who happens to have the hots for you."

"Which is why I've kept him at arm's length." Imani felt her fingers tingle with the memory of their time together. "Zander helped with the bins and then with the painting and the porch stairs, plus he drove over Grandpa Arlo's Green Grabber, which Ryker managed to get running again, so I've seen him plenty. Just not unsupervised. I even took Gigi with me as a chaperone when I brought him gulyás and peanut butter cookies I'd made to thank him."

"You sound like a heroine in one of Leann Bellamy's old Regency romances! You're thirty-one years old. Why can't you see a man unsupervised?"

Imani gave her a look. "Because spending time alone with him ends up with me stuck to his face like a lamprey."

"You're such a romantic," Kate said with a giggle. Her expression became crafty. "Although there is one item on your summer to-do list that you're going to need his help with, no doubt about that: replacing Gigi's broken tiles."

Imani frowned. "I never should have shown you my list."

While she'd managed to get every speck of the nail polish up from her mishap with Lancelot, the three broken tiles made the whole fireplace look sad and incomplete, like a smile missing teeth. While her grandmother said it was okay—that the fireplace matched her now and was showing its age—Imani got sick to her stomach every time she passed the parlor.

"I know you've looked online for vintage tiles, but I'm telling you from experience. When one of the butter-yellow ones on our antique parlor fireplace cracked, there wasn't any good option to replace it other than asking Zander to make us a new one. He's a genius with ceramics, and I challenge you to find the tile he created now—it blends right in with the ones that were fired over a hundred years ago."

Imani glanced at the leather bracelet Zander had given her, still on her right wrist, the mindfulness charm dangling there.

Heart.

Now.

She sighed. "Maybe I'll call him. Later."

"As the youngest Matthews brother would say, 'There's no better time than the present,'" Kate said, and before Imani could stop her, Kate had unlocked Imani's phone and hit a button.

"Hey, Zander," she said. "It's Kate. Someone here wants to talk to you."

Bugging her eyes at her best friend, Imani took the phone. "Hi. Um, I think I'd like to take you up on your offer to fix my grandmother's tiles."

"I'm sorry." It was clear he was pretending to be confused. "Who is this?"

"Shut up. You know who it is."

"Oh! This is the woman I let borrow my ladder, helped

fix her porch step, and saved from an imminent African gray parrot attack—all without a glimmer of hope for a first date?"

"First date?" she sputtered, then remembered she was on Drake and Kate's front porch. Standing to leave, she glared at her best friend, who did a smug finger-wave goodbye. Imani lowered her voice, fast-walking down the sidewalk to where she'd parked her grandfather's old car. "We slept together, Zander! Isn't it a little late for a first date?"

"Not in my book. And besides, my offer was to help *you* fix the tiles. Which means *you* get to learn how to create new ceramic tiles to the same dimensions as the old ones, fire them, glaze them to match, then fire them again. That's..." His voice trailed off, as if he were having difficulty with the calculations. "...three different classes with me. Pro bono, of course."

"Classes?" Imani pushed through the Matthews's spider-web gates, winding around the few gawkers still hoping for a chance to see the famous horror writer today. "Those sound suspiciously like dates."

She could almost hear him shrug.

"It's not a date. It's my work. You wouldn't call it a date if I came to watch you do...publicist stuff in your fancy Manhattan office, would you?"

"I don't know. Publicist stuff can get pretty wild."

"Are you in?"

"Fine."

"Say please, and I'll fit you in now. Studio's closed for the Fourth of July."

She sighed, exasperated. "Please."

"Say 'pretty please,'" he said, "and I'll throw in lunch."

"You're being immature." Imani's stomach growled loud enough she was certain he heard it. She groaned. "Okay, fine! Pretty please with a cherry on top!"

His low chuckle maddened her even as it quickened her pulse. "Aw, you don't have to give me your cherry. But I'm humbled and honored by your offer."

Imani pressed her lips together. It was no use calling him on his antics. Kate was right. She needed those tiles replaced—visions of having the fireplace back to normal made her bite back a sarcastic retort. Instead, she kept her eyes on the prize: a completely done to-do list before her grandmother went in for surgery tomorrow. Then she could focus on Gigi's recovery. And her own. It was only that and nothing more that made her agree to his offer.

At least that's what she told herself.

"I'm getting in the shower. I'll be over in an hour."

Zander hummed in a wicked way that made her nipples sit up and pay attention. "Or...you could come over now. My shower here is big. Fits two people. Just sayin'."

Imani huffed a breath. "You're relentless."

"It's part of my charm."

She hung up.

But damned if the images of a shower with him weren't dancing through her head.

Imani started the Green Grabber, looking down at herself in dismay. She had dirt smudges on her. And this had to be the ugliest T-shirt and shorts combo she owned, plus she had on a pair of I'm-working-out-in-the-yard-today granny panties.

Then she brightened.

She wasn't going to shower. Or change. She'd go to the studio dressed exactly like this. And she was going to remember she had on terrible granny panties that no man would want to see.

Just in case her resolve weakened.

# CHAPTER 12

Six minutes later, Zander heard a knock on his door.

"Hello?" Imani called, and his heart leaped, like it had every damn day he'd been with her, helping out at her grandmother's. He wished he could put a finger on exactly why he couldn't get this woman out of his head, but it defied logic. Sure, she was funny, graceful, and so damn organized it was downright spooky. She was hot as hell, too, but nothing explained why he was torturing himself with this this whole let-her-be-in-the-driver's-seat thing, which he could kill Ryker for even suggesting in the first place.

"C'mon in!" he shouted, shaking his head at the mystery. "I'm at the wheel."

He glanced up as she rounded the bar and his mouth went dry. She was wearing faded denim cutoff shorts and a black tee with the Barre Belles logo on the front. Her feet were in a pair of Converse sneakers, and her hair was in a windswept ponytail with little flyaway wisps that curled at her forehead and at the base of her neck like tiny corkscrews.

She was stunning.

His foot lifted from the pedal on the floor, and the

wheel's spinning slowed, then stopped. He took his hands from the clay, waggling them in the air.

"Sorry. I'd give you a good-morning hug, but I'm filthy."

"Morning?" Imani checked her phone with a raised eyebrow. "It's twelve-thirty."

"Hmm. Lost track of time. Can you give me a few minutes while I finish this mug? My client wants a set of six by the end of the month, and I've got to get it into the heat box so it can dry. Then we can eat and start your tiles."

Imani shrugged. "I can wait. My grandmother is busy whooping it up with her friends. There's a massive Fourth of July card game at Mrs. Nowakowski's, apparently."

"How's Gigi? She goes in for double knee surgery tomorrow, right?"

"She does, and she's totally ready to go under the knife. I swear, my grandmother is afraid of nothing."

He nodded. "My nana is the same. There's a box of my mom's strawberry-rhubarb muffins over there and a pot of coffee. Oh, I forgot—you prefer tea. There's a decent chai in that canister, and the hot water is in the carafe."

She set her black purse on the table and wandered over to the bar. He focused on his work until she sat down at the stool of the pottery wheel nearest him, taking a massive bite of muffin and dunking her tea bag into the water as she watched him.

"Mmm. These are amazing. I could sit here and eat PattyCakes goodies all day." She swallowed, exhaling with a sigh. "Keep working. I've never seen anyone throw pottery before, so I'd love to watch."

He nodded, looking back down at the half-molded clay,

glad for an excuse to tear his gaze away from Imani's tongue as it darted out to catch errant crumbs.

He pressed the foot pedal and the wheel whirred, filling the studio with a pleasant white noise. He wet his hands, delicately urging the mug taller with the lightest of touches. Unbidden, memories of that night after Drake and Kate's wedding came to his mind, the silky feel of her under his palms, her every reaction as he adjusted his approach to zero in on those things he did that made her gasp...

He toggled off the pedal, the wheel slowing to a stop as he rolled his neck on his shoulders, willing the desire to ebb. *Take it slow.*

Ha. As if. He needed a damn distraction.

"Pottery is not a spectator sport." He stood so fast his knees popped in protest. "Grab yourself an apron, and I'll get you some clay. You're gonna get dirty with me today."

She snorted but, to his surprise, popped the rest of the muffin in her mouth and headed for the black aprons hanging on the hooks at the far wall.

"I've wanted to do this since coming to your studio for Kate's shower last week." She grinned as she tied the strings around her to the front where she formed a bow, the ends perfectly even. She followed him to the back, where he pulled out a bag of premade clay. "Are you going to teach me the rules of throwing pottery?"

"In this studio, there are no rules."

"Why doesn't that surprise me?"

Zander ignored her sarcasm, dumping the two pounds of clay onto the wedging table and then giving her a "go ahead" gesture.

"We're going to make a mug on the wheel, but first,

you've got to wedge the clay—that's ceramics-speak for leveling it inside and out. Because this is leftover clay from another client, the outside is dryer than the inside. You need to make it all consistent before you can put it on the wheel." He mimed pushing on the clay with the heel of his palms. "Knead it like bread dough."

"Like this?" Imani lightly pressed the clay, her fingers smoothing over the top.

"You're not romancing the clay, you're wedging it. Get aggressive. Use the heels of your hands to mash it into the table. Really go after it, or you'll have an air bubble, and when you fire it, it'll explode or crack in the kiln."

"I thought you said there weren't any rules?" Imani adjusted her stance so her legs were shoulder-width apart, her hips leaning against the table. The skin between her brows puckered as she worked the clay harder, the muscles in her arms on display.

He'd never been one for waify, petite girls like his sister-in-law. He loved Imani's height and the toned strength that vibrated within her. God, she was incredible.

He crossed his arms over his chest. This was not a date. Yet while he'd made the vow to wait for her to take the next step, he wasn't going to miss this opportunity to get to know her. So he'd try to pretend she was just another ceramics client.

"The beauty of working with clay is it's an organic process. You put your hands on it, you work with it, and you let it evolve," he said, giving his standard spiel. "It's a metaphor for life."

"Your version, anyway." Imani grunted, flipping the clay and putting her back into it now. "Mine is more about making a game plan and sticking to it. Speaking of, what's your business game plan? Kate told me you have this place, plus two other studios in neighboring towns. Are these the first steps in your bid to take over the clay-molding world?"

Zander laughed as he watched her attacking the clay. "The pursuit of happiness is my only game plan. Isn't it yours?"

Imani pursed her lips. "Mine is a little more complicated. I mean, the pursuit of happiness is a great sentiment, but I've got bills to pay."

"Money doesn't buy you happiness."

Imani scoffed. "Maybe not. But it sure does buy you choices."

Zander shrugged. "Fair enough. All right, you've beat that clay into submission. Let's get you some tools and set you up on a wheel. You can make your first mug while I finish my order, and then we'll get to your tiles."

Five minutes later, she had used the wire tool to slice the clay in half. She set one portion on her wheel and the other on the stainless steel shelf above the wheel next to a cup of water and a shaping sponge. She listened carefully to his directions on how to use the foot pedal to increase the wheel's speed. As much as he wanted to put his arms around her to show her how to brace one elbow against her hip, keeping one hand motionless on the clay so it wouldn't kick up at her while she centered it on the wheel, he stuck to his guns—no touching. He could only use his words.

It was maddening.

But the good news was, he sensed she was equally frustrated by their lack of contact.

"Are you sure I'm doing it okay?" she asked as he sat next to her at his wheel. "I feel like my hand isn't stable enough. Can you...show me again?"

He shrugged. "You'll get the hang of it."

He forced himself to return to his mug, using some water to wet it down again as he toggled the pedal, spinning the wheel, feeling her next to him, smelling the scent of her sun-kissed skin and something floral.

No. He wasn't going there. He glared at the mug, focusing on his fingers moving infinitesimally closer, crafting the lip at the top as he thought about the questions he'd wanted to ask Imani but, since they always had an audience, hadn't dared.

"Does living in the Bronx bring you joy? Is the job secondary to where you've always wanted to live?"

Imani gave a surprised laugh. "My teensy studio is on the third floor with no elevator, no central air, and no yard. It's not exactly euphoria-inducing, but it's only two blocks to the subway station, making my commute to work an easy half hour."

"Your job, then. It must bring you happiness." He flicked a glance to check her reaction as she mulled over her answer. "And don't think because you work with my brother that you can't tell me the truth. I won't tattle."

She was silent for a long moment, her hands on the spinning clay between her knees.

"I've spent so much time and effort achieving this position within Cerulean Books, and it's paid off. I'm proud of going from being a communications major and a dance minor to being an intern, then an assistant, and now a publicist for bestsellers like Drake at one of the biggest publishing houses in the world. Now my boss wants me to take a higher position—work with only big authors, many of whom already also have a publicity team or brand manager. Plus I'd manage a team of people doing my old job. It's a huge step." Imani looked pleased, but she bit her lip as she added, "I've achieved the American dream."

He let the juxtaposition of her expression and tone sink in. "Have you?"

"Not everyone gets to flit around and play with clay all day." Imani visibly ruffled, like her grandmother's parrot after being denied another treat.

"My bills are paid. The lights are on. What's the harm in enjoying each day to the fullest?"

"You don't even post hours of operation for your business. It's all parties by appointment. I couldn't stand the instability. After we lost my mom, the house, and everything in the fire, I had to live with Kate and her family while Dad stayed with a friend until he'd earned enough for a first and last deposit on an apartment." Shadows flitted across Imani's face. "See, the insurance money barely covered the mortgage he'd had on the house, and my parents had no contingency funds. The fire literally took everything we had. It . . . shook me, that experience. Doesn't it keep you up at night, the lack of steady income? A contingency plan?"

"Planning only gets you so far. I realized long ago that none of us are made of Kevlar. Instead of wasting time chasing a fictitious bulletproof job, I'm searching for a feeling of happiness and contentment." Zander gave a harsh laugh. "This past year, I've been searching a lot harder than I'd anticipated."

"Why?"

He wished he hadn't said that. It was too personal. He kept his eyes on the spinning mug. "It's because of Drake and Kate. They've ruined my buzz. It fell together so effortlessly for them. They zinged from single and career-focused to married and starting a family, like entering this next phase of their life was as easy as breathing. It's..."

"Maddening," Imani finished, startling him as she laughed in agreement. "I think they zinged too fast. How can they know it'll last? How does she know he won't wake up one day and find some other girl who zings...better? Happened to me years ago with my ex, and I thought we were perfect together. He, obviously, did not and was sending dick pics to my friends. Happens every day. People leave, fall out of love...or die."

Zander scowled at the thought of the moron who broke her heart. He pressed the pedal with his heel, turning off his wheel to face her.

"Any man who leaves you is a fool."

Imani's brown eyes widened and her voice was low and throaty as she whispered, "He must have never felt that...zing with me."

"His loss. You always know when things come together just right. Like us at the reception." Zander's gaze met hers. Imani's cheeks reddened, but she didn't contradict him. "It's that feeling we're searching for. Ways to rediscover it. Reignite it."

Imani leaned closer, her eyes closing, and Zander's heart leaped as he closed the distance between them. But before their lips touched, there was a wet thud.

Imani shrieked, her hands flying to her face.

Standing so fast he put his thumb through the mug he'd so carefully crafted, he cupped her cheeks. Other than streaks of gray clay water spattering the right side of her face, neck, and most of her apron, he couldn't see anything wrong.

"Are you okay?"

"Yes." She choked out the words between snorting laughter. "My whole mug went flying off the wheel. What did I do wrong?"

Zander chuckled, grabbing his clean towel from the workstation. "Stay still." He used a corner of it on Imani's face, wiping away a rivulet of clay-speckled goop before it got in her eyes. "All set. Your clay became off-balanced, and unfortunately your mug is trashed, but that's okay. So is mine."

Her face fell. "Oh no!"

He wiped his hands clean, then clapped her on the back. Like a friend would do.

"Working with clay is much like life. If things become off-balance, you don't have to throw it away. You pick it up and start over."

Although she stared at him, her mind was elsewhere. "But even though I've been leaning into it—trying so hard to shape it into the mug I'd planned—it keeps spinning faster and faster, and suddenly it's not the form I wanted and it's out of control. Is my only option to start over?"

Zander held out his hand, helping her off the stool. Why had he thought it was a good idea to go poking around in her head? Damn, though, if he didn't want to take it back—keep things light and airy and superficial.

Like he did in every relationship.

The thought made him pause before he answered.

"I find sometimes instead of me shaping the clay, it's the clay shaping me. Let the mug create itself. Or not. Because sometimes when you try and force a form, it all goes to shit."

She nodded, and her quiet contemplation unnerved him.

So he went to his go-to: lightening the mood. "I have one more secret," he said, like he was sharing a real confidence.

Her eyebrows went up and her right hand twitched, as if she wished she had a pen and paper to jot some notes.

"What?"

"I do my best work when my belly is full of roast beef sub. And I know you will, too." He threw his arm around her shoulders, acting like the pal she wanted him to be as he led her to the washup sink. "While we eat, we'll solve the world's problems. When we're done, we'll get your grandmother's new tiles started. Not too bad for an afternoon's work, right?"

And as she laughed, standing shoulder to shoulder with him as they washed their hands, he felt his entire world unbalancing and tilting in her direction.

So much for letting the mug create itself.

# CHAPTER 13

Despite her intention not to enjoy herself with Zander, Imani found herself doing just that all afternoon and into the evening. She'd even taken Kate's advice and deleted the email app on her phone so she'd have to log in with her laptop to see anything work-related. She also had every call that wasn't from her grandmother or Kate sent directly to voicemail. She was fully immersed in her experience in Zander's studio.

It felt...liberating.

And because she was alone with Zander, being liberated was also terrifying. It was more than their physical attraction. Did she still want to get naked and leap into his arms every ten seconds? Hell yes. But being with him, without distraction, made her aware of how his lighthearted spirit lifted her up. How when she talked to him, laughed with him, joked with him, she forgot her to-do lists. Entirely.

"Wouldn't it be better if you made the tiles? You're the expert, after all," Imani said after they'd polished off a sub together.

But he wouldn't be swayed. "It's your project. You can do this, and I'll be here to help."

At first, it frustrated her that he wouldn't take the reins. He made her do everything, from prepping a large bag of clay with grog to measuring out the dry material to wedge into the clay according to his specs. He'd done research about the age and make of her grandmother's tile and had come up with a specific recipe based on his experience replicating vintage ceramics. He even made her create the tile-shaped template from cardboard, content to call out directions to her as he spun mug after mug on his wheel.

"You need to increase the measurement by twelve percent to account for shrinkage," he said, as she labored with the ruler and calculator.

"I'll bet you use that excuse with all the girls," she shot back, and was rewarded with his deep, baritone laugh that made her toes curl in her sneakers.

By the time she left his studio, she'd created a mold to match the tiles' dimensions. She'd grogged the clay according to Zander's specifications so that the finished product would fire to the same texture as Gigi's tiles, then carefully wrapped the four pounds in plastic. She found herself looking forward to when she could come again.

The next day was Gigi's double knee surgery, and she spent the day in the hospital, reading the latest bestseller to her grandmother until they wheeled her into the operating room. Then she wandered down to the gift shop, buying her balloons, flowers, and candy so her room would be brimming with color when she returned. Kate stopped by to wait with her until the surgeon finished, and she admitted to her best friend that although she wasn't sure it was the wisest decision, she was falling for the youngest Matthews brother.

"He has this way of peppering me with questions designed to throw me off-kilter," Imani said. "Like yesterday, after my mug shot off the wheel. He made me lunch, then got all introspective and deep while we ate. Right when my mouth was full, he asked if I could do anything and be guaranteed success, what would it be."

"Did you answer that you'd do him?" Kate snorted.

"No, I said I'd open a dance studio," Imani said, laughing. "But yours would've been a good answer. Would've served him right for asking so many probing questions. I have to say, he's a really great listener. When I talked about what I'd have to do to start a dance business, and the reasons why they wouldn't be feasible in the Bronx or with my present work circumstances, he sat there like it was the most interesting conversation in the world. It was...sweet."

"Why haven't you slept with him again? I mean, you're single. He's single. You two are attracted to each other. What are you waiting for?"

Imani had already told Kate about the two kisses she'd shared with Zander last week, and about how easy it was to sink into his arms...or his bed...but she'd been resisting.

"I don't want to lead him on when we don't have a future together. Even if I were interested in a long-distance relationship, which I'm not, he's just not serious. He can't go five minutes without making a joke, he has no plan in life larger than harvesting his next bunch of honey...yet I can't help but enjoy our time together. He makes me calm. It's so confusing."

Kate nodded. "It was like that with Drake and me—both of us trying to keep it professional. And failing miserably. You know, much as you and I like to plan, I do think the best things in life happen off the spreadsheets. Unscripted."

Before Imani could even begin to verbalize her hesitations, the doctor came in, and Kate left as Imani was ushered into the recovery room.

"They're making me stay for three days," Gigi croaked, grumpy as she fought off the aftereffects of anesthesia.

"When you come home, I'll have everything ready for you," Imani reassured her.

"You gonna be okay without me? Maybe you can go to Katie's, or go throw clay with your muscle man?" Gigi turned to the recovery room nurse, groggy but still managing a wink. "That's what they call it nowadays, don't you know? Throwing clay."

Knowing that if her grandmother was cracking dirty jokes, she was feeling fine, Imani left after settling Gigi in her room, and headed to Zander's studio. He was having a ceramics party with a local bank who was using it as a team-building exercise, so she worked quietly on her tiles, taking Zander's advice to make twenty.

"That way, if some of them break in the kiln or don't fire flat, we have enough to replace the three—and maybe a couple extra," he'd said with a wink, "in case you decide to lob any other nail polish bottles around."

Although he didn't have time to spend with her other than the briefest of visits, she enjoyed listening to him, watching his joy as he painted finished plates with the group and encouraged them to stretch their artistic wings.

"As the late Bob Ross would say, there are no mistakes. Only happy accidents," he said, walking around with his hands in the pockets of his cargo shorts, peering over each person's shoulder to compliment a color blending here or a creative choice there.

The guy had a talent for enjoying the moment that she found irresistible, and it made the days after Gigi's surgery, as she recovered in the hospital, race by without the stress, insomnia, and tension headaches she'd expected.

It took her two days to create her tiles, which she set on the drying shelves in the back next to the kiln, with strict instructions from Zander to come in every day and rotate them, bottom to top and front to back, so they'd dry evenly.

It was fun—more laughter and joy than she'd had in...forever.

Zander was a one-person happiness committee. She was the lucky recipient.

Three days flew by, and then Gigi was coming home. The work rehabilitating her grandmother would be a welcome break from the ceramic studio, where things with Zander were getting hot and confusing. It was best this way, she told herself as she drove Gigi home and got her tucked into bed.

Then her cell rang out the theme from *Swan Lake*.

Zander.

"Hey," he said, his deep, familiar baritone making her heart leap in her chest. "I know you don't have time to stop by the studio with your grandmother coming home, so I wanted to tell you your tiles are looking great. Drying nice and slow, although I did move them from the top shelf to the bottom because it's been so hot lately. Won't be long before we can fire them."

"You're already in the studio?" She gave a theatric gasp. "It's nearly the crack of noon!"

"You know what they say—all work and no clay makes Zander a dull boy. How's your grandma doing?"

"Gigi, Zander wants to know, how are you feeling?" Imani asked, dragging the walker from the bedroom to the foyer so she could move in the rolling table she'd brought downstairs. She wanted to put her grandmother's lunch on something steadier than a TV tray.

Gigi snorted. "No, he doesn't. He just wants to get in your pants. Again."

Imani sucked in a breath. "How'd you . . . ?"

Gigi cackled, slapping at the top of the covers with the arm that still had a purple-red bruise from the IV's insertion. "I didn't know. Until now."

Imani gave her grandmother the finger, and Gigi flipped the bird right back at her.

"Gigi's smart mouth is apparently just fine," she said into the phone. "But the rest of her is a little hangry, I think. Her incisions look good, and the docs gave her some meds and restrictions for the next week. She won't be doing TikTok videos anytime soon."

"Says you, Shypoke."

The sound of Zander's low rumble of laughter came over the line. "Your grandmother is priceless. But tell her she's wrong about me on both counts. I do want to know how she's feeling. And your pants are cute, but way too tiny for a guy my size. One last thing—is your grandmother on any dietary restrictions? I was thinking of snagging some cookies from PattyCakes for her. Molasses, right?"

"That's her fave." Imani was impressed he'd recalled that

tidbit. "In fact, she's already got her sights set on a Texas Hot hot dog and gravy fries. I might scoot out later and snag us both some hometown goodness."

Suddenly, Imani heard the sounds of a crowd on the other end of the line and figured Zander must be getting ready for a ceramics class.

"There's nothing like them," he agreed, his voice sounding different, as if he were preoccupied. "Especially if you wash it down with a chocolate milkshake. Am I right?"

Imani smiled, holding the phone with her shoulder as she unlatched Lancelot's cage. The parrot gave Imani the stink eye, hopping to the edge of the bottom metal bar, then launching himself over the avian playground to land softly on Gigi's blanketed form, glancing over his shoulder to spear Imani with a "screw you" stare before meandering up her grandmother's bosom for attention.

"Chocolate is Gigi's fave, but I like strawberry. They're so decadent—the hand-spun ones always are."

"Mmm," Zander said, and then she heard a shuffle and more rumbling words as he covered the phone to speak with someone. Soon the shuffling stopped, and he came on the line again. "Gotta bolt. Holler if you need me, okay?"

"Will do."

She pocketed the phone, perching on the bed atop the white floral quilt, joining Gigi and Lancelot. At first, her grandmother made an annoyed face at the bird crowding up for pets, but as soon as she ruffled the feathers at his neck, Lancelot dropped his head, his black beak drifting down until it touched the top of the quilt. He made a tiny chirping noise, then closed his eyes at her touch. Gigi smiled lovingly at him.

"He reminds me of those sharks that, when you touch the right place on the underside of them, they go catatonic," Imani said. "It's like his birdie G-spot or something."

Her grandmother pursed her lips. "Don't be so vulgar, Imani."

"Oh, now I'm the vulgar one?" Imani laughed, and Lancelot cracked his eye halfway open to glare at the loud noise. She lowered her voice, shaking her head at both her grandmother and her odd pet. "When he does that—lets you stroke his neck, all trusting and bonding with you—it makes me understand why Grandpa got him. Almost."

"He's a dickens." Gigi's fingers massaged the parrot's gray-feathered neck and head, smiling fondly. "I think that's why Arlo brought him home. He'd been diagnosed with prostate cancer, and he must've known we'd both need something to laugh at to get through what was ahead. Lancelot was a rescue, don't you know? He came to us with four cuss words and the sound of a fire alarm as his only verbalizations. They have the intelligence of a three-year-old, which is how he picked up so many other words from your grandpa. He used to whistle 'Take Me Out to the Ball Game,' too, but he stopped when Arlo passed. I miss him whistling that tune."

The midmorning sun draped over the three of them on Gigi's quilted bed. Imani fingered the charm Zander gave her, making it glint in the light.

Mindfulness.

Living in the moment.

Instead of jumping up to do the next task on her list—tackling the clutter in the dining room so they could eat at the table there in the near future—she sat in the sunshine, watching her beloved grandmother stroke her demon bird. The parrot made contented cooing chirps as Gigi stroked his neck, her fingers moving up to caress his bird cheeks and the space between his eyes. As Zenned out as the bird was, Gigi's face was equally contented, a half smile on her lips, her brown eyes soft and reflective as if watching pages of an old scrapbook turning in her mind.

Imani sighed.

Here.

This slice of perfect peace.

It was worth every ding to her checkbook. Every headache of finding a person to sublet her Bronx apartment for the summer, and every dwindling opportunity as she remained undecided about the Cerulean Books promotion. As Zander said, sometimes it was good to let the five-year plan blur so you could zoom in on today.

On the now that was guaranteed.

Her gaze caught the black-and-white photo of her grandparents from their wedding—a candid shot, taken after they'd been pronounced husband and wife. Her grandmother—all of nineteen years old—grinned at the photographer with the same sparkly twinkle in her eyes as today, while her grandfather had an amused smile and an expression of unabashed adoration as he gazed at his young bride.

"Gigi, how did you know he was the one?"

She tracked Imani's gaze to the picture and smiled. "I didn't, at first. He was a pain in the ass, always mooning over me and asking me out via mutual friends in biology class. I must've turned him down a half dozen times. But then came Valentine's Day, during our senior year in high school over in Wayland," her grandmother said, naming a nearby town. "Arlo had memorized my schedule and skipped out of his classes early to be sure he caught me in the hall so he could hand me a different valentine each hour. They were cheesy ones with silly puns, like a cartoon drawing of a boy with a telescope that said, 'Valentine, you're out of this world.'"

Imani's heart melted. "But that's so sweet. Why did you think he was a pain in the ass?"

"Because I was dating the captain of our basketball team at the time, and Arlo was ruining my game," Gigi explained, as though it were obvious. "But Chet—he was my boob thing at the time—"

"Boo thang, Gigi. Nobody says 'boob thing.'"

"Well, by the end of the day, Chet had only managed to give me a piece of notebook paper that said 'Happy Valentime's Day,' putting an 'm' instead of an 'n' in 'Valentine.' I knew then I'd made a mistake. There I was, wasting time with a boy who couldn't spell 'Valentine,' when right in front of me was Arlo, with his adorable Hungarian accent and seven sweet valentines for me." Gigi nodded wryly. "Best decision I ever made was to dump Chet on Valentine's Day and go down to the soda shop with Arlo for a malt. And the rest is history."

"You knew after one malt shop date that he was the one?"

"Hell no!" Gigi scoffed. "But after dating him the rest of our senior year, I knew I'd be happy if only I could spend the rest of my life with this man. Plus, he snuck into my bedroom window for two months, so I got to kick the tires before I bought the car, if you know what I mean."

"You did not! You're so naughty." Imani leaned over, kissing Gigi on the cheek, breathing in the rose scent of her face powder. She was careful not to disturb Lancelot, whose eyes popped open at the commotion, but then slowly slipped closed as his massage continued. "What ever happened to Chet?"

"Oh, he found another girlfriend within the week and ended up marrying her, knocking her up, and leaving her. Then he repeated the same process with two other girls." Gigi shook her head. "I am so thankful Arlo was persistent. That's how you know the guy is a keeper. He kept his hat in the ring and his hopes high while he waited for me to see what he'd seen all along—we were good for each other. He reminds me of your Matthews boy."

Suddenly, there was a knock at the front door. Leaning back on Gigi's bed, Imani spotted Zander's Prius parked in front of the bungalow.

Apparently Gigi saw it too. "See? He can't stay away, because he's smitten. Just like Arlo and his valentines."

Shushing her grandmother, Imani glided to the door, her heart doing happy little spins in her chest.

"Hi," she said, opening the door, trying to tame the huge smile on her face, but failing. Although he was dressed in his typical shorts and a tee, Zander looked scrumptious—the way he filled out his shirts made her want to rip that super soft cotton off him and trace every muscle with her fingers. Or her tongue...

"Hey." His smile was as bright as the summer sun as he lounged against the doorway. "I didn't want your grandmother to be without her food cravings as she starts her first day of recovery. I know when I was Ry's caregiver at

Walter Reed, there was nothing like good, greasy food to lift his spirits. And mine."

He held out two bags that smelled like heaven. If heaven had a well-seasoned grill and the secret recipe for Texas Hot sauce. In the crook of his arm, he juggled three large milkshakes.

"That's so thoughtful." Imani did her best to rein in her libido, ignoring her grandmother's cackling I-told-you-so laugh as she waved him inside.

He deposited the bags onto the round table by Gigi's bed and dipped close to give her hand a quick squeeze, followed by a pet on Lancelot's head.

The bird immediately dipped into a bow, letting Zander massage his neck as well.

Figured.

"Well, hello," her grandmother said, a naughty gleam in her eye. "We were just talking about you."

Rushing to the bed, Imani interrupted before Gigi could say something embarrassing. "Here, let me get the bird out of the way." Imani coaxed Lancelot back into his cage, scattering some of the brand-new seed-and-nut mix she'd bought. Then she spun with a bright smile, changing topics. "The orthopedic surgeon said Gigi's knees were shot. She was amazed my grandmother held out so long. I told her Gigi's tough as nails."

Gigi turned her attention to the food. "Are you planning on opening that bag, or do I need to get out of bed and do it myself?"

The food was piping hot. Zander helped her drag in two kitchen chairs, and they crowded around the table by Gigi's bed, chatting between bites. Zander had been standing outside of Texas Hot when he'd called, trying to figure out a way to ask what they wanted while still surprising them, when Imani had told him Gigi's cravings unbidden.

"All I had to do was get it ordered," he said, after Imani and Gigi both thanked him, mouths full of sopping-wet gravy fries.

"It's so decadent." Imani reached for the strawberry milkshake then snatched her hand away. She'd used her last Lactaid pill when she'd had wings so she could enjoy the blue cheese...and forgotten to replace it. She'd done enough embarrassing things in front of Zander.

No way was she adding uncontrolled dairy farts to that list.

"I almost forgot!" Zander stood so fast his thighs rattled the table. His hand went into one of the many pockets in his tan cargo shorts and came out with a white pill bottle.

"Oh, now this *is* turning into a party!" Gigi said, delighted. "It's still pretty early, but what the hell—go get the Fireball whiskey, and let's light this candle!"

He set a bottle of Lactaid on the table.

"In case you needed some. For the milkshake."

Talk about hitting her right in the lactose intolerant feels!

"Well, that's no fun." Gigi pushed out her lip in disgust. Then she brightened, mopping up the last of the gravy with her fries. "Get my purse, Shypoke. I brought something home from the hospital for your Xanax."

"It's Zander, and we are *not* having a pill party," Imani hissed, but retrieved her grandmother's purse and handed it over. What in the world could she possibly have brought home from the hospital for Zander?

Gigi wiped her hands on her napkin, then rummaged

through the ginormous, fire-engine-red pleather bag, filling the room with the sound of coins jangling, paper crinkling, and pills ramming into the sides of plastic containers.

Finally, she raised a fist in triumph.

"Here they are! Directions for how to play May-I. Had the nurse download and print them off the internet so he could learn how to be our fourth." Gigi grinned triumphantly and opened her mouth to add something, surprising herself with a huge yawn.

"We can teach Zander later. Why don't you rest your eyes, Gigi, while I show him the broken ceiling medallion in the dining room? The doctor said you should take it easy for the next few days, remember? We don't need an infection in those joints."

She whisked the lunch remains off the table, then eased Gigi back onto her pillows.

"Well, maybe I will rest my eyes for a minute." She nodded toward Lancelot's cage. "Can you close the blinds? It's time for his siesta, anyway."

Imani closed the blinds as Zander stacked both chairs together, lifting them from the room effortlessly, the muscles in his arms and chest flexing. She made herself look away from his pecs, closing the parlor's pocket doors behind her.

She didn't speak until they were in the kitchen, Zander arranging chairs around the scarred wooden table while she stuffed bags in the garbage under the sink. Washing her hands, she bit her lip, wondering if this was a good idea or not.

Then, as she spotted her strawberry milkshake, sweat condensing down the side of the white container and pooling next to the bottle of Lactaid, she decided to take the leap.

"So I was thinking," she said, spinning around.

He held up a hand, that sexy, come-here-and-kiss-me-now smile on his mouth. "Say no more. I saw the cracked medallion around the dining room chandelier, and I've got plaster of Paris back at the studio that'll make it as good as new." He fished his phone out of his pocket. "In fact, I'm going to take a picture now, so I can bring the right tools with me to sculpt the missing curves on the roses and vines."

"Oh, right." She followed him into the dining room, watching him zoom in on the fixture as he leaned over the photo boxes and crap she still had all over the dining room table, never once sending any of the precariously balanced items crashing down. The phrase "bull in a china shop" applied to him only in the sense that he was thick and strong. Zander, like some professional dancers she'd worked with over the years, had amazing proprioception—the awareness and sense of your body's movement and the flow with which you interacted with your environment. Then again, he was a Marine, and he'd played on the offensive line in football, so his natural balance made sense. It was also sexy as hell.

She could watch him move. All. Day. Long.

But that wasn't going to get him to ask her out on a date. He'd told her she was in charge, and if the past few weeks were any indication, he wasn't kidding.

She swallowed, tightening her ponytail. "I was thinking, maybe this Friday, since your studio is closed for the balloon rally—"

His phone rang.

She stopped speaking as he frowned at the screen. "It's Ryker," he said, then answered. "Dude, what's up?"

Imani waited patiently, watching Zander's expression transform from concern to jubilation. When he looked over at her, he smothered the smile, turning slightly to respond to something his brother said. Feeling as though she was eavesdropping, she pivoted toward the kitchen but caught the next thing he said.

"Perfect—you are amazing, Ry. Have I told you lately you're my favorite middle brother? Okay, I've got the keys to her place. I'll meet you there in ten."

Her.

He'd said he had the keys to *her* place.

Imani stewed in the kitchen, her arms folded across her chest. She leaned against the kitchen sink, waiting for Zander to finish his conversation, wondering who the woman was. She must be important if Zander had keys to her place.

Imani knew she had no right to be possessive. But as her throat grew thick and her face grew hot, she recognized she was jealous.

Very.

By the time Zander reentered the kitchen, she'd cycled through all five DABDA stages of grief but was seesawing back to anger and bargaining.

"Hey, sorry," he said, waggling his phone before stashing it into his cargo shorts again. "I need to meet up with Ryker to help install something."

"At a woman's place," Imani said, trying for conversational but hearing her tone turn shrewish instead.

His thick brows shot up. He nodded slowly, as if

puzzling out how he'd suddenly ended up on a land mine. "The property is owned by a woman, yes. I'm finishing up a...project there. Sanding floors, painting, that sort of thing. Shouldn't take me long, and I can be here later to fix your ceiling medallion before my ceramics class starts." He stopped talking as he spotted her dubious expression. "What?"

"I mean, I don't want to be in the way of your busy schedule," she started, then threw up her hands at his confusion. "And for the record, you could have told me you were dating. Then I wouldn't have..."

She trailed off as he approached her.

"Wouldn't have what?" he asked, his tone curious.

Imani debated not answering, then remembered her conversation with Gigi. What if he was her Arlo and she never bothered to find out?

"Then I wouldn't have spent this whole morning screwing up the courage to ask you out this Friday. That's what." She felt her chin jutting out like Gigi's did when she was working up to a real pout, and she didn't care to fix her face.

Instead of responding, he fumbled for his phone. Tapping his thick fingers on the touch screen, he managed to pull up a picture. Flipping the phone toward her, he said, "This is what Ryker and I have been working on. It's the old Super Duper grocery store."

The picture was a run-down, curved-roofed building Imani vaguely recalled seeing on one of the streets off the downtown area. The building was situated underneath an overpass, the roof perfectly curved to match the bridge.

"This is the property you're working on?" At his nod,

Imani ventured the next, crucial question. "Why are you doing it for this woman?"

"The woman who owns it was best friends with my Aunt Beth, who died by suicide years ago. Cathy's not technically my aunt, but after Aunt B died, she became like a surrogate in our family, helping Mom with us boys while she grieved and filling in every time Dad was out of town on Marine business." He took his phone to pull up photos until he held up one of a woman with short-cropped blond hair. She had a friendly smile behind thick glasses that magnified the deep crow's feet radiating from her eyes. "That's her, Cathy Costello."

"Oh." She looked over at the kitchen's kitty-cat clock, whose eyes were glancing back and forth, wishing Lancelot or Gigi were here to provide a distraction to what was quickly becoming the most embarrassing day this summer—a high bar to pass, yet she felt like she'd vaulted far over the mark as she searched for words to make this better. "Sorry. I didn't know."

Zander's stern expression didn't leave his face.

"Do you find me so intimidating that it took all morning to work up the bravery to ask me out?" The twinkle came back into his eyes. "Because if that's the case, I need to ratchet down my chest and shoulder days. I don't want to be so buff I intimidate badass girls like you from saying something I've been waiting a year to hear."

Imani's stomach unfurled like a fist opening, and she felt the corners of lips twitching toward a smile. "It's not always about your buffness, Zander."

"No? Then do it. Ask me."

"Fine." She narrowed her eyes at him, but soon her

expression gave way to a tentative smile. "I was thinking, since you have the day off for the balloon rally on Friday, we could do something."

"There's no ask in there," he commented, and as she reached out to swat at his chest, he caught her hand. His face had that easygoing smile again—the one that lit up the dark corners of her mind and made her feel floaty and buoyant. He pressed his lips to the back of her hand. "Ask me, Imani. Please."

She let him pull her into his arms, loving the solid, immovable feel of him. She touched his cheek, shivering as her palm rubbed the whiskers against the grain, creating a delicious friction and warmth that twirled down to her belly where it leaped and spun, as if a dozen miniature ballerinas were performing en pointe piqué turns.

"Will you go on a first date with me, Zander Matthews?"

# CHAPTER 14

Zander took the bungalow's porch steps two at a time. For the last three weeks, he'd tried to do exactly what Ryker had said: show Imani he cared, that her happiness was his ultimate goal, and wait, patiently, for her to make the next move.

Damned if it hadn't worked.

"It's only a date," Zander said to himself under his breath. "You've asked out dozens of women in your life. Don't be neurotic."

"Keep talkin' to yourself and they'll put you away."

He jumped. He hadn't seen Mrs. Foltz sitting huddled in an old quilt on the far porch chair until she'd spoken.

"You're here just in time," she said, standing with some difficulty. Zander moved to help her, and she waved him away, turning her head only minutely before bellowing, "Imani! Your Zamboni is here!"

Imani came out of the bungalow, wiping her hands on a dishtowel, her hair up in a ponytail that accentuated her high cheekbones and drew attention to her sparkling mocha eyes.

"Gigi!" Imani shook her head, exasperated. "For the

millionth time, his name is Zander. Zan-DER. Like...like cat dander, only it's a Z. Zander."

Zander and Mrs. Foltz looked at each other. Both hid their smiles, deadpanning.

"Did she just compare me to cat dander?" he asked.

"Yep. And think. You were going to ask her on a date. Poor Dander." She turned to her granddaughter. "Can't you say yes to this poor fellow with his unfortunate name? He has helped us quite a bit this summer. And you've been climbin' the walls like a dog in heat."

"I have not!" Imani protested, and Zander enjoyed the splash of crimson on her cheeks. "I've been taking care of you, Gigi!"

Ignoring her, Mrs. Foltz clutched his arm in a viselike grip. "Tonight's the first night of the balloon rally, and the weather's perfect, so they'll launch for sure. You take your girl down to the festival and get her out of my hair for a while. Did you know she's alphabetized my spice rack? Like I want to wade through the coriander before I can find the Hungarian paprika! She's got too much energy—she needs to be lunged, like a horse. Can you do that for me?"

"Lunged like a horse." Zander nodded obediently. "Got it."

"But, Gigi, are you sure you're ready to be left alone?" Imani bit her lip, glancing at Zander. "Maybe I should stay, just to be safe?"

Zander patted Gigi's arm. "Or Mrs. Foltz could come with us to the balloon rally—I'll make Imani give you shotgun. Better yet, let's ditch your granddaughter, and you can be my ride-or-die tonight."

Gigi cackled, waving him off. "It's too damn cold out

here for me," Gigi said, despite the fact it had to be pushing eighty degrees in the late-afternoon sun. "No, Lancelot and I are going to have an early night. I'm going inside and putting on my pajamas, then I'm going to do my crossword until I fall asleep. I've seen more balloon rallies than you can shake a stick at. You kids go and have some fun."

Zander noticed she did look tired. Maybe she wanted a night without her granddaughter fussing over her? He couldn't imagine anything hotter than Imani playing nurse...but that was different. He cleared his throat, offering a solution to what he assumed was Imani's guilt over leaving her grandmother out of the festivities.

"How about we bring you something from the fair?"

Gigi's face lit up. "I wouldn't mind some saltwater taffy, if they have banana. I haven't had banana taffy in a month of Sundays!"

"Banana taffy it is." Zander helped Mrs. Foltz into her room with Imani hovering like a butterfly at the fringes. He glanced at Imani and saw she was in shorts and a T-shirt. "You're going to want to grab a jacket. It'll get cold when the sun goes down. And I don't mean to rush you, but the balloons are launching soon. If you want to see it, we have to go."

Imani's eyes widened, and she touched her hair. "But I was going to change. Do my makeup and stuff..."

Zander shrugged. "If you do, you'll miss it. You look perfect for the balloon rally—it's Wellsville, not some swanky Manhattan club. Let's go! Time's a-wasting."

"You're flustering me," she said, spinning in a circle, her hand on her forehead as she scowled. "I feel like I'm forgetting something..."

"Here's your coat. Tick-tock." He thrust the windbreaker he'd spotted on the foyer tree at her. "We've got to roll. We'll be back later with taffy, Mrs. Foltz. Don't worry—your granddaughter is in good hands."

Zander checked his phone as Imani kissed her grandmother and she shooed them out the door. He was pleased to see his friend had come through for him—in spades. His stomach got that jittery night-before-Christmas feeling. His step was light as he beat Imani to the Prius and held the passenger door for her, giving her time to fold those long, luscious legs into the car before shutting it and sprinting to the driver's side.

"Have you ever seen the rally before? I know you used to spend summers here as a kid."

Imani shook her head. "It always conflicted with dance camp. A few years ago, as I was driving into town, I saw the balloons already overhead, but that's the closest I've come."

"Another first with me. I promise to be gentle and to hold you afterward."

Imani swatted at his arm, chuckling. "You're such an ass."

Zander put on the turn signal, waiting for the local cops to wave him over the tiny bridge to Island Park. They had about forty minutes before the first balloons would launch—still plenty of time to find the taffy vendor before the surprise he'd arranged.

Just as the police officer motioned for him to go, Imani shrieked, causing him to spike the brakes in the middle of the intersection.

"Shit! I forgot my purse!" Then Imani proceeded to go through the most bizarre yoga contortions he'd ever seen performed in a Prius. She stuck her head between her legs, searching the floor at her feet, then yanked herself over the console, wrapping her whole body around the front seat in an effort to see the entire passenger-side back seat behind her, and then thrust her head under Zander's arm resting on the steering wheel to peer between his feet. As if her purse might magically appear next to the brake.

The officer glared and jabbed her index finger first at him, then emphatically toward the tiny bridge on his right, in a gesture hard to misinterpret.

As soon as Imani had flopped back into the seat, he hit the accelerator and roared into the dirt parking lot, stones zinging against the Prius. He snagged a spot only his compact car could fit into and slammed it into park before turning to her.

"Seriously? You can't shriek like that when I'm driving. Very uncool."

"We've got to go back. It's right in the kitchen, I know exactly where I left it, so you can pull to the sidewalk and I'll hop out and—oh my God!" Imani interrupted herself, her face morphing from terrified consternation to wide-eyed awe as she focused on something over his shoulder. "They're going up!"

"Not yet. They're filling them now, but the balloon meister will be calling time soon. We'd better hurry so you can see the whole process for the thirty-six balloons scheduled to launch, from start to finish." He put out his hand as Imani started to object. "You don't need a purse. This date is my treat, so your cash is no good here."

She bit her lip, the action tugging down one side of her

full, luscious mouth in a way that made him clench his jaw against the surge of desire.

"What if I need something in there?" she asked. "Like my phone?"

"I've got mine right here." He pulled it from his pocket. "Fully charged, and I've got Kate's, Drake's, and your grandma's numbers programmed in my favorites. You can call anyone you want, whenever you want—I have no lock code on it."

"What if I need...my ID? If I have to drive because you drank too much?"

"I won't drink. I'm driving."

Her eyes shifted to the sight of the balloons filling over his shoulder, and he saw her excitement win over her purse insecurities.

"You'll take pictures for me?"

"Enough to fill a scrapbook." He grinned. "Is it official? Has our first date begun?"

"Fine...do your worst."

Twenty minutes later, they'd cruised most of Island Park—now crowded with food vendors and bounce houses that jockeyed for position between roped-off areas for balloonists, who were in various stages of launch preparation. Zander did his best to be an informative but flirty tour guide. Apparently, he was doing better with the former than with the latter, as Imani's head was on a swivel, her attention anywhere but gazing into his eyes adoringly, which is where he'd wanted them to be.

It didn't help that she'd skipped lunch and moaned every time they'd passed a food truck. Although he'd eaten lunch and downed a protein shake right before picking her up, her face had deflated when he'd admitted he was full, so he found himself packing in a ginormous assortment of junk so she wouldn't have to eat alone. After locating the banana taffy for her grandmother, Zander bought them both shoestring fries, and they'd split a hot dog, and then she'd convinced him he needed something sweet. They'd found a fried-dough stand, and he was doing his best to pick from the edges, chewing slowly to pretend he was keeping pace with her.

If she didn't let up, he was going to puke. And that would ruin all his plans.

So he kept running his mouth, telling her about the origins of Wellsville's most famous rally, and when he'd exhausted that topic, he moved onto the science involved in balloons, themselves.

"See how they're using those huge fans to fill the balloons still on the ground?" At her nod, he gave the paper plate to her on the pretext of needing to use his hands to explain. In reality, if he held the fried dough any longer, what he'd eaten was going to make a dramatic reversal. "They're filling it with cold air first, checking to see if the balloon's envelope—that's the bright-colored pieces of nylon fabric—has any leaks. Once they've determined it's safe, they'll light up the propane burners and heat the air inside until it rises off the ground."

"Mmm," she said, nodding and licking the powdered sugar from her lips in a slow, methodical manner, as if purposely trying to give him a public boner. "No wonder you know so much about balloons. You're both essentially the same."

He searched for something witty to say. "You mean, big, majestic, and burning hot?"

"I meant showy and full of hot air." She burst out laughing when he made a disappointed face, and the gust of laughter blew powdered sugar from the top of the fried dough like an updraft of fine, white snow. It left her with a faint, Kris Kringle–like mustache and eyebrows. A few tiny specks of it caught at the tips of her long lashes, clinging as she blinked so she looked like a sugar-plum fairy.

He slipped his phone from his pocket, toggled it on, and clicked a picture.

"Boom. Karma."

"Gimme that." She reached for the phone, then paused, taking in the mess of her fingers. It looked as though she'd dipped her fingers in wax, followed by a dollop of white flour. "See this? If I had my purse, I could pull out the wipes I have stashed in there and I wouldn't be so…"

"Sticky?" Zander filled in as she giggled, pitching the empty paper plate into a garbage can as they passed. When she turned to him, gazing helplessly at her splayed-out, sugar-coated fingers, she looked so beautiful standing there, the sun glinting on her chestnut hair, all childlike and full of sweets, he did something impulsive.

Ducking his head down to hers, he planted a soft kiss on her cheek.

"That was my way of saying you're scrumptious, especially dipped in powdered sugar and cinnamon."

She glanced up at him, startled, but still smiling. Then, to his surprise, she stood on tiptoe, her soft lips brushing his as gentle as a whisper.

"That was my way of saying…I loved the fried dough." Then she glanced self-consciously around.

Passersby were weaving their way around them, most watching the closest balloonists, who were still filling their crafts. But a couple of locals paused when they saw them, and Zander gave the one-handed wave accompanied by the chin nod in their direction—the universal sign for "Hi, I recognize you, but you can see I'm busy with this gorgeous girl right now, so keep your distance"—and so far, nobody had come over to them asking after Drake's next book, or checking in on Ryker, or wanting to book a ceramics party at the studio.

Imani saw everyone who did a double take. "Is there a bathroom nearby so I can clean up? I feel like I'm getting hard-core judged. Your dates probably aren't usually so messy."

Zander cocked an eyebrow at her. "You think there are hordes of them—my dates? What if they're looking at us for the opposite reason: that I never have a date with me, especially at events like this?"

She raised an eyebrow in disbelief. "As if."

They rounded the corner, and he spotted the bathrooms. Gesturing with his chin, he told her, "Head on in. I'm going to grab us some drinks. Can't have you distracted by a full bladder or sticky hands where we're headed."

She took a step in the direction of the ladies' room, then paused. "Wait. Where are we going?"

"Surprise," he said, checking his phone, and reading a portion of the text from his boot camp buddy. "Five-minute warning. Hustle now."

He hid a grin as Imani double-timed it to the ladies' room. Usually, it was a nuisance to live in a small town where everyone knew your whole family, but today his large network paid off. Big time. He'd called his old Marine buddy, determined to make this moment, this night, count.

These past weeks at his shop and at Mrs. Foltz's many house visits, he'd known they still had chemistry. Question was, did their connection have the legs necessary for a relationship run, or was it like Imani insisted—a distraction, a temporary zing?

This was his chance to make a lasting impression. Damned if he didn't want to blow her mind!

"Hey, I brought you a little something," Imani said, coming up from his blind side, making him jump. She held a dripping brown paper towel in her hand.

"Oh." He took the sopping wet mass with an exaggerated pincher-like motion, as he wrinkled his nose, letting it drip onto the grass between them. "Your used paper towels. You shouldn't have."

She put her hands on her hips, and with her long legs gleaming tan under her shorts, she stood like Wonder Woman did when she was ready to put a hurting on a bad guy.

"They aren't used. I wet them down for you so you could wipe off your sticky fingers."

He put his cell back into his pocket before using the disintegrating towel to wipe his mostly sugar-free hands. Then he flung the wad into a metal trash can where it made a sloppy *smack* noise as it connected with the plastic lining before sliding out of view.

"Thank you." He dried his hands by flopping them in the air, flinging droplets of water on her until she laughed. Then he put his hand into his other pocket, tugging out the tiny thing he'd bought this morning from a downtown merchant. "I've got a treat for you too. And it's not made of recycled newspapers."

Imani gazed at his fist, and when he had her attention focused there, he opened his fingers, revealing a balloon-shaped pin. He'd spent almost half an hour at the vendor, searching for the perfect one.

"How fun! I love pins." She took off the back and tacked it to her shirt above her heart.

"It's more than a fashion accessory, it's your only clue." He crossed his arms. "You have exactly five minutes to find the balloon that most closely resembles the one on your shirt. The pilot has your surprise in his basket, so you'd better get searching, because they're going up—"

Before he'd finished speaking, she was sprinting down the path that wound next to the river. Her head was on a swivel as she jogged by gawkers, women push-ing strollers, and everyone else moving at a more sedate pace.

Zander loped behind her, zigzagging through the crowd. God, but this woman made life so much fun! He hoped her bravery would extend to what was about to come next.

In three minutes, she'd come to the farthest end of the park and skidded to a halt down the hill from a balloon with vibrant red and orange stripes that was almost fully inflated. She turned to grin at him.

"You didn't think I could find it this fast, did you?"

He shrugged. "You've found...what, exactly? Still two minutes left. Better get to it."

Frowning, she tugged the pin and the shirt along with it to her face, revealing some of her midriff. He remembered her silky skin under his fingers when he'd put the towel on her cut there, and beyond that tactile memory was one where his hands roved over the smooth expanse of her body as she writhed and moved under him.

"This is the balloon. It's got to be. It's the only one with red and orange stripes on it." Imani put her hands on her hips as if she wanted to call him out for reneging. Then her face cleared. "Wait. You said to check with the pilot."

She brushed past him, putting her shoulder down as she did so, making it more of a standing tackle then a breezy pass-by, and he heard her chuckle under her breath as she made him move slightly, his breath coming out in an unexpected *oomph* sound.

"I'm not sure how roughing me up is helping your cause to get more clues for your surprise," he observed, following her.

"You love being roughed up by me, and you know it." Her red lips curved into a saucy grin as she wound past the crush of people to the roped-off, balloon-filled area.

He raised his hands to shoulder level. "Guilty as charged."

Suddenly, a voice came over the din of the crowd, boosted by a microphone and a good pair of speakers. "Good evening and welcome to the Great Wellsville Balloon Rally." The announcer stood on an overturned milk crate. "I'm Gordon Childs, your balloon meister, and I'm thrilled to announce we are five minutes away from the first round of launches. Let me take a moment to recognize this year's sponsors..."

As the man droned on, Zander tapped at his wristwatch, giving Imani a pointed look as he mouthed the words "Tick-tock."

"No fair! This is as close to the balloon as we can get. It's roped off!"

Zander caught the gaze of his Marine buddy, Tucker Owen, the pilot of *Someday Came*. He waved, firing the burner repeatedly, the sound so deafening he had to yell in her ear to be heard.

"You're going to let a rope keep you away from the surprise of a lifetime?"

She gawked at him, then at the rope and the pilot watching from the inside of the balloon's basket. He knew she was turning over in her head if she could break the rules—flout the convention that they had to be behind the rope like a bunch of cattle—and he was delighted as he spotted the instant her eyes narrowed and she decided to toss the rule book aside.

*Atta girl*, he thought to himself, grinning.

She backed up three huge paces, then shouted to the crowd around her, "Look out! Coming through!"

With that, she raised her chin, took five rapid steps, and sailed over the waist-high rope in a graceful, toes-pointed, white-sneakered leap.

Zander held his breath, sure she was going to face-plant, but she breezed by, clearing the rope by a good four inches, landing on one graceful foot.

Dancer. Right.

Zander straddled the rope, crossing the barrier in a much less graceful but arguably more efficient manner, following Imani as she ran to the wicker basket attached to the red-and-orange-striped balloon.

"Hi," she said to Tuck, sticking out her hand to shake. "I'm Imani Lewis. And this joker behind me says there's a surprise in your basket for me, and we had a bet I wouldn't get it on time. But I did, because you're still here."

"Nice to meet you," Tuck said, grinning and clasping her hand in a firm shake, then reaching out to Zander to do the same before goosing the propane burner. "I'm Tucker Owen. My friends call me Tuck, but that joker behind you can stick with Mr. Owen after he sicced my ex-wife after me."

Zander clutched his chest. "I didn't know you and Michelle were quits. I just needed your new cell number, that's all."

"Sorry I didn't reach out before then—been crazy busy out in Arizona, but I'd meant to see which day you wanted to reserve this year," Tuck said, then jerked his head to Imani, motioning for her to join him in the basket. "Welcome aboard *Someday Came*."

Zander boosted her in, and she climbed over the edge of the brown wicker basket. She looked around, her face alight with curiosity.

"This is cool. I've never been inside one of these." She gave the propane burner a wide berth as she explored the confines of the basket. Finally, she turned, shaking her head. "Okay, I give up. Where's the surprise?"

"You're in it," Zander said, stepping into the basket's square, cut-out step and grasping Tuck's hand as he climbed into the basket to join her. He put on his most teasing face. "I thought you'd like to see what it feels like to go where the wind takes you for once. It's going to push the limits of your comfort zone. No plan. No direction...no purse."

Tuck adjusted his trucker hat. "Unless you can't handle it. I owe this lunatic a favor, but that doesn't mean

I'm gonna take up some girl who's fainting or shriek-ing the whole time. You've got about five seconds to decide, because they just gave us the green light to ascend."

Her throat moved as she swallowed, her wide, brown eyes darting from the propane blasting flames behind her to the wicker basket under her feet to the cheering crowd.

"I . . . I mean, I didn't know we'd be doing this, and I . . ." She trailed off, and Zander saw panic flit across her face.

"Imani," he began, yet before he could tell her it was okay to back out, she took a deep breath, held it with her eyes closed, then opened them, releasing the air in a whoosh.

Her eyes were bright with excitement, colored with a heavy dose of adrenaline-laced fear as she grinned.

"Hell, yeah. I'm going up in this balloon, and if I die, I'm going to kick your ass, Zander Matthews." She gave him a wicked smile. "And if we live, I may just do the same."

"Forewarned is forearmed." He cupped her elbow with his hand, tugging her slightly to one side in the small basket. "Seriously, you don't have to go. We can do some-thing else. I thought it would be—"

"—a once-in-a-lifetime experience," she finished, nod-ding and standing ramrod straight as the balloon meister started a countdown from ten. "I'm manifesting the words in the bracelet charm you gave me. Living in the now. Let's do this."

Tuck motioned to one of the guys in his chase crew, who began unstaking the basket as the emcee's count diminished.

"Five . . . four . . . three . . ."

"You sure?" Zander asked, eyeballing the last of the

tethers being unhooked from the basket's corner. "We can still jump, but we have to do it now."

"Two...one! Balloons fly!" the balloon meister said into the megaphone, and the crowd shouted and cheered as the pilots goosed their burners at once. The sound erupted around them, as if they'd been dropped into an inferno.

Imani's fingers gripped the side of the basket so hard her knuckles were white, but she stood firm as the basket lifted from the ground, her cheeks flushed as she spoke in a breathy voice.

"Up, up, and away."

# CHAPTER 15

Up, up, and away," Imani whispered, but in her head, she was shrieking, *Holy shit, holy shit, holy SHIT!* as she gripped the soft, suede-like top of the rectangular balloon basket. It was as thick as her arm, and the whole interior was only large enough for the three of them and the tanks of what she assumed was fuel.

She wasn't sure what the rules were, and as the crowd cheered and the balloons to each side of *Someday Came* lifted off, she yelled in Zander's general direction, afraid to move her head and do something to unbalance the basket.

"Do I...do I stand here, then? Is there some sort of seat belt I should wear? Or a parachute?"

Tuck, the pilot, laughed. "Nope. This is a giant, hot-air-filled parachute. If we run out of propane, we're gonna drift down to the ground. Pretty simple physics. Warm air rises, cool air falls—we can go up and down but have to catch an air current to move directions."

The red-and-orange-striped balloon began to ascend. The basket didn't jolt but sort of floated above the ground, with no sense of speed or velocity.

Well, other than the fact that everything below them was rapidly diminishing as they rose.

The ground was visible between the weave in the wicker, and it was as though she'd been shrunk to Lilliputian size, placed in an Easter basket, and tied to a helium balloon to sail away. She jerked her head up, as watching the earth recede between her feet was giving her vertigo, and reached out for the most solid thing she could find.

Zander.

He stood next to her, his mouth smiling, his blue eyes watching her carefully, a smidgen of worry shadowing his gaze as he clasped her hand on his forearm.

"You good?"

The pilot blasted the propane burner, and suddenly Imani's back was as hot as if she were standing close to a bonfire. Her heart hammered against her chest, yet it felt more like the thrill of a roller coaster ride than like the gut-churning sensation she got after making a bad decision.

Imani nodded. "I'm good."

She refused to turn toward the inside of the basket or take the coward's way out by staring at the clouds above or at Zander. Although the latter was looking so fine in his casual T-shirt and cargo shorts—his summer uniform, apparently, and why not? If she looked that good in cargo shorts, she'd wear them every day too. Then she spotted something: a rope dangled from their basket in the air and seemed to be attached to...another balloon?

"Oh my God," she gasped, her fingernails biting into Zander's arm as she indicated the dark-orange tether dangling between the two rising crafts. "Someone forgot to detach that, and now we're hooked to that other balloon! Are we going to crash?"

Zander and Tuck both laughed.

"No, I forgot to tell you, Tuck's balloon and the local Carpet Town store's balloon are teamed up for the ribbon race this year," Zander said, pointing to the blue-and-white-striped balloon at the far end of the tether that Imani could now see was a ribbon. "We're competing against those two over there to see which one of us can stay tethered together by this ribbon the longest. Winner gets a bottle of champagne, but more importantly, we get bragging rights on the balloon rally website."

A competition? Not only were they rising far above the earth in a freaking oversized Easter basket, but these guys were making a contest out of it? Yet she couldn't help but watch the other two balloons—a rainbow-colored one and an orange-and-white-checkered one—her inner competitor eager to win as they rose, filling the evening with vibrant colors and the roar of propane burners.

Releasing her death grip on Zander's arm, she took it all in—the fear, the exhilaration, and every nuanced emotion in between. She watched the people waving below and waved carefully back, turning her hand back and forth in a queenly wave, still afraid any herky-jerky motions would upset the basket's balance.

"Ah, damn!" Tuck said, five minutes later, chuckling as their ribbon was the first to break. He waved to the pilot in the Carpet Town balloon, and the guy shrugged back, shouting, "Next time."

Zander reeled in the broken ribbon—a burnt-orange grosgrain one—and handed it to her, dragging out his phone. "Here. Let's take a picture. A memento for your scrapbook."

She leaned in, pressing her face to his, clutching the ribbon as he snapped the shot. Then he took a few more of Tuck and of the ascending balloons around them before putting his phone and the ribbon away.

"I'll keep it in my cargo shorts along with Gigi's taffy for you when we land," Zander said, stuffing it into one of the voluminous pockets down at his knees. "Now you can relax. Enjoy the ride!"

Imani faced back out, taking in the wonder of balloons rising below, and others ascending next to and above their own. While her heart hammered in her chest, she gripped the basket's side and watched as the park, then the town below, grew teeny and insignificant.

Just like her worries.

She breathed in, the late-afternoon sun warm on her face as it cast balloon-sized shadows on the green park space beneath until the balloons were too high to cast shadows. It was the oddest feeling—rising up, with no wind or breeze. Logically, she knew that was because they were moving with the breeze, so she wouldn't feel it blowing against her, but still, it was such a strange sensation to rise, like bubbles on the wind.

"Fun fact: hot air balloons originated in France during the 1700s, and not a whole lot has changed about the basic design since then." Zander tapped her hand, directing her gaze to the gauges inside the gondola. "That burner Tuck keeps pressing heats the air to 250 degrees Fahrenheit, which is why he's wearing those big fireproof gloves. It'd burn him otherwise."

"How fast are we going?" Imani asked.

Tuck answered, "We go as fast as the wind, which is currently around five miles an hour. Anything over ten miles an hour and I won't launch. Too dangerous. Once we get around a thousand feet, we'll hit a southerly air current that'll take us over some beautiful country. At least, that's the plan the chase team and I had this morning. That's the thing with balloons—you have to learn quickly how to give up control to the air gods. Still, it's the safest aircraft in the skies."

Imani's eyebrows rose in surprise. "How come?"

"Fewest mechanical parts to break down." Tuck hitched his thumb toward Zander. "Like the professor over there said, it's the same basic construction and flight theory as it was three centuries ago."

A few of the balloons had followed their general direction, but Imani noticed many were ascending more slowly and had apparently caught another current, as they moved in the opposite direction. She leaned a little over the basket's edge, watching with fascination as the landscape scrolled beneath them, growing smaller as they floated above, like in a dream.

"How do you two know each other?" Imani asked after they'd left the town behind. The houses looked like Scrabble tiles beneath them, the sky bright and cloudless and so, so peaceful. She felt comfortable enough now to let go of the side of the basket to stand unaided, but still close enough to Zander she could smell the scent of his soap and fried dough and his warm, yummy goodness.

"He's what we Parris Island recruits call a 'Hollywood Marine,'" Zander said, "because he did boot camp in San

Diego, far from the sand fleas we endured. But Hollywood Tuck and I ended up in the same deployment in Afghanistan. He's a combat engineer, like me. We played with rockets and blasted down doors and walls—you get to know a guy when you blow shit up together."

"We Hollywood Marines at least know how to pack a sea bag." Tuck snorted, shaking his head and grinning at Imani. "This dumbass forgot his underwear. Who forgets skivvies when they're deployed? So I loaned him a couple of mine until his momma's care package came in."

"Speaking of packages," Zander said, doing the hands-on-hips Superman pose he did when he was about to brag, "it was a lucky thing your briefs were made of super stretchy material. I almost couldn't fit it all in."

"Har-har," Tuck said, jerking his thumb at Zander. "Have you noticed the guy never stops joking?"

They bantered back and forth, the conversational references to Marine life so rich with acronyms, jargon, and inside jokes she didn't bother to interrupt the flow to ask questions. It occurred to her this was the first true friend she'd met of Zander's—not a coworker, a relative, or a random local he'd helped out in his past. She was curious, and she was also impressed. Their closeness was like hers with Kate—one forged from hardship, camaraderie, and a sense of loyalty and love that had nothing to do with family bonds. It warmed her heart while it also pinged something within her.

If he could maintain a best friend for almost a decade, despite being in different states, time zones, and careers, surely he could maintain a long-distance relationship.

With her.

Imani shook the thoughts out of her head. Today was for enjoyment. No plans. Just enjoying the now, like she'd promised. She took advantage of a lull in the conversation to ask Tuck the question that had nagged at her since embarking on Zander's surprise goose chase.

"So, what's the meaning behind the balloon's name?"

Tuck adjusted his hat to ride lower on his head, all but hiding his dark eyes. "There was a lot of downtime on patrol in Afghanistan, and if there's one thing Zander knows how to fill, it's downtime. Has this guy given you the 'If you could do anything and be guaranteed success, what would you do?' quiz yet? It's his favorite way to drill into people's heads, for kicks." At Imani's snort of laughter and nod, Tuck rolled his eyes. "He does it to everyone. Makes you think about shit. So I told him the most ridiculous wish I had—to fly a hot air balloon. I thought it'd shut him up, but he never forgot. Every chance he had to ask someone about piloting a balloon, he did."

"It's a good thing. Turns out our corporal's dad owned a balloon," Zander put in, coming around Imani, the wicker creaking underneath him as he shifted position to stand behind her. Although ostensibly his hand was resting on the thick, rolled edge of the basket at her back, it also felt a little like he was putting his arm around her.

She liked it.

She refocused on the conversation. "What did he say when you asked about it?"

Tuck's lips twisted in a half grin.

"Corporal Davis told us, 'If you two bullet catchers make it through your deployment, look me up and I'll make sure my dad gives you a damn lesson,'" he said, and Zander joined him, both of them speaking the last sentence in unison, "'Now get out of my damn face.'"

They both guffawed at the memory, and Imani turned slightly as if to face Zander while she asked a question, but really it was to turn in to his arms. He smelled so freaking good, and the cotton T-shirt clung to every glorious inch of those pectorals.

"What's a bullet catcher?" she asked, and Lord help her, she even gave him the doe eyes—something she hadn't done since she was in college. But her flirt game must have been off, because he didn't throw his arm around her shoulder like she wanted. He just stayed in the same position, looking and smelling like some sort of demigod.

"Dark humor. That's what they called the new recruits. We were the guys most likely to catch a bullet." Zander gave her a soft smile, holding out his hand.

Imani stared at it for a beat, then remembered his rule: if she wanted this to progress, she had to make the moves. He'd told her more than once—she was in control.

She took her hand off the basket, slipping it into his. A blush crept up her face, and she turned to gaze at the view until she got control over her reactions. Blushing like a high schooler because the guy was holding her hand? She'd already slept with him, for Pete's sake. Wasn't that like closing the barn door after the horse left or whatever the idiom was?

Luckily, Tuck picked up the story thread, ignoring her blush. "Neither one of us reenlisted, and after we got out, damned if this guy didn't remember the corporal's promise. He met up with him at some bar in Washington, DC, wasn't it?"

Zander nodded. "I was staying there while Ryker did his PT at Walter Reed. I'd heard a bunch of guys from our company were in town, so I went down to the bars, hitting each one until I found him."

"He bought Corporal Davis a drink. But before he handed it to him, this ballsy son of a bitch reminded the guy about the deal he'd made four years ago. Told him I was out of the service and ready for my lesson." Tuck pressed the propane burner. "I was stocking shelves at an Illinois grocery store, going exactly nowhere. Out of the blue, Zander phones and says he's bought me a plane ticket to Arizona for the balloon festival, and a hotel room under my name. He said he'd rip my balls off if I didn't get my free lesson."

Zander rolled his eyes. "I don't think I was quite that dramatic."

Tuck threw Imani a knowing look. "You know what I'm talking about. Once he's got an idea in that melon, he is relentless."

Imani laughed, squeezing Zander's hand. "It's one of his most...endearing qualities. So I'm guessing you had your lesson?"

"And then some. Turns out, Corporal Davis's dad was retiring. Giving up the balloon. And he offered it to me. Somehow, this guy," he said, gesturing to Zander, "had found out and put up the scratch for a down payment and pilot lessons. I quit my grocery store job and spent the next year learning from one of the best, becoming commercially licensed in all fifty states. I do tours over the Grand Canyon. As a job. Can you believe I get paid to fly this beautiful lady every day of my life?"

Imani grinned. "I'm a sucker for happily ever afters. So why the name?"

"Because every time I'd tell Zander to quit yapping about my dream—that we were just a couple of bullet catchers, passing the time—he'd say, 'Someday it'll happen.' And—"

His voice cracked, and he broke off.

She finished his sentence, her voice soft. *"Someday Came."* Imani's chest panged in sympathy as the man fixed his trucker hat, his Adam's apple bobbing as he struggled with some emotion. "That's . . . that's so perfect."

"Nah." Zander reached around to clap Tuck on the shoulder. "You're my brother, man. I wore your tightywhities for a month until my mom's care package arrived with, you know, some man-sized ones. I owed you and your tight-ass underwear."

Tuck laughed, angling away from them to wipe his eyes on the cuff of his leather gloves.

Zander gave her wink.

"Besides, it was a good business decision. He repaid me during his first year as a commercial balloonist, and I got the best end of the bargain—rides every year at the rally."

Imani's inner romance reader sighed with a mixture of adoration and lust. Zander was just so good! Maybe he was right, like he'd been with Tuck, that she needed to trust her heart and get out of publishing? Find her zen? Chase her dream?

Kate had called it long ago—the Matthews brothers were the good guys. The real-life heroes. People you could count on, pour your heart out to, and they'd always have your back. Maybe it was time to let some of her heart show to this man?

She leaned against him as the two continued to talk, sliding her arm around his waist, and she felt Zander's body jolt a little, as if in surprise. Then he wrapped his arm around her shoulder, holding her gently, securely against him.

She still didn't know what to do about her job, but she had figured out one thing: Zander Matthews was more than a two-night stand.

She tapped his waist with her finger, and he bent his head to listen as she whispered, "Zander, thank you so much. This is the first time I've let go of the chokehold I've had on life since my mom died. It feels so freeing to...drift. Just be. I get it now. Your bracelet charm and your life philosophy. Honestly, this is the most perfect date of my entire—"

"Oh shit-balls!" Tuck yelped, startling them both.

Zander's head snapped up at the pilot's tone, and Imani felt him stiffen.

Tuck stared at his cell phone, tapped against it with a finger, swore again, and stuffed it into his pocket, stepping over to check the balloon gauges before swearing louder.

"Is everything okay?" Imani asked, her body pressing Pause on the calm feeling and numbness taking its place.

Tuck took off his trucker hat, ran a hand through the matted black hair there, then slammed it back on his head. He smiled, but it was more like a grimace.

"That depends on your definition of okay. We've got a problem."

# CHAPTER 16

Zander released Imani to examine the gauges, his heart galloping at the barely disguised panic in his friend's face. "We've got plenty of fuel. Is there some freak storm? Lightning? What's wrong, Tuck?"

"My chase car was in an accident. They rear-ended a semi. They're okay, thank God, but the car is totaled. Can't get it off the road without assistance."

"Send them the GPS coordinates when we land, and I'm sure by then they'll have another vehicle lined up," Zander suggested.

Tuck winced, pointing to a metal tower in the distance. "Problem is, we're headed south, away from the cell tower, and I can't drop lower to catch a more easterly wind because of the hills. Soon as we pass over this section there," he said, pointing to the hills in the distance, "we'll be in rural Pennsylvania, and the signal's going to be nonexistent."

"Does that mean we're . . . not landing?" Imani asked, and Zander was surprised by the fact her tone was calm, as if the thought of a problem hundreds of feet in the air didn't bother her at all. Her follow-up question was as un-Imani as it could get. "I mean, can't we stay up here, high above the trees, and wait until morning?"

Tuck shook his head. "Not safe to fly at night. We'll have to land as soon as we clear these hills. Be on the lookout for a big, open area. One without fences or powerlines either, unless you want to end this date sizzling like fried chicken."

Zander's eyebrows drew together. He'd promised to keep Imani safe. Yet, as he glanced over, worried about how Imani was taking this scary news, he saw...

She was grinning.

He returned to her side, concerned her expression might be hiding her underlying fear. Putting a hand on her back, he rubbed in soothing circles. "Imani?"

She snorted a giggle, covering her mouth as he looked at her. Then another giggle, followed by another, and soon she was bent over, whooping with laughter as he and Tuck gazed on, bewildered.

"You...okay?" Zander asked, as her laughter dissolved into high-pitched hiccups. He handed her a bottled water, which she waved away, chuckling and snorting between her attempts to take deep breaths.

Finally, she regained control, wiping her eyes. "I am literally living out my worst nightmare. We're thousands of feet above the earth, no cell phone service, no rescue coming, and no plan except to find some field to land in before dark." She choked down a giggle. "And my purse, even if I'd had it, wouldn't have done a thing to help us. After today, I'm ditching that ugly-ass bag. I'm buying myself a damn Prada."

Zander nodded slowly, still wary that a crying jag was

coming. Yet Imani continued to laugh to herself as the balloon descended to lower and lower altitudes, racing the sun as it set over the hills.

"There!" Zander spotted an area where Tuck could land the craft. "That field is big enough, and there are no power lines."

Tuck agreed it would have to do...

Except it was full of cows.

"Balloons don't float nicely to the ground without assistance. If we hit that field, even doing five miles an hour, it'll bust up my basket and might throw us out, to boot." Tuck gave Zander a look. "You're going to have to swing out. Be my chase crew and haul us slowly down while I keep the thing aloft long enough to avoid any major boulders."

"Roger that," Zander said, accepting the pair of leather gloves Tuck shoved at him.

"Jump out when I tell you, hanging onto this rope," Tuck instructed, handing him a coiled rope that was secured to the basket's side and the basket itself. "Keep your feet moving, like you're running in the air so that when you hit the ground you don't break a leg. We're doing about six miles per hour, so it'll be like stepping onto a treadmill moving at a good clip. I'll do my best to slow us down here with the parachute valve, but I'm not going to lie—this is a great way to bust your ass. Hold the rope and keep those legs churning, and you should be fine."

Zander nodded, shoving his fingers into Tucker's gloves, knowing the rope sliding through his hands would shred the skin on his palms otherwise. Adrenaline raced through his body like it had done during his time blowing up walls in Afghanistan. Yet, oddly, he was calm.

"Be careful," Imani said, her earlier humor gone. Her face was flushed, and her brown eyes held...was it? Yes. It was concern.

The balloon descended, all deceptive serenity, clearing the fence at the edge of a pasture.

The cows lumbered away from them, lowing, their eyes rolling in fear as the craft neared the field.

"Now!" Tuck yelled, and Zander swung out in a Tarzan-like move that—a corner of his brain hoped—looked as cool as it felt.

He ran in midair, holding himself up with his upper body until his feet neared the ground. Then he touched down. The impact made his teeth clack together hard as he sprinted, furiously keeping pace, his sneakers flying over the rutted pasture, leaping over the big rocks. The balloon floated higher, and he slowed his pace, yanking on the rope hard as it slid through the leather gloves, leaving bits of stringy fiber behind as he tugged with all his strength.

Finally, he was able to halt the balloon's drift. He stood, his legs braced in a wide stance, tugging the basket to him, hand over hand on the rope, watching the red-and-orange balloon drift down and Imani's concerned face grow closer and closer.

Until she was there.

Tucker tossed out a metal stake.

"Tie her off to this and stomp it into the ground while I start letting out the air."

A breeze hit, tilting the craft to the left and yanking Zander to his toes as he held the rope, trying to stake it. On the second attempt, he did it, tying a sailing knot to hook the balloon's tether to the stake.

"Yes!" Imani raised her hands above her head, whooping. Suddenly, it was worth every bit of adrenaline release to see her shouting for him.

Tuck flicked off the gauges, jumping out as the balloon deflated.

"C'mon and help us catch the envelope before it gets tangled." Tuck gestured for Imani to bail out, but before she could leap, Zander was beside her, his arms outstretched.

"I got you."

He handed her out of the basket, loving the way she felt in his arms, loving the way she was looking at him as he set her gently down in the field next to him.

"That," she breathed into his ear, "was pretty impressive. I have a whole new appreciation for your skills, Zander Matthews."

"About damn time." Zander grinned back.

"Hey, Romeo," Tuck said, jerking Zander's attention away from Imani's upturned face. "Get over here and help me."

He released Imani, and he and Tuck moved to quickly gather the deflating nylon material, stretching it out into a long line on the ground.

When they were done, Tuck pulled out his phone, then called over.

"You got any bars on your phone? Because I got nothin' on mine."

Zander pulled his cell from his pants pocket, noticing Imani slapping at her shoulder for her purse, then at her pocket for her phone, until remembering she'd left both behind.

He toggled his phone on.

No service.

He shook his head, and Tuck's shoulders drooped.

"It's going to be full dark soon, so I'm going to follow those cows." Tuck jerked his thumb at the herd moving up a hill in the distance. "I figure they've gotta be heading to a barn or something, and hopefully I'll be able to get to a house or the road. You two stay here and roll this up. Guard my baby so that any wayward heifers don't get tangled in my ropes."

Tuck trudged off, and Zander and Imani teamed up to fold the balloon's nylon envelope into a strip about thirty feet long and a foot wide. Then they worked together to roll it up, Imani ensuring the slippery sides stayed folded and tucked as Zander rolled it like a snowball toward the basket.

"There." Imani put her hands on her hips as they pushed it as close to the craft as possible in the gloaming dark. "Looks like a giant red-orange Life Saver."

Suddenly, her expression changed as she shifted her gaze to the ground.

And the multiple piles of cow dung littering the field.

"Noooo! Please let me not have stepped in it," she moaned. She lifted one leg to eye level, then the other, in a feat of flexibility that parts of Zander clearly recalled from their weekend in Niagara Falls.

He forced his mind from the gutter. She was in control. Her. Not him. If she wanted this date to go further, or for it to extend to a second or third date, she'd have to be the one to tell him. Ryker was right—Zander knew his feelings. Now he had to wait for her to come to him. To make her own decision.

So he surreptitiously adjusted his cargo shorts and put on a mock-serious face. "Looks like you avoided the land mines."

She took off her sneakers, holding them in one hand. "I don't know about you, but I'm not sitting anywhere in this field. I'm going in there until we're rescued. If we're rescued. Give me a boost?"

He lifted her easily, swinging her long legs over the basket until she'd landed, barefoot, on the wicker, making it creak as she caught her balance.

She grinned, looking over the lip of the craft.

"Plenty of room in here, if you want to join me...but you've got to leave your shoes. Probably your socks, too. Looks like you scored a big jackpot on the left one."

He glanced down. She was right. His left Nike was covered up to his ankle in dark goop.

Great.

So much for hoping she'd amp up the romance on this date. Nothing said "you're not making out" like cow shit on your socks.

He slipped his feet from his sneakers and used the toes of his clean right foot to pull down his left foot's sock, holding onto the wicker basket—and Imani—to avoid toppling over. When he was done, he gave a massive leap and landed in the basket with a creaking thud.

The bottoms of his feet felt like he'd stepped on shattered clay, and he hotfooted around until he figured out no matter where he stood, it was going to hurt.

"You don't spend much time barefoot, do you?" Imani giggled, watching him shuffle from foot to foot. "My feet are so covered in calluses from dancing that I feel nothing. You'd better sit down."

He didn't bother to pose like he wasn't in pain but plopped down immediately, then patted the area next to him. Although he hadn't planned it, he'd sat down facing west. "Plenty of room to watch the sunset with me."

She sat next to him, her shoulders brushing his as they watched the sky turn pink, then purple, as dusk turned to dark.

"Best. Date. Ever," Imani said.

And then she kissed him.

Her lips were soft, and when she opened her mouth, he tasted her and groaned. How was it she always tasted sweet?

His fingers twined through her silky hair, cupping her head as he deepened the kiss, his thumb stroking the velvety skin of her cheek. She was all feminine softness but with that tough, resilient core he'd come to respect and love over these summer days and nights. Her graceful efficiency of movement and her direct way of pursuing what she wanted, whether it was checking items off her lists, or now, as she guided his head down to her neck, showing him the places that made her light up inside, was as impressive as it was arousing.

Even now, her hand crept up his shirt, those elegant fingers exploring his chest, toying with then lightly pinching his nipple. He gritted his teeth, willing self-control as she moved her mouth to his neck, adjusting herself until she straddled his lap, her lips on him in so many places that he thought he'd explode if he didn't touch her back.

So he did.

His hands crept up her T-shirt, and she shifted on his lap to give him greater access. His fingers played over the top of her lacy bra, loving the way her breath hissed in when he skated over her nipple, mimicking her move by squeezing her flesh there lightly, then more forcefully as she groaned, her lips leaving his neck to arch her back, pressing more of herself into his hands.

It was hot as hell, and Zander's fingers moved fast, unhooking her bra, shoving it up along with her T-shirt until he had total access to her smooth, warm skin.

"That feels so good," she whispered, easing back to place her hands on his legs behind her, so she could arch toward him more fully, giving herself to his hands as she ground against his erection. Even through his shorts and her pants, he could feel the heat of her, and he had to quickly think of something else.

He focused on relearning her body. Seeing exactly what pleased her.

Cupping her breasts in both hands, he lowered his face to her beautiful chest. He kissed the flesh there, taking her nipple in his mouth and sucking her gently, then switching to the other breast, fondling her pebbled flesh, soaking in every hissed intake of breath, every soft, moaning exhale, and repeating what she most enjoyed until she put her hand on his shoulder, panting.

"We've got to stop." She snagged his hands in hers, then grabbed the back of his head for another deep kiss.

"Okay," he breathed. "We can stop. But why?"

"Because I don't have my purse."

This time, he was the one to pull away from the kiss, raising an eyebrow.

"What does that have to do with us stopping?"

"Well, my purse has certain supplies," she began, and at

his puzzled look, she rolled her eyes, the expression clear in the moonlit night. "A condom. I have a box of damn condoms stuffed in the side pocket of my purse. You know, just in case. And since I don't have my purse, I don't have anything, so that means we have to stop."

He chuckled, nuzzling her neck until she tilted her chin, giving him free access there with a sigh.

"I'm hurt you think I can't handle basic Man 101 prep. Don't judge—I didn't have many options, but I slid one in my wallet this morning." He heard her low laugh and answered with one of his own. "I promise it's brand-new, bought for you. As a just-in-case, of course."

"I'm not judging." She found his lips again in the dark, pressing her body into his willing hands once more. "In fact, you get the gold star tonight for preparedness."

"Hold off on that gold star as I work." He eased her shirt and bra over her head, tossing them into the basket behind her, tearing his off in the next breath. "I'm going for the whole damn galaxy."

# CHAPTER 17

When they'd descended into a farmer's field and Zander had done that wild maneuver, swinging out to stop the balloon like some sort of Viking superhero, Imani decided there and then she was tossing the rules out the window and going with the flow, although she knew it would lead to his bed.

*Especially* because she knew it would lead to his bed.

Now, with Zander's hands and mouth igniting fires and fanning flames everywhere his fingers and lips traveled, she wondered why in the hell she had waited so long. Put up so many rules and guardrails. Why had she denied herself time with a man who was giving, kind, and always searching for ways to put her first?

"You sure about this?" he asked, as she unbuttoned his shorts, blindly reaching inside the elastic waistband of his jockey shorts.

She took the length of him in her hands, feeling the silky skin of his shaft and burning with want as he groaned, the sound guttural, coming from a place of urgent need.

"Hell yeah," she breathed, replacing her hands with her mouth to prove how sure she was.

Too soon, he dragged her off, his breath erratic.

"There is way too much fabric on you for my liking. Let me fix that."

His large, dexterous hands had her shorts unzipped and down in a flash. When he got to her underwear, he halted, his fingers tracing at the fabric there.

"Hold up. What are you wearing?"

"Tap pants," she said, out of breath and annoyed. Why was he stopping for a thing like that? She added to her statement, hoping it helped her cause to get laid. "Little black lacy ones."

"Stand up," he said. "Give me a quick spin. Pretty please."

"Since you asked so nicely..."

She stood. Although the moon shone down, most of Zander's face was in shadow, showing only the gleam of his eyes as he watched. Her nipples were hard as she grew bold enough to put her arms up in fourth and then fifth position, as she'd do in the studio standing at the barre. She elongated her torso, coming up to her toes to execute a slow, full turn.

When she was done, she returned to flat feet. He shook his head, grinning, his teeth catching the moonlight.

"Tap pants are the best things ever created." He'd slipped off his shorts, and as she sat, he hooked his thumbs into her tap pants, easing them down her legs. His voice was low but filled the night as he nuzzled her neck, wrapping his arms around her as she straddled his thighs. "Thanks for the private dance. You are the most beautiful woman I have ever seen. Do you know that?"

Instead of answering him, her mouth found his, and she kissed him, desire pounding through her. He answered her passion with his own, his hands and mouth doing a dance along her body.

Without clothes between them, his hard shaft rubbed the slick spaces between her thighs, and when he asked her to pause while he put on his condom, she gripped his shoulders, her brows drawing together as she held back the tide of longing surging through her.

As soon as he was done, she moved herself on her knees until her chest was at his face level. His mouth found her breast, and he licked his way to her nipple while she positioned herself over him. The wicker was hard and unyielding on her knees, but she didn't care, as long as it meant the pulsing need within her was answered. And soon.

Slowly, she lowered herself onto him, enjoying the way he stretched and filled her. Once she'd taken all of him, she tightened her muscles, gripping him inside. He stopped in his attention to her chest, tossing his head back against the gondola's side with a long hiss.

"Jesus, Imani. You're killing me." His voice was rough and rumbling deep in his chest. "Don't stop."

She obeyed, moving slowly at first, kissing him as she made small motions on him, reveling in the way her body adapted and made room for his thickness. Soon, though, small movements weren't enough, and she worked over him, their bodies slick with sweat, their breath mingling as they kissed. His hands roamed over her back and then lower, gripping her ass, his hips coming up to meet hers in a sweetly punishing rhythm she enjoyed even as she recognized the rapidly approaching cliff.

"Zander," she gasped, wanting to warn him she was close. But it was already upon her.

She shouted, tossing her head back, climaxing so hard the stars danced and whirled in her mind's eye, and when he came moments later, the aftershocks were still coursing through her, and she clutched his shoulders, wringing out every last pulse until her orgasm subsided and all that was left was a wonderful lethargic tingling.

He leaned his forehead against hers, heaving one last, shuddering breath. Then he kissed her lips, cupping her face.

"You are amazing—"

Suddenly, light beams penetrated the darkness around them, and someone shouted in the distance.

"Zander? Imani? You guys in there? My chase crew arrived, and we're ready to load up."

Imani had never moved so fast in her entire life.

She crouched in the basket, giggling like a loon as Zander cursed and fought to get his shorts on. By touch, she'd found her tap pants and shorts, and had slipped on her shirt over her hastily hooked bra just before Tucker and his crew reached them. Imani's face felt like it was glowing, it was so hot with their almost-public-indecency moment, and she kept glancing down at her knees, where an impression of the wicker's weave was embedded in the flesh there. Thankfully, the darkness disguised it as she slipped on her shoes and tromped over the cow pasture with the others. Her hand sought Zander's, and he squeezed it in their shared post-sex adrenaline rush.

Although she was introduced to Tuck's crew, Imani was so busy fixing her face so it didn't look like she'd recently climaxed, she promptly forgot their names. Luckily, it was Tuck and his new girlfriend, Carrie, who drove them the thirty-two miles from Pennsylvania back to Wellsville, and Carrie was more interested in retelling her brush with death than with Imani and Zander's silent, satisfied presence in the back seat.

"Can I borrow your phone and call Gigi?" Imani asked Zander as soon as they reached a more residential area. Noting the time was 10:45, well past her grandmother's bedtime, she opted to text her instead.

She sent a quick note that she'd be late getting home and not to worry, ending with the fact Gigi should call this number, Zander's, as her cell phone was in the kitchen. She held his phone for a second to see if Gigi was going to respond, but nothing appeared.

"She's probably sound asleep. You must have a spare key somewhere, right?" Zander pocketed his phone as they talked in low tones in the back of Carrie's SUV. "You can let yourself in, and I'm sure she'll sleep right through it."

The cherry-sweet after-sex glow still vibrated through her as Imani leaned into to his Irish Spring–smelling body.

"Or...I could spend the night at your place instead?"

He put his arm around her, pulling her close in the back seat.

"I thought you'd never ask."

Soon, they arrived at Island Park, now deserted except for Zander's Prius. After extending their thanks to Tuck one last time, they piled into Zander's car and he drove the short distance to his studio, checking with her again to see if she wanted to stop at Gigi's first.

"No," Imani said, not letting go of his hand—not

wanting to ever let go of his hand—and bringing it up to her lips to kiss. "I'm not ready for my night with you to end. In fact, I'm not ready for my time with you to end."

Zander jolted, taking his eyes off the dark road momentarily to spear her with an incredulous glance. "What do you mean?"

"I mean, I'd like to date you. Again. Several times, in fact, and maybe even see how we can make a long-distance thing work between us." Imani's pulse quickened, and although the idea of that kind of commitment and its unplanned, tenuous nature made her nervous, she forged on. "You'll have to give me time to figure it out, but maybe there's a way. People do the remote work thing all the time now, and although it'll be hard if I take this manager position, maybe I can finagle things so we could...see each other after I go back to the city?"

"I waited a year for our first date. I'm ready to wait however long it takes for you."

The next morning dawned hot and sultry, and they had to use the Prius's air-conditioning in the early morning hours on the way over from Zander's studio to Grover Street.

Zander's sweet words rang in her head, like the last note of an orchestral finale as she snagged the spare key from under the cushion on the porch rocker. Despite the fact she and Zander had just enjoyed an evening in each other's arms, using his stash of condoms and her dancer's flexibility in the most creative, thrilling ways possible, she'd never felt so refreshed and rested. Worries about her career goals and life plans seemed miles away as she smiled happily, waving Zander off as he mounted the second porch step.

"Get, now! It's only seven o'clock, and if we wake Gigi, you're going to get an earful," Imani stage-whispered to him. "She lives to embarrass people, and she won't miss the chance to mess with you."

Through the closed door came the sound of Lancelot screeching.

She chuckled. "Now we're both caught."

Zander paused on the step, a frown creasing his brow.

"I think I'll hang right here until you get inside," he said. "Lancelot sounds distressed. Maybe he escaped again?"

Feeling that warm, tingling feeling again at his desire to watch over her, Imani thrust the key into the lock. She used her hip to bump the sticky door open.

"Suit yourself. That bird always sounds distressed—"

The word died on her lips as the early-morning sun's rays illuminated the foyer and staircase.

And the splayed, prone body of her grandmother at the bottom of the stairs.

# CHAPTER 18

Zander's heart stopped as Imani's scream slashed through the peaceful morning like an axe through dry wood.

"Gigi!" she shrieked. "Oh my God! Gigi!"

He was up the stairs and into the house before the last syllable had left her lips, dreading what he'd find.

Imani's grandmother lay half on her belly, half on her side. Though her eyes were closed, Zander could see the shallow, in-and-out movement of her ribs. She was breathing. He saw no blood, but something in the way she lay wasn't quite right. Her baby-blue cotton night-gown was shucked up to her thighs, revealing her pale, blue-veined legs, which were canted at an odd angle to her hips.

As Imani reached for her grandmother's shoulder, Zander called out, "Don't move her. I think she fell. Looks like she might've been climbing the stairs and took a tumble."

"Oh my God." Imani's hand detoured from her grand-mother's shoulder to her face, then darted to her forehead, gasping. "She's burning up! Why in the hell was she going upstairs? Where's my phone? We need to call 911—"

"Here. Use my phone." Zander tried to yank his cell out

of his pocket, intending to toss it to Imani, but it seemed to get snagged on something.

"No, the landline is better so they can send the address to the dispatch quicker." She vaulted to her feet and raced toward the kitchen.

"Mrs. Foltz?" Zander leaned over, but before he could do anything other than ascertain the woman had a pulse in her neck and was breathing, the parrot was flapping toward him, claws aiming for his eyes as he swooped down from the upstairs banister.

"Son of a pickled BITCH!" shrieked Lancelot, his gray feathers rustling as he came to a stop on the prone woman's shoulder.

"Okay, boy, let's get you back in your cage, huh?" he cooed to the bird. Placing his hand out, he made a kissing noise and gently touched the bird right below his gray, feathered chest. The bird cocked his head at him, giving him a dubious, beady-eyed stare, then stepped up, one black-clawed foot at a time. He ruffled his feathers in an all-over shiver, then bent his neck until his dark beak was against Zander's palm, as if seeking pets.

Zander covered the short distance to the cage in the front parlor and locked the bird inside. He'd just knelt next to Mrs. Foltz again when Imani raced back to the front of the house, phone in hand. She shoved him out of the way before he could do anything more than take one of her grandmother's arms to touch the weak, thready pulse at her wrist.

"I've got it." Imani's lips were pale and her hands shook as she toggled the cordless phone to life.

"Let me get the pulse for you, and you can tell them—"

To his surprise, she slapped his hand away. "I should never, *ever* have left her last night," she breathed, dialing 911. "You don't ever leave sick people alone. And I let you talk me into it anyway."

*Whoa.*

Zander eased back and was opening his mouth to reply but stopped as she began talking to the dispatch.

"Yes, this is Imani Lewis, and we need an ambulance! My grandmother, Georgina Foltz, must have…" Her voice skipped, but she steadied herself on the next inhale. "She must have fallen. She's lying by the stairs, and she's got a fever and I can't rouse her."

Zander watched as Imani listened to the dispatcher and shook her head.

"No, she's got a pulse. She's breathing. It—it looks like she's sleeping. She recently had surgery on both knees…"

Imani continued talking to the dispatcher, and Zander rose, figuring out a way he could be helpful. He strode to the kitchen to grab a clean towel. Twisting the faucet knob to Cold, he wet the towel, wrung it out, and dashed back to Imani and her grandmother. Kneeling on the opposite side of the older woman's prone body, he applied the cool cloth to her hot forehead as Imani finished verifying the address of the bungalow.

"Hey, Mrs. Foltz?" he asked, crouching down to pat her hand as he held the compress to her head. "It's Zander. Can you hear—"

"Stop that!" Imani hissed, snatching the dish towel from his grip. "Stop touching her!"

Zander recoiled, settling his weight onto his heels. He watched Imani apply the cool towel herself, folding it over into a rectangle that exactly covered her grandmother's forehead. With delicate fingers, Imani smoothed back the blond-brown hair on Mrs. Foltz's head, her mouth set in a tight, grim line.

He knew she was distraught, but didn't she know he was here to help? He tried for a soothing tone. "You've got to calm down, Imani."

As soon as the words left his lips, he regretted them. Based on the way Imani's eyebrows rose to her hairline and her eyes bulged, he'd missed the mark soothing her in any way.

"I've got to. Calm. Down?" Her words were sharp and staccato. "Do you have any idea who this is, and what she means to me? And I left her here to...to—"

"Don't worry. She's a tough old bird." Zander tried a reassuring smile. "She's going to be fine."

"How can you possibly know that?" Her voice was high, teetering on shrill. "Look at you, smiling away. Not a care in the world. Reason number fifty-three why we won't work as anything more than a distraction."

Zander swallowed convulsively. "Is that all we are to each other? A distraction?"

"What else can this be, Zander?" Imani stopped smoothing back her grandmother's hair to pierce him with a glare. She threw her hands up. "Look, you're a good guy, but I was wrong. We're through. It's better for you, for everyone, if I go back to New York City."

"Just like that? You can turn what we have—what we've started—off like a light switch?"

"If it weren't for you, I'd have been here!" she shouted. "I should never have gotten involved with you. You're as

permanent as my lipstick color—a summer fling. All your
talk of 'being in the moment' means you're not ready to face
grown-up plans, like mortgages and retirement accounts and
kids. You act like working for permanent things—freaking
stability—ruins your vibe. I need a great partner in life—a
man who wants to be tied down forever. Embrace a future
plan. Not just float with wind, like some hot air—"

"Stop the damn yelling," Mrs. Foltz said in a voice
that sounded like sandpaper on rough wood. Her mouth
puckered in a grimace as her hand came up to flutter
aimlessly then settle back down by her side. "Can't a body
sleep around here?"

"Gigi?" Imani paused, mid-rant. She leaned over, brushing back her grandmother's hair with a shaking hand. "I'm
here. It's going to be okay."

"Amira? Is that you?" The old woman's hand rose feebly,
and her eyes cracked open, but she didn't turn her head.

Imani captured her grandmother's hand, chafing it and
kissing it as first one tear then another fell from her eyes,
racing down her cheeks.

"No, Gigi. It's me, Imani. Amira's daughter."

The sound of a siren wailing brought Zander's head
around and he stood. Putting aside Imani's words, he
strode out onto the front porch. Directing the EMTs into
the house, he held the door while they put Imani's grandmother in a neck brace, then on a backboard, and lifted her
onto the stretcher. He suggested that Imani get her purse
and her keys to follow the ambulance. She didn't answer
but raced to the kitchen, thankfully missing the part when
Mrs. Foltz cried out in pain after they jostled her while
hefting the stretcher into the ambulance.

Imani's face was frantic as she came tearing back into the foyer.

"Is she okay?" she asked, following the EMTs to the ambulance.

The EMT gave Imani a nod. "Looks like it's her hip, but we'll get her to the hospital so the doctors can see what else is going on and why she's running a fever. We're taking her to Jones Memorial if you want to meet up with your grandmother at the ER."

Zander walked behind them as they loaded Mrs. Foltz into the ambulance, taking it upon himself to reassure Mrs. Nowakowski as she came running down the street in a white bathrobe.

"She must've taken a spill in the night, and she's hurt her hip," Zander explained as the ambulance doors swung shut. Then he turned to Imani, his brain searching for and finding some way he could be helpful. "Leave your spare key in the same spot, and I'll bring over Ryker's old wheelchair for you. He doesn't need it now, and it's an ultralight one, so it'll be much easier for you to use when she recovers. Don't worry, she's going to be fine."

Imani spun to him as soon as her grandmother was loaded up, her hands trembling as she pointed at him. "There you go again, with the 'don't worry' attitude. I'm glad that works for you. I really am. But just saying she's going to be fine won't make it so. That is what reality looks like. I screwed up. I should've ended this weeks ago. In fact, I should've never let it start up again with you." She backed away.

"Imani, stop." He took a step toward her.

But she shook her head, tears skating down her cheeks. "I knew better. I did."

Then she turned, sprinting toward the car. Away from him.

Ten minutes later, he'd extracted himself from Mrs. Nowakowski's inquisition and drove to his mother's bakery, his hands shaking on the wheel as he put the Prius in park. He'd never been more relieved his mother owned a bakery than he was that morning, with the lights on and the sound of cheerful, sugared-up customer chatter greeting him as he opened the door and stepped onto the black-and-white-checked floor of PattyCakes.

His mom spotted him right away, her smile of welcome melting as she read his expression. He'd no sooner settled in a window seat far from the other patrons than she'd bustled over in her pink, frilly apron carrying two steaming mugs of coffee and a massive sweet roll on a chintz plate.

She slid the pastry to him and sat on the other side of the old, 1950s-style table with its boomerang print on top, handing him a fork as she settled into the chair.

"Tell me what happened."

And he did, starting with the balloon rally, alluding to the overnight stay, and ending with the awful last scene.

"Sounds like Georgina might have an infection in one of her knees or maybe a urinary tract infection making her feverish—that happened once to Nana Grace." His mom sipped her coffee. "Those UTIs can put you in an altered state pretty quick. It would explain why Georgina attempted the stairs in the first place. What about Imani? I'm guessing she's pretty broken up right now. Why aren't you with her?"

Zander shook his head. "She doesn't want my company

now. Or maybe ever again. She said...she couldn't be with a man who jokes all the time. She had the nerve to shame me for not having a mortgage and a damn 401(k) or whatever, as if those things matter in life. She's upset about her grandma, and I get that."

He was assuming his mother would jump to his defense. Be as flabbergasted by Imani's hurled accusations as he'd been.

Instead, she gazed at him over her coffee mug. "So you don't think there's any truth to her words?" his mom finally asked, pinning him with an "I expected more from you" expression that made him squirm.

"No, I don't see it. I run three ceramic studios in this county, and big deal—I don't want to post business hours. It's my shop, and it works for me." The back of his neck felt scalded as he continued to speak. "And so what if I don't own a house? That's not happiness, Mom. That's stuff."

"Zander, honey, you know I love you and your happy-go-lucky spirit." His mom put a hand over his on the table. "But you're not getting any younger. You can't afford to pretend you'll never be my age. That you'll never need a retirement account or the equity in a home you've paid off."

"By that time, I'll have equity in my businesses," he argued. "That'll be my retirement fund."

"Will it?" His mom cocked her head. "You rent the space for your other studios, but your brother owns the building here in Wellsville. Drake knew you'd missed out on a whole year of earnings by being at Walter Reed as Ryker's coach. He gifted you a fresh start."

"And I made good on that investment," he said,

defensive, his good humor gone. "I've expanded that into three studios."

"With whose funds? And with whose credit? It's none of my business, but you're sitting here in my restaurant, where I own the business and hold the mortgage. If I go under, the only one who's out money and whose credit history goes in the toilet is me. Can you say the same?"

Zander's jaw dropped open, and he closed it with a click. "I—I never thought about it that way."

"I'm so proud of you for your ceramic studios, honey, but there's a reason you've never been able to keep full-time employees for long. It's because you don't have regular business hours and the income stability that goes along with that. I'm not saying it's wrong to live for the present. I cannot imagine the pain you carry from your time overseas and as Ryker's support coach." She held up a hand, halting the objection bubbling up inside him. "But with Imani's past—her mother dying in a fire, and she and her father losing everything—can you blame her for wanting more stability than you seem able to offer?"

His arguments froze in his chest as he thought about it. He managed a chain but didn't have much to show for it. He rented the studio and the apartment above from his brother, and while he'd never paid back Drake's initial loan, he'd never figured his brother wanted or needed the money. That could be looked on as...being irresponsible. Truly, his only possession in the world was a Prius—a leased one, at that. While he had a couple of stocks he'd invested in for fun to learn the market during one of his finance classes, he'd never saved up for any sort of future cushion, and he hadn't cared...up until now.

His mom grabbed his hands in both of her own, shaking them for emphasis as she spoke.

"Son, I've never seen you happier than with Imani this summer. Maybe spend some time thinking about what's more important to you: living as a captive to your life's philosophy, or tethering yourself to a life filled with the love you deserve?" Releasing his hand, she stood, dusting off her apron and glancing guiltily at the queue of people forming in front of the bakery's curved glass display case. "I've got to go help Melissa. You take your time here. I love you, my sweet baby boy."

Zander stared at the cinnamon roll in front of him, blindly cutting into it and shoving a sticky, gooey piece into his mouth. He chewed woodenly, barely tasting it as he thought about his mother's words.

She was right.

It was time to examine his life with an ice-cold eye.

What, exactly, had he done with himself, after his active duty in the Marines and being Ryker's coach? Sure, he was there for his brothers and had helped out his fair share of people in the community, but was that all? He made a decent set of mugs and knew how to throw an epic ceramic-painting party. He'd dated a bunch of women for a few weeks, maybe a couple months, tops. But even though he was still friends with them, they'd likely give a similar reason as to why they hadn't worked: he was more of a plan-of-the-week, spur-of-the-moment, dancing-through-life guy.

He wasn't ever going to ever be "the one."

Unless he changed.

Nobody—not his brothers, or even his mother—knew

the real him, the person he was inside, what made him tick. Nobody knew how he still struggled with food and body image. Nobody knew he read philosophy about bees at night to make sense of things, or that he was a joker—a constant mood lightener—because that was a comfort zone for him and how he fit best into his family dynamics. Nobody expected him to be anything else but chill.

Nobody knew these things about him...except Imani.

Reaching into his shorts pocket, he found a pen. Snagging a napkin from the silver dispenser, he wrote out a to-do list based on a "now" plan and a "future" plan. Three cinnamon rolls and seven napkins later, he was done.

He examined his lists, and his course of action was obvious. He had hopes that this might demonstrate to Imani he was more than her perception of him. But as he stared down at the napkins covered in scribbles on the table, he realized it wasn't only about her or their relationship potential. It was about him. He'd spent years of his life looking down his nose at those who painstakingly sacrificed the now for a nebulous future. Since his time in Afghanistan—or more accurately, since the time spent with his brother as he recovered from his war injuries—he'd dedicated his life to Present-Day Zander. He'd also done his share to help out present-day friends and relatives, to be sure. But his single-minded focus on today, he now realized, came at the price of his future.

Present-Day Zander had been robbing Future Zander of happiness.

And that shit was not okay.

He didn't fully understand the steps necessary to get himself back on track. But he was blessed to know a lot of people smarter and better equipped to correct his course.

He pulled out his phone, scrolling through his contacts until he found the numbers he needed, and he began to dial.

# CHAPTER 19

Imani sat in the hospital room, watching the peaceful rise and fall of Gigi's chest as she slept. Although she'd never been much for praying, Imani made up for it during the days after her grandmother's emergency hip surgery, and she sent up another one now.

"Please let her hip be the only damage she's suffered."

The doctors said the worst of the infection had abated, and she'd come through the hip surgery with flying colors. Although she'd been awake off and on after the surgery, the pain medication had made her grandmother's conversations foggy and disjointed—nothing like her normal Gigi-like directness.

For good luck, she'd even worn the top Gigi had bought her—the vintage white Hermès shirt with the keys printed along the neckline. She'd just picked it up from Ray's Dry Cleaners, and the man had magically restored it to new, as Zander had promised.

Imani frowned at the thought of the youngest Matthews brother and their last exchange. She stared down at the speckled composition notebook on her lap, examining the journaling prompts written in the happiest pink gel pen she owned.

The only benefit to Gigi's emergency surgery was that it had been the final straw breaking whatever stupid reasons Imani had concocted for not calling her therapist. She'd reached out that very day Gigi broke her hip, requesting and getting a telehealth appointment, and was currently working on the assignment the clinician had given her— four questions she needed to answer.

*What's the best thing that happened to you yesterday?*
*Same for the last month?*
*How about in the last year?*
*In your life?*

Clicking her pen, she poised the tip over the empty blanks under the questions, determined to fill them in. On the surface, the questions sounded deceptively simple, yet she was struggling with them all the same.

She thought about the first question.

What was the best thing that had happened to her yesterday?

"Nothing." She snorted softly. Yesterday and the day before had held little joy other than watching her grandmother wake up now and again, unless she counted the ten-minute visit Kate had paid to the hospital, her arms full of flowers, her face full of worry.

"It's not your fault," said her best friend, giving her a fierce hug. "You let that guilt go, Imani. I mean it. It's not healthy, and it's not true."

But it felt true.

Gigi's accident had resurfaced Imani's memories of that tragic call at ballet camp. How gutted she'd been to learn the house fire that killed her mother was the result of a stupid mistake—leaving a candle burning during a nap. If she'd only been there to blow it out for her, like she'd done dozens of times before, her mother would still be here. And now with her grandmother...had Imani only been home, she'd have seen that Gigi was getting disoriented. Maybe she'd have heard her downstairs, moving around in the middle of the night, and would have met her before she'd gotten on the staircase and fallen...

Imani dashed the sudden tears from her eyes, determined not to cry again. Instead, she focused on the question and wrote down that the best thing that had happened to her yesterday was seeing Kate's sweet face and knowing her best friend was there for her, like a solid rock foundation, never crumbling, never failing to hold her up.

Scrawling that in the journal, she went to the next question.

*Same for the last month?*

What had been the best thing that had happened this month?

Her mind immediately flashed upon her time with Zander. At the studio wheel. Creating the tiles. Eating lunch with him and Gigi, laughing and joking.

Then there was the hot-air balloon ride and the sense of wonderful wholeness that had overtaken and buoyed her with a swell of rightness so full-bellied it felt as though it were she, not the balloon, lifting the basket to ascending heights.

Before she could second-guess herself, she wrote this down, including the sensation she'd had soaring over the fields, trees, houses, and river below—the belief that she was limitless. Free. But it was more than the ride that made her feel that way. Objectively, it was Zander, not the activities this past month, that had made her less stressed.

Imani glanced at her grandmother, still dozing, her pale, wrinkled face looking so much older and more fragile when at rest.

Sighing, she glanced back at the journal. The last question was the one she'd most dreaded.

*How about in the last year?*

Imani screwed her forehead up in concentration. Beyond this summer, what ranked as the best thing this year? She propped her feet on the rails of her grandmother's hospital bed, tapping the pen against the journal as she racked her brain.

Well, from a career perspective, it was probably being offered the coveted raise and promotion at Cerulean Books. Arguably, it was the best thing that had happened in the years she'd worked for the publisher. She wrote it down. Then she drew a line through it, skipping to the next question.

*In your life?*

She heaved another sigh.

Was this question answerable for anybody? Except for Zander, could anyone pinpoint the "best" thing that had happened to them in their whole life?

Imani thought for a moment. Kate would definitely be able to answer it; she was sure her best friend would quickly state it was falling in love with and marrying Drake, followed by becoming pregnant, which would likely soon be eclipsed by having their baby.

Absent that, Kate would have said it was her career.

It was something she'd always been envious of, how Kate had gone after her dream of being an event planner. She'd disregarded her family's dismay when she didn't pursue medicine, instead going all in on what made her happy. While Imani arguably had a career that was just as financially viable as Kate's, she lacked the daily passion her friend still had after years of planning weddings and other events.

Imani frowned, swiping away the tears that never seemed to end.

The problem was she wasn't sure how she'd define "best" any longer.

Since getting to know Zander, her value system had altered. Now the word "best" wasn't interchangeable with "success." To use Zander logic, "best" had little to do with money, promotions, the size of her apartment, or her 401(k) account. Now "best" meant what filled her bucket of bliss—things that made her thrilled to wake up in the morning.

"I don't know anymore." A ball of guilt and grief thickened in her throat. "I have no bliss moments. Nothing to fill a bucket, for sure. What in the hell am I doing with my life?"

"Damned if I know."

Her grandmother's gravelly voice made Imani jump, upending her journal and pen, which clattered to the floor. She gripped the side rails, leaning over to see her grandmother's dark-brown eyes open, blinking owlishly at the light.

"Gigi?" she asked, wiping tears from her face and snatching up her grandmother's soft, pale hand. "You're awake! How are you feeling?"

"Like I've been ridden hard and put away wet." Her voice was a hoarse gargle. "I'm thirsty as hell, and my right side feels like I was kicked by a mule."

Imani scrambled for the water pitcher on the nightstand, pouring a bunch into a plastic cup. She angled a bendy straw to Gigi's lips for her grandmother to drink as she explained what had happened.

"You're in Jones Memorial Hospital, where you were taken by ambulance for an emergency hip surgery two days ago. You had an undiagnosed urinary tract infection, and you spiked a fever in the night, became disoriented, and...you fell. B-but the doctors say you're going to be fine..." Imani trailed off, pressing a hand to her throat where the knot of guilt had lodged itself. "Maybe I should page the nurse, or something? Tell them you're awake?"

She searched for the call button on the metal bed frame, but she wasn't able to distinguish the right button among the tubes and wires attached to her grandmother. Her eyes swam with tears, making everything blurry.

"I can't find it." Her tears spilled over. She'd thought she'd cried herself out of tears over the last two days, but it was like she'd turned into a never-ending fountain of shame.

Gigi's hand covered hers, stopping her frantic searching.

"Take a breath, little Shypoke." Gigi squinted, patting at her own face. "Where are my glasses?"

"They're right here." Imani took the glasses off the bed-side table and eased them onto Gigi's nose, securing the frames behind her ears.

"Much better. Now, can you move the head of this bed up so I can see you?" Gigi waited as Imani found and pressed the button to raise her to a sitting position. Her grandmother's eyes were brighter now, regaining their former sparkle as she looked around the hospital room. Then she focused on Imani, her lips pursed. "If I'm going to be fine, why in the hell are you crying?"

Then, like jabbing a hole into a full bucket of water, Imani sobbed out her story—how she'd left on a date with Zander, forgotten her purse, gone up in a hot-air balloon, then gotten stranded in a cow field in Pennsylvania.

"I tried to call," she said between hitching breaths, "but Zander's phone had no cell service, and by the time the pilot came back with the chase team, it was late and I didn't want to wake you. I...I spent the night with him, Gigi."

"It's 'bout damn time."

Imani forced herself to look into her grandmother's eyes as she admitted, "But if I'd come home, I'd have known you had a fever, and none of this would have happened. If only I hadn't been—"

Her grandmother cut her off before she could say "so selfish" and took the sentence in a different direction.

"—living your life. Like you should be at thirty-one years old." Gigi shushed her, patting Imani's hand. "Stop crying now. Dry your tears."

Imani plucked two rough-as-sandpaper tissues from the oblong box on the bedside table and wiped her eyes, then blew her nose.

Her grandmother nodded once. "There, that's my girl. Now listen to me. None of this is your fault. I felt fine when you left, and I went to bed. I don't remember getting up, and I don't remember falling down, but I do remember one thing—how happy I was you were going on a date with your young man. Zander."

Imani goggled her eyes. "You remembered his name?"

"What do you mean? I always knew his name." Gigi reached for the water, and Imani attempted to hold it for her again, but her grandmother shooed her hand away. She drank deeply, then settled her head back against the pillows, handing Imani her cup as she speared her with a look. "If I'd have felt sick in any way, I'd have called Noreen, or Aggie, or even 911. No different than if you weren't in town. I asked you to stay with me this summer not because I wanted you to wait on me, but because I thought you needed a break—just like on summer vacations from school when you'd come here for a month, and we'd play May-I, weed the garden, and eat a whole lotta gulyás. You've got this guilt over not being around for me, for your mom, for your best friend, and you've got to let it go. Your only job, Imani Regina Lewis, is to live your life and *be happy*."

"I don't think I know how to do that anymore, Gigi," Imani whispered.

Gigi jiggled Imani's hand for emphasis.

"It's like riding a bike. And that sweet Matthews boy can show you how to live—how to grab life by the balls and *uumph*!" Her grandmother raised a fist in the air and squeezed it, shaking life's imaginary testicles violently before letting her hand drop. "You do know that boy loves you, don't you?"

Imani sighed. "I'm not so sure anymore."

Four days later, Gigi's doctors declared her ready to go home, although she still had to report to physical therapy three days a week to regain full functionality of her legs and hip. Imani drove the few short blocks to Grover Street, rattling off the doctor's restrictions to her grandmother again—more for her own benefit than for Gigi's.

"When are you going home again?" Gigi grumbled, listening to the list and Imani's strict tone. "You're starting to be no fun at all."

"Two weeks, and you'll be rid of me. At least, for a little while." Imani flicked a look to her, and, figuring she was healthy enough for this news, decided to tell her grandmother her new plan—one she'd concocted as a result of her therapy homework. "I've decided not to take the manager promotion, Gigi. I know it's more money, but it's also more headaches and offers less of what I like most about my job—working directly with authors. I've talked to my boss at Cerulean Books, and we're going to figure out a way for me to work remotely. The details aren't ironed out, but I'm not renewing the lease on my Bronx apartment. I'm ready for something . . . different."

Gigi reached over to put a hand on her arm. "I knew you'd eventually figure it out, Shypoke. You always do."

Imani pulled up to Gigi's bungalow, racing to unlock the door and get things inside.

Just as promised, Zander had dropped off his brother's old wheelchair. She grabbed it from the foyer and jogged back out to the car, setting it up for her grandmother.

By the time Imani yanked the wheelchair, with her grandmother in it, backward up the four porch steps and into the house, she was winded—and thankful she'd spent the nights stress-cleaning and widening the area next to Gigi's bed. By shoving the full-size bed against the far wall, she'd been able to create a large central spot for the wheelchair to maneuver, helping the transfer from chair to bed and back again.

Lancelot popped his gray head out of a pair of red jockey shorts and gave a cheerful wolf whistle. "Bitch? Good boy get a treat?" Gripping the bars of his cage with his black beak and claws, he slid down the length of it like a fireman's pole, plopping onto the newspaper-covered bottom so he could be closer to Gigi's bedside.

When Imani unlatched the cage so Gigi could toss in some treats, the bird didn't look at the scattered fruit and nuts. Instead, he flew to Gigi's shoulder and started whistling the song Imani had played on repeat since Gigi went to the hospital.

Her grandmother's jaw dropped open. Then she smiled, her face softening as her eyes misted with tears.

"You got him to whistle 'Take Me Out to the Ball Game' like he used to with Arlo. How in the world did you do that?"

"Lancelot and I have spent some quality time together while you were in the hospital."

Before Gigi would agree to be tucked in, she insisted on seeing the cleaning and organizing Imani had done while she was away. Obediently, Imani wheeled her and Lancelot from room to room, showing her the patched ceiling medallion she'd repainted white satin so you couldn't see the repair Zander had put in. Then she took Gigi out to the back porch to show her the newly planted garden with zinnias and dwarf sunflowers, all weeded now so you could see the rosebushes and peonies in bloom.

By the time she wheeled Gigi back to her room,

Imani made a mental note to drop off a thank-you card and homemade dinner to Ryker this week for his loan of the ultralight chair. Sure, she'd met the guy a couple of times throughout the years working with Drake and most recently at the baby shower, but she didn't know him well enough to warrant this equipment loan. It was all because of Zander—to whom she owed so much this summer—and her heart pinged again.

Most of all, she owed Zander an apology.

A guilty knot formed in her stomach, and she pushed the thought of seeing him out of her head. She still didn't know what to say. She'd deal with that later when she had more time to think. Now she needed to focus on her grandmother.

"There." She propped Gigi up on a mound of pillows, wincing every time her grandmother's lips tightened in pain as she settled in. "Now, what can I get you? I made some macaroni salad for us, or if you're not feeling that, I can heat up some tomato soup. What sounds good?"

Instead of answering, Gigi looked over Imani's shoulder toward the fireplace. Her face relaxed in a soft smile. "Oh, you fixed it! You little Shypoke. I didn't think you'd pull it off, but sure enough, I can't tell which ones were broken."

Imani spun around.

The fireplace tiles were all in place. No longer did the antique fixture look gap-toothed and dilapidated, and the colors she'd mixed for the underglaze, per Zander's advice, were the perfect shades of rose pink and variegated green, matching the originals. He'd given them the final glaze and firing, then grouted them in to match the rest, using the key under the porch rocker's cushion for more than the wheelchair.

He'd wanted everything to be perfect for Gigi. For her.

Even though she'd said awful things to him, he'd still kept his word and fixed it, because he knew how important it was.

Her throat tightened, strangling the words as she spoke. "It wasn't me. I made the tiles. But Zander did the rest."

Imani gazed at the beautiful work he'd done to fix her grandmother's favorite piece in the whole bungalow.

"That Zander is a sweetheart," Gigi said, her voice pleased but weary. "Looks like he left you a note."

Imani spotted the envelope on the fireplace mantel, next to the framed picture of Gigi and Arlo on their wedding day.

Crossing to the fireplace, she saw his handwriting—all blocky, uppercase letters, as precise and careful as a drafts-man's hand. When she lifted the envelope, she noticed there was something bulky inside.

Ripping it open, she was disappointed not to see a note from him. Instead, it was a piece of thick, creamy paper with a Wellsville address on Madison Street—written in those same blocky letters, signed with a 'Z' in a flourish at the bottom, with a key taped underneath.

"What the hell is that? Is it a key to his studio, do you think?" Gigi peered over from her bed. "Bring it here and let me see."

Imani did, and her grandmother read the address and shook her head. "That's not the studio. His place is over there by Veterans Memorial Park." Gigi eased her head back, looking somehow disappointed. "I thought he was going to give you his key, telling you to come over so you could talk. Work things out. But that address is in the business section of Madison Street. Why do you think your boyfriend wants you to go to some store, and why do you need a key to do it?"

"He's not my boyfriend," Imani whispered around the lump in her throat. "I've told you that a million times."

And for the first time, the truth of those words stung like acid.

Suddenly, her cell phone rang, startling Lancelot into a fire-alarm imitation. He flapped his wings rapidly, hovering in the air until he landed on Gigi's chest, chirping and chittering in irritation before settling in to let her pet his neck feathers.

At first, Imani's heart had bounced at the ringing phone, assuming it was Zander giving her a chance to thank him and apologize, or at least checking in on her and explaining the mystery of the key and address.

But it was Kate, and her heart fell back into a regular rhythm as she swiped to answer, putting her best friend on speaker, figuring she was calling to wish Gigi a speedy recovery.

"Hey, Katie. I just got Gigi home and tucked into bed—"

"Imani!" Kate's voice was panicked, her breath coming in puffs that made her voice on speakerphone go all snowy-windy sounding. "Either I peed myself or my water just broke. Drake's not answering his cell. He's with Ryker, testing out Ry's new build, and they must be somewhere out of cell range. I'm having contractions. I think—I think this baby is coming early!"

"Okay. I'm on it." Imani stuffed the letter with the key in

her shorts pocket to figure out later. "But you're still three weeks early, so maybe it's those cramps you're supposed to get—those Brandon Hickey things."

"Braxton-Hicks," both Gigi and Kate said in stereo.

"Babies don't care about due dates," Gigi said. Then she spoke to the phone. "Kate, honey, you need to relax and quit puffing like a train or you're going to hyperventilate. Breathe deep and slow, and keep reminding yourself this is what women have done since the dawn of time. You are going to be fine."

"I can't remember when to *hoo* or *ha* anymore, and I don't know which outfit to put in the hospital bag, and I haven't even washed the new baby blankets in Dreft yet, so I'm not sure if I should pack that, because what if the baby is allergic to whatever starch is on it, and— OHHH!" Kate's panicked list of worries halted as if she'd run into a wall.

Imani heard a gasp, followed by a low groan on the other end of the line that morphed into a string of cursing that used the f-bomb as a noun, verb, adjective, and adverb in an impressive stream-of-a-sailor's-conscience way.

"Katie, are you okay?" she asked when the cursing stopped.

"She's all right," Gigi said, with a wry laugh. "But that was no Braxton-Hicks. I've been at the bedside of more than one laboring woman, and that was the sound of a contraction. A fierce one. Baby Matthews will be here sooner rather than later. Kate, put a bath towel between your legs. Imani is going to be there in a jiffy to drive you to the hospital."

"But what about you?" Imani asked, panicked by the

thought of leaving her grandmother, but equally panicked by the thought of not being there for her best friend.

"I'll call Noreen to come sit with me, so you won't be a worrywart."

Imani kept Kate on the phone as she threw some focus items into her black tote, got herself a bottled water, and waited until Mrs. Nowakowski pulled up to the curb, tires screeching. She met the woman, who was dressed in an embroidered balloon T-shirt, at the door. Shoving a piece of paper with her cell number on it into her hand, she explained what had happened and asked the old Sunday school teacher to call if Gigi started feeling poorly.

"Are you sure you're okay, Gigi?" Imani asked, muting the phone to turn to her grandmother. "Last time I left you—"

"Oh, for Pete's sake," Gigi said, waving her away. "I'll be fine. Noreen and I can catch up and play some cards. We might even shoot a TikTok video to show off Lancelot's new skill. You take care of Kate and find Drake."

"Lord help that man if he's not there to see his baby entering this world. That kind of thing will land him in the doghouse for months." Mrs. Nowakowski nodded knowingly. "Drake thinks he knows horror? Try being shut out of the sweet shack until the snow flies. I've seen it happen."

Imani grimaced. She never could get used to the no-nonsense, sex-talking, embroidered-shirt-wearing bluntness of the church lady.

Carefully, she unmuted the phone.

"Katie, Mrs. Nowakowski's here, so I'm on my way. I need to hang up with you now so I can reach Zander. If anyone can track down Drake and Ryker, it's him. He won't let Drake miss his child's birth." Imani raced out the front door, the truth of her words ringing in her voice as she spoke them. "I guarantee it."

"But if he's with his brothers, he may not have reception—"

Kate stopped speaking as Imani jumped in the Green Grabber and twisted the key, the car roaring to life.

"Katie? Are you okay?"

The other end of the line was filled with whooshing breath sounds, like a class of little ballerinas after a three-minute, dance-out-the-wiggles session in between ballet and tap classes.

Another contraction.

Imani checked the car clock as she pulled away from the curb. She couldn't be sure, but she thought she'd checked the time on her phone during the last contraction, and this one couldn't be more than five minutes later. She noted the time so she could track it accurately as she came to a stop at a red light two blocks from the Matthews mansion.

"Katie?"

"I'm fine." Her friend's voice was shaky and scared and miles from the land where "fine" lived. "Front gate is unlocked. Call Zander and I'll meet you at the door."

She hung up, and Imani used the stoplight to her advantage, toggling on her cell phone to her Favorites menu and pressing the number next to Zander's name. He answered after the first ring.

"Imani? I was hoping you'd call when you got the envelope. Can you give me five minutes and I can meet you down there?"

For a second, Imani didn't know what he meant, but then she remembered the address and key in her pocket.

"I can't. I need your help. Actually, Katie needs your help. My help, too. Our help—"

"Whoa. Slow down. Tell me what you need," he said in that confident, capable baritone she'd missed so much these past few days.

Imani updated him on Kate's contractions and the fact that her best friend couldn't reach Drake. By the time she'd finished, she was screeching to a halt next to the bat-winged gates of the Matthews's imposing brick-red Victorian.

"I'm picking up Katie now. Can you find Drake?"

"I'll have him there in time," Zander said, and she heard the *ding-ding* sound of his car's ignition sequence. "Promise me two things. One, you will drive safely. The hospital is five minutes away, so you don't need to speed. Two, keep your cell phone on. When this is over, we need to talk."

Imani gave a nervous laugh as she vaulted out of the car and toward the front gates. "Deal."

Forty minutes later, Kate was admitted to a room, examined, and put into a hospital gown. She was busy huffing out breaths with Imani as the doctor watched her contraction via a monitor attached to her belly.

As soon as the contraction ended, and the heart-monitor-like contraption started trending down again from the spike, the doctor—a no-nonsense woman dressed in scrubs, her white coat, and a pair of blue glasses—nodded in satisfaction.

"You're beginning transition," she said, the word ping-ing in Imani's head from class as the time when things start to go southward, from a pain perspective, fast. "I would imagine you'll be pushing in under an hour."

"B-but," Kate panted, her face painted with worry, "I thought with the first baby your labor lasted for hours? My husband isn't here yet, and I only started contracting an hour ago. Have you seen my birth plan? While I took Lamaze classes, I said I wanted to see how the contractions were before deciding whether to have it naturally. And now that I've had an hour's worth, I'd very much like to have an epidural."

The doctor checked her watch, a half smile on her lips.

"No time for an epidural, Mrs. Sweet-Matthews. You're already nine centimeters dilated and almost completely effaced. You'll be pushing in probably forty-five minutes, plan or not." The doctor chuckled ruefully. "You first-time moms and your birth plans. I've had three kids, and let me tell you, birth will not be the first time they don't do things according to your schedule, so get used to it. Oh," she said, stopping before she left the room, "tell the father if he wants to see his child born, he'd better get here within the hour. You're moving fast for a first-timer."

Kate gave Imani a look of sheer panic. "What do we do?"

Despite wanting to panic right along with her, Imani thought about what Zander—Mr. Zen himself—would do in this situation. She gazed at the charm dangling from her wrist.

Now.

Heart.

Love this moment.

Imani pinned on her most Zander-like smile, all cocky

and assuming something epic and insanely fun was coming, and she grinned at her best friend.

"Katie, Zander will find Drake and get him here before you deliver. Meanwhile, we're going to take it one contraction at a time, because in a little while, we're going to meet your new baby. Isn't that incredible?"

Like a wrinkled sheet that met a hot iron, Kate's face smoothed. Her green eyes lit up and she squeezed Imani's hand, smiling with wonder.

"You're right. I can't wait to see who the baby looks like—"

And then her best friend stopped talking, turning abruptly to the right. She clutched the kidney-shaped basin she'd been given.

And she puked.

Imani held her best friend's hand, breathed through her mouth, and fervently hoped for a happily ever after.

# CHAPTER 20

Zander knew Ryker was a creature of habit. If he was going to show off the pizzazz on the '68 Chevy Impala he'd just restored, he'd do it where speed limits didn't matter.

Like on the unused side of the airport runway, far from traffic. And cell reception.

Zander pulled into Wellsville's tiny airport, which sat high atop a wooded hill a few miles from town. His brothers both knew the owner—Ryker because of his abilities with engines of all kinds, and Drake because he flew in and out of the airport in a helicopter he leased for trips back and forth to his publisher. The airport's owner was always happy to let them take over the long strip of straight asphalt carved into the hilltop as long as no flights were scheduled to land or take off.

The Prius complained as he goosed the accelerator down the runway until he found his brothers. He flagged them down, and Ryker pulled up so their driver's-side windows aligned. His middle brother's close-shaven, military-stern face was flushed and alight with the happiness that came only when he was driving. Fast.

"Hey, did you decide to join us?" Ryker jerked his thumb

toward the back seat. "Drake's already riding shotgun, but you should be able to squeeze your ass into the back seat, as long as you leave your ego behind."

Before Zander could reply, Drake's eyes widened behind his chunky black glasses. He leaned over Ryker to pin Zander with his infamously intense writer's gaze.

"It's Kate, isn't it? She's gone into labor?" At Zander's nod, Drake's face brightened. But then his mouth pressed into a tight line. "She's early. By three weeks. She must be frantic."

"Imani's with her at Jones Memorial." Zander checked his phone as it chimed with a text from her. "She said they're admitted, and they're in room 316...the doctor said she's almost ready to push. You've got to go. Now."

Drake nodded. "Get me there, Ry."

Ryker gunned the Impala, leaving a strip of rubber on the pavement. Yet when the matte-black Chevy reached the main road, his brother was cautious, looking both ways and staying well within the speed limit the whole way to town.

"It's not as if there's a baby coming or anything," Zander growled, gripping the steering wheel as he putted behind his normally lead-footed brother.

While his car felt mired in molasses, his mind raced. Imani had called him first in an emergency. That had to count for something. Didn't it?

No.

He wasn't going to torture himself anymore. She wasn't interested in a relationship. And he wasn't interested in a fling.

They were at an impasse.

Even so, he'd busted his ass this week. Sure, some of it was his final gift to her—a gift he hoped showed how serious he was about her—and he was proud of the results. But that was nothing compared to the work he'd done for his future self these past few days.

A meeting with Leo, his boot camp buddy turned financial adviser, revealed his finances were in worse shape than he'd thought. A mess, actually. Nothing Zen about it.

"You're going to have to make some tough choices," Leo said. "You don't have any liquidity the way you're running your business. You're paying too much in rent and you're bleeding money in redundant equipment, supplies, and staff. You need to downsize."

This week, he'd closed the Friendship and Cuba locations, welcoming those staff who could manage the commute to work in the Wellsville studio, where he posted standard business hours: Tuesday through Friday from four p.m. to ten p.m. and Saturday from ten a.m. to four p.m., with evening parties still by appointment. He sold off the extra pottery wheels and supplies he didn't need to Alfred University's art program and used his contacts there to secure a ceramics teaching gig two mornings a week—something he'd been doing, albeit casually and inconsistently—for art students there for years.

Some of the money from the sold equipment went into starting a savings account that he would add to monthly until he'd paid back the start-up funds, plus interest, that he'd borrowed from Drake so many years earlier. Of course, since neither his brother nor sister-in-law would hear of taking money from him, he'd used a more circuitous route.

He'd set up a savings account for the baby. His future

niece or nephew could use the funds someday for college or maybe a first car.

The rest of the funds and his saved rent were going toward closing costs.

With the help of a cheerleader he'd dated in high school, who was now a fancy commercial lawyer, he had a contract pending on the building where he lived and worked. Drake had been surprised by his request, but understood Zander's need for this autonomy and had agreed to Zander putting up the down payment and fees required to remove Drake's name from the mortgage and the deed. In just thirty more days, he, Zander Freaking Matthews, was going to own something for the first time in his entire life.

He had a plan to take care of Future Zander.

Planning felt good. Damn if Imani hadn't been right all along.

His last remaining task was to pull her aside and tell her. Everything. Lay it on the line one last time.

Zander pulled in behind his brothers at the hospital. They sprinted through the entrance and were quickly given directions to room 316 on the maternity floor.

"Dude, it's going to be fine," Zander said as Drake—fidgeting, tense with worry—and Ryker stared at the elevator's buttons, as if the circles with *L*, *1*, *2*, and *3* contained the mysteries of the universe. "It's Kate. She'll have it under control. Plus, with Imani at her side, I wouldn't be surprised if the two of them have their planners out, using every spare minute between contractions to create an event spreadsheet for the baby's baptism."

Drake adjusted his glasses, flashing a brief smile. "You're probably right."

They exited the elevator as soon as the doors opened, heading past the nurse's station toward room 316.

A woman could be heard yelling in the distance, and Drake looked at Zander. "Wait. Decorations? Do you think I should have picked up balloons? Or flowers?"

"C'mon. We're talking Kate and Imani here," Zander said, giving his biggest grin.

Drake smiled back, relieved. "You're right. Those two have probably already..." Drake trailed off as they stopped in front of the closed door to room 316.

The woman inside yelled in pain. As soon as the low, guttural noise cut off, there came the sound of Kate's voice in an angry, un-Kate-like tone. "Where is my damn husband?!"

Drake pushed the door open.

To bedlam.

Zander and Ryker flanked their older brother in the door-way where they stood frozen, taking in the wild tableau of room 316.

Zander's artist's eye noted the stuffed tiger balanced on Kate's bulging belly and a pink plastic emesis bowl on the table. Next to it was a planner open to a page with a printed Excel spreadsheet. Only the head and upper shoulders of the doctor could be seen between his sister-in-law's legs, which were jammed in gleaming metal stirrups that pushed her knees practically up to her ears. Kate's face was a mottled red and white, and her pretty features were screwed up in a ferocious grimace. Her auburn hair hung in lank, sweat-damp hanks. Machines were hooked up to her in an assortment of tubes and wires, and a nurse stood to one side of the doctor, dipping out of sight under the covering across Kate's legs with a white bunch of gauze. The material was bright red with blood when she reemerged to dispose of it in the hazardous-waste bin at the side of the room.

It was a lot to take in.

His gaze sought out Imani in the chaos.

She stood like the Marine outside the Tomb of the Unknown Soldier, at attention, gazing with military focus at the wall over the bed as Kate gripped Imani's wrists with both hands to stare at . . .

Imani's sneakers.

Imani held her running sneakers in one hand, while the other hand braced Kate's shoulder. Kate muttered something under her breath. As soon as Imani spotted them entering, she sent a warning look at the door.

All three men interpreted it correctly, staying where they were.

Kate huffed a series of *hee*s and *hoo*s, intermingled with a couple of choice curses that Zander was surprised his sparkly, sunshiny sister-in-law knew.

"Stop pushing, Mrs. Matthews," the doctor said as she popped her head up from between Kate's knees. "I can see the cord. I need you to breathe while I try and shift it so your baby's oxygen supply isn't compromised."

Drake stiffened, and Zander put a hand on his brother's shoulder at the same time as Ryker did on the opposite side, both comforting their oldest brother while at the same time holding him back as the doctor worked.

Ten tense seconds later, Kate's grimace eased and the panting stopped.

"That's it." Imani's voice was light and easy. "Now take

a cleansing breath, and look at who's arrived. Just in time, as promised."

Kate swiveled her head to the door, sinking back into the pillows with exhaustion. Her deeply bloodshot eyes swam with fear and relief as she smiled.

The doctor looked up from between Kate's knees once more, taking in the crowd at the door. Her face was calm, but serious.

"I think I got the cord shifted from around the baby's neck, but we're going to get a quick ultrasound to make sure everything's okay. Until I tell you, it's critical you don't push, Mrs. Matthews. Understand?"

Kate gave a tense nod, then refocused on her husband. Her eyes filled with tears. "Drake, I was so worried. Thank God you're here. Imani, can you fill him in so he can take over for the next contraction?"

Quick as a flash, Imani skirted around the bed, dressed in a melon-colored shirt and a pair of white shorts, her no-show socks skidding slightly on the gray hospital floor tiles as she halted in front of them.

"Here's the deal." Imani focused on Drake without sparing time for a hello or a smile. "She's at the end of transition, so she's puked twice, and the pain is pretty intense since there wasn't time for an epidural. The focus objects I brought were a fail, but the good news is she likes these." Imani thrust her Brooks running sneakers at Drake.

He took them in one hand, brow wrinkling in confusion. "What should I do with them?"

"Hold them. She counts the holes in the top here." She pointed to the teeny, mesh-like air vents along the sneakers' toe boxes. "She'll have another contraction in about thirty seconds, and when she does, do *not* move the shoes and do *not* talk until it's over. Don't breathe on her, either— point your mouth toward the bed, so your breath doesn't touch her skin. It distracts her from counting, and she says the pain is worse when she doesn't count. She's using the Lamaze method to resist the urge to bear down. The monitors on the baby's head are showing lower heartbeats than they'd like to see, and you just heard the rest from the doctor."

"Got it. Thank you for being here with her." Drake squeezed Imani's arm then strode past his publicist and to his wife's side, kissing her head and murmuring to her.

"Let's give them some time alone." Imani swept Zander and Ryker out of the room with her. Once the door closed, her expression changed from serenity to stark horror. Imani's gaze went from Zander to Ryker, her voice hollow when she next spoke. "Trust me, unless you don't *ever* want children, you don't want to stick around for the next contraction. I have never seen another human being in so much physical pain before. Until we figured out the sneaker trick, she was writhing on the bed like she was trying to escape the prison of her own body. It's terrifying. Watching it makes you feel—"

"Helpless," both Zander and Ryker said at the same time. Zander caught his brother's gaze over Imani's head.

They knew. It didn't take bro-lepathy—just their shared experience at Walter Reed.

Anyone staying there—coach or patient—had encountered the wretched, bone-rattling combination of fear and helplessness when you, or someone you loved, endured pain that ratcheted up the scale to an unbearable threshold . . . then went beyond.

Ryker's face got tight. "I'm going to the gift store. Buy some flowers or a congratulations card."

He executed a perfect pivot, his hands cupped at his thighs so that his thumbs pointed down the seam of his trousers—an exact execution of the form drilled into recruits from day one in the Corps. Then he strode down the hallway, opting for the door that said *Stairs* instead of the elevator. Zander knew his brother well enough to know he'd likely sprint up and down those stairs for a good ten minutes to work off that emotion.

Imani's face looked stricken. "I . . . forgot he lived that pain," she whispered. "That was so insensitive of me. I should go apologize."

Zander waved his hand in dismissal. "No, he isn't freaked out by Kate's pain. He'd be the first to tell you what every Marine has heard a billion times by the time boot camp is over—pain is just weakness leaving the body. He's more freaked out there will be a new Matthews baby, and he's the godparent for the rest of his days. My bro has just realized there will now be a tiny human looking up to him forever. And it's wigging him out."

Just then, Kate yelled from behind the door—that same guttural noise they'd heard upon exiting the elevator, except this time it was followed by two sibilant words.

"Ssstaaayyy ssstiiillll!" Kate hollered in a way that sounded like her jaw was wired shut.

Imani grimaced. "Drake moved the sneakers. You do *not* move the sneakers. I told him that."

Zander chuckled. "He'll learn. Let's take a seat." He gestured to the two chairs under the window beside Kate's room. "I'm guessing she's going to be a while, and you look like you need to get off your feet. Besides, if they catch you without shoes in here, there will be hell to pay, focus item or not. Nurses are hypervigilant about the possibility of slipping, trust me."

Imani glanced down, startled, as if she'd forgotten she'd given her sneakers to the cause. She settled in the seat next to him, perching on the edge, with her long, tanned legs crossed in front of her. Then, as if realizing that put her shoeless feet on display, she tucked them under the chair, crossing them at the ankle.

Her shoulders slumped, and she turned to face him. "Thank you so much for bringing over Ryker's old wheelchair. And for grouting in Gigi's tiles. They turned out beautiful, and it was such a lovely surprise. I was going to reach out and thank you, when Kate called. Then it got all crazy."

He shrugged off her thanks. "You did the work. I just stuck them up there."

"I wanted to tell you more than that. I'm truly sorry, Zander. What I said to you when we found Gigi on Saturday was rotten, and it wasn't true. None of what happened to my grandmother was your fault." Her expression was bleak, as if she had little hope he'd accept her apology. "I've still got control issues—carrying this guilt of not being there to save my mom. My therapist says I probably always will. When I saw Gigi lying there..."

"I get it. And what you said that day wasn't all wrong." He leaned over, bracing his elbows on his knees. God, this was hard. Admitting he'd been living in a way that had precluded anything but the most superficial romantic relationships made him feel shallow and immature. He licked

his lips, reaching for words to explain the painful intro-
spection he'd engaged in these past three days. "I've been
thinking a lot lately. Talking to my family and friends, and
it's pretty clear to me—"

Room 316's door burst open, and the doctor came out,
peeling off her latex gloves in one fluid, practiced motion.
Her face was grave as she motioned for one of the nurses at
the central nurse's station.

"Need a hand to the OR," she snapped.

Both Zander and Imani shot to their feet as the nurses
wheeled Kate's cot around, pushing her headfirst out of the
door. His sister-in-law's face was pale and shiny with sweat.
She was covered by a sheet, but he saw no visible blood. He
figured that was a good sign.

But the vibe he was getting was definitely not.

Drake followed at the foot of the bed, holding Kate's
purse, the stuffed tiger, the pink puke bowl, and Imani's
sneakers. His brother's eyes were wild behind his glasses.

"Baby's heart rate is decelerating," he said, shoving
everything into Imani's waiting hands without looking, his
gaze focused on Zander. "Kate's going in for a C-section,
and I'm going in with her. Mom should be coming soon.
Make sure you update her. Where's Ryker?"

Just then, the door to the stairwell opened, and Ryker
stepped onto the maternity floor holding gift bags, balloons,
and a giant bouquet of flowers. He spotted them, and his
eyes zeroed in on Kate being wheeled out, with doctors,
nurses, and IV stands moving with her. Zander could tell
his brother wanted to escape back into the stairwell, but
he gave him credit for stepping up—just as he always had
done in his career and in life.

"We moving this party somewhere else?" he asked.

"The operating room," Drake said, his scarcity of words proof his writer's mind was in crisis mode. "C-section."

Ryker's blue eyes widened. Then, mustering it up from somewhere deep in his reserve, his middle brother put on a big smile and winked at Kate.

"Let the record show *I* was the first one to bring you and the little one gifts—not the baby brother or the boss brother—the *middle* brother. Now, you hustle in there so I can meet my godchild, will ya?"

"I'll do my best." Kate gave a tiny salute, then gasped out as they wheeled her toward the maternity ward's operating room. "Imani?"

Imani jogged with Zander and Ryker, following the retreating cot, her smile still relaxed and calm for her friend.

"I'm right here, and you're doing so great! I spoke with your mom, and your folks are on their way. Drake got them a VIP flight on his friend's helicopter, so they'll be here to welcome Baby Matthews in a little while. And I'm *so* writing this up for the scrapbook so this little one will see how much drama they caused." Imani beamed. "Because you'll forget it all when you see your beautiful baby!"

Kate's answering smile vanished, and she arched her back, her eyes clenched shut.

"Don't push," Drake, the doctor, and the nurses said in unison as they approached a set of massive double doors. The doctor smacked the automatic open button, while at the same time gazing over the patient to the group trailing Kate's hospital bed.

"Okay, Mr. Matthews, you're coming in with us to gown

up if you still want to be there for the birth—without any passing out?" At Drake's vigorous nod, the doctor gave a smile of approval. "Good. The rest of you can take a seat in the surgical waiting room, and we'll be out to update you as soon as we can."

The nurses pointed to a room off to the side with a name plaque announcing *OR Waiting Room.*

They all peeled off, watching Drake leave with the nurses as the doctor directed Kate's bed beyond the doorway. It swung closed, like two giant tomb doors clunking shut at the end, and Zander heard Imani take a shuddering breath in.

"You okay?" He held the waiting room door for her. She entered, with Ryker following, lugging his balloons, flowers, and gift bags, his face Marine-serious and his eyes darting everywhere.

"I'm fine," Imani said, the words a dead giveaway that she wasn't. She set her black tote, Kate's purse, the stuffed tiger, the pink emesis bowl, and her sneakers on one of the waiting room chairs and dropped into the one next to it. Perching on the edge, she put on her shoes.

"It's easier to be under anesthesia. This waiting blows," Ryker said, dumping the gifts on another waiting room chair. He folded his arms across the chest of his short-sleeved camo T-shirt, his expression morphing into his typical resting bastard face.

Zander hummed in a derisive, "must be nice to be you" sort of way. "Well, lucky for both of you, I'm a pro at waiting for people to get out of surgery." Noticing the way Ry's eyes were darting toward the door, he decided to give his brother the kindest gift he could under the circumstances.

"Why don't you go downstairs and wait for Mom so you can bring her up to this waiting room, instead of room 316? Oh, and can you snag me some fresh coffee? And a chai for Imani, too?"

"I'm fine," Imani said, repeating her usual don't-worry-about-me mantra.

But Ryker was a doer. Not a sitter. Zander knew every task he assigned relieved the Marine from thinking. The more difficult and obscure the task, the better.

"Oh, and see if the cafeteria has any high-protein snacks. I'm starving." Zander added to the scavenger hunt. "But no hard-boiled eggs or tuna. Nobody needs to smell that in this closed-up space. Oh, and no dairy. Imani is lactose intolerant."

Imani opened her mouth, scowling, but Zander gave her a shake of the head. He stared into her eyes, willing her to understand this wasn't about her—it was to help his brother wait out his time in the hospital without losing his freaking mind.

She closed her mouth, shaping her lips into a reluctant smile as Ryker repeated the orders.

"Coffee. Chai. Protein snacks—no eggs, fish, or dairy." Ryker stood, his shoulders straight and his chest full of purpose. He leveled his icy-blue stare at Imani. "If they don't have chai, do you want another type of tea? And do you need sugar?"

Zander knew she didn't take sugar, but apparently, she'd gotten the gist of his nonverbal message.

"If they don't have chai, I prefer Earl Grey, but any black breakfast tea is fine. As for sugar, I'm not sure what tea you'll be able to find so…" Imani paused, cocking her head as if in deep consideration. "Could you bring me up one of each of the sugar packets they have? That way, I can match it to the tea. Can I give you some money for it?"

But Ryker had already executed a perfect ninety-degree pivot to the door, his only answer a vague, dismissive wave of his hand as he left.

Zander nodded at Imani. "Thanks. He hates hospitals, although he won't admit it, and he couldn't have taken another minute in here. This'll keep him busy for a while."

She shrugged, lacing up the last sneaker. "Katie's the same way when she gets anxious. If you ask her about the nitty-gritty details of her spreadsheet or add some minute point she missed, it'll occupy her for hours. That's how they de-stress. By doing. Transforming stress into action. Me? I clean, or bite my nails."

She waggled her nubbed fingers at him just as her cell phone rang. Descending on her black tote as if she'd been given five seconds before the bomb went off, Imani clutched it to her, her face brightening in recognition of the number.

"It's Kate's mom."

She swiped to take the call.

"Hi, Kasey," she said, and Zander remembered the three times he'd met Kate's parents: at Drake's book launch, Drake's wedding, and most recently at the baby shower.

Kasey and Kevin Sweet were both orthopedic surgeons on Long Island, and after meeting them, it'd been easy to see where his sister-in-law had gotten her type A tendencies. Those two put the "tense" in "intense."

Imani listened to Kate's mom, nodding, until finally fitting in a word edgewise. "Good. Sounds like you'll be here in plenty of time, then. Kate's doing great, but the baby's heartbeat had a rapid deceleration the doctor didn't like the looks of, so she's taking Kate for a C-section. Drake's in with her now."

Imani paused, gave some murmured response, then ended the call.

"Drake's helicopter pilot friend, John, said they were ten minutes out. Kasey didn't sound alarmed that Kate was going into surgery. Although, knowing the Sweets, they'll demand emergency privileges to scrub in, just to supervise." Imani seemed relieved at the thought of their arrival. She met his gaze across the room, and her eyes grew troubled underneath knitted brows. "Are—are you still mad at me?"

The simple, childlike question, paired with her worried expression, caught him off guard. He felt as though the words chiseled away at the ice he'd attempted to form around his heart these past few days, and he gritted his teeth against the anticipated pain of her leaving again. The clock ticking in the room couldn't be a more apt metaphor for how fast he felt these next two weeks were likely to go before she returned to New York City, and he shook his head.

He made a decision.

He'd put it all on the table. To hell with holding back and letting her make every move. It was time to tell her how he felt.

"I was never mad at you," he said, then amended himself. "Well, maybe when you teased me into thinking you were in a car wreck in my Prius that time, or when you yanked a shard of glass out of your freaking ribs."

The last memory elicited a small smile, which only made Imani's expression more miserable. He would say or do whatever he had to in order to make her misery go away.

"But I'm not mad at you for lashing out when your grandmother was injured. Both Mom and Drake were on the receiving end of my stressed-out tirades more than once when I was Ry's recovery coach, so I get that knee-jerk impulse." He paused. "No, I'm mad at myself. Because you were right—my whole life's philosophy was designed to keep me away from failure. In relationships and in business. My determination to live only in the now has kneecapped me and cost me my relationship with you. As you said, I'm like a damned hot-air balloon, just drifting whatever way the wind blows. For the longest time, I thought not having a future plan meant freedom. Now I can see it's just . . . lonely."

Imani's expression changed as she processed his impromptu soliloquy. Then she got up and joined him on the awful, apricot-tinted couch.

When he flipped his hand over, palm side up, she slipped her fingers inside his. Then she tucked up next to him, her side molding against him until they were like two bookends pushed together, arm to arm, hip to hip, and thigh to thigh.

She laid her head on his shoulder. "I missed you, and I'm glad you're here. Listen, what you said earlier—"

Suddenly, the door flew open. Ryker burst in, his mom on his heels.

Patty scanned the room, her expression at once excited and frantic. "Sorry I'm so late. Did she have the baby? Is Kate okay? How's Drake holding up? Does anyone want a cookie?"

The questions came out as one long, worried stream of words, ending with her thrusting a massive, pink PattyCakes box out toward where Imani and Zander sat. Zander got up, tugging Imani with him so that they stood together in front of his mom.

"No. Yes. Good. And absolutely," he answered her questions in sequence, reaching for the box. In truth, his stomach was like a massive piece of hardening clay, but it made his mom feel better when people ate, and he could always find room for cookies.

Imani smiled at Patty, filling her in on the latest with Kate and checking her watch to verify how many minutes ago she'd been taken back.

His mom nodded, then surprised Imani by throwing her arms around her shoulders, gathering her in for a tight embrace.

"You've been Drake's publicist for years, and I feel as though you've become a welcome extension of our family. I was so sorry to hear of Georgina's accident, and I can only imagine what you've gone through this past week." She clutched Imani to her, speaking into her hair. "I know what it feels like to want to trade places with the one you love and bear their pain as your own. But I'm so impressed by your strength for your grandmother as well as Drake and Kate in their times of need. We are so blessed to have you in our lives. Thank you, Imani. Is Georgina feeling better, then?"

With one last squeeze and pat on the back, his mom released her. Imani stumbled a bit as she retook her place next to him. Zander saw she was wiping away tears with a shaky hand.

"That—that's so sweet," she managed. "And yes—she

got home from the hospital today. In fact, I'm going to step out and give her a ring."

Zander felt her squeeze his hand, and she left with her phone to the hallway.

"Thanks for the cookies." Zander snagged a peanut-butter-cup one and downed it in two bites. "Oh, and you'll be happy to hear I took your advice."

"You did?" His mom sat down, tucking a strand of salt-and-pepper hair behind her ears, her brows raised in surprise. "Well, that's a first. Which bit did you listen to?"

"Everything. As of August 17, I'll be the proud owner of All Fired Up, lock, stock, and...kilns." Zander couldn't help but give a proud smile. "Aaand...you're looking at the next associate adjunct something-or-other at Alfred University's ceramics program."

"Whoa, did you hear all that, Imani?" Ryker asked, motioning to Imani, who stood still as a statue in the doorway. "As if his ego weren't large enough, now we're going to have to add associate to the list. I believe they abbreviate that with a-s-s, is that about right?"

"Ryker!" his mom scolded, shaking her head as if scandalized. Then she wrapped her arms around Zander's waist, giving him a squeeze. "Good for you, honey."

"Congratulations!" Imani's smile was wide and genuine. "I'm so—"

Just then, Drake burst through the waiting room door. "It's over, and Kate's okay!" he shouted, as if they'd been talking and he'd had to be overheard in a crowd. "And it's a girl!"

Imani whooped. "A baby girl! And she's healthy? Katie's okay?"

Drake nodded, shoving his black glasses up and wiping tears from his face with his forearm as Zander thumped him on the back. Drake took a second to collect himself, swallowing several times as he beamed, his joy bringing an instant lump into Zander's throat. What must it be like to have your own epic love story come true?

"Kate's doing great. She was such a warrior in there," Drake said, awe in his voice. "They're stitching her up and monitoring the baby. Turns out, the cord was wrapped around her neck. Twice. Our doctor got the first loop off during labor, but she hadn't known about the second loop until the baby's heart rate started tanking. Thank God she took Kate in for surgery in time to avoid anything…" He stopped talking, his throat moving convulsively.

"All's well that ends well." Patty engulfed her son in an embrace. "I'm so thrilled for you both."

Ryker came up, squeezing Drake's shoulder. "When am I going to meet my goddaughter? And I want to congratulate Kate, of course. I *am* the only one here with balloons and flowers. That ought to count for something." Ryker gestured to the loot on the chair.

"They should both be back to the room shortly," Drake said.

Then a commotion in the hallway made them all turn.

"Kasey! Kevin!" Imani called out to a thin redheaded man followed by a willowy woman. Kate's parents. As the surgeons spotted Imani, smiles replaced their worried looks. They quickly gave her a hug and brief kiss on her forehead.

Imani updated them, and they turned as one unit to Drake.

"Congratulations," Kevin said, pumping Drake's hand.

"When can we see them?" Kasey asked, after giving him a brief hug and waving at Patty, Zander, and Ryker in one brief motion. "We are doctors, so they shouldn't have a problem with us coming back with you, as long as we gown up, right?"

"Uh," Drake pushed his glasses up his nose, his handsome face grimacing. "Actually, before Kate leaves the OR, she wants to see Imani."

Imani's eyes widened in surprise. "Me?"

Drake nodded, motioning for her to follow him. Then he halted, snapping his fingers. "Oh, and she told me to tell you to bring your Mary Poppins bag. Whatever that is."

Imani spun to go back into the waiting room to find her purse, but Zander had it already, hanging from one hand.

"If it requires the bugout bag, it's a job for you." He gave her a reassuring grin. "Go. Work your Imani magic."

# CHAPTER 21

After multiple reassurances that she'd bring Kate their well-wishes, Imani was released from Kate's parents' hold to follow Drake inside the surgical doors. She'd been relieved to see the two who'd stood in for her parents during her entire freshman year of high school after her mom died and their house burned down. When her dad was so broken he couldn't parent, they'd cared for her and loved her as if she were one of their own, as if she were a middle sister between Kate and Kiersten. She'd always felt that additional connection to the Drs. Sweet, even now, and was buoyed by the thought they'd be here to help Kate, but also to help her as she waited to hear back from Cerulean Books on the biggest decision of her life.

"Are you sure I'm allowed to be back here?" Imani asked as Drake whisked her into the gowning area. A nurse helped her into a thin, yellow plastic gown that tied behind her back, as well as a set of gloves and a surgical mask.

"Yes," Drake said. "They're stitching her up, and then she'll be in recovery for a few minutes before they let her back to her room. Before the C-section, she pushed..."

"With her face," the nurse said, taking the liberty to

finish Drake's sentence with a flourish. She chuckled, leading them into the tiny recovery area. "She burst the blood vessels in her eyes and some on her cheeks while she was bearing down. It'll go away in a few weeks, but until then, she looks a little like something out of her husband's novels."

Drake nodded, and although Imani couldn't see his face behind his mask, she knew from the squinted expression he was grinning.

"I'd never tell her this, but she looks...like an attractive demon. She has no white left in her eyes. It's just her green iris surrounding by a sea of red, like someone chummed the waters of her eyes."

"That'll be in one of your next books, I'm guessing," Imani joked, knowing her client recycled every single thing into his horror books, and—lately—into his romance novels.

"Best not," said the nurse, before opening the door. "In my experience, new moms have absolutely zero sense of humor about these things for at least the first seven...years."

"Imani." Kate grinned from the hospital bed, waving her over with one hand, while the other held a tiny bundle wrapped in a gray-and-white-striped receiving blanket against her chest. "I'm so glad you're here. Come and meet your goddaughter."

Imani left Drake, bustling over to her best friend's side. It wasn't until she was about three feet away that she saw the damage to Kate's eyes and face.

*Yikes.*

Her best friend was suddenly part zombie, with little blood vessels broken in her cheeks and up around her eyes, the burst veins so thin and spider-wispy, it looked like they were drawn on with a makeup artist's bright-red, fine-tipped brush. Kate's face was swollen, and she must've bitten down hard sometime in the process, because she had a mark on her lower lip and dried blood in a fissure there. Her hair was sweat-damp, sticking out in wild auburn stalks, and her eyes were so terrifyingly bloodshot, it was hard to look at them and not wince in sympathy.

But the happiness radiating from her best friend erased the unfortunate damage from the birth trauma, and the way she gazed down at the bundle in her arms gave Imani shivers. Kate had never looked that way about anything— not a well-executed event, not landing a spot on a TLC show, not even her husband.

The look she gave the baby in her arms was next-level devotion.

Creeping closer, Imani peeked at the infant. She was ruddy-cheeked and serene with a shock of dark hair on her head. She was tiny, and while her eyes were mostly squeezed shut, they appeared to be light-colored. Her mouth moved in a smacking motion, and then she squinched up her tiny nose.

"Look! She's got your expressions—that's exactly what you do when an event is not jibing with your spreadsheet's plans." Imani giggled softly along with Kate, being quiet so as to not disturb the baby. "She looks like you in the face, but she's got Drake's dark hair. She's beautiful. You've created the perfect 'Aww!' moment once again, Katie."

"She is." Her best friend smiled. "I'll never top this one. Unless she gets a brother or sister..."

Kate gazed down at the bundle in her arms with a look Imani could only describe as transported by joy.

To love something so much...Imani's heart squeezed in a pang of yearning that made her breathless.

"She's so gorgeous, I think I just ovulated in some sort of sympathetic response." Imani mimed grabbing at her lower left side. "What are you naming her?"

Drake interrupted, making Imani jump—she'd forgotten he was still in the room, he'd been so quiet. "We promised Kate's parents not to announce the name until we were all together as a family. Apparently, it's a tradition on their side. So as soon as you get Kate ready, we'll tell everyone in the room."

Imani nodded. She'd lived with Kate's family for a year in their spare room, then for so many weekends and vacations afterward, she couldn't begin to tally the amount of time she was an honorary Sweet. She knew that while they were pretty relaxed with many things, some traditions were sacred.

"You brought your Mary Poppins bag?" Kate asked, tipping her head up to see over the baby. When Imani raised it in triumph, Kate sagged in relief. "I refused the mirror in the OR, but I caught a glimpse of myself as we passed a stainless steel cabinet. And I am *not* going in there until I look...human. Can you work around the baby, or do I need to give her to Drake?"

Imani dug into her bag, mentally going through her supplies. She had a tiny bottle of Visine, a travel version of her foundation—which was a few shades darker than Kate's alabaster skin but would have to do—and she had a brush and a tube of lipstick.

"Nah. Little girl is happy right there. You relax. I'm going to make you the hottest momma on this delivery ward—a bomb-ass warrior who absolutely did *not* code brown when she was pushing."

After Kate was wheeled into room 316 about twenty minutes later and she'd been hugged and congratulated by everyone, Zander did what he did best: ask the hard question.

"So, what are you naming her?"

The room went silent.

"Elise, after Nana's middle name," Drake said.

The whole Matthews clan whooped in approval.

Then Drake looked at his mother-in-law at the head of the bed next to Kate.

"And her middle name will be Kasey, after her grandmother."

In the years Imani had known Dr. Kasey Howard-Sweet, the woman had never been at a loss for words. Which made her open-mouthed expression even more priceless. Her chest and neck got the same mottled red her daughter's did when she was flustered, and she stood there, clutching her daughter's hand while her husband hugged her by the shoulders as if he were holding her to keep her from falling apart.

"Elise Kasey Matthews," Imani said into the silence, coming to the rescue of the woman who'd been so kind to her when she'd needed kindness. "It sounds so beautiful. It's perfect."

Kate, to everyone's surprise, lay back and let her husband lecture everyone about washing their hands and masking up before they could hold the baby. Her pale, exhausted face wore a happy smile and her eyes—while still a beet-red that no amount of eyedrops could fix—gazed at Drake with amused adoration.

Imani made her way over to Kate while everyone was cooing over the baby in surgical masks, only their eyes showcasing their joy and happiness. She grinned down at her best friend. "You did great. Despite the fact it didn't go according to plan, this is your happily-ever-after moment. I'll make sure you have a bomb-ass scrapbook, and this will be backed up to every server known to man."

"I appreciate it, but nothing could erase this moment from my heart." Kate squeezed her hand. "And I couldn't have done it without my planning partner in crime. Thank you for getting me here. I'm sorry for everything I said when I was contracting."

Imani laughed. "Forgiven. Besides, I was breathing on your face, and nobody can count sneaker mesh holes with any accuracy when the holder keeps fidgeting." Imani tucked away a wayward lock of her friend's auburn hair.

"Thanks for fixing me up so I don't look like dog balls for the pictures."

Imani snorted. "As if. I've got your back, like you've always got mine. My Summer Fling lipstick is your Summer Fling lipstick."

"Speaking of summer flings." Kate motioned with her chin toward Zander, who leaned against the doorjamb, all casual-sexy nonchalance as the female nurses eyed him hungrily. "Yours is coming to an end. Or is it? You know, now that you've turned down the promotion, can I throw in another option? As long as you're remote-working, why not consider coming to work with me as an associate with Sweet Events? You could do some of the heavy lifting with this brand management stuff for Drake while I stick to my wedding clients. I need the help, especially now that baby Elise is here."

"Well..." Imani paused, risking a long look at Zander, who was taking his turn holding Elise now, the infant looking impossibly small in his arms. The scene was so melt-worthy, she could practically feel her ovaries working overtime. She turned away, refocusing on her best friend. "I am already entwined in Drake's life and your life forever as Elise's proud godmother. And we do make a great team..."

"Perfect!" Kate beamed, although her red eyes still glowed like embers. "I'll draw up the details for you, and we can work together to transition from Cerulean Books whenever it's feasible. I'm so excited!"

Imani laughed, hugging her friend. "Looks like I'm going to be involved in every aspect of the Matthews family for the near future."

"Every aspect?" Kate's gaze probed her face for clues. "Including a certain Matthews brother who shall not be named?"

"I think that ship has sailed." Imani's smile dimmed, her heart heavy with the admission.

"I wouldn't be so sure," Kate murmured. "Looks to me like your ship's leaving the doorway and is coming this way with my baby. Can you find my hand sanitizer for me? Otherwise, Drake is going to lecture. Honestly, I'm going to force him back to his writing desk soon if he's going to hover."

Zander made his way effortlessly through the crowded hospital room, people parting around him like ocean waves before a cruise liner.

"Here's Momma." Zander laid Elise carefully in Kate's arms, cradling her head in his large palm until the baby was securely nestled before stepping back. Imani couldn't help being impressed by his obvious comfort with the tiny baby—his giant hands holding her as if he'd held dozens of babies.

The guy was like an onion, with levels and layers yet to be revealed.

Imani sincerely hoped he'd forgive her and she'd have the opportunity to peel those layers back. But from his distance earlier, she worried that opportunity had passed her by like the string of a runaway kite.

Elise was fussing, her tiny face screwed up, eyes squinted against the room's lights as her little pink tongue darted out of her mouth.

Imani laughed. "I think she's hungry. At least, that's my guess. Because I'm starving, and we both sort of have the same pissed expression if there's not something ready for us to eat right now."

Kate's face got a worried, tense expression. "Damn. I've got to try and breastfeed her, and my boob is almost the size of her head. So this ought to be fun." She flashed Zander a desperate glance. "Do you think you can corral them out? Except Drake and the nurse. I'll need their help, because while I've read about the football hold and the cross-body hold to feed her, I have no freaking clue how to do this without smothering this poor child."

"Will do." Zander pulled down his mask and gave a short whistle, drawing all eyes to him like a magnet. "Okay. Kate and Drake need some time alone with the baby, so you don't have to go home but you can't stay here."

"But I didn't get a chance to give her my gifts," Ryker said.

"Dude," Zander said, "she's got to breastfeed."

Ryker immediately halted in his attempt to close the distance to Kate's bed, pivoting to the door, instead. "Gifts are on the chair. See you tomorrow."

Imani filed out with everyone else and dumped her mask and surgical gown before giving last hugs to Kasey and Kevin with promises to see them later. When the hall cleared, it was only Zander left.

He shifted his feet, a hand coming up to rub the back of his neck.

"Did you, uh, have a chance to read my note?"

Imani gasped. "Oh my God, I forgot about it. It was an address, but I didn't recognize it. What's that about, anyway?"

"I think it's better if I show you."

Imani followed Zander's Prius to the address off Main Street and pulled the Green Grabber into a parking lot off Madison Street, which abutted a warehouse-like building with a dome-shaped roof. The windows and the double front door had been treated with some sort of tint that made them opaque, showing only their reflection as she got out next to Zander.

The late afternoon sun danced off the glass door, creating dazzling sun spots in her vision. She shielded her eyes.

"What did you want me to see?"

He stood next to her, his hands stuffed into his pockets.

"Did you know this place used to be a grocery store called Super Duper in the late 1970s? This is what I wanted you to see."

She raised an eyebrow. "Are you starting a grocery chain?"

He gave a short laugh. "No. Definitely not. Your going-away present is inside. Go ahead and use the key. We have permission."

Frowning, she turned to the door and inserted the silver key into the lock, twisting it until she heard the tumblers clink and the bolt retract. Instead of opening it, she bit her lip.

"Listen, Zander, I'm not sure what this is about, but I've been wanting to tell you something all day—"

"Open the door. Please."

His expression gave her pause. He—Mr. Zen himself—was nervous.

"I...okay." She shrugged and shoved against the glass door's handles with both hands.

Inside was a vast space with gleaming hardwood floors. The sun shone through the tinted windows and bounced off a bunch of massive mirrors leaning, haphazardly spaced, against the wall opposite.

"It's pretty in here." She loved the way her voice carried in the open, happy space. "But why—"

Zander handed her a present wrapped in a large, burnt-orange ribbon that was sitting by the front door. "Open this first."

Puzzled, she took it. The box was surprisingly heavy, but the orange grosgrain ribbon caught her eye. "This is the ribbon from the balloon race, isn't it?"

Zander only nodded.

Puzzled, she continued to open the package. Inside the wrapping was a shadow frame that held four tiles—extras that she'd made with Zander at his studio for Gigi's fireplace—which were placed in a square. Inside the square was a picture.

She gasped. "That's—that's our selfie from the hot air balloon. Aw, and I love the caption. 'Until we get carried away again.' What a beautiful gift, Zander, but as far as me leaving town, I wanted to—"

"Wait. Before you say anything, there's more." Zander's hand shook as he took out a folded sheaf of papers from his cargo shorts pocket. "This is a six-month lease for this space, rent-free."

Her heart trip-hammered in her chest.

She turned to him. The questions she wanted to ask were smashing into each other in her brain, getting tangled and tumbling helter-skelter from her mouth, refusing to line up neatly.

"I—I don't understand."

Zander reached one hand to the left, flicking up a group of switches, then gently guided her to the middle of the space.

Industrial fixtures flickered on from the white-painted, duct-lined ceiling. They bathed the space in light that reflected and bounced off the gleaming hardwood floors, revealing some details she hadn't seen before. Next to the stacks of mirrors stood almost a dozen swivel stools from Zander's art studio—the ones he'd kept in the back and had pulled out for Kate's shower. She spotted two built-in-shelves to either side of the window bank, perfectly sized to hold the speakers she recognized from the pile of

Grandpa Arlo's old garage junk Zander had agreed to haul off for her.

"What is this place? Is this...a dance studio?" She whirled to him. "Why? What...?"

"It could be. This is Cathy Costello's building that Ryker and I cleaned out for her. In exchange for the work, I made her a deal—I'd sand and refinish the floors, if she allowed it to be used rent-free for six months." He gestured around the space. "I couldn't find a barre to install, but I did salvage those mirrors from a local gym that was closed down, and I guess you recognize the speakers from your garage. They're wired to an old stereo system I found in Drake's attic. I warn you, though, you'll have to find a bunch of vinyl albums to play on it until you can afford to upgrade it to this decade. But I found a bunch of classical music and some eighties pop stuff from Mrs. Nowakowski, who was cleaning out, so you'll at least have some records to choose from. This place is so vast, I didn't think a Bluetooth speaker hooked up to a phone would cut it."

Imani's mind was spinning. "You mean...you did this for me?"

Zander lifted his shoulders in a shrug. "I didn't do much but run an orbital sander and give it a few coats of stain and varnish. The rest was free. There's a tiny unfurnished apartment above, although the hot water tank's only good for about a seven-minute shower. But it's yours to try out for the next six months if you want. No strings attached. And it's also totally fine if you don't want to try it. Nothing is permanent, and I can move it all out in under an hour. I just wanted to give you...an option."

"You...you got me a freaking dance studio as a going-away gift? Are you serious right now?" Imani thought her head was going to explode as she attempted to wrap her thoughts around this. She stared at the man who shrugged in an "it's not a big deal" sort of way. "I mean, most people give gifts like a nice set of those blue-green mugs that you make. Maybe a pair of throwing axes, just to keep my skills sharp. But, no, Zander Matthews decides to gift me..."

Her voice drained to a whisper as it snagged against the lump forming in her throat. She gulped air, spinning to face him. "A dance studio. Why?"

"Everyone deserves the chance to chase their dream," he said, and she swore he was flushed under his perpetual ten o'clock shadow.

A wave of feeling surged within her. It was the chime of her soul realizing that while she'd spent her whole life chasing a job, she'd missed out on chasing this: the transcendent joy of fulfillment. Yet it was also something more.

And that something more was directly related to the man standing next to her.

She gazed around, her eyes catching their reflection in the mirrors of the studio—of *her* studio for the next six months, if he was to be believed—and she spotted the charm on the bracelet she still wore, dangling from her wrist. The sun, gleaming through the window, highlighted the calligraphy characters for mindfulness etched in the onyx surface. She recalled the literal translation of the Chinese symbols:

Now.

Heart.

Like a curtain opening, she glimpsed a new stage, with a new setting, and a new scene...

And a new Imani.

One who wasn't afraid of taking chances. Not anymore.

She felt a surge of excitement shoot from her heart to her toes, making her want to leap at him. Smiling, she opened her mouth to tell Zander what she'd been trying to tell him all day—that she loved him.

He put up one finger, and she held her tongue, as he clearly had more to say.

"No matter what you decide about me, or this place, or your career, I want you to know one thing. Although I joke most of the time, I am serious. Serious about my future. Serious about my business. Serious about my feelings for you." He stood as if bracing for a blow. "I'm ready to be an anchor, a tree, a dock, a big-ass mountain—whatever you need to feel stable. And loved."

"Loved?" she repeated in a whisper that bounced back to her ears in the empty space. "You love me?"

"I fell for you last August as soon as we danced the bachata, then I tumbled the rest of the way, head over heels, these past weeks with you. But I want you to know that this"—he swept his arms to encompass the vast studio—"is part of my journey to adulthood. One I've put off until you helped show me that it's not so scary to be invested in the future. None of this obligates you. No strings attached."

Imani squinted an eye. "None? Not even one?"

He never flinched as he shook his head.

Damn. He meant it.

Her whole being felt filled with light, but she forced herself to ask another question.

"But...what if I want one?" She took her feet out of first position to glide closer to him. She wrapped her arms around his neck, rising to her toes as he held her waist, almost like he was readying for a lift. "What if I told you I wanted a tether—from my balloon to yours—for a while? At least eight or twelve more dates. Possibly more. What would you say to that?"

Zander's blue eyes widened. "What are you saying, Imani?"

"Only what I've been trying to tell you all day long." Her lips were inches from his mouth. "I've turned down the promotion at Cerulean, and I'm going to start working remotely. From Wellsville. Gigi is thrilled to have me as a houseguest for a while longer. Plus I might eventually be joining forces with Kate to be Drake's brand manager, which excites me on so many levels. So there's only one more thing you need to know."

He'd stopped breathing, his chest absolutely still as if worried he'd miss her words.

She smiled up at him. "I love you, Zander. And there's nothing I'd like better than to soar with you forever."

He did lift her then, kissing her until she was breathless.

"Now," she murmured against his mouth, kissing him one last time, "why don't you take me upstairs to that little apartment you mentioned, and we can...christen the place properly?"

Imani tugged him toward the metal spiral staircase next to the office space at the back.

"Uh, there's no bed up there," he said.

Imani shrugged, giving him a saucy wink as she climbed. "When has that ever stopped us before?"

# EPILOGUE

## *Eight Months Later*

Imani's heart thumped wildly, her stomach full of a million shooting stars as she watched her entire dance troupe take their final bows on the makeshift stage at the back of her studio. The twenty-six girls and boys, ranging in age from five to eighteen, were onstage taking their class-by-class bows to the song that had stood in as their finale as well as her recital's theme: "Up, Up, and Away."

Although she hadn't had the funds to rent the local high school auditorium or the stage at the library, she'd done exactly what Zander had taught her last summer—she'd trusted that somehow, it would work out.

And it had.

A bunch of lumber had come her way from the surplus at a construction site in a nearby town, and one of her dance parents had delivered it to her. She'd worked with some handy parents to craft a makeshift stage at the back of the studio space. Then they'd rigged black fabric onto PVC pipe that hung from the ceiling rafters as a curtain that had to be manually pulled back on both sides and tied with a braided rope during the performance.

It was janky.

And the most magical day of her life.

As the last bows were taken and her studio's first dance recital wrapped up, the crowd on the metal chairs and stools at the far end of the studio stood, clapping wildly as she joined her dancers onstage. She gestured first to her dancers, then to the audience, and she took her own bow, her eyes misting over.

What an amazing night—worth every bit of the time she'd been here before her day started at her new job as the only associate of Sweet Events and Associates—a job she adored because it kept her working with Drake and his brand, plus their new client, Leann Bellamy. The best perk was her almost daily visits with her goddaughter, Elise, plus the extra evening and weekend time she used to teach dance classes.

She took a breath in, determined not to cry. Determined to soak in this moment, as she'd tried to soak in every moment during the roller coaster of months since her grandmother's surgery.

Imani took the microphone, another found gift from one of her students' parents who'd been in a band thirty years ago, and she began to speak.

"Thank you so much for coming out to our first recital. It was my absolute pleasure to work with your children, and I am honored by your commitment to our little studio."

She continued for a minute more, thanking specific people who had come in clutch, finding them easily in the crowd of family and friends gathered in her studio. She was elated to have her dad and his new wife and kids here for this special day. They sat, clapping madly in the back row, having been part of the crew running lights for her during the performances.

"Your mom would have been so proud," her father told her last night when he'd flown into town with Belinda and her stepbrothers. "She was never happier than watching you perform."

Today, her dad gave her a thumbs-up from the back as she pointed him out to the crowd, including him in her list of gratitude.

"Big thanks to my dad, who not only worked with my stepmom and stepbrothers to run the door and lights tonight but also is one of the reasons I was able to relocate from the Bronx to Wellsville in time to start classes in September. I owe him—and my wonderful stepfamily—so much."

Imani had to blink several times as she noticed her dad was tearing up—he'd been more supportive than she'd anticipated when she announced her life changes to him last August.

She continued, spotting her best friend's face in the crowd. "I'd also like to thank Kate Sweet-Matthews, who's responsible for strong-arming every downtown business into donating so we could have these beautiful recital programs and a trophy for each of these talented dancers on the stage tonight." Imani pointed out Kate, who sat next to Drake. He was watching over little Elise strapped in her stroller, happily gnawing on a teething ring. "Katie and I were in dance class together for almost a decade, and maybe one of these days, I'll get her up onstage to do her tap number."

"Not likely," Kate called cheerily, and the crowd laughed.

"I'd also like to thank Ryker Matthews, our sound guy." Imani pointed over to the studio's windowed office, where

Ryker had stood the entire time, switching out records on the old stereo turntable wired to her Grandpa Arlo's old speakers.

He gave a stern-faced wave to the clapping crowd, but Imani thought he'd secretly enjoyed being the DJ, with his headphones and all.

"And where would we be tonight without our backstage manager? Everyone, please put your hands together for my grandmother, Gigi Foltz, who has been here since the beginning, helping out with everything from sewing our curtains to putting stage makeup on our dancers tonight. C'mon, Gigi! Get out here!"

The crowd roared as Gigi reluctantly came out from behind the stage's backdrop, waving off the applause as she joined Imani, walking spryly and without a limp. You'd never have known she had both knees and a hip fixed eight months earlier. She wore a pair of black pants and a black, glittery top that matched the clipboard in her hand, and her blond-brown hair was done in perfect, orderly curls.

Imani nodded to one of the girls' parents in the crowd who'd helped her arrange a special surprise. The woman handed Imani a massive floral arrangement of the brightest, loudest flowers they had at the local florist. Imani passed it to Gigi, who gave over the clipboard to take the arrangement, her mouth widening in a delighted smile.

"This woman deserves so much more than flowers. Honestly, I would not be here today—in more ways than one— if it weren't for my grandmother." Imani forced her voice to remain steady as her eyes filled with tears. Memories, thick as molasses, flowed through her—summers spent at Gigi's house; her sage, no-nonsense advice; and her wicked sense of humor that had gotten Imani through so many difficult times. "I'm blessed to have her in my life, and she has been such an integral part of opening and running the studio this year. I know every dancer on this stage will agree with me when I say she is the wind beneath our wings."

The dancers vied to be next to the older woman, sneaking in hugs as she marched off toward the backstage area holding her flowers, dashing tears off her face but grinning from ear to ear.

"Lastly, I'd like to thank Zander Matthews." Imani looked around, as the dancers around her started to titter. Imani had seen Zander throughout the performance, helping to bring in extra chairs, fixing last-minute issues with the bathroom and the makeshift changing area, but he'd disappeared once the recital ended. She frowned, shading her eyes against the glare of the bright lights. "Well, when you see him, make sure you thank him. He's the reason I decided to take a chance on my dream and embark on this wild, incredible flight of owning a dance studio, and...there's a lot more, but I should wrap this up. Thanks for making our first recital a huge success!"

Imani switched off the microphone and stepped offstage to congratulate each of her students in her black leotard with its floaty black skirt that was as airy and light as her heart.

She hugged them to her, smiling for pictures even as her eyes scanned the crowd, searching for Zander. She'd wanted a picture with him on this stage with the backdrop he'd painted to look like a sky, which reversed for other dance scenes to look like outer space with planets and whimsical shooting stars covered in so much glitter it glimmered and sparkled, despite the substandard lighting. She cast her eyes around.

Where was he?

She was chatting with some of her students' parents when five of her dancers approached, forming a semicircle and clutching small, white poster boards in their hands.

"What in the world?" Imani grinned at them, her eyebrows raised.

"This is for you," said Camilla, her oldest student, with a shy grin, handing Imani a bouquet of roses in a riot of yellow, pink, white, and red blooms.

But the vase they were in caught her eye. She recognized the elegant design and trademark blue-green variegated glazing.

Her heart lifted.

Zander.

She spotted him behind the five dancers, dressed in a black T-shirt and shorts, his uniform while helping with scenery changes backstage. He looked alternately happy and nervous, and Imani gazed around curiously when the noise of the crowd died down. People shushed each other as Zander stood, his hands by his side.

"Two years ago, when I danced with you, you swept me off my feet," Zander said, his deep baritone making the shooting stars in her stomach zip and zing. "I haven't regained my footing since."

Some people whispered, "Aww," but Imani's attention was focused on the man she loved stepping between dancers until he stood a foot from her in the center of the semicircle of her students.

"I'm not as eloquent as my older brother. So I thought I'd ask these talented ballerinas to help a guy out."

And then Zander knelt on one knee.

Imani gasped, putting her hand to her lips.

Slowly, he pulled a square box out of his shorts pocket. Then he grinned, calling out behind him, "Girls, can you help me out?"

At his signal, the dancers flipped their posters, revealing four words:

*Will You Marry Me?*

The room went silent, and Imani wasn't sure if it was because the crowd was hushed or because everything had narrowed on the only thing that mattered: the sweet man kneeling in front of her as he held a diamond ring in his huge, trembling hand.

"Imani Regina Lewis, will you please marry me?"

Imani didn't have to think about it. What had started out as physical attraction and a two-night stand had blossomed into friendship and love, as natural and easy as breathing. This man—this Zenned-out, gorgeous, clay-flinging hunk of a man—had given her so much: a fresh career outlook, stability, and a newfound appreciation for the present. He'd shown her the ways she could soar if she only trusted in the now with all of her mind and all of her heart. The only thing her future lacked...was him.

Her heart and throat were full with emotion as she tugged him up, cupping his face in her palms.

"Zander, I love you," she said, kissing him deeply.

"Eww!" the children around them chorused as the adults cheered and clapped.

He chuckled, pulling away long enough to slip the

ring on her finger, where it glittered and winked like the brightest star in the sky. Then he wrapped her in his arms, grinning.

"You didn't officially answer."

"You didn't ask with a pretty please," she countered, raising an eyebrow.

"Pretty please." His voice was low, his smile sweet. "With a cherry on top."

"Then how can I resist? Yes!"

He whooped, twirling her in his arms.

Imani clung to him, laughing.

Her eyes caught sight of her dance studio's name reflected in the mirrors behind them—Dancing Through Life—and she marveled at how what she'd once thought of as this man's biggest fault had become the reason he was now her whole world.

DON'T MISS RYKER'S STORY,
COMING IN SUMMER 2023.

# HUNGARIAN GULYÁS

Traditional Hungarian goulash, or gulyás, is very different from the Americanized version, and eats more like a thick stew. The word "gulyás" means "herdsman" in Hungarian, because the dish originated with the shepherds who cooked meat and vegetables with paprika and water over fires in heavy iron kettles. Known as Hungary's national dish, gulyás may be prepared various ways. This recipe is from my Hungarian grandmother, and is the perfect comfort food! —Dylan

## Ingredients

- 3 strips thick-sliced bacon
- 1½ pounds chuck roast or stew beef, cut into ½-inch cubes
- 2 medium onions, chopped
- 1 (12-ounce) can of your favorite beer
- 2 tablespoons Hungarian sweet paprika
- ¾ cup beef broth
- ¼ cup red wine
- ¼ teaspoon salt
- 1 medium green bell pepper, sliced into ½-inch-thick slices
- 1 medium carrot, cut into ½-inch-thick pennies
- 1 tablespoon cornstarch (optional)
- 3 cups dry medium egg noodles
- 1 tablespoon butter
- Sour cream (on top, as desired)

Serves 4

### Directions

Cook the bacon in a Dutch oven or stewpot, simmering over medium heat until the fat is rendered (bacon is cooked, leaving only the grease behind). Remove the bacon slices from the pot and feel free to snack away—bacon makes an excellent appetizer as you prepare the rest of the gulyás.

Add the beef cubes to the rendered bacon fat and richly brown on all sides. Remove the beef and set aside in a bowl.

Reduce heat to low and add the onion. Cover and simmer until softened and opaque. DON'T ALLOW THE ONION TO BROWN OR BURN. Add splashes of the beer (or water, if you prefer) so the onion doesn't dry out while simmering. Drink the leftover beer. ☺

Stir the paprika into the onions. Return the beef to the pot, and stir to coat. Add the broth, wine, and salt. Stir and reduce heat to very low. Cover and simmer for 1 hour.

After the first hour, add the bell pepper and carrot slices to the pot. Re-cover and simmer for 1 more hour.

Check the tenderness of the beef and simmer longer if needed. Add more broth if needed, but not so much as to make it soupy. If the sauce is too thin, mix the cornstarch in a small cup with just enough water to dissolve it, then add it to the pot and stir until the sauce is thickened.

Meanwhile, cook the noodles per package directions. Drain and place them in a bowl with the butter, mixing together until the butter melts.

Divide the noodles into wide, shallow bowls. Top with gulyás and a dollop of sour cream. Enjoy!

# MAY-I CARD GAME INSTRUCTIONS

*May-I is a card game my family has played for decades, and while it's similar to Continental rummy, the version we play is unlike any other. It's strategically cutthroat, but addictively fun. Pour yourself a drink, pull out a couple of decks of cards, and enjoy!* —Dylan

## CARDS

You need two 52-card decks, including jokers, to play the game with 3–4 players. Add a third deck for 5–6 players, and an additional deck for 7–8 players, etc.

## OBJECT OF THE GAME

The object of May-I is to be the player with the lowest penalty points after playing all 7 hands.

## THE DEAL

Everyone draws a card, the high card deals, and the subsequent deals are passed to the left. Each player is dealt 12 cards, facedown, and the remaining cards are set on the table, with the top card flipped next to the deck to begin the discard pile. Jokers are wild.

## THE HANDS

The game revolves around contracts, or hands, of books and/or runs. A book is three or more cards of the same face value (three queens, or three 7s, etc). A run consists of four or more cards of the same suit, in sequence. Aces may be either high card or low card, but not both in the same run (e.g., you can't have a run of king, ace, 2, 3). No book or run may be the same as that of another player who has laid down their contract, nor can you duplicate books or runs of your own in the same hand (e.g., you cannot collect six kings and separate them into two books).

| Hand | Description |
|------|-------------|
| 1 | 1 Book and 1 Run |
| 2 | 2 Books |
| 3 | 2 Runs |
| 4 | 2 Books and 1 Run |
| 5 | 2 Runs and 1 Book |
| 6 | 3 Books |
| 7 | 3 Runs |

## THE PLAY

Play begins with the player to the left of the dealer, who must either draw a card or pick up the top card on the discard pile. If the player does not select from the discard pile, any other player can say, "May I?" to claim that card, but that person must also take a card from the top of the deck as a penalty for picking out of turn. If several players ask, "May-I?," the first to yell it out gets the card (in my family, it pays to be loud!). Each player is allowed to ask, "May-I?" only three times per hand. Whether or not a "May-I?" happens, the original player must finish play by drawing from the deck or the discard pile, then discarding one card so the play can move to the next player. You may not lay any cards on the table until your turn. If you are granted a "May-I?," you may not play cards until it is your regular turn.

Play keeps going like this until players are able to lay down their contract, and play ends for that hand when one player discards all remaining cards in their hand. The exception to this is the final hand; players must hold the final hand until they have exactly enough cards to lay down and go out on their turn, or lay down and discard their only remaining card. During all other hands, players may lay down their contract on their turn, and once a player goes out, all other players must count any remaining cards as penalty points. Only one person will lay down on three runs—the rest must all count the cards in their hands as penalty points.

As a point of strategy, players might say, "May-I?" for a card that is not directly useful, in the hopes that the penalty card will be useful, or with the knowledge that taking that card may prevent another player from gaining an advantage. This is where it gets cutthroat, and Foltz's Fiery Fizzers may help ease tension.

Once a player has the requirements for a given hand, they may lay down the books and/or runs on their turn. They're then free to play (in that same turn and in subsequent turns) additional cards onto existing books or runs already on the table (their own or others'). A player may not put any cards into play until they've gone down.

Jokers may be used to fill in missing cards in a book or a run, but you may only have one joker per book, and one per run of four cards. Once placed on the table, the joker is fair game to be taken by another player who may have the value of the missing card. For example, if a player lays down a book of kings that contains a joker, another player (on their turn and after drawing or picking up a discard) may offer up a king and take the joker into their own hand. In a run, if the joker stands for a specific suit, the replacement card must also be the same suit to be removed/taken by another player. Jokers may be held or played at the player's discretion for any card and any suit.

## THE SCORE

Once a player has gone out (laying down their contract and discarding any remaining cards), players must tally the penalty points by hand. We keep a scorecard with the hands written in the left column and the players' names written in a row at the top so we can tally penalty points by hand and by player, with the following penalty points assigned by card:

Joker: 50 penalty points

Ace: 15 penalty points

Face cards (king, queen, jack): 10 penalty points

10 and under: penalty points equal to the value of the card

The May-I winner is the player who, by the end of all seven hands, has the fewest penalty points in total.

# ACKNOWLEDGMENTS

If writing a romantic comedy during pandemic lockdown was hard, attempting it without a village of support would have been impossible. While it is difficult to thank an entire village in a few paragraphs, I will do my best.

First, I wouldn't be here without my agent, Cori Deyoe at 3 Seas Literary, and my editor, Leah Hultenschmidt at Forever. Thanks also to Estelle Hallick, Dana Cuadrado, and the rest of the Forever team. You all are a powerhouse of talent, and I'm thankful for your hard work!

A huge thank-you to the artisans and potters at the Wellsville Creative Arts Center who allowed me to interrupt with my newbie questions, and to WCAC studio manager Christina Rhodes, who explained the ins and outs of a pottery studio. I am so thankful for the time you spent instructing me on the massively fun yet incredibly difficult art of throwing clay. Thanks, also, to my mom, Patty Nicholas, for being my pottery partner, and to Terry Lounsberry for the inspiration behind Foltz's Fiery Fizzers and for glazing my fired pieces. The tall one is a vase. Really.

As always, my beta readers came in clutch with their

book advice and motivation. Rhonda Kauffman, Annette Miller, and Faith Powers—you ladies are amazing, and words cannot express how much I appreciate you! I also owe my mental health to the lovely (and productive) Molly Call, who ensured my butt left my desk chair to work out.

I'd be remiss if I didn't mention the role libraries and sequestered library spaces had in writing this book. Thank you to Taylor Keeran, Eric Head, Nic Gunning, and all of the librarians and library staff at both the David A. Howe Public Library in Wellsville, New York, and the Citrus County Library System in Florida—I appreciate you.

I'd like to thank the following Marines for their service to our country and for sharing with me their Corps knowledge, experience, and grit for this story, and the series: Sergeant Jonathan da Cruz, Sergeant Michael MacHose, Corporal Jamey Clovis, and Infantryman Josh Langston White. They were invaluable resources, and any mistakes are entirely mine. Ooo-rah!

Thank you to the readers and book cheerleaders in my Newton Neighborhood Facebook group, my dedicated ARC Leaders and Readers, and the supportive Bookstagram lovelies—you rock! A special shout-out to Amanda Newton for her dance knowledge, and to my spunky grandmother, Yolanda Szabo, for her Hungarian gulyás recipe, which was lovingly recorded and perfected by Kris and Eva Thompson.

I owe much of this book's goodness to my daughters: to Devon for her poolside plotting expertise, and to Ava for her wise words: "Just sit down and write, Mom. You're making this harder than it needs to be." I'm blessed beyond measure with you both!

Finally, always, this is for my husband. I could write a thousand romance books with every hero inspired by you, yet I'd never truly capture all that you are to me. Love you, Mike.

# ABOUT THE AUTHOR

DYLAN NEWTON was born and raised in a small town where the library was her favorite hangout. After over a decade working in corporate America, Dylan quit to pursue her passion: writing books. When she isn't writing, Dylan is pursuing her own happily ever after with her high school sweetheart as they split time between Florida and Western New York with their two much cooler daughters and a tone-deaf cockatiel.

Check her out at:

DylanNewton.com

Facebook.com/DylanNewtonAuthor

Instagram @AuthorDylanNewton